Ronin of the Dead

Book One

By Keith J McIntosh

Acknowledgements

There's a lot of people I would like to thank that helped me get to this point. This, of course, is not in any particular order.

I would like to thank Pete Chaffe for introducing me to George A. Romero's movies, and pretty much the entire concept of zombies. For listening to my bullshit over the years, and for giving me a wall in which I could throw ideas against. We did it, old friend!

Of course, my wife and family for supporting me. Especially my wife, Renee, who sat with me and helped edit this monster during those long, winter nights. When it was just you, me, and Microsoft Richard. I love you.

I'm extremely grateful for my good friends, the Fergusons. Sorry, guys. It's just easier to lump you together. The pains of being married, I guess. Jason, for reading the first edit of the book, which was painful. I know. But even after reading that hot mess, he still believed in it. Bobbi, his wife, for teaching me the cold-hearted, merciless art of editing. We sacrificed much in this journey, but we will always have the orange flickering glow.

A special thanks to Robert Belland, my high school friend, who helped me put the technical side of this project together. He helped a lot with the actual formatting of the book, as well as coming up with the amazing cover art for it.

Another special thanks to Kathy Carter. My first fan. Another poor soul who suffered through the very first version of the book. Chapter by chapter she climbed this mountain with me, encouraging me to finish. Demanding that I finish. And at some points, threatening violence if I didn't finish.

This is dedicated to my Dad, Don McIntosh.

Miss you.

Contents

Chapter 1

Kenshiro

The spear tip exploded out the rear of the undead woman's head. Kenshiro saw the slight spray of gore that jumped out the back. She was the first one of the trio of undead to fall. It was early, Kenshiro could still see the fiery orange hues of the morning light on the clouds in the eastern sky. There was barely enough detail to make out the grotesque injuries of the two remaining zombies. Thankfully.

The second zombie lunged at Kenshiro, it was a man in jeans and a tattered biker vest that had a gap in the top row of its teeth. Kenshiro could see its black gums clearly as the zombie viciously snapped its jaws at him. He darted back, almost playfully while he brought the sharpened point of the seven-foot length of half-inch steel rebar low and forward in a swooping motion. It caught the undead man on the inside of its knee joint. Kenshiro saw the joint buckle under the impact and heard the sickly snapping sound that broke through the morning air. The zombie dropped down onto the ruined joint and Kenshiro promptly kicked the undead man firmly in the chest, which sent him back onto the asphalt of the highway. Kenshiro then swung the spear at his side before he stepped forward and brought the point down on top of its forehead.

Two down.

The last one was another male zombie, this one dressed in some form of uniform that Kenshiro didn't recognize. It lumbered forward towards him as he twirled the spear overhead once before he brought it around to smash into the side of the zombie's head. Kenshiro watched with great satisfaction as the zombie's skull was violently propelled to the side, and the body was carried with it as the corpse settled into the overgrowth of the highway's shoulder. Once again, he was alone on the road.

There had only been three of them waiting for him this morning. Kenshiro heard their low groans from atop of the tractor-trailer unit he slept on last night. Not a great way to start the day, but there were only three of them. Not enough to worry about. He could have speared them from the top of the trailer if he wanted to. Kenshiro felt like starting the day with a bit of exercise, so instead, he climbed down and dealt with them. It still served as a reminder that there was no safety to be found in this world anymore. The wrong sound or the wrong movement can get you killed, or worse. *Overwhelmed. Devoured. Turned.* They were the only three things that still worried him, and they went together like a choreographed dance. One led to the other, which led to the final nightmarish end.

If that was the end at all.

In the past, Kenshiro pondered what happens to the consciousness when a person turned. Does the mind die? Do you fade to black as the human mind dies away and the soul leaves the body before the zombie mind can awaken? Or are you trapped inside your body for all eternity, helpless to watch the horror behind dead eyes as your body stumbles mindlessly on? Kenshiro didn't know. He wasn't afraid of it though, and in some way, he figured that was important. He couldn't even admit to being afraid of getting bitten. He was cautious of it, sure. Always. But if it were to happen, the next decision would be easy. So incredibly easy. Kenshiro tried not to think about that too much. Bad thoughts led to bad actions.

Even the lonely mornings held little comfort because

they didn't last. They couldn't. Mornings could be filled with bloodshed, screams, and rotting mouths chomping down on warm flesh. Admittedly, that didn't happen much anymore. He was too smart for that bullshit. In the beginning, when he was on his own in the new world, he had been so incredibly stupid, and made so many mistakes. It was hard to believe he had survived that first month. Millions of people didn't.

There was one night; he was exhausted from running literally all day from one thing to the next. At the brink of collapse, he foolishly opened the back door of some posh SUV, climbed over the rear most seat and hid in the back cargo area. Kenshiro fell asleep immediately, huddled into a tiny ball and tried to make himself as small as possible. The next morning, he woke up to a nightmare. The SUV was surrounded by black mouths and rotting hands scratching at the exterior, and he could see more on the horizon coming towards him. If that SUV hadn't had a sunroof, he would be dead. The two most important rules to sleeping in the new world: *Don't sleep where they might see you.* If they can see you, they will surround you. Secondly, *always leave yourself a way out.* He didn't know that then, but he survived. Though, he'll never forget the sound of the undead hissing and snarling outside that SUV. Like a throaty roar of desperation. They didn't just want to eat him. The undead *needed* to devour every inch of him.

Last night, he awoke from a familiar dream. It left him with the usual dark feelings of failure and regret. Kenshiro looked up to the clear starry sky that opened up the universe to him. It was all just laid out above him. Growing up, he had only lived in two places. Tokyo, and then after the death of his mother, his father had moved them to Los Angeles. Both places had black evening skies where only a few stars were able to poke through the pollution. He had grown up with it that way and never learned what stars were supposed to look like. Admittedly, he never appreciated the night sky before. But last night, for the first time, he saw the splendor of the universe. *Did it always look like that?* Kenshiro remembered wondering as he witnessed its sea of multicolored diamonds, too many to even consider counting, with the blue/green hues of the Milky Way that just seemed to glow in the darkened sky. It was haunting. He gazed at the infinite expanse above him and was crushed by the realization of just how small he was in the grand scheme of things. Once humanity was consumed from this planet, the zombies would eventually rot, or maybe not; maybe they would walk the earth for the rest of eternity. It seemed cruel to think that after the buildings of the world fall to ruin, after nature reclaims the roads and highways, after all the steel rusts away to dust; *they* may be the last thing to remain. A decaying monument to humanity's failure. The universe, however, would continue to spin. It would be completely unaffected by their tragedy. Humanity's demise wouldn't even be felt or noticed. After all he'd been through, all he'd seen, all he'd done and had failed to do, none of it mattered. It was a somber moment.

But that was last night.

"*Sorera o subete korosu tame ni,*" he whispered to himself as he moved back to the truck. *To kill them all.* It was his mantra. It neatly defined why he kept going. The promise of vengeance. The unattainable goal that kept him focused on the here and now.

It was a beautiful morning. Not that that changed anything. His day had started, and it was time to focus on surviving it. The air was still cool, but the day ahead promised to be warm. Kenshiro could see far down the road in both directions. There was a valley stretched out past the guard rails on Highway 160. Its gentle beauty contrasted solemnly by its vast emptiness.

He slept fully clothed, of course, with a 9mm Beretta in a holster that was strapped to his right thigh. Fully loaded with one in the chamber. *"There's no point having a fucking gun if it's not loaded and ready to go."* His former mentor, Trevor Dixon, the man responsible for his continued survival, had often said. Kenshiro wore a medium-sized knife sheathed and fastened to the front of his right leg. He also had a long-curved knife sheathed on his left leg. Another Dixon habit. He had insisted to the point of blows that a good sturdy knife, *not one of those pussy ass folding deals*, was the best hand-to-hand weapon against zombies. *I fucking love knives. You can never have enough knives*, Dixon had said on more than one instance. Kenshiro wore them every night and only took them off on those rare occasions he bathed.

Which he sorely needed now. He sniffed the air but only smelled his own odor, and if he could smell it, it must be bad.

He moved towards his rolled-up sleeping bag he had tossed down from the trailer's roof. It was still fairly new and was considerably warmer than his last one. Last night, he didn't even have the sides zipped up. Kenshiro threw the sleeping bag into the box of the truck with little enthusiasm.

The climb down from the trailer was easy enough. He parked his red and black pickup truck close to the rear of the trailer the night before. After the zombies had stirred him, he climbed down onto the pickup's hood and then down to the ground, cautious as ever. *Minor injuries could lead to major problems*. If needed, he could have jumped from the trailer to the truck's hood, climbed into the box and from there into the cab through the back window he had removed long ago. A tidy escape, if needed. *Always have a way out*. In the box of the truck, he kept a jumble of useful things he had collected along the way. He had two ten-gallon jerry cans full of gas. It was a good amount, considering he still had half a tank in the truck. Fuel, for the time being, was the most vital commodity to be collected, because of its scarcity. Food, clean drinking water, and bullets were also vitally important, but so far, those things were fairly easy to come by. If you knew where to look.

Guns were handy, to be sure, but they came with a fairly significant problem. They were loud. The only thing that attracted zombies more than sound, is blood. Zombies had surprisingly good hearing. Kenshiro once saw a zombie through a pair of binoculars, he sneezed and when he peered through the binoculars again, that zombie turned and started walking towards him, and it wasn't alone. The more you shoot, the more you attract, and no matter how good of a shot you are, guns are useless once you run out of bullets. The Beretta on his hip was meant more for people than zombies. Kenshiro had a .22 semiautomatic pistol and a rifle he used for the undead when the time came for it. The rest he picked up to use on other people. Some guns he did that job quite effectively.

Also, in the box were two water cooler jugs. One sealed, and the other had a plastic hand pump fastened on top. Kenshiro had also put an expensive looking mountain bike in the box some time ago. He thought it might come in handy if he ever ran out of gas, and it didn't take up much space. He has yet to use it. There were two long duffel bags along the driver's side of the truck's box, one a solid black color, and the other was green with a narrow red reflective strip down the middle of it. The heavy black bag held the long guns, all his ammunition, a few spare hand guns, and a small tool kit he kept for cleaning and maintenance. He dropped the tailgate of the truck and reached for the green bag; that was the survival bag. The *Go-Bag*. Its contents were of vital importance to his continued survival. It held all his food, a first aid kit, another knife, half a dozen bottles of water, a heavy sweater, and various other handy items. It was also where he kept his Road Atlas of the United States of America. The *Atlas*.

He sat on the tailgate, unzipped the green survival bag, and pulled out today's breakfast. Today he selected a can of baked beans, and a vacuumed sealed packet of apple and orange slices that had been freeze dried. There were tastier things he could have chosen other than beans, but they were high in protein. Kenshiro always felt guilty eating canned peaches or his favorite, mandarin oranges, first thing in the morning. The beans would have tasted better if they were warm. He could have cooked them if he wanted to, but it would require making a fire or pulling out the gas stove, and then pulling out the cookware. There were half a dozen things he would have to do. It would take time, which meant more exposure. Kenshiro put down three zombies already, and more would be on the way. No, he simply unzipped the side pouch of the duffel bag before he pulled out a can opener and a spoon.

He shoveled a generous spoonful of cold beans into his mouth and then fished out the Atlas from the green bag. The Atlas had the dimensions of a legal pad but was as thick as a dictionary. It was huge, and over time, the once pristine pages had become weathered with use. It also had several colored bookmarks protruding out passed the top-edge of the book. He marked the pages that featured the various safe houses and supply dumps he had made thus far. It was a useful item to have in his possession. He wrote down all the noteworthy things he had found while on the road.

Without people to maintain them, the highways had developed a lot of different hazards. Even on the good stretches of road, tuffs of grass and vegetation have begun to poke through the asphalt. It wasn't unusual anymore to see the occasional sapling poking through the middle of a secondary highway. Kenshiro used to take the time to pull the sapling out, in an attempt to preserve the roads as long as possible. He didn't want to have to worry about rogue trees growing in the asphalt down the line. *Better to fix a minor problem now than a large one later.* He didn't do that much these days, though. Kenshiro felt like he had enough on his plate already, he shouldn't have to worry about holding off the inevitable.

There was enough to worry about, a bridge out, a highway that's impassable due to traffic congestion or storm debris. The Mississippi river, for instance, could only be crossed north of Memphis. All the other bridges to the south were destroyed. Whether by nature or by desire, he didn't know.

In his first year heading east Kenshiro tried to cross at a bridge on the 278 north of Vicksburg only to find the bridge gone. He wasted a week looking for a crossing to the south only to find them all impassable, and Kenshiro spent another two weeks backtracking before heading north where he finally found a bridge on the 155, near the Tennessee border.

Whatever he came across of interest on the road, Kenshiro wrote it all down in the Atlas. At first, it had been a hobby. Something to keep his mind off his day-to-day struggles to merely exist. He would cross out the stretches of roads that he found to be impassable, marked off the bridges that no longer existed, and the towns he's been to. Most importantly, he marked off the locations of the safe houses he had established across the country. He wrote the details of these safe houses in the side columns, in Japanese.

It was also vitally important for determining where he went next. He didn't want to make the mistake of mindlessly travelling the roads from place to place. He enjoyed knowing where he was, where he could go to find a safe place, and

Kenshiro couldn't describe how important he felt it was to know where he should go next, well ahead of time. The Atlas helped him target small towns while avoiding anything that resembled a city.

Cities had tens of thousands of slowly rotting corpses just walking around waiting for fresh meat, and thousands more you couldn't see because they're tucked away out of sight. Cities were death traps.

Interstates could be pointless more often than not. Kenshiro noticed most were often clogged with thousands of abandoned vehicles along the stretches near major centers. Most of those vehicles, if not all, had run out of gas and had been thoroughly searched and stripped of anything remotely valuable. In some spots, even the shoulders and the ditches were littered with abandoned vehicles to the point the road was basically impassable. Never mind the roadblocks. For relatively easy traveling it was smarter to stick to the state highways and the rural roads.

The Atlas was also indispensable when it came time to approach towns to attack. Without it, he would go in essentially blind with no idea where to go if things went bad. Then the panic would set in, the adrenalin would start pumping, and mistakes would be made. He'd seen it happen before. Many times.

Kenshiro had the page he wanted bookmarked in the Atlas. La Veta, Colorado. He had been through this all the night before, and the night before that, and the night before that. He was planning on staying and setting up camp in the town for a while, and that meant every one of the undead had to be put down.

If he kept going on Highway 160, it would meet up with Highway 12, and it would eventually lead to La Veta. His target. A tiny speck on the Atlas between the two larger centers of Fort Garland to the west, and Walsenburg to the east. It was also far enough away from both that it was isolated. To the south was another small town, Cuchara. It was the likely next stop for him if La Veta went badly, but it was too soon to worry about that yet. Highway 12 seemed to run straight through the town, but he had no intention of going *through* the town. Not yet.

Kenshiro couldn't explain the undeads's behavior. He didn't know the exact psychological nature of the collection of habits and compulsions the undead seemed to have. However, he had witnessed it enough times in the past to plan for it. History had shown that the bulk of a town's infestation could be found in the places they would have congregated if they had been living. Like stores or gas stations, and places like that. Mostly he expected them to just be uselessly shuffling around the streets, but the undead at those locations would have higher concentrations. As if they were trying to imitate their prey, or worse, some inner part of their brains still functioned and recognized those places. Memories of their former lives driving them as if they were being guided by an invisible hand. To his knowledge, the dead only had one purpose. To devour people, and when there were no people left to eat, they went into standby-mode. When that happened, he guessed maybe half would become roamers, and they'd walk forever in whatever direction they were facing until they came across an obstacle. It was like watching a robot vacuum. Zombies would bump into something, turn slightly, and walk off in whatever new direction it was facing. The rest didn't leave the general area it originally died at, but those undead were still drawn to places they were familiar with.

However it worked, the end result was a mass of them always lingered in the town centers. According to the Atlas, Highway 12 ran straight through the heart of the small town. Kenshiro had no intention of approaching on Highway 12, though. In the Atlas, he traced his finger further up from his location to a smaller rural road numbered 450. It was likely gravel, but even so if he took that to the 440, then follow it around a bend that headed south, Kenshiro could hook up with the 430 going west and take that straight into the town. Far enough away from what he guessed would be the town center, he felt safe trying it. He would have to see it to know for sure. Kenshiro was hoping for a nice, open area. That's what he liked about this part of Colorado; not a lot of trees. If he took his time, he could get there within the hour. Then he could take the rest of the day to scout the town and get a feel for the local population. Plus, he planned to stop at whatever farms he may pass to search for supplies. Farms were great places to find fuel. He could start the assault the next day when the air was still cool.

He was ready.

The spoon rattled a bit as he tried to scoop up the last of the thick juice at the bottom of the can. He added some water to it, and then splashed the water around to mix with the bean juice before he swallowed it down as well. Satisfied, he tossed the can over the guardrail on the side of the highway where he was parked. Kenshiro stopped worrying about littering long ago. Next, he washed it down with a generous gulp from the plastic water bottle he retrieved from the green bag. He tore open the packet of dried fruit. They looked like odd colored potato chips. Kenshiro pinched a couple and put them in his mouth. They were dry but sweet, and most importantly, it was food. In his old life, he was a picky eater and would have probably turned his nose up at a can of beans and dried fruit. These days, if you weren't eating dog food or human flesh, you were doing good. Practically a gourmet.

He would run out of the dried fruit packets in another

couple of days, and he only had a dozen cans of food left. He drove through the Rio Grande National Forest believing it would be quiet and scenic. Which it was, but there was nothing to be found there. Worse yet, on three occasions, he had to clear fallen trees from the road. At the first stop, a single tree had fallen, but it stretched across the whole road. There was no going around it, and he had nothing to cut it with. It took him about a day to find an axe. Kenshiro found it neatly tucked away in the back of a tool shed. It took hours to finally remove that tree. Then he had to do it twice more. It was enough to make him rethink driving through national parks.

He chewed another mouthful of fruit before washing it down with some water. After he swallowed, Kenshiro paused. The next moment, a flock of birds zipped silently overhead and down the road, followed by an alarming quiet.

They're coming.

He froze. Keenly listening to the wind for the telltale sounds of the dead, but none could be heard. He had time. Kenshiro upended the packet of dried fruit into his mouth, dropped the wrapper to the ground, hopped down off the tailgate and moved towards the driver's door. He paid no attention to his reflection in the window. It had been a hard three days, and he didn't need to be reminded how rough he looked. He felt it. He opened the door and checked his surroundings as he put on the baseball hat from where he left it last night on the dash, to keep both the sun and his hair out of his eyes.

On the driver's seat was his combat vest. He scooped it up and promptly put it on. He found it in the trunk of a police car that was abandoned on a gravel road in South Dakota. It was all black and had a holster on the left breast that fit his Walther automatic pistol nicely. Below that were three small pouches with a Velcro flap for magazines. They made the vest for larger caliber ammunition in mind, so those pouches fit two magazines of the smaller .22 caliber bullets. It was a squeeze, but they fit. On the bottom right quarter were two larger Velcro pouches. He wasn't sure what they were meant for, but he used one to house three more magazines. The other held a multi-tool and a small flashlight. The pouch above that was about the size of a large cellphone that was placed on its side. He could stash two more magazines in there. Once fully suited up, he had a nine-millimeter with forty-five bullets, a .22 pistol with one hundred and sixty-five bullets, and two knives. The vest had a weight to it, but it felt good to have it on again. Kenshiro zipped it up and buckled it at the bottom.

He left the driver's door of the truck open in case, for some reason, he needed to bolt. The keys were in his pocket, and all he had to do was get in and go. Not yet though. He had work to do.

He approached the back of the trailer the pickup was parked behind and carefully peered around the corner. It was there on the road, maybe a hundred yards in front of the tractor-trailer unit, shuffling towards him. It was clear by the listless way it moved, the zombie was not aware of him. The dead have fair eyesight. At a distance, though, they would only respond to an obscene amount of movement. From his position, it wouldn't recognize him until he moved to the center of the road and waved at it like the zombie was some long-lost friend. He had plenty of time. Kenshiro scanned the entire area ahead of him, then moved to the rear of the pickup truck, and checked down the road. He went to the shoulder and peered up the road on that side, and then out past the guardrails to the valley. There were no others, but experience told him to expect a few more out there somewhere he couldn't see. He went back to the truck bed to grab the rebar spear.

Kenshiro's muscles came alive as he felt the familiar weight of it in his callused hands, but he wasn't burdened by it. It moved freely in his hands as he spun it side to side, like the spear had become emboldened by a sense of purpose and was eager to get to it. After a couple of spins to warm up his arms, he moved out from behind the truck confidently. The zombified man halved the distance between them while Kenshiro was getting ready.

By the look of the gray flesh on its ruined face, it had been dead, or rather undead, a long time. The undead man had originally died wearing a dark-colored suit, that was now in tatters that hung from the zombie like rags. Its left arm hung limp and useless by its side. Somewhere along the way, its collarbone had been broken. The undead figure spotted Kenshiro immediately as he strode out into the middle of the road. He kept his eyes on the zombie and saw its behavior change when it recognized the fresh meat in front of it.

It was like an electric jolt had coursed through its body. Its eyes fixated on him as its dry lips peeled back and an angry snarl passed through its black teeth. The listless shamble it had been doing turned into a full-on hurried stumbling trot. Like a newborn who knew how to walk, but lacked the muscles and coordination to do it well. Its good arm clawed at the air for him like the thirty feet still between them didn't matter and Kenshiro was just within reach. Its bad arm wiggled and flopped uselessly at its side. This lurching, snarling mass of rotting meat devout in the purpose of consuming human flesh, was horrifying on every level.

The sight of them didn't bother Kenshiro much these days, though.

This one didn't even look that bad. Kenshiro had seen some dead walking around that didn't even look human. Zombies could survive just about anything. The only thing that kills zombies is destroying the brain. Anything short of that is a waste of time. Decapitating the dead doesn't even kill them. The head on the ground is still very much intent on biting anything that happens into its mouth. Kenshiro lovingly refers to them as, *undead landmines*. Missing limbs, abdomens torn open with blackened guts spilling down the front. Any horror that could happen to the human body, they could survive it and continue to function so long as its brain remained intact. They technically didn't breathe, so they couldn't be drowned or poisoned. Although he had never been remotely near cold temperatures, Kenshiro suspected extreme temperatures affected them.

He had seen a zombie drop dead from what he imagined was heat exposure. It happened last year, in the Nevada desert. Kenshiro had just discovered Las Vegas was on fire. The whole damned city seemingly ablaze. A giant black smoke plume larger than anything he had seen before, enveloped the entire eastern sky. It was mid-afternoon but all the land in front of him was cast in darkness from the shadow of the smoke. In a way, it was beautiful. On the road in front of him was a zombie wearing only a pair of running shorts, approaching him. Kenshiro stopped the truck, but before he could get out, the zombie suddenly pitched forward and dropped to the pavement. That day had been sweltering; the sun baked his skin. After a quick assessment, it was obvious the zombie wasn't moving. He stabbed it in the head, anyway. Kenshiro couldn't explain why the zombie fell, other than to imagine the heat had finally baked the zombie's brain enough that it completely shut down. After all, when you light a zombie on fire, it's not the flames that eventually drops it, it's the heat. Extreme temperatures could kill zombies, but they would kill Kenshiro a lot quicker.

Kenshiro and the undead man closed in on one another.

He gripped the spear with both hands and lined up the point of the spear to his target. After some experience, he had concluded the best place to aim for, if you were stabbing the front of the face, was the eye socket. It wasn't wise to risk the spear glancing off the skull because it suddenly moved to the side or something. If you went for the mouth, which was a larger target, you risk missing the brain entirely and just pushing the spear through the back of its neck, and the spear was always harder coming out than going in. A flailing zombie at the end of it didn't make it any easier. At that point, Kenshiro might be forced to abandon the spear altogether if there were more undead around to deal with. It took him some practise to hit a target with the spear's heft, but once he adjusted to the weight of it, and developed his two-handed thrust technique, he found the spear to be more than an adequate tool for destroying them. He stepped into the stance he was taught so long ago. The undead man was almost in range. Kenshiro could see how the fury of its bloodlust contorted the edges of the desiccated flesh on its face. It took another step and its snarl grew louder as its bony grey fingers clutched at him. Kenshiro breathed in and struck.

The spear's point found its target and buried itself into the zombie's right eye before it proceeded straight into the brain with ease and burst violently out the back of the skull. Kenshiro yanked the spear back out with practised ease before the corpse hit the road's surface. After, he was surrounded by silence again. He carefully scanned his surroundings with the spear out in front of him, fully prepared to deal with the next one if needed. After a moment, Kenshiro found he was alone again.

He breathed out and let the tension go from his muscles.

"Baka," he cursed the body on the road quietly as he approached it to clean the gore-stained tip of the spear on the zombie's ruined blazer.

Kenshiro walked back to the truck and lifted the tailgate closed before he put the spear in the box point first so the handle protruded out the back slightly for easy access. He then reached in the bed and grabbed the green bag with the stripe. Kenshiro put the Atlas back in its place and zipped it back up. He moved to the driver's door and paused to look at the carefully wrapped bundle on the passenger seat while Kenshiro fished the keys out of his pocket. He thought about what it was, who it belonged to, and why he still carried it, before he climbed into the driver's seat. He sighed deeply as he closed the door and he put the key in the ignition.

The pickup came to life with gusto.

Whoever had owned this truck before had taken good care of it. Kenshiro planned on continuing that effort. He relied on this vehicle. While also fully aware of how dangerous that was, it was a necessary risk given what it afforded him. The truck was another tool of his survival. Just like the spear he always kept sharp, and the survival bag he tried to keep stocked. He maintained the vehicle to the best of his ability. Kenshiro turned on the cassette player and let it play as he steered out onto the road. The cassette tape had been in the truck when he found it. It was music he had never heard before. He didn't listen to it often, but it would be a good start to the morning. As the song went along, he translated the lyrics into Japanese and kept the volume low while he sang along quietly. He cruised down the road at thirty-five miles an hour. He didn't drive fast. He didn't have to. Given the condition of some roads, the things that might be abandoned on them, and the things that could stagger out onto the road at any time; it made a lot more sense to take his time.

Besides that, he had all the time in the world.

Chapter 2

Elliott

Elliott woke up late in the morning, stretched out his body, and decided to try and sleep for a while longer. Laying there with his eyes closed comfortably, he wondered, as he often did, if today would be the day Momma and Daddy would come back home.

Elliott missed them so much he ached and sometimes before bed, in those moments after closing his eyes and before falling asleep, when it's just him and the darkness; he wondered if his parents missed him as much as Elliott missed them. Elliott was embarrassed to admit that if they walked in the door now, he would cry. He would run to them and wrap his arms around them and never let go. Elliott wouldn't care if daddy teased him a bit or called him a baby for crying. He would wrap himself in them, take in momma's sweet flowery perfume, feel daddy's scratchy chin on his cheek. All of it. It would feel so good to hold them. He may never let them go again.

After a short time, Elliott opened his eyes again and breathed out in frustration. Sleep would not come anymore today. When he closed his eyes, all he could think about were all the things he missed. Like chocolate. His mouth watered when he thought about chocolate and how he liked to just hold it in his mouth, then let it melt on his tongue. Almond M&M's were the best for just leisurely sucking on. First, he'd roll it around in his mouth until he got past that candy shell and then the chocolate would just seep into his mouth; once the almond center was exposed, he would then chew and mix it all up in his mouth before swallowing. Delicious.

He missed television, playing with his Transformers on the carpet, and hanging out with Daddy while he watched his favorite shows. After most dinners, Daddy would want to watch the news while he and Momma cleaned up the dishes, and then after they would all sit down and watch their programs. At bed time, Elliott would hug his parents both goodnight, brush his teeth, and hop into bed. His nights usually ended with Daddy shutting off the light before saying, "Good night, son.". He missed the warm feeling of those hugs, and the gentle reassurance those words gave him. Elliott knew he wasn't like the other boys. He wasn't good at writing, or math, and although he liked to read, he couldn't read the books the other boys could. That warm feeling at night he got from his parents before he closed his eyes made him think, maybe it didn't matter.

He missed his best friend and neighbor, Jenny. He missed all his friends, but he missed her most of all. She laughed at his jokes and called him funny all the time. She was kind of like his big sister. She punched Johnny Witmore in the face when he called Elliott stupid. After that, Elliott knew she would always be his best friend, no matter what. She left with her family when the grey people first started showing up on all the news stations. He hasn't seen her since. He prayed she was alright.

"No!" Elliott said aloud to his empty room when the first sting of tears came to his eyes.

He promised himself some time ago he would try not to get sad anymore. Defiantly, he threw back the covers and swung his legs out of the bed and went to get up, only to feel the room spin dangerously. Elliot quickly sat back down on the bed until his head cleared. This had been happening more and more lately. He didn't know why, but now-and-then Elliott would get kind of woozy. The world seemed to move around him even though he was pretty sure he was standing still and he would feel kind of… distant. Like everything was sort of far away. It would pass with time. Usually, he had to steady himself until it did. A few times, he had actually fallen. Like his legs suddenly became jelly and refused to hold him up anymore, and down he went. This time wasn't too bad. After a few moments and some deep breaths, his vision cleared, and the world settled around him.

More cautiously, he stood, and after a few seconds testing the waters, Elliott made his way to the bathroom. He still felt a strange tingling in his legs as he went, but that also disappeared as he exited the bedroom door. He didn't think it was something he needed to worry about. His feet made little slapping sounds against the hardwood floor as he made his way down the hall.

It was a small bathroom, but Elliott had kept it tidy all this time. Just like Momma would want him to. Keeping his little bathroom clean was one of the few chores his parents entrusted to him. He took it seriously because Daddy had explained to him, they trusted him to do his chores, like a big kid, and he would not let them down. The bathtub was to the right as he entered and the toilet was on the opposite corner. Beside it, was a five-gallon bucket with enough water to flush the toilet. At first, he would flush the toilet and then fill the tank, but over time, he found it was just easier to pour the water directly into the bowl. He lifted the lid, dropped his pants, and peed. Elliott looked at the stream and decided not to bother flushing this time around. He went to the sink without looking in the mirror. On one side of the faucet was a tiny bar of soap, a tube of toothpaste, and his toothbrush in a little blue cup. By the side of the sink, in a plastic container that was roughly the size of a thermos, was the rinsing water. Elliott grabbed his tooth brush and the toothpaste and brushed his teeth like he always had, and while he did, he ran through the things he could do today to pass the time until it got dark.

He could start by checking his list. He wrote all the things he could do when he was bored down on a piece of paper, and he was bored a lot. Of course, there was housework, which momma would be proud to know he hadn't let slip. The house was spotless, even by her standards. Working the brush in his mouth, Elliott smiled to himself at the thought of what momma would do to reward all his hard work. He didn't do housework every day; he didn't need to, so he made sure the list included other things. Fun stuff, like throwing the ball around outside, if no grey people were around. He also had a large assortment of puzzles he could do. Momma loved puzzles. So, Elliott did too. It had grown to be one of the things that they enjoyed doing together. In the past, they would talk while they slowly assembled the puzzle. Momma would tell stories of when she was little and asked Elliott about stuff that was happening at school. There were games he could play, board, and card games. He knew how to play solitaire, but it rarely held his interest long enough to finish a game. More often than not, he would end up using the cards to build houses. He enjoyed that, mostly because it took a lot of time.

Some time ago, he had searched the house and found they had about a dozen different decks of cards and used them all to create a card city in the living room. Dozens of unique structures littered the floor, some were small one-bedroom houses, others were larger multi-story constructions. Elliott had impressed himself with some of his designs. He supposed he could do that again today. There were other things he could do, but he couldn't think of them just now, which is why he took the time to write them down. He didn't have the best memory normally, but these days it was getting hard to keep a thought straight in his head.

When he was happy with his brushing, Elliott spat into

the sink and was disappointed to see blood in the sink. He looked at his teeth in the mirror, his gums were bleeding again. A few teeth on the side had bright crimson oozing out from the gumline. He took the water container from the side of the sink and rinsed his mouth before spitting the pink fluid out. Elliott poured a little water around the sink to clean what remained, before replacing all the items in their proper places and heading back to his bedroom. *Maybe I'm brushing too hard*, he thought as he padded his way into the room. If that was the case, the problem would take care of itself when the toothpaste ran out. In the beginning there had been a lot of it, momma found a good deal on it and bought in bulk, she did that sometimes when she could find a bargain. But now, there was only one container left in the cupboard after the one he was using ran out. Elliott didn't know what he'd do after the last tube ran out as well.

His bedroom was tidy, even though the rule in the past was bedrooms were special places and could get messy. With all the time on his hands, it was hard not to clean something when it needed it. He went to the closet and selected a simple outfit, jeans, a white t-shirt, and a blue hoodie. He was sure it was summer because the thermostat on the porch was well into the eighties, but Elliott still felt cold most days.

Another problem was, he wasn't the boy he was when this all began and none of his clothes fit him anymore. He was taller, by how much he couldn't say, but Daddy had marked lines on the wall of his room to show how much he's grown since he was a toddler. When Elliott checked his new height against the line on the wall, he was noticeably higher than the last line. Elliott didn't mark it, though. He wanted daddy to see for himself just how much he grew. Daddy would also be pleasantly surprised to see Elliott had lost weight. Like a lot of weight. He said nothing to Elliott about his weight in the past, but he knew it secretly bothered his father. Before, Elliott couldn't even see his feet if he looked down while standing. Now, not only could he see his feet. When he took off his shirt, he could see his ribs poking through the skin a bit. He was skinny now. With his clothes on, the cuff of the hoodies' sleeves barely reached his wrist and the hem of his jeans hovered above his ankles slightly. Everything sort of loosely hung on him like an oversized robe, and without his belt done up to the last notch, his pants would fall to his ankles.

He took his pajamas and hung them on the side of the laundry basket for later. The basket was only a quarter full, and Elliott didn't really like doing laundry by hand, so that could wait for now. He went downstairs, being sure to hold on to the railing in case he felt dizzy again. At the bottom he quickly eyed the three baby carrots he left on the kitchen counter from last night. His pinkie finger was larger than those carrots. They looked more like small orange twigs than carrots. They probably shouldn't have been picked for months yet. But he had to eat something. Without thinking, he walked over to the counter, scooped up all three carrots and put them in his mouth.

While chewing thoroughly and sucking on the carrot's juices. He decided he would start his day working in his garden. It used to be momma's, but after last winter, Elliott doubled the amount of space used for the garden. He simply needed it to produce more. So, after that, he proclaimed to no one in particular that it was now *his* garden. Until momma got back anyway. His stomach growled loudly, the carrot-twigs did nothing more than to remind his stomach how empty it was. Elliott rubbed his stomach as if trying to sooth it, and went about checking the windows to see if there were any grey people in the yard. He went from window to window on the ground floor and spent a few moments at each looking for any movement.

From the living room, he had a good view of the big, metal swing gate at the end of the lane leading to the road. That's usually where he saw them, if they were out there at all. Grey people didn't bother him much, but he kept to daddy's rule; *when you see one of them, you go inside, and you don't come out until they're gone.* That led to him being confined inside the house for days, like a prisoner trapped inside his own home, but that was preferable to bashing their heads in with a rock.

He'd had to do that a couple times as well. Elliott had a hard time thinking of anything else in this world he'd rather do less than hitting another grey person over the head with a rock. First time he had done it, Elliott was ashamed to admit he cried a bit. It was so horrible. The smell, the sound the rock made when it connected with the grey person's head. The grotesque way its skull just seemed to give way under the force of the throw, the black goo that splashed out of the wound, and the god-awful smell of it. He knew he had to deal with them. Elliott knew he couldn't hide in the house forever, but if he could avoid it, he would.

Luckily, they haven't been too much of a problem, and Elliott felt if he left them alone that maybe, the grey people would leave him alone too. He checked the windows repeatedly, and saw no movement. He felt it was fairly safe to go outside. He approached the front mud room, where the family kept all their coats in the closets along the wall, and went to the shoe shelves by the far wall and took out his work boots. His running shoes would be lighter, but he didn't want to get them dirty in the garden. When momma bought those shoes, she bought them a size bigger so he would grow into them, which he did, but they were the only shoes that size. The rest still fit, but it was a tight fit that gave his feet cramps after a while. He tried daddy's shoes on, but they were still too big for him. Regardless, Elliott put his boots on and felt his toes cram together inside before he moved towards the door. He peered out the window at the door through the crack in the curtains. Nothing. He slowly opened the door, careful of the noise he made, and walked onto the porch.

He tip-toed across the porch to the stairs and down onto the paved walkway at the bottom. Once there, he knew he could relax a bit. Before he went to work in the garden, he carefully looked around the yard for grey people. Grey people could be silent as well, and Elliott didn't want any of them sneaking up on him while he worked. He went to the barn first and checked all around it, careful to peer around the corners first before walking around it. He made the full circle of the building and found nothing. He did the same with the chicken coop, keeping his distance so not to rouse the last two chickens he had. Nothing there. Finally, he went to the round metal quonset where Daddy parked the various vehicles they had. Elliott let out a breath when he found nothing there as well. The yard was clear. He turned the corner of the quonset and walked down the lane a bit to the front gate and was relieved to find it was free of grey people, too. Thankfully, this was typical, but whenever he was outside, he was on the lookout for them. Elliott wasn't concerned with checking the fields. He had never seen one come from that direction; only from the road.

Elliott made his way to the garden on the other side of the house. Since his expansion, it ran the entire length of the barn. Before, it had only come about halfway and was maybe twenty feet across. It was obvious at what point momma's garden had ended and where Elliott had expanded it. The new section still had ugly looking serrated edges from where he pulled the grass up months earlier, and the rows were not exactly straight, but he didn't consider how it would look when he did it.

His tiny crop comprised of peas in the first row. Green beans, which he didn't really like, in the second row. The third row was carrots. He could see the bare patches in the neat row from the few carrots he had already picked, but they weren't the only scavenged plant. The fourth row had fist sized lettuce plants. He didn't know what kind of lettuce exactly, and he could see on the plants where he had torn away a leaf or two to eat two days before. Towering over the entire garden at the back was the corn. They were about three feet high, but he didn't see any cobs growing yet. In the corner, where the corn row didn't quite reach the edge of the garden, he had planted a few potatoes. It was a good sized garden, but was it enough?

Momma often talked about making the garden bigger but usually ended the thought by complaining it would be too much work and the weeds would eventually take over. Back then, Elliott didn't quite understand why momma even bothered having a garden. They purchased most of the vegetables they ate at the local supermarket, which in his experience was a lot easier than tending a garden for fruits and vegetables. However, that was then and this is now. Now the garden was vitally important because the garden and his two remaining chickens were his last remaining food sources.

Before Momma and Daddy left, their house was stocked with all sorts of food, and if Elliott had known just how long he was going to be alone, he might have rationed the food better. Looking back, he couldn't believe how much he had eaten in that first month. He had three meals a day, each comprising of several courses. His favorites to start with, then after those were gone, he experimented. He tried not to think of the food that he threw away for no better reason than it didn't suit his palette, or simply because it didn't look appetizing. In those days, he usually capped off the day with a sandwich before bed, usually peanut butter and jam, and a tall glass of juice from a powdered mix. That didn't even include the snacking. Elliott's stomach protested loudly as he knelt down into the garden to weed while thinking of all the snacks he had in the beginning. If he had only known it was going to be the last bag of Cheetos he was ever going to eat...

They had been his favorite.

When his parents left, there were three bags in the house; Elliott ate them all that first night. Back then, he didn't even consider the possibility that Momma and Daddy would not be back when they said. When his father was giving him instructions on what to do while they were gone, and Momma was sobbing softly while smoothing his hair, Elliott thought about raiding the pantry.

"We'll be gone maybe an hour, son. Don't go outside and remember what I told you," His father had said before he walked out the door. But all Elliott was focused on was that when they were out of the driveway, he was going to tear open one of those bags of Cheetos and have just a few handfuls.

Later that night, when they didn't come back, he continued to munch down on the powdery nuggets. When he was well into the second bag, he looked out of the window so he could see the headlights coming back down the road from Aunt Kelly's house. The next morning, he had woken up to three empty bags, orange fingertips, and a lonely house.

Now that the Cheetos and all the other food that was in the house was a distant memory, there was only the garden and the chickens. He never had to work so hard for so little. Elliott tried to focus on the garden and put all thoughts of food as far away from the here-and-now as possible. He fussed over the garden daily so really there wasn't much that needed to be done. There were only some baby weeds strewn in with the plants. Elliott was amazed by the it ability to grow so fast overnight.

He went plant by plant. Row by row. First, he inspected and pulled what weeds he found. Then, using his hands, he would build up the mound around the plant again to help funnel the water towards the stem. Elliott had a small container with him. Any worms or slugs he came across, were placed in the container so he could feed what he found to his chickens. He had tried eating worms once. He didn't like them, and he found he couldn't swallow them. Like his body wouldn't allow it, even though it was starving.

Starving.

Elliott tried not to think about that word.

Maybe the chickens would have an egg for him today. The last egg was four days ago. Molly, the one covered in feathers the same color as milk chocolate, had produced it. Or was it five? He couldn't remember, the days sort of blurred together into one long day, but he was pretty sure it was four days ago he found the egg under Molly. Elliott remembered he could barely contain himself when his hand closed around it. He had been drooling all the way to the house to cook it up.

The one thing he still had, his last real convenience, was he still had a working stove. It was a simple gas range that fed off the huge propane tank on the other side of the barn. Elliott didn't know how much propane they had left in that tank. His father had turned off the furnace at the onset of the grey people invasion, so as far as Elliott knew, the only thing draining that tank was the stove.

He made scrambled eggs with a little water and a bit of pepper. Egg days were always the best days. Elliott hoped for an egg today as he plucked a slug from the infant lettuce plant he was tending to and placed it into the container. *I feed them, and they feed me.* He smiled at the simplicity of their unspoken arrangement. They were survivors, him and those chickens, and maybe if they kept working together as they have been, the three of them would make it out of this.

When he finished what he wanted to do in the garden, he felt a cool sheen of sweat on his brow and underneath his clothes, but somehow, he still felt cold, and Elliott suddenly realized how breathless he was. Like the air he breathed in didn't have enough oxygen in it. *I thought when I lost all that weight, I'd be healthier*, Elliott thought to himself. He certainly didn't feel healthier at that moment. He sat down by the peas to rest a bit. He chose a few thumbnail sized pea pods, picked them and ate them. *I have to stop doing this. I have to wait!* He cursed himself as he chewed. If he didn't stop, there would be nothing to harvest in the months to come because he would have picked it clean by then, but he couldn't help himself. *Starving.* He pushed the thought deep down and without realizing it; Elliott had sunk down in the grass.

He was looking up at the clouds, but he didn't remember lying down or even wanting to. The sky was beautiful though, deep blue color with little fluffy white clouds slowly drifting across his vision. He closed his eyes, and thought about his parents and how when they got back, they would have bags and bags of groceries in the back of the truck when they pulled up. Daddy would pat him on the head and…

Elliott awoke violently sometime later, confused and afraid. His eyes snapped opened, and he frantically scrambled away, his hands furiously pedalling backwards while his legs kicked at the grass for purchase. All the while searching desperately around him for the thing he was trying to escape from in his dream. He had sworn he felt something grab his leg. The more he looked around him, the more he realized it wasn't *something* that he thought grabbed his leg. It was the grey person from his dream. Elliott remembered its cold, dried fingers wrapping around his right ankle. He was sure of it. He frantically looked around for the source of the assault, but he was alone. Elliott was in the yard, but he couldn't remember how he had gotten there. He looked around in amazement, like somehow, he had been transported to that spot from his bed. Elliott tried to think but his mind was foggy, and it was hard to focus on a single thought. He looked beside him and saw the container he used for worms on the ground, a quarter full of worms and slugs all squirming together at the bottom.

That was when the first pieces started to come back to him. Elliott used his hand to comb the sweat-soaked strands of hair out of his eyes, and waited as it all came back to him. *Stupid! Stupid idiot. Dummy*! He was mad at himself for being so careless. How could he have fallen asleep outside? Or did he pass out? It didn't matter. He remembered after the garden work was done; he felt exhausted, but he didn't remember lying down. Elliott then remembered what had woken him up in the first place and shivered; he could still feel those dry digits as they began squeezing the flesh of his ankle. It felt so real.

He sat up, feeling his heart still racing, and as the dread slowly released its grip on him, he felt little cramps all over his body. Elliott had exerted himself too much just now. He didn't feel dizzy, but his muscles were now protesting the sudden movement he frantically made a moment ago. His mouth was dry, he needed a drink. When he struggled to rise, that's when he also remembered he wasn't done with the garden just yet. It needed water as well. He let out a weary groan as he walked about a dozen paces to the hand pump where it was set in the ground close to the corner of the barn. Elliott pumped the handle a few times until the water flowed and then put his head under to let the water wash away the heat that seemed to radiate off his scalp. It felt good. Elliott backed away, opened his mouth and gulped down a few mouthfuls before reaching for the water can to fill it up.

Using both hands, he carried it back to the garden and began giving each plant a generous drink of water by its stem. It took three more trips to the water pump to finish the entire garden. He took a generous drink himself each trip, hoping the cool water would lessen the ache in his stomach.

The chickens were next, and then after that; he decided he should go back into the house and get out of the sun for a while. Elliott picked up the container and its slimy contents from where he left it by the peas, and started across the yard towards the chicken coop.

The coop was a small building that has been on the farm as long as he had, and by the look of it, probably a lot longer. It had wooden siding with cream-colored paint that was peeling in some spots. In other spots, it was worn completely away, exposing the weather-beaten wood underneath. The area in front of the building had been cordoned off with a tiny fence that kept the chickens in, but it was still low enough Elliott could climb over it without opening the gate. He didn't have to do that anymore, though. The front of the fence had a gaping hole in it from when a grey person got into the chickens.

Elliott watched the entire ordeal from the house, not knowing what to do, but knowing he needed those chickens. He had named all thirteen chickens and watched in horror as a grey person in dirty overalls ripped Sally to pieces and savagely thrust feathery bits of bloody chicken into its mouth. Thankfully, the rest of the chickens escaped through the new hole in the fence and scattered immediately away from the danger. Only two chickens found their way back to the yard. The grey person, to Elliott's relief, pursued one of the fleeing chickens down the lane and back to the road. After that, Elliott no longer allowed the chickens to go outside, not that the two remaining ever showed an interest in going outside anymore. He also closed the gate at the end of the lane and kept it that way ever since. Elliott didn't quite understand how the chickens attracted the grey person, but he realized they had, and it still stung now that if he had kept those chickens in the coup, he probably wouldn't be so desperate for food now. He'd probably get an egg a day with all those chickens. Elliott opened the door to the coop and realized if he still had all those chickens, his days would be spent constantly digging up worms for them. *Totally worth it*, he thought as he said his greeting to his chickens when he entered.

"Morning Molly. Morning Rebecca," he said and then remembered he really didn't know what time of day it was.

The inside of the tiny building had two sets of wooden shelves, one above the other, that encircled the room. The shelves held the chicken's nests. There were thirteen nests spaced out around the room, but there was plenty of space for more. His two chickens nested across from each other, one on the left side of the room and the other on the right. Elliott sometimes wondered if his two chickens didn't like each other, because they spent their time just glaring at each other. He walked up to Molly's nest first, carefully rationed out her share of the slimy food, and poured it into her feeding dish in front of the nest. Then came the moment of truth. Elliott slowly slid his hand under the distracted bird while she was busy pecking away at her dinner. His fingers came across the warm smoothness of a shell. Elliott pulled his hand back as if in disbelief and pumped his fist in celebration.

"Yes!" Elliott cheered quietly but enthusiastically, and then turned to the chicken. "Thank you, Molly," he said and meant it. He would eat today because of that bird, and he couldn't help himself but to be grateful. Using his two fingers, he gently stroked its tiny neck and down its back. If Molly liked the attention, she gave no sign of it and simply continued eating. Elliott couldn't blame her. He then looked at the other chicken, Rebecca, and moved towards her. He emptied the rest of the container into her dish. She too began to furiously devour the slimy treats, and once again Elliott slid his hand under the bird.

Holy Balls!

Elliott couldn't believe what he was touching. He pulled out the second egg and just stared at it in his palm for a moment. Two eggs. In one day, it was a miracle. He felt his heart pound in his chest and heard his stomach groan at the promise of the actual food that was in the palm of his hand, and he had two of them. Elliott went over to Molly and collected the other egg; they were both a good size, both fitting nicely into the palm of his hand. Now he had to get them safely back to the house, which shouldn't be a hard task. He'd done it countless times in his life. This time was different, though; he felt it in his bones, the grim importance of what lies ahead; of what he must do without failure. Elliott took in a deep breath and tried to steady himself for the next few minutes. He planned it all out in his head. He'd open the door, walk to the house, go inside and place the eggs in the bowl he had already prepared for just such an occasion. The round soup bowl with the cloth inside, Elliott's own nest. He visualized the kitchen counter in his mind and saw the bowl there by the far-right corner of the sink. Elliott breathed out and moved towards the door of the coup.

Elliott faced a new dilemma as he made his way towards the house. He held the eggs close to his body and kept his eyes on the ground in front of him. Carefully mapping out his steps ahead of time; this was no time to trip on a root, gopher hole or some stray pebble. After the first few steps were out of the way, his confidence grew and some part of his mind wondered aloud inside his head. *Should I eat one egg or both of them*? Immediately, an all too familiar voice piped up for the first time in a while. *Eat, Eat, EAT*!! It growled inside his head.

"No," Elliott said solemnly, not even realizing he spoke the word. He knew that voice. Elliott had listened to that voice before, too many times in the past, and it had cost him. He had eaten everything, like an idiot, for no other reason than he could. He knew this time would be different because this time he understood. When he was reunited with his parents, he would tell them of this day. The day a miracle happened, and it blessed him with two eggs, and for once in his life he wouldn't eat all he could. Elliott would make them proud by showing his parents how grown up he could be.

He got to the front door and moved the egg in his right hand to his left and opened the door and went in. Elliott didn't bother to remove his shoes; he was too close to the finish line now to stop for minor details. Plus, a dirty floor would give him something to do later. He walked right to the bowl and deposited the eggs, safe and sound. It was then his knees gave out, and he sank to the floor, overwhelmed by what he felt. The two eggs wouldn't last. He knew his days of stomach pains weren't over, but today he won a minor victory. He sat there for a moment, basking in the warm glow of his success, before his stomach called him into action. Elliott rose off the floor and fished the frying pan out of the large drawer by the oven where momma kept her cookware, turned the dial on the range and waited for the burner to come to life before setting the pan on the tiny circle of blue flames. With a wide grin on his face, Elliott cracked the egg he believed to be Molly's with practiced ease and cooked his dinner. The smell coming off the pan while his egg cooked was intoxicating. After he finished eating the egg, as custom demanded, he licked the plate clean. Elliott felt slightly better. Stronger. Tomorrow would be a good day too. From where he sat, he could see tomorrow's egg nestled in the bowl by the sink.

Hours later, Elliott sat at the kitchen table, quietly working on his puzzle. Tonight's puzzle showcased a close-up picture of a fairy girl that was dressed in rags and had big butterfly wings sprouting from its back. Judging from the picture, it was flying through some fantastical garden. It was a hard puzzle to assemble, a plethora of soft colors and sparkles with very few solid colors. This will be his fifth time assembling it. He spent a long time at the start just blankly staring at the colored pieces. Slowly, he constructed a good starting place to begin with. It was a fifteen-hundred-piece puzzle, which was one of the few harder puzzles he had. He and momma usually tackled five hundred. Elliott didn't *exactly* like putting puzzles together. Before, it was something he could do with his mother, and they would snack on cookies or carrots while doing it, and just talk about stuff. All kinds of stuff. Now, sitting there in the dim light the setting sun provided, he didn't have the company of his mother, and he found putting those little oddly shaped colored pieces into their rightful place gave him a feeling of longing. The puzzle of his life was missing a few important pieces.

Tomorrow he would spend a little extra time and try to dig up extra worms for his chickens, and he would take the time and clean out their nests. He felt they deserved the extra effort.

Elliott looked down at the piece in his hand and decided it was time to stop. It had become too dark to bother going any further, and by looking at the fading light on the horizon, he concluded nothing else could be done today. He went around the house and checked all the windows and the front door before heading upstairs to his room. He took off his clothes; put them into the hamper before putting last night's pajamas on and climbing into bed. The house was deathly quiet.

Before the crisis, the moments in bed before sleep finally took him were normally a calm time. He would lie awake listening to the sounds of the night. Just about every night, he could hear the television downstairs playing his parents' favorite tv shows. Sometimes he could hear them laughing over the sounds of the television. On the nights his father watched hockey, he would hear the announcer frantically calling out the game just loud enough so Elliott could hear it, but not so loud he could make out exactly what he was saying. His father would cheer or curse, depending on how his team was doing. There were even those rare occasions his parents would argue about something, usually money, and when they did, they would walk outside into the yard because they wouldn't want Elliott to hear them shout, but he did anyway. Even when his house was quiet, there would still be the sounds of the countryside he had grown accustomed to. Throughout the night, he could hear coyotes howling and barking off in the distance. He'd hear the neighbor's cows moo now-and-then, and owls would sound off in the darkness. Maybe a vehicle would drive by the road out front. There was countless sounds Elliott had grown accustomed to hearing at night, back then.

But now, there was nothing like that. On windy nights,

he would hear the wind rattle the leaves in the tree, or else the house would give off a spooky-sounds as it shifted in the night, and the sound of his breathing. Those were the only sounds to push back against the dead silence that consumed the world at night. Every night now, he laid in bed and tried not to feel the nothingness closing in around him, and some nights he was ashamed to admit the bitter silence got the best of him. Doom and doubts would creep into his bones, and try as he might, Elliott would still think of terrible things.

It was hard not to think that maybe Momma and Daddy weren't trying to get back to him at all. Maybe this was what they wanted all along, and they abandoned him to die while they were off somewhere safe. Maybe they were happy to be rid of him once and for all. Maybe they went to his aunt's house and picked up Aunt Kelly and Uncle Jerry, but instead of coming back home to him, they looked at each other and just decided they were better off without him around and just kept driving down the road. It was an easy thought to have, and once it was in there, it just bounced around his head, getting louder and louder. He would cry, not a simple weeping either. It would rack his whole body with uncontrollable sobs and he would scream into his tear-soaked pillow until his throat was raw. When it was over, he would feel nothing still. Nobody was there to soothe him back from the edge. There was no comforting voice or a warm touch to break through the darkness. Only the silence to greet him once more.

Tonight, however, he didn't feel he had to worry about that, although he had eaten quite a delightful meal and his stomach no longer bothered him; he still felt dog-tired. His day had put a toll on him, he knew that, but it had ended better than it began. And these days, that was rare. He let his head sink into the pillow and almost immediately fell asleep and was dreaming.

A thin smile passed over his lips. He was dreaming of Thanksgiving dinner at Grandma's house.

Sitting in his usual place with his aunts, uncles, and cousins all around him, Elliott looked towards the kitchen at the exact moment his grandma was bringing out a big fat turkey on a giant silver platter that he didn't really remember her ever having. He could almost taste it. He looked at his family and was unsettled to find they had dry grey faces with cracked lips covering black teeth. Their hair had faded to a dirty grey and had thinned to the point their scalps were clearly visible on each of them. They still talked and laughed as they passed food around the table, as was normal. He even took the plate of buns from Kurt, his cousin who was five years older than he was, and their fingers brushed against each other and Elliott briefly felt the cold dry flesh of Kurt's fingers. Elliott thanked him and took a bun, all the while fixated on the cracked skin of his scalp and feeling there was something he was forgetting. The smells of the table were intoxicating and drew his attention away from what he was thinking about before; he breathed it in and let the aroma fill him. *I'm home*, he thought, *I'm finally home*. Like he had been away for a long time, but he didn't remember ever being anywhere else other than right here. He quickly dismissed the feeling as he began cutting the meat on his plate. Whatever it was, it didn't matter. He was here, and *this* is where he belonged.

Chapter 3

Kenshiro

By the time he was satisfied with his reconnaissance of the small town of La Veta, Kenshiro was convinced the western approach was the only logical option.

He first followed the highway into the town on the north and stopped the truck atop a small hill that overlooked La Veta. He had a nice view of the road heading into the small town, and he didn't like what he saw one bit. The first intersection was cluttered with abandoned cars, and the sides of the road leading to it was congested with overgrown shrubs. Worse yet, he spied a small apartment complex on the east side of the road before the town limit.

The south wasn't much better. Again, the sides of the roads were lined with trees that obscured his view. Posh little acreages lined both sides of the roads, and each had mature trees marking the boundaries of the properties. Which limited his visibility and was guaranteed to have pockets of zombies that would find a way in behind him. Kenshiro didn't even bother with the eastern approach because the western approach was perfect for his needs. Nothing but wide-open space with a clear line of sight into the town. The gravel road was almost completely straight for a half mile before it hit a T-intersection right before La Veta. The two branches ran for about a hundred yards before they both turned into the town. It left a beautiful football field-size patch of barren land right before the first line of houses. It was a perfect killing field.

Kenshiro looked up and saw the sun dipping down into the western sky and decided it was time to find a place to hold up for the night. He spied a little farm on his way to the west side of La Veta. It was situated on the south side of the road right after a lazy bend. The quaint looking farm was far enough away from the town to be isolated, but close enough he could retreat back to it if he needed to tomorrow.

Kenshiro pulled the truck into the long driveway of the farm and slowly drove up to the house. It had been the trees that lined both sides of the paved entrance onto the property that attracted his attention first. Tall, slender trees that reached up towards the sky, easily the tallest things around for miles. They followed the approach towards the house and then encircled an area around the bulk of the property. Driving slowly, he saw the driveway ahead spread out into a large paved parking area, and beyond that, he saw the front of a barn. On the left side, Kenshiro saw the beginning of the porch that led up to the house. He couldn't see the house yet, but from what he did see, he was expecting it to be rather impressive. Farms were good places to find things. His plan was to stay here tonight, and start into the town in the morning. It was still early enough he could spend what daylight there was and have a look around for anything he might need or want. As Kenshiro slowly pulled up the driveway, he daydreamed about an above ground fuel tank with a gravity fed hose complete with a nozzle, a pantry with shelves filled with food stuffs, and properly preserved food in jars each labeled with easy-to-read dates and the seals still intact. He could hope anyway.

Kenshiro was trying to get a better look at the house ahead when he saw movement to the right and saw a zombie lurch out from the tree line in front of him. This was not unexpected. He slowed the truck to a stop fifty yards from the house, knowing full well the zombie was locked onto the truck, and him inside it. Kenshiro simply watched it approach and waited. The zombie obviously had been a teenager before. It wore camouflaged cargo shorts, and a muscle shirt with a band logo Kenshiro didn't recognize. The zombie wore no shoes though. It must have been walking a lot because Kenshiro could see bits of torn flesh peeking out from under its feet from where the meat of its sole had been scraped away. Slowly, the zombie walked out onto the road and lined itself up with Kenshiro, or more precisely, it lined itself up with the driver's side of the truck as it stumbled forward on the asphalt road. It was then that Kenshiro let off the brake, and the truck began to roll forward, gathering speed as it went.

The trick to running over zombies, was not to do it fast. Mainly, because it presented too great a chance of not putting the zombie down so much as turning it into an undead landmine. Essentially immobile, but still just as ready and willing to bite whatever happens by, and all it takes is one. Second reason is to not damage the vehicle. The safest way to deal with zombies using a vehicle was to treat it the same way you would a speed bump. Kenshiro lined the lurching figure up with his driver's wheel and slowly approached it, and slowed down even more right before the impact.

If done right, the bumper merely nudges the zombie, but with absolutely no balance to speak of, the zombie falls back almost comedically. Then, like he would a speed bump, Kenshiro slowly rolled over top of it. He felt the bones crunch under the wheels, until he heard the familiar crackle and pop of the skull giving way under the tire. The hardest part of the whole process was trying not to pay attention to those sounds. Kenshiro drove on and spied three more emerging from the trees along the side. He made a mental note of them as he drove by and continued up to the house.

The house was on the east side of the driveway, partially hidden behind more trees. It was a large two-storey house with a steep sloping roof and a brick chimney on the side. The comfortable-looking house at one point must have been a bright blue with white trim. Now, the colors were muted by a thick layer of dust and grime. It had a large porch that wrapped around the house to the back with a white waist-high railing, and thick pillars that were spaced out evenly that reached up to meet the roof. The front had a staircase leading to the porch, and on each side, there was a flower bed Kenshiro felt might have been well kept and colorful at one time, like it had been someone's pride and joy. The woman of the house maybe? The house had large bay windows in the front. Kenshiro also noticed the second level had decorative shutters on each of the windows, and the front door was also white and had a large stained-glass window in it. Yes, in its day, this house must have been a shiny jewel compared to the other houses he had seen along the way.

Now, however, the house bore the scars of what it had been through. Kenshiro's eyes immediately locked on the blood-stained drapes in the front window that had been partially torn down on the side. Kenshiro noted it and moved on. The once colorful flower bed now had been taken over extensively by weeds, most notably were dandelions, but there was a variety of invasive plants that have established its dominance in the tiny flower beds long ago. A section of the railing on the front porch had been broken through; the pieces lay scattered in the flower bed where the center section of it had been flattened. From the driver's seat, Kenshiro could see bloodstains on the remaining broken end of the railing. *People have died here.*

The stairs leading up to the porch, and the porch itself was covered with leaves from the year before. In the yard, he could see piles of leaves and rubbish that had collected from where the wind blew it. He parked directly in front of the rustic red barn. It reminded Kenshiro of the kind he had seen in movies and television shows, complete with red paint and white trim. Two wide wooden doors that swung out marked the front, and he guessed there would be a matching set at the back as well. Like the house, dust dulled the colors of the barn slightly, but also like the house, the barn was in great condition otherwise. On the west side there was an extension that had been built onto the side. The paint looked a little newer, and there were windows built into it that looked more modern than the rest of the barn. He suspected this was a vehicle shed, garage, or workshop of some sort and not a *barn* in the traditional sense.

Kenshiro pulled up to the center of the driveway, a safe distance away from anything, and stopped the truck. For the time being he left the truck running, the gentle hum of the engine would attract any zombies within ear shot, and make for a quick getaway if need be. He scouted the property from the road and he didn't see any real numbers to be concerned about, but it was good to have a backup plan.

Kenshiro heard them as soon as he exited the cab.

He left the driver's door open and proceeded to the back while looking for the source of the snarls. Kenshiro immediately saw the three he had seen on his way in. There was also a female zombie in a bloodied summer dress with a flower print that came into view from behind the house. Two more moved into the afternoon light from the far side of the barn, and as soon as he saw them, his eyes caught the movement of another coming through the trees on the opposite end of the driveway. As always, the sight of fresh meat electrified their stiff muscles, and propelled them into faster motion. Their arms reaching and clawing at the space in front of them, their jaws automatically snapped at the air as their legs propelled them forward with renewed vigor, and their normally quiet, breathless hiss became their signature throaty snarl.

Seven, but there'll be more coming soon. Kenshiro visualized their positions in his head and started planning as he slid the spear out of the back of the truck. He reminded himself to find a pair of gloves because even though the spear was a fine weapon, it was still rebar, and the coarseness of the shaft blistered his hands after a while

This won't take long.

He kept the spear in his right hand as he approached the three coming up the driveway towards him. With quick strides, not running exactly, Kenshiro moved towards them. He wanted to get some space between him and the other four from behind. Kenshiro imagined if others came, it would be from behind the barn. He hurried up on the three. They were nicely spaced out, and Kenshiro planned his attack. He grabbed the spear with both hands and stepped into a left stance a moment before thrusting the spearhead through the female zombie in the badly soiled summer dress. The spear slid into its eye socket with ease and into its brain, seemingly without obstruction, and its body fell for the last time as he jerked the spear back out. He then swung the spear low and towards the back, took a full step forward, and he brought the spearhead down on top of the nearest zombie's skull. There was a splash of dark fluid as a sharp crack filled the air, and its skull collapsed inwards. Kenshiro didn't wait to examine the damage. He simply swung the spear overhead, took a quick step to the side where the remaining zombie was, and brought the full weight of the steel shaft crashing into the side of its head. The zombie violently leapt to the side and landed motionlessly in a heap onto the driveway, and did not stir again.

Three down in less than thirty seconds. It felt good, but it was an insignificant victory. Zombies don't block, they don't move out of the way, and as far as he could tell, they didn't seem to even notice the incoming attack. As the American saying goes; it was like shooting fish in a barrel.

He spun to face the remaining four, which swelled to eight, as a tight group of zombies rounded the corner of the new extension on the barn. Kenshiro added them to his mental tally. They were a ways off still, and it would take them some time to enter the fray. He darted back to the truck and walked around the open driver's door just as another undead female in a flower print summer dressed came stumbling awkwardly down the porch stairs. He waited until it took two steps on the driveway towards him, before Kenshiro swung the metal spear like a sledgehammer to the side, and watched with a cold indifference as the spear made contact right above its shrivelled ear. The female's whole face distorted and shifted as the impact destroyed its skull.

Crunch!

Without missing a beat, Kenshiro took two quick steps towards the two closing in on him, swung the spearhead down and back to gain momentum, before he brought it down on top of the left one's head. The spear made a tiny channel in the zombie's forehead as it sank down into the skull to its eyebrows. Kenshiro winced in disgust, as bits of blackened skull and brain matter jumped up from the wound. Pulling the spear back hard to his right side he thrusted the tip into the face of the other one and watched it enter under the right-side cheek bone. The bodies fell where they had stood, and Kenshiro violently yanked the spear free before checking his surroundings.

The single zombie from the trees was rounding the back corner of the truck. Kenshiro swiveled on his heels and swung the spear low and caught the zombie on the inside of its front knee. There was a wet sort of snapping noise and the joint turned a weird angle as the impact reached the bone, and the zombie mindlessly fell to the ground face first. An instant later, its skull was broken apart as Kenshiro smashed the spear point down on the back of its head. He looked back at the tight group of newcomers and waited. Looking behind him, Kenshiro saw two more walking up the driveway towards the house, and through the trees he could see another one approaching awkwardly. He had time. He was okay. Kenshiro took in a deep lung full of air and positioned himself behind the corner of the truck, so the truck was between him and the group of newcomers.

As if on cue, the four new zombies split into two groups, walking around the truck in different directions. He decided on the pair coming up on the passenger side and dealt with them first. He walked around the truck towards the pair. They were a man and a woman who were of similar age, and walked together like they were an undead couple. Kenshiro stabbed the undead man through the face and landed a heavy front kick on the woman. The zombie woman landed hard on its back on the driveway, and before it got its bearings, Kenshiro brought the spear down on the center of its face, collapsing the whole front of its skull inwards. When he lifted the spear up, he could see the point was covered in bits of gore and hair, but he couldn't let that bother him now.

The other two were rounding the truck to come up behind him. Kenshiro quickly darted around the front and came up behind them just as they were turning towards the front of the truck to face him. The pair had been walking together closely and Kenshiro hadn't noticed until he had come upon them that someone handcuffed these two together. They were both wearing grey coveralls that could at one point have been white, it was hard to tell. Each also had a thick, solid stripe going down the side of the arms and similarly down the side of the pant legs. *Convicts.* They were trying to pivot towards him, but the handcuffs made it impossible and the pair lacked the coordination and brain power to even comprehend how to maneuver as one. The one on his right twisted sharply and tried to lunge at Kenshiro, but the cuffed hand twisted sharply behind him and tugged him off balance forcing him to step down onto the fallen remains of the zombie with the collapse skull. Its foot landed awkwardly causing both of them to fall in almost a humorous way. The one that lunged at Kenshiro landed hard on the driveway and its companion toppled down right on top of him. There was a wet snap as one of their bones gave way from the collision. Using both hands, he brought the spear point down hard and the sharpened point drove through both their skulls and struck the pavement underneath. He planted his boot on the top zombie's back and violently yanked the spear free, and then stepped around the bodies to approach the two coming up the driveway. He figured the one he saw through the trees would still need some time to navigate the tree line. Zombies didn't do well on uneven ground.

The closest one on the driveway had been a woman, middle aged maybe, wearing a tank top with a knee length pair of shorts. She wore shoes meant for walking, and her dirty, thinning brunette hair was in a ponytail at the back. Kenshiro could see a bite sized chunk of flesh missing from her upper arm, and the dark trail of dried blood on her arm and down the side of her top. *She looks fairly fresh*, Kenshiro thought morbidly as he calmly approached it. Its skin was a light shade of grey and still looked relatively healthy. It wasn't dry or cracked and its face didn't look desiccated. Its eyes had yet to fully recede into its skull, Kenshiro could still see the dulled colored irises, and he could still tell this one had had green eyes at one point. *Couldn't have been undead for more than a couple months*, he thought as he brought the spear point forward. It was getting to be a rare occurrence seeing one that fresh these days. Its body slumped to the ground and Kenshiro didn't give it another thought as he stepped over the corpse.

He saw from the back of the truck, the farther of the two zombies had some sort of abdominal wound and as he stepped closer, Kenshiro could see this one had its stomach ripped open. He noticed the messy edges of the flesh on the wound, and beyond that he noted the abdominal cavity itself had been emptied. Kenshiro didn't even want to think of what a person would have to go through to get a wound like that. A quick thrust later and it, too, fell to the ground. Kenshiro let the spear point rest on the pavement. It was a mess of black clotted blood with wet bits of flesh and hair stuck to it, and he could even see little white bits of bone mixed in.

Kenshiro knew from experience that the zombie gore did not cause a person to turn. It was vile, and it had a distasteful smell that filled the open air around it, but from what he had seen, it didn't cause a person to turn. He even had the unpleasant experience of getting some of it in his mouth. Back in the beginning, when he thought the best way to deal with zombies was to blast away at them with a handgun, it was the Beretta on his hip he had been using. Pistols were so quick and easy it was hard to see the downfalls. He had been surprised by one coming through a doorway and Kenshiro shot it in the face at close range. The 9mm bullet blew apart the top of its skull. The zombie's blood and gore rained down on him. The effect of getting the foulness in his mouth was immediate and severe. He spit it out as soon as he tasted it, but his body didn't agree that was enough. Kenshiro threw up on the floor in front of him before he even knew he was sick, spilling the morning's meal, and he was momentarily paralyzed as his body seized up as he retched for the next few minutes. That put him in a tough spot for the rest of that night, and probably for most of that week. Even after he felt better, he was terrified he would get sick and eventually turn. It never happened, but Kenshiro still changed how he did things. He didn't think zombie gore could turn somebody, he's never seen it happen, but he recognized the fact he now lived in a world where what he didn't know, could also kill him. So, why take chances?

From where he was, Kenshiro could see the lone remaining zombie still struggling towards him in the tree line. Kenshiro just stood there for a moment and carefully looked around himself for others that might be closing in on him. He could hear the one in the tree line growling in frustration off in the distance, but there were none to be seen. Kenshiro looked at the fallen bodies on the driveway as he approached the tree line. With a forceful thrust, he ended the last zombie, and left it where it fell amongst the trees. It was dirty work to be sure but, on some level, he took satisfaction in knowing there were fewer zombies in the world because of him.

Kenshiro lifted the spear into his right hand and calmly walked back to the truck with the tip pointed to the pavement. He scanned the area in front of him from left to right as he approached the truck on the driver's side, and then reached in and turned the ignition off. It was safe now, he felt. The immediate danger had passed, and now he was just wasting gas. He looked to the house and tried to see any movement inside through the large bay window in the front. There was none, so he would check the house last. If there were any undead inside, he wanted a chance to lure them outside to be put down. He was planning on sleeping in that house and he didn't want the stink of a rapidly decaying zombie corpse ruining what could be a rather pleasant night.

The search of the yard went surprisingly well. As

hoped, Kenshiro found two cylindrical gas tanks on raised metal scaffolding around the backside of the barn. They were tucked away beside two semi-trucks that were neatly parked back there. Kenshiro tapped the gasoline tank and was thrilled to find it still had some fuel in it. He also found the leather gloves he was looking for. They were just waiting for him on the seat of a riding lawnmower he found in one of the sheds behind the house. They were a touch large, but they would work.

When he believed the yard had been cleared, Kenshiro walked the full perimeter around the property inside the tree line once more. This time, Kenshiro checked darkened corners and even looked under the porch where he could. He searched every nook and cranny he thought a zombie could be. Again, he found nothing of interest and the wind carried only the sounds of the leaves rustling.

With the yard done, Kenshiro moved to the back of the big red barn and once again peered into the space through the window in the man-door. He cupped his hands around his face and leaned into the window for a better look. If Kenshiro had to guess, he would say this was a repair shop, like a professional one. This space looked like it used to be someone's source of income. From where he stood, Kenshiro could see a row of workbenches along the wall with an industrial drill press fastened to the bench farther down. In the far corner, he could see three hydraulic, lever-operated floor jacks of various sizes all lined up against the wall, ranging from small to large. Kenshiro guessed the larger one might have a twenty-tonne capacity. Next to the jacks, also lined up neatly in a row, was a matching variety of stands to accompany them. From what he could see, it looked like a very organized space.

Kenshiro didn't see any movement, so he knocked loudly on the door and looked again. Nothing moved. He leaned the spear, with the point down, against the wall of the barn and tried the door's handle. It was locked. He'd run into this a few times, so almost as a reflex, he reached for the knife on his right hip. It was narrower and therefore better suited for this kind of job. He simply pressed the point up to the center of the window, and using his free hand, Kenshiro gave the back of the hilt a slight slap. The knife pierced the window in an instant and the window spider webbed and a hundred tiny pieces of glass fell inwards. It looked like a cascade of gems. He used the knife to scrape any loose pieces from around the frame before returning it to its sheath and waited quietly in front of the door. It would have been foolish to simply reach his arm in immediately to unlock the door. That's a good way to lose a chunk of your arm.

He had all the time in the world, so he looked in the window from a safe distance, checked his surroundings, and then checked in the window again as he pulled out the .22 pistol from its holster on his chest. He clicked the safety off and moved the pistol to his left hand and approached the window. Using the barrel of the gun almost like a third eye, Kenshiro leaned slowly towards the open window. He looked to the right, and then down to the floor where the glass had spilled, and then twisting his body slightly he looked to the left. When he was satisfied with what he saw, Kenshiro then reached in with his right and unlocked the door. No bodies moving around, no bodies on the floor, and Kenshiro couldn't see any blood stains from the door. This building might still be untouched since the crisis began, which Kenshiro then assumed should not be that surprising given where he was. He was literally in the middle of nowhere. La Veta was one of the smallest towns listed in the atlas for Colorado. He hadn't been there before, but those were the two things that drew him to this place. Kenshiro clicked the safety back on the gun, and holstered it before using his right hand to draw the long knife out before entering the barn.

Out of habit, he looked down and stepped around the glass on the floor to avoid making any unnecessary noise. Once inside, he turned and closed the door quietly behind him. The inside of the barn smelled of dust and grease. It was a strong smell, but not entirely unpleasant. It was how a shop should smell. It reminded Kenshiro of the one that he worked at for a time, it was owned by the father of one of his friends from class, Michael. He didn't like the smell at first, but then he gotten used to it and then learned to love it. *Those were good days.* The inside of this shop had a high ceiling with a large chain hoist that was on a track that was suspended twenty feet off the floor. Presently, the hoist was stowed off to the side. The roof above had a series of skylights that allowed a good amount of natural light in, but the dying afternoon sun left the side dangerously shaded. However, Kenshiro could see well enough. There was a panel of light switches on the wall that he didn't bother trying because he knew they wouldn't work. Against the opposite wall, he could see a large red tool box, probably fairly new, but even from where he was standing, he could see a generous film of dust covering the once shiny exterior. At one point, it had been someone's pride and joy, but now, it just sat there in a corner of some forgotten barn in the middle of nowhere, probably never to be used again. Kenshiro looked a little closer at the truck in the center of the space and that's when he saw a figure sitting in the front seat.

Then he saw it move.

The head twitched to the side in one sharp motion, like some invisible fist had struck it. Whoever it was in there, it was clear it wasn't living, and strangely enough, there also seemed to be something on its head. Cautiously, Kenshiro moved up to the passenger side window to have a look inside, and as he did, he monitored the vehicle's sole occupant. Kenshiro expected it to move or thrash around inside the passenger compartment, but it just sat there calmly like it was waiting for something. Kenshiro looked in the passenger window and saw a man in jeans and a denim jacket sitting in the seat, wearing his seat belt with his arms pinned under the belt. He could see it fighting weakly against the seatbelt, to no avail. It had a dark sack of some sort covering its head completely, but by the way it was moving, Kenshiro was sure it knew he was there. There was a muffled sound coming from it. *Must be wearing a gag.* What he didn't see was a wound of any kind or any bloodstains on his clothing. After a moment, Kenshiro noticed the keys were in the ignition and he could see they had left the ignition on. After that, he assumed that the battery would be long dead and probably useless, and the gas tank would be empty as well.

He realized what had happened here.

There are all kinds of tragedies in the new world. They marked the landscape and were as varied as road signs. Kenshiro saw all kinds of horrors on his journey; suicides were not uncommon. So much so, Kenshiro has theorized there are only two main reasons for suicides since the crisis began. There were the people who knew they would not survive. These were usually the people who got bit, and instead of facing the slow degradation of the body as the organs succumb to the undead infection, they swallowed a bullet. He would find the bodies sometimes slumped in a dark corner somewhere with a bite. Sometimes severe and gory, while other times, as slight as a single digit missing. Some people find a nice quiet place outside before blowing their brains out, some don't even bother with that. Once he found a man with a bite on his leg slumped against a lone tree on a tall hill that overlooked a wide river valley. The last thing the dead man had seen before he ended it had been the expansive vista before him. The quiet beauty of the landscape was not lost on Kenshiro. He was envious of the man and hoped when his time came, it would be as peaceful. The other reason for killing yourself was that you didn't even want to try to survive. Kenshiro could empathize with those people, even though he harbored a subtle contempt for them. The hard truth of the new world was survival came at a cost. Worse yet, it wasn't a onetime charge; it was a fee you kept paying when the bill was due. He understood, sometimes the price was too high for some people. Considering what Kenshiro was looking at, he could only imagine what lay ahead for him in that house.

On the passenger seat was a note. A piece of folded paper with, *to whom it may concern*, written in big letters on the front. Kenshiro moved to the driver's side and promptly ended the zombie with a quick thrust to where he guessed the temple would be. The knife slid in so easily, it was like it belonged there. The shrouded zombie violently twitched once and went limp in the seat. Kenshiro looked at the note again. It didn't concern him. He didn't want to know. On a pleasant note, ten minutes later he found another twenty-liter jerry can.

When he felt he was done, Kenshiro opened the door, loaded up the jerry can while still holding onto the knife, and then he took one last look back at the corpse in the truck with the note on the passenger seat. Kenshiro sadly pondered if that note would ever be read if he didn't read it.

"Watashi wa kinishinai," he said quietly aloud before walking out the door, knowing full well he would probably never return. *I don't care.*

At the house he found the bodies of the wife and a young girl, that were left in the living room, which was a mess. Before he killed himself, the man in the hood must have laid them side by side and covered each with a white blanket. *Why didn't he bury them?* Blood had soaked through the part of the blanket covering the heads and had turned an ugly brown a long time ago. There were other stains on the blanket from other fluids that seeped through while the bodies underneath rotted.

On the wall by the entrance, was a picture of the family that he assumed was fairly recent. The wife had flowing brunette hair that cascaded around her tanned features. Her smile was full, and she looked happy in the picture. The girl was adorable, full cheeks with a hint of freckles on the bridge of her nose. She, too, was a brunette, but had noticeably lighter hair than her mother. She was missing a tooth from the top row of her smile, and she almost seemed proud of it. The man had his arm around his wife and wore a checkered plaid shirt that clashed somewhat with the white flowing dresses of the girls. He had a square jaw, and a weathered face of a man who didn't believe in sunscreen. In the picture, Kenshiro could see tiny wrinkles at the sides of the man's eyes from his smile. They cut his sandy hair short. He had a look of a man that liked to keep his work space neat. They were all here, all accounted for, and the doors had been closed when he got here. So, none should have been able to enter.

Kenshiro searched the house anyway. When he first entered, Kenshiro had followed his usual routine of knocking loudly on the door and waiting to see if anything stirred. Nothing did, so he walked further into the house like he still expected trouble. That's when he saw the scene of the mother and daughter on the floor. There had been a struggle in the living room at some point. Someone had swept the contents of a coffee table to the floor, and upended the small table as well. Long ago, someone had smeared blood on the couch's flower print cushions, and Kenshiro could see bloodied footprints on the wooden floorboards that led further into the house, so he left the covered bodies and followed the trail into the kitchen. They had spilt a lot of blood in this room. It was everywhere. The counters, the sink, and the appliances all had splashes and smears of blood. The floor by the sink had a large pool of blood in front of it that dried long ago. All that remained now, was a dried, cracked stain that had corners that were peeling and flaking away.

The footprints started at that stain. Looking around, Kenshiro saw a staircase leading upstairs that also had dark brown patches of dried blood on the carpet. Kenshiro stalked upstairs with the knife clutched firmly in his hand. He didn't expect trouble but it was better to be ready. The blood trail led to the girl's room.

Kenshiro cautiously peered into the room. It was painted in a soft yellow color with lacy white curtains that were drawn closed, but still allowed plenty of light into the room. There was a wooden dresser in the corner complete with a mirror that was inhabited by a plethora of childish bobbles he didn't recognize. Next to it, was a tiny desk that, by the looks of the piles of colored pages on it was primarily used for coloring and drawing. The bed had a bedspread that featured a variety of Disney princesses he couldn't name on it. It looked like your typical American little girl's room. Except for the mass of blood that had at one point been spilled onto the bedspread and ran down onto the white carpet by the side. Kenshiro marvelled at the strange contrast of the stain to the rest of the room. It didn't belong there. That much was clear, but more than that, the stain seemed to defile everything this room stood for. It corrupted it.

In the back of his mind, he was piecing this tragedy together. He couldn't help it. It was like watching a terrible mystery unfold in front of him, and he just couldn't bring himself not to look. *This is where it started*, he thought as he stepped into the room. The room was empty, so he moved onto the rest of the house. In the main bathroom by the toilet, he saw a hard plastic container with a biohazard warning label on it. Inside were hypodermic needles, and in the trash can, were several empty vials. The prescription label had a girl's name on it, and the name of a drug he didn't recognize. *The girl's medicine*, Kenshiro guessed. It made the most sense to him and fit nicely into the chain of events that explained the horror that befell this family.

The last two rooms were the parents' bedroom, which had a nice spacious attached bathroom, and a spare bedroom that also seemed to serve as an office of sorts. They were both empty and untouched. Kenshiro went back downstairs, satisfied the house was free of the undead. Once on the main level, he went looking for where the lady of the house kept the fresh linens. He found them in a closet in the main hallway. Kenshiro grabbed a couple of fresh sheets and laid them over the mother and daughter. He wouldn't bury them. He didn't see the point of doing that. Instead, he dragged the bodies out of the house and placed them neatly off to the side by the barn with the others.

On the way back to the truck to gather his things for the night, Kenshiro ran through the scenario in his head. The family decided to wait out the crisis. They ignored the mandatory evacuation orders, and decided they were safest right where they were. Not entirely unusual, he had come across the remains of many who did the same. They may have been okay, for a while, but the little girl was sick. Kenshiro guessed the medicine in the trash was for her. He didn't know what exactly she had, but it was serious, and required regular injections, maybe as much as daily. Though eventually their supply of her medicine ran out. Kenshiro imagined those were hard nights, lying there knowing your little girl was dying, and outside, the world was going to hell around you. Knowing the pharmacy with the drugs they needed was so close, but still so impossibly far away.

At some point, though, the girl's end stopped being a possibility and started becoming an eventuality, and priorities shifted as they sometimes do. Kenshiro didn't find any firearms yet, but he assumed when the man finally did risk the trip, he had to have been armed in some fashion. Maybe he told his wife he was just going to have a look, and the plan was if it was too bad, he would try the next town over and so on. Kenshiro imagined they embraced before he left, the tight sort of hug where you bury yourself in the other person. The kind of hug you give someone if it was for the last time. Left alone in her room, Kenshiro pictured the tiny body of the girl quietly breathing its last breath underneath her princess covers. Sometime later, the mother checks on the daughter and, of course, as most people would be, is lost in the sorrow of what she found. Probably reached in to grab her baby's body and held it tight to her one last time, and that's when she probably discovered the one thing about zombies people at the time didn't realize.

You don't have to be bit to turn; you just have to die. Humanity didn't have time to learn that little nugget of information until the lights went out for the last time. He pictured the little girl's teeth sinking into the mother's neck, the shock, the horror. The mother pushes her baby away with one hand using a force she didn't think she could ever use on her sweet little girl, while using her other hand to stop the torrent of blood pouring out of her neck. Another fun fact about zombies is, their saliva is a powerful anticoagulant. With blood pouring from her, the lady of the house was faced with fight or flight. So, she backpedaled away in horror and ran, bleeding the whole way. Once in the kitchen, she must have flailed around looking for something, bandages maybe, but she came to rest by the sink. Kenshiro assumed the man returned empty handed. How could he not? When he did, they must have surprised him, the two of them caught him off guard by the door shortly after he entered. A struggle ensued, a savage battle for life. Kenshiro imagined the man's instinct to survive blinded him for a time. A simple grace that didn't allow him to see who he was attacking and just showed him what he had to do to survive. He had subconsciously chosen fight, and had to stick with it until the end. When the dust settled, the man was left with the two most important people in his life gone forever, because he had just crushed their skulls a moment ago. The last decision was probably the easiest at that point, and Kenshiro was thankful the father had taken a moment to consider the *after* part of his death and took a few steps to ensure the next guy's safety, because that next guy was Kenshiro.

At the truck, Kenshiro paused for a moment to have a good look around. The driveway had suitable cover from the road and surrounding area, and he had been almost silent the whole time he had been here. He expected a quiet night. There might be some that would wander in through the night that he would have to deal with in the morning, but that shouldn't be more than a half dozen.

No big deal.

Kenshiro chose to bunk in the parents' room for the night. The attached bathroom sealed the deal on that decision. Kenshiro walked up to the spacious bedroom and unceremoniously unloaded the bags onto the bed. Then he returned to the truck and grabbed the opened water jug with the hand pump. Kenshiro then reached into the cab and retrieved the cloth bundle from the passenger seat and walked back to the house. He placed the water jug in the bathroom and placed the bundle neatly onto the parent's dresser. The sun was beginning its final descent into the western sky. Kenshiro guessed he might have a few hours of light left in the day, and although he wasn't especially tired yet; he was looking forward to a bed tonight.

Some part of him then relaxed slightly. He let out a deep breath and with it, went the tension in his body Kenshiro didn't even know he was carrying with him. He went around the main floor and checked the windows, peering outside to see if anything moved. On the south side, off in the distance, he could see a shambling figure working its way across the distant scrubland, but other than that, it was clear. When Kenshiro finished with each window, he closed the curtains tight except for, of course, the big bay window in the living room that had the curtains closest to the door half ripped off the hooks at the top. He left that room alone; Kenshiro wouldn't be spending much time in the living room, anyway. There was still a hint of fouled meat in the room's air.

Kenshiro, once inside the main bedroom, opened the window to let some fresh air into the room. He then went around the room and gathered up the few personal items of the parents. Pictures, both on the wall and in frames on the dresser, he put neatly under the bed. The mirror on the dresser had a few pictures the little girl had drawn in crayon. In one, the little girl drew a trio of stick figures holding hands beside a two-dimensional house that was placed on top of a hill that had a solitary tree on it, and a bright yellow sun hung in the sky. The other one was a shaggy brown dog with white spots and strange looking ears that, after a moment, Kenshiro thought could have been horns. Maybe it was a cow? He didn't know, and as he pulled them off the mirror, he figured it really didn't matter anymore, anyway. Those went under the bed as well. *Out of sight, out of mind.*

Once he removed everything he could find that

reminded him this wasn't his room. Kenshiro sat on the bed, unzipped the combat vest, and let it slide off his shoulders. He breathed out, knowing the hard part of the day was over. In some ways, he knew he could relax now. He didn't need the vest anymore. Besides, with two knives and a holstered berretta, he was hardly defenceless. He left the vest on the bed and went back downstairs to retrieve a few more items.

The kitchen was an absolute horror show, even though whatever happened here happened a long time ago. He still didn't want to eat in this room, much less cook in it. He searched through the cabinets and drawers for what he was looking for and hauled them upstairs to the bedroom for later. When he came back down, he went down the back hallway to the back porch door and opened it, as he expected, there was a good-sized stainless-steel barbeque off to the side of the door. He almost expected it to be there because it was the one area of the porch he couldn't see from the window, and considering it was rural Colorado, it would have been more surprising if they didn't have a barbecue.

Kenshiro promptly unhooked the propane tank on the side after he tested the valve to ensure it was closed, and pulled it free. It wasn't full, but there was plenty of gas left in it for his purposes. He hefted the tank upstairs as well and placed it on the floor by the dresser. Kenshiro felt he had everything he would need for the night and closed the door to the bedroom.

The next hour he was sort of on autopilot while he made his dinner. Now that his day had all but ended, and the looming sense of doom had subsided enough to allow him to deal with his more basic needs. Twenty minutes later, he was sitting on the floor with his back against the bed eating his food. Tonight's meal was macaroni and cheese, with the half can of beans that was left over from lunch. Kenshiro occasionally washed it down with a simple glass of water, while staring at the wall in front of him, trying not to think about tomorrow. With little luck.

Part of the misery of the new world was the things he had to do to survive. Deep down inside of him, some part of him still recognized the zombies, on a level, as being human. If they *were* human, he would be the single worst mass murderer in history. He didn't keep count or anything, but the number of zombies he put down is easily into the thousands, and it wouldn't surprise him if the number was into the five-digit range. All he knew for sure was sometimes when he closed his eyes, he saw them. Their dark, twisted faces haunted the darkness behind his eyelids.

Kenshiro finished his meal and felt a warm satisfied glow from a full stomach. He got up, placed the plates next to the pot and saucepan. He briefly entertained the idea of doing the dishes, but in the end, it came down to being unwilling to waste good water to clean them. When he walked through the bathrooms, he checked the toilet tanks for water. They both were half full, so it guaranteed him one good flush from each. He could technically wash what few dishes he had in one of the toilet tanks, but somehow washing dishes in water that has been sitting in an uncleaned toilet tank for almost two years seemed to defeat the purpose of washing them in the first place. Kenshiro left them on the dresser and instead reached down and shut off the valve on the propane before he unscrewed the fuel hose and packed the burner back in his bag. He zipped it up and placed it on the floor by the door, then placed the black one next to it. Kenshiro didn't have a use for it but he didn't want it left outside, and because all the ammo was in there, it was too important not to be in the same room as him. He finished tidying, by taking the vest off the bed and propping it up on the chair in the corner before heading to the bathroom.

Kenshiro stared at his reflection in the bathroom mirror for a time, taking in all the features of the long-haired shaggy stranger that was looking back at him. It had been well over a month since he had shaved, even though he realized a clean-shaven face was a luxury. Something in him still wanted to appear neat when possible. It made him feel more like a normal twenty-five-year-old Japanese man and less like a zombie killing hobo.

A quick search of the cupboard and drawers provided everything he needed, and he placed the items neatly on the countertop. He pulled the lid off the toilet. He didn't have a problem using two-year-old toilet water to shave, and lathered up his face and slowly began shaving the mass of hairs on his face. It wasn't too thick. It was a beard of a young man and nothing to really be proud of, anyway. He took his time and was careful not to cut himself. When he finished, he looked in the mirror and checked for smoothness, touched up a few bits, and then tossed the razor in the bin beside the toilet. Next, he grabbed the small pair of scissors and the comb he had found in the drawer. Kenshiro leaned into the mirror and, using the comb as a guide, started snipping off lengths of his long, black hair. He had only done this once before.

Last time he did it, it took an hour, and he looked like a crazy person. He had tuffs of hair sticking out in some places while other spots were so short you could see the scalp. It was one of the few times he was glad no one was around to see him. He was careful to position himself so the black locks of hair would fall gently into the sink. When finished, he looked in the mirror and was happy with the finished product. It didn't look professional, but it was good enough. *Fight hard and leave a good lookin' corpse*, Dixon would say that as a toast after he already had a few, and that was the first thing Kenshiro thought when he saw his new clean-cut face.

He still didn't recognize the face on the other side of the mirror. It was him, or rather a version of him, but it wasn't the face he identified with. His face never seemed angular, his skin never used to look as tight around the contours of his face, and his eyes never looked that severe.

The last thing he wanted to do was to bathe. Removing his clothes, he could smell the days old funk and made a promise to himself to start wearing deodorant again. Normally, smelling good wasn't an important factor to his survival, but smelling that shirt made him rethink that. He put the holstered pistol and the sheathed knives on the bed and threw his soiled clothes into the laundry hamper by the wall.

His *bath* comprised of three one-liter pours of tepid water over his head. Kenshiro held his breath as the first pour of water ran down his exposed skin. He shampooed his hair furiously into a thick lather and then took the bar of soap on the side of the tub and scrubbed his way down his body and then back up again. He measured out the second liter and deliberately poured it over his scalp in a tiny circle in order to wash out all the suds, and then in the same fashion rinsed himself a second time. After that, he toweled himself off, and it was done. Ending his bath may have taken two minutes and usually left him a shivering mess afterwards, but here the heat of the day was thankfully quick to return.

He went back to the room and went through the drawers and closet, looking for a change of clothes. Luckily, he and the man in the hood had been close in size. Kenshiro's guess was the man was taller and maybe thicker than he was; the clothes fit well but were maybe a size too large. That suited him just fine. Kenshiro had always preferred loose-fitting clothes, anyway. Unfortunately, the man had been fond of briefs, which was not Kenshiro's preference, but it was the only clean underwear available unless he wanted to try the lady's on for size. In the closet, he found a nice pair of tanned denim slacks, they looked like sturdy work pants, along with a plain cotton t-shirt. The closet also had a rather fine selection of colored plaid shirts. An entire row of them, he could probably wear a fresh shirt each day for an entire month and still not run out. Kenshiro picked out two more changes of clothes, folded them neatly and placed them on the floor by the foot of the bed. He didn't know whether he was going to take them with him. There was a good chance he would need to change his clothes a few times over the next few days, or should he leave them here and simply come back to this house if he needed them. The house was far enough away from the town. He could use it as a respite if he needed it. For now, he would leave them there and decide in the morning what he was going to do.

The light cast through the window had a distinct orange tinge to it that told Kenshiro the sun had set. He strapped the knives back into place first, and then the holster. It felt good to have them on again. He climbed onto the bed and stretched out over the covers. It was glorious, and the bed welcomed his whole body into a soft embrace. Kenshiro moved to the center of the bed and spread out his arms and legs, and closed his eyes. While he waited for sleep to come, he visualized what tomorrow would be like, what he may face, and tried to prepare himself for what he may have to do.

Luckily, he didn't have to wait long before sleep came.

Chapter 4

Elle

Elle opened her eyes to a new day, and instantly regretted it. She knew she had a headache before she even opened her eyes. The signs of a classic hangover were all there. She had been laying there awake for some time now, unwilling to face another day in this vertical prison. On a normal day, it was hard enough. However, feeling the way she did right this instant, made the prospect of handling another day at The Prescott seem impossible to cope with. None-the-less, she took the first step. She slowly peeled back her eyelids, and the light of the morning instantly assaulted her. It wasn't direct sunlight. They bunked on too low of a level to see the full sky unobstructed. The light burning her eyes reflected off of the neighboring building windows, and somehow, that just seemed to make it worse. Her head pounded mercilessly as her eyes fought to adjust and focus. Clumsily, she brought her hand up to first rub her sore eyes and then shield them from the offending light. She breathed in deep and her nose got the scent of a foul, yet familiar scent. She moved her hand away and opened her eyes fully.

That's when she saw it.

Elle saw the wastebasket with part of last night's dinner, mixed with generous amounts of beer, vodka and Kool-Aid. *That's right*, Elle thought to herself regretfully as she closed her eyes again, and rested her palm on her forehead right above the spot where her head was pounding. She rarely threw up. Normally, she was what her mother would refer to as a 'polite drinker', but last night she let her defences down. Then Jacob started wagering shots of his disgusting version of 'sex on the beach' during the poker game instead of the normal chocolate covered peanuts, things just went downhill from there.

They weren't supposed to be drinking at all last night, but Bill brought a few bottles of his wine and, to his credit, it had been civil in the beginning. Bill had left earlier than expected to get some sleep and Kate, or Kat as she wants to be called now, eventually got bored and retired to relax in their room as well. That left her with Jacob, Blaine, Marty, Darcy, Elizabeth and Jolene. At twenty-two she was the youngest in the room by at least ten years, and that may have factored into her decision to abandon all sense and drink that much. They finished the wine bottles. That she remembered clearly, because she was already quite drunk at that point and was disappointed the night may end. But then, Jacob brought the vodka and Kool-Aid mix and things started getting blurry. At some point, she had decided it was time for bed, or maybe someone told her it was time to call it a night. She didn't remember, and by that point it really didn't matter. The night had come to a close, and she stumbled awkwardly down the stairs to her floor and somehow made it to her couch without incident.

"Shit," she cursed silently so as not to anger her already throbbing head. She realized *without incident* was not accurate at all. Hazy pieces of last night seemed to drift into her memory, and one of those pieces included throwing up in the hallway between the receptionist's desk and the conference room they bunked in. She looked over to her shoes besides the couch to confirm it, because the memory included her getting a good splash of vomit on her shoe as well. The shoes were on the floor with the left one featuring the dried crust of vomit across the front of it. It had been a rough start to the day, to say the least.

Against her better judgement, she rose. Elle still held

her head in her hands on her way up to a seated position on the couch, and immediately felt the world around her spinning cruelly. The room was sweltering, and her clothes were damp with sweat that had leaked from her during the night, and yet somehow, she felt a chill in her bones that caused her to shiver uncontrollably. A knot formed in her stomach after she once again caught a whiff of the bucket of puke by the couch. She didn't remember using it last night, but it was pretty clear from its contents that she had. She felt her core clench painfully and her ailing stomach once again purged itself of its contents.

Thankfully, she had the presence of mind to at least turn and put her head over the foul-smelling bucket before she retched. Her throat burned as a small amount of bile spewed into the bucket, but her body didn't know her belly was empty and just kept on heaving. Elle closed her eyes and pushed through the painful spasms and when it finally subsided, she spit whatever remained in her mouth into the bucket without opening her eyes. Elle moved her face away from the foul brew, and just sat there breathing deeply. She was sweating profusely now from the exertion of dry heaving for what felt like five minutes, with her head in her hands and her elbows resting on her knees. She watched the space on the floor between her feet as the occasional drop of sweat traveled down her face and eventually fell to the ground with a silent splash. It was strangely calming. It gave her something small to focus on. Something easy and pure.

Mom would be proud, she thought, and with that bitter jab, her already fragile morning fell apart. When the tears came, she didn't fight it. When the weak sobs became somber weeping, she watched the tears hit the ground right beside the sweat as she thought of her mother. *Just let it out. It's okay, it's okay. Sometimes you need to cry.* Her mother would sometimes say on these occasions. She would run her hand down her neck and rub Elle's back in the way only a mother could. When the gentle weeping became loud body shaking sobs, Elle didn't even notice the transition, she probably wouldn't have cared if she did.

Sophia Russo, Sophie, was *a rock*. Growing up, people would always tell her that, her grandparents especially, and that she never cried. *Tough as nails*, they would say in admiration. Elle knew the truth of it though. She still remembered those first few months after her father died in the car accident, her mother had cried plenty. Elle never actually saw it, but at night when her room was dark, she would hear her mother through the walls crying in her room. The next morning, Elle would wake up to smiles, hugs, and breakfast like the quiet sobs in the night might have been a dream. This cycle would continue, and some mornings, Elle wondered if she should mention something. She hated hearing her mother cry and always felt responsible somehow. She never did though. Sophia Russo was the kind of mother that if she wanted you to know something, she would tell you, and the things she didn't tell you were none of your concern. Even though in that instance, it did concern Elle, it concerned her so much some nights she would cry in her bed too.

Years later, she looked back on those days and realized she only *saw* her mother cry three times. The first time was when the Fire Chief came to the house to tell her about the accident that took her husband's life. All Elle remembered of the night was her mother came running into her room sobbing uncontrollably. She scooped Elle up in her arms in a tight embrace and shattered Elle's fragile world with a few quick words. They just cried together. The next time was saying her vows to Joe, her second husband, on the day they got married. Elle had been there too. Her mother, of course, had made her maid of honor and she was right there beside her mother with tears running down her face as well. It was a special day.

The last time she had seen her mother cry was when the nurse put Kate into her arms. It had been a difficult pregnancy, and if she was being honest, most of the difficulty in the beginning was Elle coming to terms with her mother having another man's child. Marriage was one thing, but having a child with Joe just made it feel more like her mother was moving on from her past life, and maybe that meant moving on from Elle as well. It was a stupid, selfish, childish thing to think, and she was still ashamed of some things she said to her mother in her fits of rage. Luckily, her mother saw right through it and made sure she was involved throughout, which included being in the room when she gave birth, which was the last place Elle wanted to be. Thank God for Joe. He held it together and when Kate came into the world, all the Russos in the room were crying. It was a beautiful moment.

Unlike this one.

Elle's sobs finally subsided to a quiet whimper as she looked down at the dark stain of tears on the fine carpet of the office they had converted into a bedroom. Once again, she came face to face with the cold reality that she was nothing like her mother. Elle had her dark hair and tanned skin, her cheekbones, and Elle's jaw line looked similar to her's. She also had some of her mother's curves, but to a lesser extent. Sophia Russo was a full-bodied woman, whereas, Elle thought she still had a bit of a girlish figure, like she was still in high school. Her mother was graceful, independent, and always knew what to do in any given situation. Elle was none of those things, and sometimes that fact cut like a knife.

She looked up at the clock on the wall and it surprised

her how late into the morning it was. She had missed breakfast, which wasn't much of a disappointment. Elle was still thankful because there was a half hour until lunch started in the common area. That gave her twenty minutes to get her shit together, and ten minutes to make the trek up to the common area on the fortieth floor. She wasn't looking forward to doing in her present state, but as foul as the prospect was at the moment, she still needed to eat. Elle took a couple of deep breaths and tried to steady herself. She wasn't built for this life. Elle knew that, but there was nothing she could do about that. Everybody knows there was no real escape; this building was probably the safest place in the world right now, even though most days it felt more like a prison.

Every day, she saw the same faces and walked the same halls. She filled her days with routine, maybe subconsciously, because she felt it would help deal with the boredom. Like it would give her some feeling of purpose, and maybe in the beginning it had. But now, all it seemed to do is merge the days together so it felt like she was living the same day repeatedly. She wasn't the only one either. The others had their little routines and habits as well, it helped to bring some semblance of normalcy back into their lives.

Any given day, you could see Bill watching the sunset on the roof. He said it was something he used to do with his kids; he was sentimental like that. Darcy, that giant nerd, lived a simple life of waking up and hitting the exercise bike that was rigged up to car batteries and an inverter to power one light socket they all used to charge their devices. He would do that in the morning to charge his fancy laptop, and then after lunch, he would play games on it until dinner. After which, Darcy would charge it again before retiring to his room to watch movies and probably jerk off to porn before bed. Sadly, if that was true, Elle would be kind of jealous because he still had it in him to bother with masturbating.

Elle placed her palms on her knees for leverage and was about to push off the couch when her eyes caught something. She turned to look at it. On the floor, by the end of the couch her head had been resting on, was a full bottle of water with a tiny bottle of aspirin beside it. On the top of the bottle was a post-it note that had a rudimentary drawing of a cat puking that was unmistakably Kate's handiwork. It also had a drawing of a heart underneath it with a large capital U beside it. Elle momentarily choked up at the gesture of kindness. She leaned over to grab the water and the pill bottle. Her head was still throbbing like her brain was about to pop out her ears, so she shook out three pills and washed them down with a gulp of water. It tasted good. So good, in fact, she kept drinking down the sweet liquid until the bottle was empty. It felt good to wash some of the foulness out of her mouth, but it wasn't enough. She eyed the note again and noticed there was more writing on the back.

I put another bottle in the bathroom. Don't be late!

She could appreciate the subtle bit of manipulation. Kate obviously had learned that from their mother, even though right now she would have appreciated the second bottle even more if it was right beside the first. However, at least it gave her the extra bit of motivation to push off the couch and walk past the now defunct elevator bank to where the washrooms were.

The law offices of Pierceson, Spectre, and Litt were designed well for the modern era. A lot of open spaces, plenty of neutral tones, and glass. Everything was glass. Most of the offices seemed to be constructed solely out of it, so much so you could see unobstructed from the north side all the way to the south side of the building. There were glass doors to the offices, they made some desks out of glass, they made most of the coffee tables and conference tables out of glass. The lobby had a glass art piece behind the reception desk. Elle was sure back in its day these offices must have been impressive to be in, but walking to the bathroom with a disastrous hangover at the end of the world, all she noticed was the sun glaring into the space through all that damned glass. At the door to the ladies' washroom, there was a hook on the wall with a flashlight hanging by a cord on it. As was the routine, she grabbed the flashlight off the hook and entered the pitch darkness of the washroom.

These were one of the few rooms on the floor that didn't have windows, so the space descended to utter darkness once the door closed. But before that happened, Elle switched on the flashlight and proceeded to the sinks. By the middle sink, close to her and Kate's toiletries was the second bottle of water. Without hesitation, Elle placed the flashlight on the counter so the beam would flash towards the ceiling and cast the whole room in a somber glow from the reflection off the ceiling tiles. She would only drink half of the bottle and save the last half so she could brush her teeth and finally clear out the awful taste in her mouth that was leftover from last night. Elle would try to get her hair straight, it doesn't have to be runway-beautiful, but she should at least attempt to be presentable. The haze of the night before was wearing away as she planned out the next few hours of her day, and then she looked at her reflection in the mirror.

"You little bitch!" On both sides of her mouth, someone had used a marker to draw in three, not so tiny, cat whiskers. "Aw, you-, "she said and then spied the heart that was also drawn on her right cheek, and on any other occasion she might have thought it was cute, but today this was just insult to injury. "I'm going to fucking kill her."

Elle put herself together in a frenzy of activity in the darkened bathroom, partially spurred on by her rage at her sister's infantile bullshit, but mostly at not wanting to be the last one to lunch. Sometimes in the past, latecomers had to settle for whatever could be scraped out of the pot, a granola bar, or a can of something people aren't usually excited about eating in the first place. Like beets, that's what Elle got stuck with on one occasion and she vowed to never be that late again. When she left the bathroom, she replaced the flashlight on the hook for the next person and headed to the stairwell on the opposite side of the elevator bank. Like the bathrooms, the stairwell of the building had no windows, and without power for the lights, the stairwell was permanently pitch black, except whatever light escaped from under the doors to the floors. Also, like the bathroom, there were communal flashlights hung on the walls. All the occupied floors had them. The system they worked out was you take from the floor you're on, and you drop the flashlight off at the floor you arrive at. That way, people didn't have to carry flashlights around with them all the time.

She casually grabbed a flashlight from one of the many hooks and entered the stairwell, grateful to be leaving the constant glare of Pierceson, Spectre, and Litt's offices. As Elle climbed the steps in as much of a fury as she could muster in her given condition, she played out the tongue lashing she was going to give her sister. However, by the time Elle reached the fortieth floor, she was out of breath, sweating slightly and resigned to let the matter go. Something about climbing six flights of stairs with a hangover took the fight right out of her, and instead, all she wanted was the bland oatmeal that was on today's menu. There was also a chunk of bread that Emilio makes in his automatic bread maker, and a tiny bowl of fruit from a can. Elle especially like the peaches, but they ran out of that a few weeks ago and it would be a few more weeks until they made another supply run. Major John Mason rarely makes a run until the need was there. Given the dangers out there in the world, she didn't blame him.

She leaned into the push-bar of the fortieth floor, opened the door, and hung up her flashlight on the hook on the wall to her right. There were many hooks on this floor because they all agreed this floor would be the common area. They would all share it, and judging by the number of flashlights already hung up, she was no longer worried about missing the meal. She didn't bother to count them, but she figured about half their numbers had shown up for lunch. There was a small hallway that led around the elevator bank into the floor. It was here that Emilio, who was the sole member of their group who volunteered for the job, operated as the group's cook. He had worked as a line cook in some posh restaurant on the upper east side. Emilio had said he was mainly in charge of the salads, but nobody cared. They were all just thankful someone took on the responsibility.

The offices of MobileCom on the fortieth floor weren't offices at all. It was a giant open space that consumed the entire floor. The only space on the floor that could even loosely be called a room was the lunch area that was partitioned off from the rest of the space. It came complete with enough four-person tables that they could easily seat all of them with a few dozen left over for good measure. On the far wall, was a cafeteria style stainless-steel counter where Emilio served the meals. Behind the serving area, was a complete kitchen that looked professional, as everything was constructed of stainless-steel as well, which Emilio kept spotless at all times. The rest of the space was a college frat boy's dream. The desks had been moved out long ago and now the space housed two basketball hoops, a ping-pong table, a foosball table, and a pinball machine that was hooked up to a stationary bike in the same setup as their charging station. You could play it as long as someone was willing to pedal the bike to power it. Many leather couches and beanbag chairs littered the area by the windows and they had put a bookshelf in a while back with a few choice paperbacks neatly lined up on the shelves. She saw Jolene laying on one couch as she rounded the corner into the space. She too, apparently, was nursing a hangover as she did not look well at all. She looked up and waved weakly but said nothing. Elle returned the wave before turning into the partitioned area.

Let's get this over with, she thought and Elle steeled herself for what was about to come.

In the fifth grade, her best friend at the time was Jennifer McGregor. Jen convinced Elle during a sleepover that she could cut and style her hair better than her regular professional stylist. She was wrong, so terribly wrong. Her mother took her to the salon the next day to try to fix the horror show that was on her head. When Monday morning came, she walked through the school doors with her new haircut and was in tears before she got to her class. Nobody said anything but she could feel their eyes on her, judging her, mocking her. It wasn't the stylist's fault. She did what she could, but combined with her thin, yet to hit puberty frame, her fresh hair cut made her look like a boy. She had long hair her whole life up to that point, and without it, she felt vulnerable. Walking into the cafeteria, Elle knew this was going to feel a lot like that day.

Immediately she saw her sister sitting off to the side with Bill, who had his back to her, but she could still see her sister clearly. and when their eyes met, Elle sneered at her and walked right up to the serving counter. First things first, she was still ill, but her stomach had awoken on the climb up and now the prospect of eating wasn't so vile. She grabbed a tray and walked over to the spot where Emilio served the food. As usual, he was in the same full cook's uniform he had on when he first arrived. When he worked in the kitchen, he always had it on. Emilio was busy wiping down the already spotless countertop.

"Good morning, Elle," he said in his usual cheerful manner. Elle figured it was best to get it over with and looked straight at him.

"Morning, chef," she said, trying poorly to mask her frustration. On cue, Emilio looked up from the spot on the counter he was wiping and Elle was sure he was about to comment on being called 'chef'. Few people still bothered with the joke anymore, but Elle knew it was more than a joke to Emilio. There had been nights when she and Emilio had talked about stuff, like the dreams they had for themselves before the world went to shit. Emilio confessed to wanting to open up a small restaurant, or maybe even just a food truck. Just cooking his own food for people. So, he liked it when people said 'chef' to him, normally he responded cheerfully, but today he looked at her and froze. At first, he looked confused, but then the pieces came together. Last night's drunken exploits would have already made the rounds by now. They were a small community and word travels fast.

That's when the laughter started.

"That's right, get it out of your system," Elle said to Emilio, unimpressed. To his credit, Emilio tried to suppress his guffaws by laughing into his fist, but after his face turned red, it became obvious he was amused.

"Shit!" He said finally, a little breathless. "I heard you guys tied one on last night. Sorry I missed the party," he said between snickers as the moment passed. He gestured to her face, "Did Jolene do that after you passed out?" He asked, but before she could answer he sucked in a big breath of air. By the look on his face, she could tell Emilio had just realized who the culprit had been. "No. It was Kate," Emilio said like he had just solved a big murder case. "She said she had a surprise for me that would make my day, and when I asked what it was, she said you'd bring it to me when you came to lunch." He smiled and crossed his arms in front of him, obviously proud of himself. "That's funny," Emilio said absently as he replayed how he thought the events played out in his mind. But when he snapped back to reality, he must have seen the resting-bitch-face Elle had on, because his smile drooped slightly. "Don't worry about it, though. It looks good. Well, maybe not good, but it doesn't look bad or anything. It's not like she wrote *bitch* across your forehead in big letters. That's more how my little sister would have handled the situation. That little turd was always pulling shit like that. It's what brothers and sisters do to each other. The more I look at it, the more I think it looks kind of-," he struggled on the next word, "-cute." *Cute?* She breathed in deeply to quell her frustration.

Everything he was saying was technically correct. It could have been a lot worse, and yes, maybe on a different day she might bring herself to a point where she could admit it was cute, maybe even tastefully done. And this *was* the exact thing brothers and sisters did to each other. They made each other's lives miserable. Which was one reason it bothered her so much. However, Elle didn't want to be comforted, and she didn't want attention drawn to her, especially like this. These were games children play, and she had a hard enough time trying to get people to see her as anything more than an old teenager. It didn't help that the only person here younger than her was Kate.

"Cute? Huh?" she said, as if considering the word. "I'll be sure to put that on her tombstone when I get done with her," she said as a joke but when she saw the hurt look on Emilio's face, she reconsidered what she said.

"Hey, come on. Don't be like that." He came back with his mock-hurt big brother's voice. "A little joking around is good for all of us. Hell, it made my day, that's for sure." He added another chuckle to emphasize his point, but quickly saw that Elle was still unappreciative of what Kate was trying to do for other people, at Elle's expense, and let it die away. "Look," he said, holding up his finger, "I know what will cheer you up a bit and maybe take the edge off that murderous sisterly rage." Emilio turned and went to the pot on the propane burner in the back kitchen area, scooped out a bowl full of warm oatmeal, and then she saw him sprinkle a generous amount of brown sugar on top, more than usual. He then placed something on top she couldn't see. He then took another bowl and filled it partially with today's canned fruit. She couldn't see what it was, but she noticed he put more than the usual amount in her bowl. He came back with a big grin on his face. "I gave you an extra helping of oranges." He leaned in close when he said it like it was a big secret and other people might be listening. He put the bowl of mandarin orange slices onto her tray. "*And then there's this*," Emilio said as he slid the bowl of oatmeal onto the tray beside the one filled with oranges, and to her shame she didn't notice it at first. She was distracted by the corny look of excitement that crossed his face. Then she looked down casually and saw what the excitement was about, and her jaw dropped.

"Is that a fucking strawberry?" She looked at him with what she imagined was utter awe. Elle couldn't believe her eyes. It wasn't a tiny little thing either, but a big fat red juicy strawberry like you would see in the ads. Her mouth watered as her brain tried to remember what a fresh strawberry tasted like, but then came back to more pressing matters. "How many do you have?" She said and then felt strangely ashamed. That was the first thing she thought of.

"That's the only one. For now. There are others still growing on the plants that aren't quite ready to be picked." He must have read her expression because Emilio held up his hands as if to surrender and said, "No. You take it. I insist. It would personally offend me if you didn't take it. You see Elle, the ultimate goal of a chef is to heal the soul through food." He then stood back and put his hands on his hips and that's when Elle knew he was into a full-blown speech. But Jesus, it was a goddamn strawberry. As far as she was concerned, he earned the right to ham it up a bit. "That is what I do. I heal your souls through my cooking-."

"The oatmeal, you mean?" She couldn't resist a tiny jab.

"*My cooking* is what brings us all together, like a big family. As the culinary head of this family, I feel it is my job to avoid CAT-*astrophes* before they occur." He finished and looked her dead in the eye. There was an awkward pause where she just looked at him unimpressed, much like a daughter would at the end of a groaner of a dad joke, before he cracked. It started as a thin tight grin and then, unable to contain himself any longer, the thirty-something Hispanic man exploded into uproarious laughter, misting her face with his spittle as he did. He was so caught up in his joke he didn't notice her go through the motion of wiping her face with her hand in mock disgust.

"I feel my job here is done," she said and slid her tray farther down the counter to where the twenty-liter water jug sat. It was like the ones people took on camping trips or to baseball tournaments. All plastic with a spout on the bottom with a twist valve on it. This one was blue and white, and Emilio made it a point of pride it was as clean as the rest of the cafeteria. After some thought, she poured herself three cups. She didn't think anyone would say a thing about the extra helping. She didn't remember the last time they ran out of juice at lunch. Most people here preferred coffee over juice with their meals, which she was thankful for this morning.

As she walked back to the table, she marvelled at Emilio's tiny red accomplishment. He first came up with the idea of a tiny garden shortly after their group got established, but at the time it didn't seem like a priority. Emilio kept on the issue, quietly mentioning it at meetings and to Mason in private until finally he got the supplies he needed to build the flower beds and plant his garden. He planted it on the roof, on the south side of the building so the garden would receive the most light throughout the day. He put it under the protruding edge of the helipad so to protect it from the rotor wash when the helicopter took off to take Mason and his team on supply runs. Elle tried to remember the last time she saw the garden, it was a while ago, and the plants were just beginning to break the surface of the soil. She made a mental note to go up to the roof and have a look at the garden at some point.

It was then that she looked down again, and noticed there was no bun on her tray.

"Meeeeooooow." The sound of the cat call broke her train of thought as she passed by the table Mason's crew sat at. The voice was unmistakeably Derek's, and it was the sort of childish man behavior she expected from him. Derek Peters was the police officer who stumbled breathlessly into the building a half hour after she and Kate did, with a look of sheer terror on his face that she will never forget. To his right, was Jackie Orr, she had been one of the three security guards on duty in the building when Manhattan fell into chaos, she was the person who guarded the door when Elle and her sister came up to it, begging to be let in. By grudgingly opening that door, she had saved them. There was no doubt about that, but as time went on, the shine of that one righteous act had dulled slightly. To Derek's left was Marty Handler, seeing him there seated with those two was a bit of a disappointment, because Elle kind of liked Marty. He was a down to earth decent person who kind of reminded her of her uncle on her mother's side. In her eyes, he didn't belong with Mason's meatheads, as she has been known to call them in whispered tones. Just because he was the group's resident pilot and flew them around on their runs, didn't mean he had to hang out with them.

When she looked towards the table, both Derek and Jackie were both grinning like idiots at her. Waiting for some reaction to spill out of her, it was the type of juvenile bullshit she had hoped she would have seen the last of when she left high school. Derek with his wide face and sharp nose, when he smiled at you, it made you feel like he knew something you didn't. Like a secret about you he was on the verge of spilling to everyone. Jackie's shark-tooth smile wasn't much warmer. The pair of them smiling at her like that made her think, *that's how jackals might smile at their prey before taking that first bite*. She wanted no part of it. Elle gave them both her best *whatever*-face and kept moving. She would have hoped it would signal she didn't appreciate their brand of teasing, but that was too much to ask from this lot. If their little group were a high school, Mason and his little crew would be the stereotypical jocks, constantly muscling their way around trying to establish some crude form of dominance over the rest of them. Elle left them to giggle to themselves at her expense.

"You're a brat," Elle said, placing her tray down at the table and sitting down on the steel stool next to Bill and across from Kate. It was her usual spot. She gave her sister a mean stare and went on. "Like thank you for the water, that was awesome of you, but this-," she circled her hand in front of her face. "-this I don't need," she breathed out forcefully, wanting to say more, a lot more, but she had made her point thus far without raising her voice or swearing. Which considering how she felt, was a personal victory. Elle didn't want to make a scene; she was trying to avoid that. It was bad enough her sister decorated her face like a five-year-old. Elle didn't have to throw an all-out tantrum like one too.

"Listen," her sister met her wicked gaze with one that almost looked bored. "In my defence, I swear I didn't know it wouldn't wash off." It was at this point Bill looked over and was about to say his usual good morning to her but the words seemed to jam up in his mouth as he saw Kate's handiwork on her face.

"Ew." It was all the man could manage to say, and before he could comment more, Elle flashed him the evil eye. Almost challenging him to say something. Bill was a sixty-something year old black man with short salt and pepper hair that in all reality was more salt than pepper. He had kind of adopted the two of them, after a while. Bill moved onto their floor a few months back, even though he also complained there was too much light. He remedied that by moving into the file room that had no windows except for the glass doors. He returned her gaze unafraid, but after a moment he returned to his own bowl of oatmeal with a sigh and a shrug of his shoulders.

"It's a marker. Of course, it's not going to wash off." Elle snapped back quickly.

"It wasn't a *permanent* marker, though." Kate stretched out the word to emphasize it. "It should have washed off. Maybe you just didn't wash your face." Kate raised an accusing eyebrow, but Elle wasn't taking the bait.

"Of course, I washed my face. I *scrubbed* it for like five minutes-."

"It does look better," Kate cut in.

"-but it's still there," Elle said and she could feel her

blood pressure rising as the throbbing inside her head kicked up a notch. She took a long breath to bring herself back down.

"Also, in my defense, I wouldn't have done it if you didn't puke all over the place." It was Kate's turn to take the offensive, and by the pissy look on her face, Kate wasn't done. "You puked all over the place; you puked in the hallway, you puked in the stairway, you puked in the bathroom. Which, by the way, I stepped in when I went to take a pee, and the whole bathroom reeked of it. The hallway too. It was disgusting." Kate's frustration was definitely showing, but Elle had to hand it to her. She, too, was keeping it civil and not raising her voice either. However, Elle was getting the feeling she might be outgunned in this matter.

"Amen to that," Bill chimed in after a spoonful of oatmeal.

Elle took a step back mentally from her little sibling spat, and tried to think back to last night. She knew she left the card game feeling ill, not sick exactly, but she definitely knew it was time to sleep it off. She knew for a fact that she did indeed vomit up the contents of her stomach at least once, even if she was still a little fuzzy as to where. Could she have thrown up more than once? One thing was for sure: she didn't remember using the bathroom, but after a moment more, she realized she didn't remember not using it as well. She was a little ashamed at how little she could actually remember of her journey home last night. *Wait*, she suddenly thought to herself. *I was in the bathroom and I didn't see any vomit*. Nor did she remember any in the hallway this morning, and on the way up, she noticed nothing in the stairwell.

"You cleaned it up," she said in a sinking voice.

"You're damn right I did," Kate said with gusto. "I was

up with the sun this morning," she gave a nod to Bill because that was one of his favorite sayings before continuing. "And I immediately could smell it in the hallway. At first, I thought it might be a zombie or something roaming the halls. You know, by the horrible smell in the air. Boy! Was I wrong. After seeing that first chunky pile of spew, I almost wished it had been a zombie. Probably would have been easier to clean up." Bill chuckled mildly into his bowl of oatmeal, thoroughly amused by this morning's drama. Elle said nothing. She took it with little more than a slightly annoyed look on her face, but that never stopped Kate before. This was, in part, her punishment for being so irresponsible last night. She would sit here and listen to her sister's embellished story of one of the few times she has had to clean up Elle's mess. God knows Elle has done more than her share of mothering to her sister without complaint or compliment, and Elle was fine with that. She was. Elle washed their clothes each week and tidied up after Kate and her constant clutter every day, and the lack of basic utilities made those once simple tasks more difficult by an order of magnitude. "-and then I went into the bathroom to clean out the bucket and I slipped on another puddle of puke. I almost fell right onto it, but I just had to do the funky chicken a bit-," Kate wiggled around in her stool, trying to look like someone who was slipping but Elle thought she looked more like someone drowning to her. "-And now I'm like: 'great, now I have to clean my shoes', but thank god I didn't fall in it.'"

"Oh yeah, that'd be nasty," Bill chimed in with a merry chuckle as he was putting his spoon into his empty bowl.

"Could you imagine if I got it in my hair?" Kate asked with a look of horror on her face. That got Bill too, his face scrunched up in disgust and humor at the thought, but he soon recovered.

"That pretty head of hair of yours would soak it right up. While you're down there, you might as well mop the rest of the floor too." The two of them giggled, and she realized what Kate was up to. She wasn't punishing Elle, well, she was, but that wasn't her primary goal here. Just a sick bonus only a little sister could enjoy. No, Elle thought she was mainly telling this ridiculous story to entertain Bill. She wasn't even looking at Elle at all. Kate focused on Bill like she was a comedian who was playing to a crowd. It was endearing.

Lately, Bill had been reserved, and he had grown into a habit of keeping to himself during the day. He still kept his puzzle dates with Kate, but she told Elle a few weeks ago that the time between puzzles was getting longer. Bill seemed to pull away from them, away from everyone in their little community, and there was little point in asking why either. Elle figured they all wore their own personal tragedies like weights around their necks. The whys of everyone's misery were obvious. It *literally* was all around them, but this seemed different. Elle kept her worries to herself though. Kate latched onto Bill like a grandfather, the likes of which she sorely needed. Probably has been good for Bill too, which has made the last couple months worrying. Kate noticed it, of course, but Elle was quick to tell her it was nothing, even though she too feared it was something. *If something is bothering him, he'll tell us.* That's what she told herself. *But would he*?

"-Then I came across the puke in the stairwell and I was like: '*Holy Mary Mother of God*'!" Kate had a look of wondrous awe on her face, like she found an enormous diamond in the stairwell instead of what Elle had left for her. "It must have been the first time you barfed because there was so much of it, and it had the biggest chunks. I could still see the corn you had from dinner."

"That's too bad," Bill said with an amused smile. "It's a waste of a splendid dinner."

"I can't argue with that," Elle replied sheepishly and returned the smile.

"The more I hear of this story, the more I think you got off lucky with a few whiskers on your face." Bill looked at Elle with that warm smile he has. Her mother would say Bill was one of those people who use their entire face to smile, and this close Elle could make out the tiny patch of dark freckles on the bridge of his nose.

"Oh, she did," Kate added. "I was tempted to write barf on her forehead."

"It's a good thing you didn't." Elle jabbed her spoon at Kate to emphasize her seriousness and then used it to point to her own face. "This is bad enough. Message received, loud and clear." She fixed Kate with her patented big sister's stare, letting her know a line had been drawn. Entertainment aside, she didn't want her entire morning to be like this. Elle suddenly remembered she has yet to touch her oatmeal, and not wanting to waste good warm food, she decided maybe it was best to leave the two of them to their banter and try to focus on her meal.

"Is that a fucking strawberry?!" Kate blurted out, staring wide eyed at Elle's bowl.

"Language," she and Bill said in unison in a practised drone. It amazed Elle it took Kate this long to notice it, after all the bright red strawberry grossly stood out in her bowl of oatmeal and brown sugar.

"Emilio's garden?" Kate looked up at her and Elle nodded. "Oh my god, that's so awesome. I hope he planted peas; I would die for some fresh garden peas. You remember eating peas from mom's garden, Elle?" Elle nodded solemnly.

"He has been awfully secretive about it. I've been asking him about it now and then, but he won't give any details," Bill said, eyeing the strawberry himself. "That's a good size."

"Has anybody ever been up to the roof to look? Do you know?" Elle asked. She hadn't, but it wouldn't have surprised her if Kate had snuck up there at some point, given her reaction to the strawberry though, she was wondering. Kate confirmed it by shaking her head.

"No," Bill said next. "He's pretty uppity about it, and I try not to piss off the people who cook my meals." Bill added, leaning into Kate as if giving some advice for something Elle was unaware of. Kate, in her typical manner, rolled her eyes playfully.

"That's good advice. Did Moses tell you that, back in the day?" The table shared a laugh at that one. It felt good to laugh, even with a nine-alarm hangover.

"It's lucky for you I prefer smartasses to dumbasses, little lady." Bill shot back, and the two of them traded jabs back and forth. Elle thought it was best to stay out of it and just focus on her meal.

She used her spoon to scoop up the bright red berry to put aside. She had plans for that later. She mixed the oatmeal and brown sugar with a couple of swirls of her spoon. It wasn't hot, but it was wonderfully warm still. She never thought sugary warm mush, washed down with tepid orange flavored water, could be so satisfying.

Her eyes caught movement from the other table. In unison, Derek and Jackie rose from the table, dropped their trays off on the counter for Emilio to collect before walking out of the cafeteria, leaving Marty alone at the table. Elle wondered if Derek and Jackie were secretly screwing some place. Elle wouldn't blame them, but the thought of those two going at it was the last thing she wanted to think about right now. Hook-ups happened in their little community, but these days they are usually kept very discreet.

As was his routine, Marty fished a paperback out of his pocket and began to read at the table. Occasionally taking sips from his coffee. Emilio knew Marty liked his coffee and usually kept a pot warm throughout the day, only for him. Being the only pilot in a community whose sole lifeline was a helicopter, gave you special privileges. Everybody knew and respected that. Hell, if Marty had turned to her and asked for her strawberry, Elle wouldn't hesitate in giving it to him. Marty wouldn't do that though. It wasn't his style. Over the time she knew him, she has never seen him ask for anything above what everybody else got. Marty never asked Emilio to make coffee for him all day, it was a small service Emilio could provide to make Marty's life a little better. Elle's contribution was doing his laundry along with hers, Kate's, and Bill's. Like Emilio with the coffee, it was an insignificant gesture, and she was happy to do it.

Elle leisurely ate her food while the other two chatted away and she gave some thought to how she would spend the rest of her day. She was seriously thinking about finding a sofa somewhere on some unoccupied floor where she wouldn't be disturbed and just crashing until she felt better. She had a book she could take with her if she wanted to read. The Prescott building reached forty-five stories into the sky. Nobody in their group occupied a floor lower than thirty-five anymore. That was Jacob and Blaine's floor. That left a lot of empty space. In the beginning everybody started out on the lower floors but as time went on, they all sort of moved up the ladder, sort to speak.

Within days at the beginning, it became apparent help wasn't coming for them, and they noticed their presence in the lobby extremely agitated the collection of undead outside the front doors. So, they moved into the building, and just as they got settled, Jacob voiced a concern that they still might attract more zombies. A quick glance down to the street would show more and more zombies gathering at the front. What started as maybe a dozen harassing them out front turned into a protest size collection of bodies pressing against the building. Then they ran out of food and the scavenging started. People frantically tore through the building and what little they found, Mason forced them to share. It didn't matter, though; it wasn't enough. Then people got worried. They moved higher floor by floor in search of food, and then one day they heard the helicopter overhead. Marty showed up like a white knight, in a suit and tie, no less. The excitement died down quickly when he explained he wasn't here to rescue them. Marty didn't even know then that there was a group of people in the building. He was wrong, though; he *had* rescued them by giving them the chance to rescue themselves. Now they all stayed closer to the top, but farther away from each other.

"Here." Elle waited for a break in their conversation before she scooped up the strawberry with her spoon and offered it to Kate. "You earned this. I'm sorry for making such a mess this morning." She struggled with the last part, but it had to be said. "You didn't *have* to clean it up, though. I would have done it when I got up."

"Aww." Kate sounded like she was looking at a baby kitten instead of a strawberry, and for a brief moment Elle thought she would decline it. But a moment was all it took for Kate to pluck the berry up from the spoon and promptly put it in her mouth. So fast someone might think she was stealing it. "So good," she said while still chewing, and by the surely exaggerated noises she was making, Kate was truly enjoying it. When she finally swallowed it, she sat back with a satisfied grin on her face. "Wow, I would *not* have done that if I were you." Kate laughed a bit, which deflated Elle somewhat. "That was awesome. Thank you, but if I was being honest, it wasn't a big deal. I know you would have cleaned it up, but I didn't want you to. You're my *sister from another mister*. I got your back." Elle winced when Kate said that, and she was positive that was the intended reaction. But honestly, *Sister from another mister? Who says that?* Kate offered her fist across the table and Elle bumped it with her own. It was their thing. They had done it since Kate was a baby. It meant all was forgiven. That was also Kate's thing. She was always quick to forgive. "Besides, you look like shit this morning."

"Gee, thanks."

"Well, you do." Kate snapped back, much like a ten-year-old would. "So, what's everyone doing today? I'm going to be exploring down below for the afternoon, unless a certain someone wants to try their luck with a crib game or two?" She gazed at Bill, who looked down his nose at Kate.

"Not until you learn to cheat better."

"I don't cheat," Kate said, putting on her approximation of a hurt face.

"Well, it's that, or you're *real* bad at counting," Bill said with a bit of a chuckle. He liked giving Kate a hard time, besides Kate probably *was* cheating. She was notoriously bad at card games. "Besides, I have a date with a book this afternoon"

"Whatcha reading?" Elle said almost instinctively as she started in on her bowl of oranges.

"Is it that book I found you?" Kate chimed in.

"Yep," Bill said and then turned to Elle. "Kate found me a copy of Stephen Prince's Christina. I read it once a long time ago and loved it. Thought I would give it another go."

"That's the one with the car, right?" Elle asked between chews.

"Yeah, I'm just getting to the point where the car is going to take its first victim. I plan to read a few chapters and then maybe I'll take a nap before dinner tonight."

"You want me to come wake you for dinner?" Kate asked excitedly. "Then we could walk up the stairs together."

"At my age, we call it *climbing* the stairs." He winked at Elle. "Yeah, that would be good. Well, ladies," Bill said with a groan as he rose from his stool to leave. "I bid you good day," he said with a nod of his head and a quick wave before he turned to leave. They watched him go and then they settled into a silence only sisters could enjoy. Elle returned to her oranges and Kate was content to wait quietly while she did so.

"Where's a good place to crash for a few hours? Preferably dark," Elle asked when she finished her bowl of fruit and then tried to gently rub her headache out of her temples.

She definitely felt better, not so nauseous, but still tired. She didn't know how much sleep she got last night, but it wasn't enough, and she had nothing pressing on her schedule this afternoon. As usual. If anyone knew a good place to sleep undisturbed for a few hours, it was her sister. She has spent much of her time just exploring the building. Elle would join her sometimes and they would just walk the empty halls of the abandoned floors, not exactly looking for anything, but just seeing what was there.

"Um." Kate thought intently for a moment. "You probably don't want to go too far either, huh?"

"The fewer stairs, the better." Elle rubbed her temples.

She made a mental note to stop on their floor for a few more aspirin on her way. Hell, maybe she would just take the bottle with her.

"I would go to the twenty-ninth floor, it's some interior design company, go left after you get out of the stairwell and follow the hallway around to the north side of the building. There's a big office, you can't miss it, it has a big leather couch and blinds on the windows." There was a pause, Elle could feel something was coming, and then finally her sister asked, "Why'd you drink so much?"

There it was. The question Elle had been avoiding all morning, and was hoping to avoid for the rest of the afternoon, hopefully forever.

"I don't know," Elle said, seemingly without thought. "I guess I just lost track of how many drinks I had." She threw that out there and hoped Kate would just accept it to be the truth. Even though, Elle knew better. It started out innocently enough. First, she told herself she wanted to blow off some steam. They all did, it was perfectly natural, and if she had stopped after the initial buzz it might have even been true. But deep down, she knew she didn't start drinking last night to feel something. She started drinking to *stop* feeling something. She couldn't quite put her finger on it, it felt like a pressure that was pushing in on her, choking her, making it hard to move. She knew she wasn't alone in this. You couldn't live under these conditions and not feel something. People talked about it. They joked about it. They agonized over it. Consoled each other from time to time, and tried to be there for others when their own personal pressures became too great. Other than that, to Elle's knowledge anyway, there was nothing to do to help ease the pressure they faced staring down their own doom in this place.

Except drink, or fuck. So, Elle drank.

"Uh-huh. Yeah, that seems likely." Kate looked at her with her classic raised eyebrow of disbelief, but thankfully, she left it at a hard look and didn't pursue it further. "I'm going to help Emilio clean up the dishes and then see if anyone wants to play some chess. Are you done with that?" She pointed to Elle's tray with its two empty bowls on it.

"Yeah, I'm done. You can take it," she said. Elle rose from the table with Kate. "Chess?"

"Bill taught me. Or should I say I let him teach me? It's actually pretty fun once you figured out how all the pieces move." Kate shrugged.

"I thought you were exploring this afternoon?" It seemed like an innocent enough of a question, but Kate still rolled her eyes at her.

"It's a long afternoon. I have a lot of time. If I go exploring, I'll keep it above the tenth floor, like you said."

"That still leaves a lot of building. What if I need to find you?" The truth of it was she didn't like Kate wondering around alone in the building. It's not that she didn't trust the people here. She did, even if some of them sometimes gave her reason not to. But what if something happened? It had become her mantra in regards to Kate. She was all Elle had left in the world. Life was precious before, back when the earth was practically overflowing with people. Now life was sacred, and given that Kate was probably her last surviving family member, that made her a miracle.

However, Kate wasn't a China doll. Elle had to remind herself that Kate would not break if she falls or else she might risk suffocating her like a new mom. Which, Elle guessed she was now. In the beginning of their stay here, she didn't let Kate out of her sight. For months, she would literally be within arm's reach of her sister. At first it brought them closer together, like they were a team, but the tension between them grew because Elle wouldn't stop babying her. To her credit, Kate was right, so she relented, but she couldn't help feeling something terrible would happen and Elle wouldn't be there to fix it.

Not that she's done a really great job fixing things so far.

"I'll stay between fifteen and twenty," Kate said with a long, frustrated groan. "I'll even keep the stairwell door open on whatever floor I'm on so you can find me easier if there is some *emergency*." That was new, and Elle had to admit that was a pretty good idea.

"Thank you."

"You know, you might want to take a break from worrying about me, to worry about yourself now-and-then." Kate gave Elle another hard look, took her tray and her own, and walked to the kitchen where Emilio was serving Walter his lunch at the counter. It wasn't exactly how she wanted their interaction to end, but given how it started, Elle might as well put it in the win category and move on. She watched Kate disappear behind the counter before Elle started off in search of a couch and some peace, wanting nothing more than for this day to end.

Elle made the trek back to their room without incident. She had been concerned that the movement might stir something up in her stomach on the way down; the last thing she wanted was to throw up again. Once in their room, she retrieved the bottle of aspirin and her phone that had her headphones wrapped around it still from the last time she used it. Elle checked the battery's charge, and it was still at twenty-seven percent, which back before the zombie outbreak wouldn't have lasted the day. But now, without Wi-Fi or internet, the phone's battery lasted a lot longer. She had a game on there she could play, or listen to music, and she also had some photos on there. She stuffed the phone and the pills in her pocket and then, on a hunch, walked over to a small tan filing cabinet in the corner. Elle had removed all the files long ago and now they use it to store some of their stuff. Kate and Elle both had their own cabinet. Kate's was black, and Elle had the tan one. She opened the bottom drawer, which is where she stored beverages, and was pleasantly surprised to find Kate had also resupplied their water. In the drawer were six bottles of water that were not there the day before. She grabbed one and closed the drawer before heading out through the door and down the hall to the stairwell door.

Elle opened the door and entered the stairwell's darkness. She pressed the button on the side of the flashlight and it came to life in her hands moments before the door closed and the stairwell fell into complete blackness. Elle aimed the beam down the stairs and started heading down.

Elle thought about what Kate had said before they parted. Maybe she *should* start worrying about herself. As much as Elle liked to tell everyone last night was just about blowing off some steam, it felt more… destructive. Like she was punishing herself. At least that's what it felt like this morning. Elle couldn't say what she had done that she would need to subconsciously punish herself over, unless simply surviving was something to be punished for. She'd heard of survivor's guilt before, people who survived something insanely tragic only by pure luck, and after, felt they didn't deserve to be alive. Elle could understand that feeling. She felt she had already been through that phase, though. It was easy to be guilty when you look at the sheer number of people who must have died by now. Though, the true number of dead would never be known because contact with the outside world died shortly after they locked themselves in this building.

She rounded the corner of the stairwell continuing her descent, thinking of the last days of Manhattan. Then there was a loud crash to the immediate left, and a blinding light flooded the surrounding area, before a tall dark figure appeared in the doorway. Elle screamed and jumped up, dropping her flashlight to the floor as the figure reared back.

"Jesus-fucking-christ!" Jacob shouted and jumped back, tripped over his own feet and landed solidly on his behind. "What the hell are you screaming about, and what the fuck are you doing out there?" He barked at her from the floor, clearly annoyed at the sudden scare. Elle had composed herself enough to grab the door before it slammed close and stood there feeling like an idiot with one hand on the door and another held up in the classic *whoa* position.

"I'm sorry," she pleaded. "I was heading down and you scared me. Are you okay?"

"Yeah, I'm fine." He admitted and then wiped his face with his palm. "You scared the shit out of me," Jacob said as he collected himself off the floor. "No joke, I thought I was going to die." He looked at her and then they broke into a shared laugh over it which was cut off when they heard shouting from further down the hall.

"What is it?!" Came the frantic cry from down the hall and around the corner. "What's happening?" She recognized the excited cries as Blaine Davies, Jacob's best friend forever in the building; they were a cute pair, although totally mismatched. Jacob was a tall, skinny, gay IT guy with a thick mass of dark curly hair on his head. Blaine was a short, somewhat round investment banker, with a bald head who was completely straight. Their friendship started with their shared love of movies and it grew from there. Jacob sometimes referred to their friendship as the Bert and Ernie of The Prescott.

There was a crash and then she could hear heavy footsteps running towards them. "Jake!" Blaine bellowed breathlessly as he continued towards them, still out of sight.

"Oh, Jesus." Jacob lowered his face into his palm and shook his head. "Here comes my white knight," Jacob said into his palm. Elle kept her eyes down the hall waiting for Blaine to appear, and then Jacob cupped his hands around his mouth suddenly shouting down the hall. "Blaine! Don't bring the-," but before he could finish whatever he had to say, Blaine rounded the corner like a charging bull, red faced and sweaty, waving a silver object Elle didn't recognize right away. "*And* there it is," she heard Jacob say in a disappointed manner.

"Where'd you get a gun?" Elle turned to Jacob, realizing it was a secret, and for good reason. One of the group's first established rules was there were to be no firearms allowed amongst the group. They didn't have many to begin with, but Mason wanted whatever they had to be stored properly until they have need of them, and only accessible by those who could safely handle them. Namely Mason and his crew, nobody argued much with that rule. Who better to be in charge of the firearms than professional soldiers? Until now, she didn't think anybody disagreed with that rule. If Mason found out, he would not be pleased.

Blaine's frantic run slowed to a walk when he saw them and saw there was no emergency that required running of any sort. As if receiving some unspoken cue from Jacob, Blaine quickly jammed his hand behind his back as if he could somehow still hide the fact he was carrying a large, silver revolver.

"It's a bit late now," Jacob complained and Blaine breathlessly looked at his friend as if to say; *what*? "You might as well have put sparklers and ribbons on that damned thing, the way you were waving it around." He then turned to her with a serious look on his face. "I'm hoping we can keep this between us."

"Where'd you get it?" She asked again. "You didn't steal it, did you?" Jacob actually looked hurt at the suggestion.

"God, no. We found it in a desk and kept it. For protection," he said casually, like Blaine was describing how he found a quarter on the street, but the look on his face told a different story.

"From what?" Elle said without thinking. Jacob looked at her as if she had spoken an unfamiliar language.

"The *zombies,*" he said as if it was obvious, and it was, or at least it should have been. Of all the things Elle thought about these days, the threat of zombies wasn't actually one of them. "In case you haven't noticed, we are surrounded by them at all times, and they have kind of taken over the earth." Jacob then turned back to Blaine in frustration. Blaine was bent over with his hands on his knees still panting, the silver revolver hung limply from his right hand. "You okay there, pumpkin?" he asked sarcastically. "You want me to see if I can find you an oxygen bottle or something?" Blaine gave him a disdainful look and raised his free hand to give Jacob the finger.

"What'd you expect? I heard you scream, and I thought something terrible was happening." He turned to her and gave her a friendly smile. "Hey, Elle."

"Hey Blaine," she replied with a friendly wave.

"What's that on your face?" He asked and Elle cringed because she had forgotten about the damned whiskers on her face until Blaine mentioned it. She was starting to think she should have let the stairwell door close and just continued on her way. Jacob turned to her and really looked at her for the first time since the door opened and his face lit up. "Did Kate do that?" Elle nodded and quickly informed them of the day's events so far.

"Oh, my god," Jacob snickered scandalously, highly amused at what he saw. "That's adorable and all, but why don't you wash that off?"

"Permanent marker," Elle simply said.

"Ew." Both Jacob and Blaine made the same noise, as if on cue. "Maybe try make-up remover," Blaine said, raising his finger, excited at his idea.

"That's a good idea," Elle said sincerely, but then immediately faced the obvious problem with that solution. Where does she find the make-up remover? She made a note to ask one of the other women in the group.

"That *is* a good idea," Jacob said, almost as if it surprised him Blaine had good ideas. "Wait," he said, pointing to Blaine suddenly. "You thought I was the one who screamed? You think that's what I sound like when I scream?" Jacob sounded almost hurt.

"Well, yeah," Blaine said and winked at Elle. "I assumed it would be a bit higher pitch, maybe a bit more girly sounding, but generally yes." Jacob was about to protest, but Blaine sternly held up a finger to cut him off. "I'm going to run this bad boy-," he held up the revolver again. It looked large this close up, and Elle wondered what kind it was. Or caliber, whatever the term was. She didn't know too much about guns, but that one looked like it could do some serious damage. "-back home, and then when I get back, I'm kind of hoping we can finally get some lunch before we're stuck with the scrapings at the bottom."

"That wouldn't be a problem if you just brought me the food, like I asked. You could have left whenever you wanted." Jacob countered and Blaine shot Elle a look as if to say; *see what I have to deal with?*

"We're not married. I'm not bringing you breakfast in bed, especially after you stay out all night drinking." Blaine said and briskly turned and walked back down the hallway to their room, gun in hand. Jacob, seemingly unable to resist, called after him.

"You say that, but that's exactly what a pissy wife would say. *And* you were there too." Blaine simply responded by giving him the finger again without even turning around. Jacob smiled affectionately and then turned back to Elle. "So, you'll keep this a secret?"

"Yeah, no problem. Don't worry about it," she said without hesitation, and she meant it. Sure, they were breaking one of the few rules the group agreed upon, or more precisely, one of Mason's rules that the rest of them went along with. The no guns rule made sense, and time had shown that there really wasn't a need for it within the building. At the same time though, she couldn't blame the boys for wanting one. There were a lot of "what if" scenarios that would be solved if one had access to a gun. "Just try to do a better job of hiding it next time." She smiled warmly when she said it, but she also tried to add a touch of seriousness to her voice. Not telling somebody about a thing and lying about it to someone's face were two very different things in her eyes.

"Hmph. No doubt. I'm not sure what got into him."

"I think it's cute," she teased. "Coming to your rescue like that."

"Stop," Jacob said and held up his hand as if directing traffic. "It's bad enough he has it. I don't need him getting all gung-ho about it. He came around that corner like he was

John Wayne, for Christ's sake. He's liable to get himself killed," he said, looking down the hall and Elle could see genuine concern on his face. "Or worse yet, me." They shared a smile at that. "Oh, before I forget, we're having a movie night tonight and you're invited. Steel Magnolias. Don't look at me like that, I didn't pick it. It was Blaine's turn to pick, and that's what he chose. He said it was his wife's favorite; he got all misty eyed about it too. What could I do? Anyway, start time will be around 9pm and there'll even be popcorn, if you can believe it." Elle didn't feel she had to say anything to that. The open-mouthed look of amazement on her face should say everything. She couldn't remember the last time she had actual popcorn. First, a juicy red strawberry at lunch, sure she may have given that to her sister, and now popcorn tonight. This was turning into a great day despite her best efforts. "Yeah, I know, right? Apparently, Blaine has been sitting on a stash of microwave popcorn, and this morning he told me he asked Kat if she-."

"Kate," Elle corrected him playfully. She didn't understand her sister's affection for the nickname, she didn't hassle her about it, but Elle didn't have to encourage it either.

"Kate-," Jacob said and stuck out his tongue at her. "If she could find some sodas for everyone as well, can you imagine? He's really going all out for this," Jacob said, almost as if he was proud. They chatted for a moment longer before Blaine came back around the corner and then they entered the stairwell together and said their goodbyes. Blaine and Jacob rounded the corner going up and Elle aimed her flashlight on the stairs and continued down to the twenty-ninth floor.

She found the office easy enough. Kate's directions led her straight to the office of Wanda Cleary, the Chief Financial Officer to Horizons Urban Design, and judging by the photos on her wall; a loving wife and mother of two boys. The office itself was fairly large. The one wall to her left as Elle entered the office was entirely wood paneling. It was a deep brown color and on that wall was where Wanda kept her various degrees and achievements, all framed and meticulously hung to occupy the space evenly. Elle took a moment to scan over them as she walked through the office. On the opposite side, was a shelving unit so large it filled the entire wall, and was made of the same dark wood. On it, Elle found all the things that she imagined were a tiny representation of Wanda's life.

There were pictures of her family, of her friends and colleagues. Books of all kinds and tiny mementos littered the shelves. Elle briefly looked over it to see if there was anything of interest, there wasn't, so she moved on. The center of the room was where the desk was, a large wooden one that still looked somewhat modern. It housed everything you'd expect from a working space. A large computer screen on an adjustable stand, and they stowed away the keyboard in a tray that slid out from underneath the desk. It had a nameplate that faced outwards with her name and position on it, as well as more pictures that faced inwards. Elle didn't check but she assumed it would be more pictures of Wanda's family. There was a desk mat on the top of the desk and it held the ancient tools of the trade; pens, a stapler, and a neat stack of Post-it notes that looked almost eager to be used. The chair behind the desk was like the desk itself in that it was simple and built for use as opposed to a representation of status. Elle had some experience with office chairs and she could see this was a good one, nice mesh backing with plenty of lumbar support. A nice cushion to sit on and cushioned arm rests at the sides. The two chairs that sat in front of the desk that were meant for guests were of a lesser quality by far, but still nicer than most chairs Elle has sat on in her life.

Elle moved over to the windows. Outside, the

neighboring buildings stood like giants made out of concrete and glass. She was low enough, so there was no view beyond those buildings. Judging by the reflection in the windows across the street, it was a bright day with few clouds in the sky. If she looked up, she could see the mid-day sky painted on the sides of the buildings, and although she couldn't see the sun directly, there were dozens of reflected sources of light beaming into the office. Elle imagined Wanda Cleary moving into the office and immediately ordering the full-length blinds installed the next day to counteract the unwanted glare. Before Elle closed the blinds, she pressed her hands against the glass and leaned in close and looked down.

She was too far up to see the area in front the building, but what she could see of the streets off in the distance, had a black stain that almost looked solid until you looked at it for a time. Then she'd notice the subtle shifting to it, almost like a ripple in a quiet pond. *There's got to be a million of them down there.* The sheer number of the undead that has accumulated on the street-level morbidly amazed her. The enemy, the devourer of humanity, the undead. She still had a hard time saying the word, *zombie.* Elle couldn't believe she lived in a world where science fiction bullshit like this could actually happen, but there they were. As real as the nose on her face. She turned away from the window, unable to look at it any longer. There was no point dwelling on it. They were down there, and she was up here, safe. Trapped, and some days it felt like imprisoned, but safe none-the-less. She closed the blinds tightly, and the office plunged into blessed darkness. There was plenty of light to see still but thankfully not enough light to cause her temples to throb.

The couch was huge. It was dark leather that was soft to the touch and had tastefully matching pillows at both ends that looked more stylish than comfortable, but she didn't care; they would do her just fine. The couch was large enough that she could easily lie down on it and have room to spare for her feet. It sat against the frosted glass of the hallway and it was practically calling out to her. In front of it was a large coffee table made entirely of glass that was currently bare, and on both sides of the couch were smaller glass tables that each housed a fashionable lamp. Before she indulged it, though, she placed the bottle of water, the aspirin, and her phone on the large coffee table and sat down on the couch. She popped opened the aspirin and swallowed two more pills, which she washed down with half of the bottle of water. Elle read somewhere hangovers were because of the body being dehydrated. All she needed to feel better was more water, and she hoped that was true. She thought about finishing the bottle and left it until later. Elle arranged the pillow and laid down on the couch. The soft leather almost seemed to suck her into a soft embrace. The office air was warm but not hot. She closed her eyes and let her body relax.

She thought about her old life in the moments before she drifted off to sleep. Before this, she had two jobs, a large circle of friends, and an on-again off-again boyfriend. She was busy, each day was planned out and full. The only things she didn't have time for was cleaning. The apartment she shared with her friend, Clara, was a mess, but it was a happy mess. If such a thing existed. She was building the life she wanted, becoming the woman she wanted to be, but that was before. Now she was stuck in limbo, with no options, no plan, just a lot of time. A lot of time to wonder how it could all fall apart.

Elle woke up hours later and although she wasn't exactly refreshed, the pains of her hangover seemed to be mostly behind her. Her head wasn't pounding and she felt sharper than she did this morning. She was still tired, and she had a thin film of sweat covering her face. Her hair was wet and sticky and her clothes felt damp, but she felt good. Better than good. She had an idea. Elle felt she knew what she wanted to do. She awoke with it fully formed in her mind. It was nothing fancy or well thought out. Just an '*I want this statement*' that crystalized in her head. At first, it was ridiculous, but the idea stuck with her and soon she was thinking; *why not*? From that, the first course of action became clear, and once it did, there was no possibility of sleeping further until it was resolved. She rose from the couch with a purpose, collected the bottle of pills and downed the last bit of water in the bottle before heading out the door. She left the office feeling that Wanda Cleary would approve of her bold new plan, if she had been around to hear it.

As she climbed the stairs, Elle thought of what she would say. A newfound energy carried her up the stairs a lot faster than she would have thought possible on her way down a few hours earlier. She quickly determined that she shouldn't make any sort of grand statement or anything that might be counter-productive to what she was trying to accomplish. In school, she learned you need to be aware of your target audience. A big long explanation of her personal history, a breakdown of her anxieties over not having a sense of purpose in this place, and a brief rundown on how this solution could change everything for her, would not impress him at all. He was a simple person. He talked little, but when he did, he got straight to the point and didn't waste many words explaining things. That's who she was dealing with. That's how she had to approach this. The first thing that came to her mind is she wouldn't ask for anything. She didn't want to go up to him and say: '*Can you do this for me, pretty please? I'd be ever so grateful*', that would be a mistake. She didn't want to appear like some damsel in distress. She was never comfortable using that act on men, but she knew in certain situations it could come in handy, but not this one. Nor could she walk up to him full of steam and demand anything. She was not in any sort of position to be making demands of anyone. It would have to be a delicate balance of the two. She didn't want to appear flighty, either. This was a big request. As she neared her destination floor, she thought about how she could best convey her understanding of the responsibility she might take on. This would be a big step for her in the group; there would be no more sitting on the sidelines after this. She would take an active role in the group's survival. It was a sobering thought, but she was ready, and she would show him she appreciated the seriousness of her request.

By the time she opened the door to the fortieth floor, she was more than sure she had the coming conversation mapped out. She tried to consider what he would say, some questions he might ask. Elle expected some push back, of course. It would be foolish to assume there wouldn't be any, especially given her age. She would be ready for that angle if he went there, but she didn't think he would. He was a sensible person, not one to assume something about a person just because of their age.

She hung her flashlight on the hooks and entered the floor. To her surprise, there wasn't anyone in the big open area. Nobody playing foosball or shooting hoops or quietly sitting on the couches. The floor was a ghost town, which made her wonder if he was even here. She checked her phone to double check the time, and it was only twenty-two minutes past four in the afternoon. Supper wasn't for another three hours. He would be here. If he wasn't, she would wait until she could get him alone again to have this talk. She didn't want an audience when she talked to him. Not that she was planning on making a scene, but she felt she would be more at ease if she didn't have to worry about anybody listening in.

She turned the corner and there at the same table he had been at this morning, sitting in the same chair quietly with the same worn and tattered paperback in his hand and a cup of coffee off to the side on the table.

Marty.

Elle didn't want to waste time and didn't break her stride as she approached the table. She calmly walked up and, without being given or asking permission, she sat down opposite of Marty. She placed her hands out in front of her, just like she had planned, and waited until he acknowledged her. A moment or two had passed. Elle was beginning to worry she might have to say something before he would look up at her. Finally, his eyes popped up over the top of the paperback and looked at her wordlessly for a time until it became clear his full attention was required. Marty slowly marked his place in the book with a bookmark and close it in front of him. He looked at her again and simply raised his eyebrow as if to say, *yes*?

"I want to learn how to fly the helicopter," she said solemnly and let it hang in the air between them. It was all part of the plan. When he inevitably asked her why, she would roll out all the points she came up with on the way up. Elle stared at him, almost daring him to ask, but what Marty said was something she didn't plan for. The childish hubris instantly struck her. She did not think to consider the obvious response.

"No," he said definitively. With that said, he apparently considered the matter closed because he picked up his book again. Marty opened it to the page he had been reading before she had arrived. He added insult to injury when he casually asked: "Are those supposed to be whiskers on your face?"

Chapter 5

Kenshiro

Kenshiro parked the truck on the dirt road about thirty yards from the T-intersection, where the road branches off to the north and south before heading into the town. Beyond it, was the large open field and the first row of houses on the west side of the town. Laying prone in the bed of the truck, Kenshiro had a perfect view of it all.

Using his binoculars, he could clearly make out the back side of a light blue house. By the look of it, the house wasn't anything special, maybe even a bit run down. However, what he liked about the house was the waist high chain-link fence that circled the entire property. It was the perfect physical barrier against the undead for his purposes; sturdy enough to keep them at bay, but it didn't prevent or hinder him from dealing with any zombies surrounding the short barrier. If all went according to his plan, that house would be where he would spend the night. If needed, he could go back to the farm house he stayed at last night, but in his mind that would be a retreat. It remained a viable option, but it was something to be done only when the circumstances called for it. This was a war, pure and simple, and that blue house was his beach head. If today was to be a success, he would have to take it, but that one task might take him all day. Before it was over, at least a hundred undead bodies would fall. Hopefully more.

His battle plan was simple enough.

In the center of the T-intersection, he had placed a battery-operated CD player that was remote controlled. Kenshiro had already checked the batteries;

they had plenty of juice, and the song had been pre-selected. Kenshiro currently paused the unit with the sound turned all the way down. The remote lay on the truck bed in front of him and to his right. When the time came, he would press play and turn up the volume on the unit slowly until he could just barely hear it from his position. That way, he could try to control the approach of zombies somewhat. Initially, the flow would be a mere trickle and he could observe where they came from. Like ants, the undead tended to follow the path of the zombie in front of them, which made their approach predictable. He would simply lie in the truck bed, under the tarp he had set-up to further conceal himself, and pick them off one by one as they came into range.

The .22 rifle he used was small compared to the rifles he had seen others use for this purpose. The tiny rifle was designed mostly to hunt small rodents like a rabbit or a prairie dog, but what it lacked in power it more than made up for in discretion. When fired, the rifle made a sound comparable to a mild sneeze. From a hundred yards out, the rifle was practically silent. At this distance, the sound of the rifle would be overpowered by the music coming from the CD player. What made it even more attractive when he first saw it was the barrel had a tiny bipod to stabilize the rifle while aiming even more.

To protect the CD player, Kenshiro took a large plastic garbage can that he had prepared earlier in the morning by cutting good sized holes in it. He then flipped the garbage can upside-down and placed it on top of the stereo.

His first attempt using a stereo to draw them out ended abruptly when the first stumbling zombie who approached it on the road lunged for it clumsily as soon as it was within range. The hapless zombie ended up falling on the compact music player he had been using, and crushed it under the bulk of its body.

The first time he used a garbage can to protect the stereo, he found the construction of the can itself muffled the music too much for it to be an effective lure. That was a simple fix, and since then he had cut fist sized holes all over the can's body to let the sound escape but protect the stereo within. Also, he tried to make sure the zombies didn't reach the music player. He knew that Swiss-cheesed garbage can might keep one or two zombies away from his stereo but a crowd of them would easily and unintentionally ruin the whole setup.

The first time he used the truck bed to shoot from, he found the hard steel interior uncomfortable. So now, he emptied all nonessential items out and lined the truck bed with a few layers of blankets from the ranch house. He was going to be laying prone for a while in the box of the truck, he might as well be as comfortable as possible.

He had maybe done this approach to clearing a town more than a dozen times. Each time Kenshiro did it, he looked for things to make the next time better. That's why his little .22 automatic pistol was lying on the truck bed off to his right with the butt end facing away from him. He found the pistol jabbed his ribs as he laid prone, but he also knew he would need it close and handy, in case some undead asshole snuck up on him from the opposite direction. It had happened a few times before. He placed the freshly opened box of five hundred .22 cartridges on his right side between the rifle and his pistol so when he needed to reload, he could use his left to pull the magazine free and use his right hand to load the magazine. Everything around him within arm's reach was the product of the evolution of this process. This was only the first phase, though.

The second phase could begin several ways. Ideally, he would lie there in relative comfort and snipe each one of the undead that came into his sights until his little box of bullets was empty, or he staunched the flow of zombies completely. It's happened only once before where he could fire off the entire box, but it was possible. However, there was a possibility the flow of zombies could also overwhelm his ability to shoot them. In that scenario, his priority would shift to defending his little stereo, because once the music stopped, he would lose his cover. At that point, he either had to press forward the best he could or abandon the whole thing and try again in a couple days.

Another possibility was he might get spotted. Zombies had poor eyesight, but they didn't need much to attract their attention. If undead eyes looked his way and noticed a muzzle flash, or maybe spotted the slight bit of movement needed to reload his weapon, or because he was facing east, they might notice the sun's reflection in his scope. Whatever got that one zombie's attention might shift the focus of the whole herd. At that point, the music would no longer be effective, or even noticed by the ones already locked onto his position. If the day went well, however, he would lay in the truck all morning lazily picking off the approaching undead until he decided he had done enough for the day. The days they forced him to leave the comfort and relative security of the truck bed and flee, those were the days that showed him he needed to work on his process more.

Kenshiro looked back to the town one last time before deciding it was time to kick this party off. He placed the binoculars to his left. Kenshiro wouldn't have much use for them once he started shooting. He took a deep breath before he picked up the tiny remote for the stereo and pressed *play*. Next, he pressed the button on the remote to increase the volume until he could just barely make out what might be the drum beat or the opening guitar riff for the song. He liked to use ACDC's album Highway to Hell. It seemed appropriate. He still couldn't make out the lyrics, but he didn't want to turn the volume up anymore until he saw if anything inside the town was listening.

Kenshiro used his right hand and placed it around the grip of the rifle and pulled the stock into his shoulder. He put his left arm out in front of him for comfort, tilted his head slightly, then looked down the scope for signs of movement. Kenshiro first checked the north and south road leading to the intersection. When he saw nothing, Kenshiro moved to the buildings off in the distance and looked in between them for any shambling figures. He was beginning to think he would have to turn the volume up higher, when the first one came into view.

Kenshiro touched the tip of his finger to the trigger.

Directly in front of him, across the field, was the light blue house with the waist-high fence he was eyeing up as his beach head. The zombie was on the south side of it when it came limping listlessly along the fence line. It was walking straight towards him. Through the scope, Kenshiro could see the undead man's fixation on the stereo ahead of him. It crept forward. Kenshiro breathed in deeply and steadied the rifle. Through the sights, he placed the crosshair slightly above the top of its head. Thankfully at this distance he couldn't make out a lot of details. Though, he could still make out the ragged pieces of flesh hanging from its face. Kenshiro breathed out slowly and focused on the slight bob of its step. He tried to time it like a drumbeat. He wanted to fire at the top of its arc. *One-thousand-one, two-thousand two, three-*

Paff!

The rifle kicked slightly against his shoulder. Kenshiro relaxed his finger and removed it from the trigger. He had aimed low. Through the scope, he saw the bullet punch through its front teeth. He had been aiming for the bridge of its nose. None-the-less he achieved his desired effect as he saw it fall to the ground like someone had yanked its plug out from the wall. *One down*, he thought to himself as he scanned the buildings and the spaces between them for any others who might have come into view. Kenshiro made a mental note of the distance of the corner of the fence and where the crosshairs would have to be elevated to compensate for the bullet drop. Every shot would be different, sure, but it would be a good baseline to start from.

Kenshiro went back to the scope and began taking his shots at the undead slowly filtering into view. He took his time with each shot and only fired when he was confident the bullet would hit its mark. The stock of the rifle pressed slightly into his shoulder each time he squeezed the trigger. He tried not to look at the faces and to separate the act from the shot. He wanted to imagine he was at a shooting range, simply aiming and shooting at the target, not monsters responsible for the destruction of humanity, not the abominations that ruined his entire life. This was a bitter business, and he needed a cool head to do it properly. So, he didn't let emotion get involved, even though he was fully aware of the grimace on his face as he was firing. He counted the bullets and after ten shots; he pulled the magazine free with his left hand and began reloading it with his right with practised grace. When he saw there were no immediate threats to his position, Kenshiro returned to the scope and lined up the next shot.

On the fifth reload, after he loaded his weapon and it was ready to go, he let the stock drop to the truck bed and reached for the water bottle.

He felt he had the scene in front of him well under control. The flow of the undead horrors was slow but relatively steady, it gave him plenty of time for each shot. Unfortunately, that didn't mean he didn't miss occasionally. He found the roads coming out from the town on the north and south were the most challenging shots to make. Especially the south. He found he missed his mark on most of those shots for a reason he couldn't explain. So much so, he decided to wait until the targeted zombie rounded the corner, coming up to the T-intersection before firing. To the north he had more success, but only because he had a lot of time to work out the aiming. The easiest shot was the path his first target took along the light blue house. Kenshiro might have had a dozen come that way already and was hoping it would continue to be a popular path for the undead. He kept a close eye on the scene in front of him as the undead continued their approach. Kenshiro took another generous swig from his water bottle before replacing the cap and setting the bottle to the side. He placed his hand on the rifle's grip and put the stock to his shoulder, breathed in deeply and simply let the air escape his lungs before he looked through the tiny scope and got back to work.

Half way between the eleventh and twelfth reload, something *bumped* into the truck.

By then, the flow of zombies had dropped off almost entirely, so much so that he was holding back his shots because he was hoping more would appear. The scene in front of him had become littered with corpses. The evidence of the fruits of his labors was apparent. There was no place he could look where he didn't see a corpse. Objectively, it was a horror show. He didn't count the bodies that fell, but he was confident there was more than a hundred corpses in front of him. A truly nightmarish scene, but in the new world, it was simply a good start to owning the town.

Kenshiro continued to listened intently. So, when he heard the soft scraping sounds traveling along the driver's side of the truck, there was no mistaking it. Phase two had begun. He wasted no time in pulling the magazine free from the rifle and ejecting the round still in the chamber. Kenshiro then loaded the spare round back into the magazine and set both the magazine and the rifle to the side. He was done with them, and a part of him was thankful to be leaving the confines of the truck bed after all this time. The tarp did little to allow air circulation, and it had become a bit of a sauna underneath it. With his right hand, he reached for his pistol on the truck bed and with his left; he retrieved a black box that fit nicely in his hand that had two metal barbs that protruded out of the top of it. The green status light on the side let him know it was ready to go. Tasers did little to the undead except to drop them to the ground for a few seconds, which is all he really wanted. He waited as the soft scraping sounds got closer, first to the truck bed, and then slowly down the length of it until Kenshiro was sure it was right beside him. He heard its low, soft moan that confirmed, without a doubt, what was sneaking up on him. Kenshiro waited. It soon rounded the corner of the back of the truck and he could see, and unfortunately smell, the soiled tattered clothes that barely covered the gray cracked flesh of the zombie's midsection . Where he could see a fist-sized hole, maybe an inch to the right of the belly button, that was currently leaking a black goo.

An instant later, Kenshiro reached out and jabbed the taser into its stomach, purposefully avoiding the leaking hole, and pressed the button on the side. The tiny box made a loud snapping sound and the walking corpse spasmed so violently, Kenshiro was sure he heard something pop. Then it fell over, stiff as a board. That bought him a few moments, and he didn't waste them. In one motion, he rose and used his arm to sweep the tarp back. Instantly, the bright sunlight bombarded him, it was both welcoming and disorienting at the same time. It didn't slow him down, though.

Without waiting for his eyes to adjust, he scanned the area around the truck with the pistol held out in front of him and his finger on the trigger. He saw to his relief that the immediate area around him was clear except for the now recovering zombie by the tailgate. Kenshiro did not want to fire the pistol in his hands because, although it used the same ammunition as the rifle, it was considerably louder. In one swift motion, Kenshiro holstered his pistol again and jumped down off the tailgate. The zombie on the ground was slowly regaining the use of its limbs. Kenshiro wasted no time as he raised up his boot, and with considerable force, brought it down on the spot on its ruined face where the bridge of its nose would have been. There was a muffled sound, like little twigs breaking, and he felt something within the undead skull give under the weight of his boot.

The undead man stopped moving and became the corpse nature intended. Kenshiro then reached for his water bottle and downed the rest of its contents in one giant gulp. He threw the bottle into the ditch and saw two more zombies coming up the road towards him. A pair who had been men once, and by the look of them, they have been undead for a long time. At this distance, they looked like walking skeletons with rags loosely hanging about their bodies. There was another one approaching across the field to the north that was wearing a light-colored dress, and was some distance away still. He saw it was having a hard time navigating the terrain. As he was looking at it, he saw its leg catch on something, and the female zombie mindlessly fell to the earth. He turned away as it flailed in the dirt, kicking up a small cloud of dust.

Looking back to the town, he didn't see any new arrivals except for one coming in on the south road. Kenshiro added it to the tally in his head. He reached down and pressed the stop button on the stereo's remote. He didn't need the music anymore. With the surrounding zombies alerted to his presence, they instantly moved towards him with a new intensity. The two bony ones up the road back towards the ranch moved only as fast as their rotten muscles would carry them. Kenshiro stepped over to the passenger door and opened it. On the seat were his two duffel bags. He went to the green one with the reflective stripe on it and retrieved a fresh bottle of water, a packet of dried peach slices, and a granola bar that he felt confident was still good. Kenshiro then quickly ate his lunch.

He was stalling.

Admittedly, this was his least favorite part of the entire operation, but he knew it had to be done, and the benefits of it far outweighed his revulsion at what it entailed. So, he did it. He didn't enjoy it. He secretly was hoping this would be one of those times he didn't throw up. Kenshiro washed down his lunch with another generous drink from the water bottle. There were four left in the bag and he hoped it would be enough to get him through the day. Kenshiro had a lot of work ahead of him, and it looked like it was going to be another hot one.

He opened one compartment on the front of the green duffel bag and pulled out a large black handkerchief which he tied around his head, so the material hung down and covered the bottom half of his face. From the same compartment, he pulled out a roll-on deodorant stick he found back at the ranch house, which he simply tucked away into his pocket for later. After Kenshiro finished putting on the pair of gloves he found at the ranch, he zipped the duffel bag shut before he locked the truck's door. He had the keys in his pocket. Kenshiro moved to the truck box and retrieved his rebar spear from where he left it this morning. That, and a half-used roll of thick nylon rope that he also had placed in the truck earlier that morning. With everything in tow, he walked down the road towards the stereo, monitoring the approaching undead. Kenshiro casually walked past the garbage can with the holes in it, and moved into the field to wait for them. He decided he would put the pyre directly behind the little blue house, a safe distance from the fence. From inside that house, he could watch them all burn.

Once at the spot he envisioned, Kenshiro drove the point of the spear into the ground and left it with the butt end pointing towards the sky. He placed the roll of rope and the bottles of water down on the ground and ceremoniously began cutting four-foot lengths of rope until he had a dozen of them lying on the ground. Kenshiro then took each length of rope and tied a slip knot on one end and made the loop big enough for a pair of feet to fit through. On the other end, he made a double knot and tightened them up against each other so they made a sort of ball at the end of the rope, a little smaller than the size of his fist. He followed the same procedure for each length of rope.

Kenshiro finished just as the first zombie came within range. He quickly stuffed his hand into his pocket and pulled out the stick of deodorant. He popped the cap and lifted the flap on the handkerchief covering the bottom of his face. Then Kenshiro rubbed the stick generously along his upper lip and the smell of evergreen filled his nose. As the day wore on, he would have to reapply. He found it helped with the smell.

It had been the zombie from the south road that would arrive first. Kenshiro had been watching them all closely as the undead stalked awkwardly towards him this entire time, and he had expected this one to arrive first for some time now. He had seen from some distance away the thick leather biker jacket the heavy zombie had been wearing. The shirt underneath had been shredded, and now at this range, Kenshiro could see the bite-sized pieces of skin that had previously been torn away from its chest. There were maybe a dozen ragged chunks missing and the entire front of his jeans was a dark brown stain of old blood. He had been a bigger man when he had been alive, but now, after being undead for so long, all that fat had decomposed away. It made it look like its flesh was melting in the sun. Kenshiro stood in place for a moment until the wiggly fleshed zombie was in the right spot and then, quick as lightning, he unsheathed the knife on his right side and drove it through its left eye with ease before yanking the knife out again just as fast.

Kenshiro waited until the body settled on the ground before he used his foot to nudge its legs slightly to position the deflated zombie the way he wanted. After he positioned its head towards the house, he tucked in the zombie's arms and legs using his foot. Then, Kenshiro cleaned the black substance off his knife using its soiled jeans. He stood up to look towards the undead housewife walking towards him on the north road. Although he was guessing the stumbling figure had once been a mother, truth be told, Kenshiro did not know what it could have been when it had been a living, vibrant woman. It had the look of a mother, though. The zombie wore blue jeans, and a faded pink plaid shirt that had the sleeves rolled up to the elbows. Its medium length blonde hair and been pulled back into a sensible ponytail. It was hard to determine what age it was when it first turned because now, even though her face was unmarked, the unnatural transformation into the undead did a great job of masking age. They all had withered features, cracked dry skin, thinning hair, and stiff joints. The only things that stood out on zombies anymore were their clothes, their injuries, and their hair. Assuming they still had hair. This one had a red stain on the back of its pant leg on the left side; he couldn't see any other injuries. It was still somewhat fresh looking; this shambling corpse didn't look like it had been exposed to the elements that long. Before it was turned, it could have been someone passing through this town, like him.

Kenshiro tightened his grip on the knife as the motherly zombie stepped in beside the corpse he had just positioned a moment earlier, and before the undead woman could take another awkward step, he struck. He used his left hand to clear its flailing arms out of the way and lunged forward with the knife. The knife easily destroyed the soft tissue of its milky brown eye as it passed on through to the brain. He always knew the moment the blade hit home, because the corpse's body would give one last tiny spasm before it would finally accept its death and fall to the ground. This one was no different, and he was happy to see it had fallen pretty much exactly where he wanted it to fall, down beside the fleshy corpse with the leather jacket.

Again, he cleaned off his knife and sheathed it so he could quickly tuck in the arms and legs of the new arrival. After, he scanned the surrounding area, carefully looking for any other clumsy figures that might look for a fresh snack. He didn't see any new ones. The two skeletons had made it to the truck and were making their way alongside it, but the one in the field that had on the light-colored dress would arrive first. The closer it got, the more it seemed to be emboldened by his presence. Its lust for fresh meat spurred it on, whereas the two skeletons just lumbered along the road woodenly, unaware of his presence and equally unconcerned of their destination. Kenshiro positioned himself for the approaching trio and waited. When the walking corpse in the flower print dress finally stepped into the spot he picked out for it, he put it down with another quick thrust to the eye and repeated the same process of arranging the body next to the one with the plaid shirt. The last two were by far the longest wait. As their dried-out bodies lumbered towards him across the uneven ground of the field, he got a good look at their ravaged forms. At this stage, the pair were hardly recognizable as human. Sure, they still had two arms, two legs and a head, but that was where the similarities ended. It was rare to see zombies this far gone, and rarer still to see two walking side by side along the road. So much so, he couldn't help but wonder if they had a connection to each other from when they were living. He didn't want to think too much about their backstory because whatever it was, it would end with him. The undead usually kept pretty good. Kenshiro knew nothing about normal decomposition of the human body, but he knew more than he liked about zombies.

Once turned, a fresh zombie is at its most dangerous. At this stage, zombies had full motor control over their bodies. They can run, they can jump, and even operate simple mechanisms like door knobs. If that wasn't bad enough, they found out later, after it was far too late, that early zombie's adrenal glands went into overdrive until it eventually burned itself out, so fresh ones were freakishly strong as well. A pack of runners is like a frenzied school of piranhas on steroids with legs. He had in the past witnessed what five fresh zombies could do to a man, and they literally ripped him apart before the sickness could take hold.

Thankfully, the runner stage only lasted about two days, and then the undead would fall into the walker stage. There they would remain for the bulk of their existence. Kenshiro realized that this stage isn't static, but a very slow decline, or rather decomposition, of the body. The first thing to go is all the useless stuff; namely the internal organs. They rot away on the inside as nature intended and then find some way to escape the body cavity. If not by some hole in the abdomen, made by zombie or man, the decomposed sludge will leak slowly out of the anus and create the foulest odor imaginable as the zombies literally shit out their own organs. Kenshiro could usually smell those zombies before he saw them. After that the hair starts to fall out, fat deposits shrink away, leaving the skin to droop slightly, which lasts until the skin dries out and then it thins as it gets pulled across the bones.

These hunched over stumbling wrecks represented what he assumed was the last stage of the undead sickness. Skeletons weren't exactly an accurate term. They were not a walking frame of bones, but from a distance it was easy to think that. At this stage, all the hair had fallen out, all the nonessential tissues were consumed to fuel the undead engine, or had rotted away and simply fallen off the body. They had no ears on the sides of their head, and the one on the right was missing its nose completely. While the one on the left still had one, but it was a shriveled mass on its face. All color had long left their eyes. They were the color of milk, and had the shape of a rotten grapes inside their sockets. The skin on their heads had dried up and stretched so tight that, in some places, it cracked open exposing the bone below. They also had no lips to speak of, the skin of the lips had long ago dried out until they disappeared completely and now it was just teeth. Two rows of jagged teeth with gaps in some places where the tooth had been knocked out or maybe pulled free from ripping flesh from its victims.

All over its body the flesh that been pulled tight over the dried-out sinew of its muscles, and at the joints, he could see where the skin had been ripped apart instead of flexing with the joint. Their hands had wasted away completely to shrunken claws that were pulled in close to their chests as they walked towards him. When he looked down, he saw their feet pulled in to look like tiny knobby little fists. Their tiny frail looking legs, that reminded him of chicken legs both in size and texture, were walking on the sides of their feet because the callused remains of their soles were so badly disfigured, they would no longer lie flat on the ground. They were abominations, but not beyond his pity.

Nothing deserves to be reduced to this.

He took no delight as the one on the right flopped forward suddenly and, after a series of pops up and down its withered body, it attempted to crawl but lacked the range of motion in its limbs to do so. Kenshiro left it and focused on the one still upright and kept leading it to its final resting spot. Once there, he dutifully put it down and arranged its body neatly next to the others. Kenshiro went to the one that had fallen and promptly pushed his knife into the back of its skull, ending its misery. It was only a short distance away from where he had wanted it, so instead of grabbing one of the pre-cut ropes, he simply stabbed the knife into the spot under where the collar bone met the spine. He didn't have to guess at the spot because he could clearly make out the bones underneath the tatters of cloth that hung off its shoulders, and used the knife to drag the corpse in beside its partner. It couldn't have been over sixty pounds and moved easily across the ground. When he finished, he looked down at the five corpses he had neatly lined up in a row for a moment, almost as if to see if he would feel something at the sight of it, at the realization that he was looking at his own handiwork, and this was just the beginning.

"Sorera o subete korosu tame ni," he breathed to the wind. *To kill them all.* As he looked at the zombies he had put down, searching for some complex emotion that maybe, at one point, he would have argued defined the human experience. Remorse? Regret? Sympathy? Sadness? Shame? He found none of those when he looked out over the field of bodies he had left behind so far. He didn't know why it was important, like a litmus test for his humanity maybe, but he thought he should feel something. *To kill them all*, he said again within the confines of his mind, and he wondered if it was enough, or if he was walking down the path to madness. "Sorera o subete korosu tame ni," he said aloud again. This time a little louder, and with a little more conviction to silence his mind. He was wasting time, and he had a lot of unpleasant work to do yet.

The pyre's construction was the height of simplicity. The bottom layer he constructed using the larger corpses in the field, as well as the bodies of the adult males. Kenshiro did a line of ten bodies before he started the next row. Then came the kindling layer. Kenshiro found an abundance of dried twigs and branches to fill in the gaps between the bodies. The second layer was reserved for women and teenagers. Again, more kindling. A woodpile beside the olive green house to the north of his beach head helped with that. The last layers were comprised of the smallest of the corpses to be found in the field. The ones Kenshiro didn't like thinking about. It was hard, gruesome work. When he was tired, he took breaks, ate some food, drank some water, and listened to the sound of the wind blowing across the barren land. When it was done, the pyre was a true monstrosity that was hard to look at.

He placed the corpses of the dozen zombies who happened onto the scene during the construction process around the pyre. He spaced them out so they formed a loose ring around the stack of bodies about four feet out from the edge of the grotesque mound. He found a shovel in the shed of the same drab looking house that had the wood pile. Kenshiro used it to dig a shallow trench in the space between the ring of corpses and the pyre. In the same shed, as luck would have it, he found a small container of gasoline. It was maybe a two-gallon container, and it was only about half full which wasn't a lot but he scooped it up anyway. He walked the container over and placed it next to the spear, that spent the afternoon stuck in the ground like it was marking some spot in the field. He set it down beside the five-gallon container and a road flare he brought from the acreage he stayed at last night. With that done, the pyre was complete and ready to go, but the big moment wouldn't be for some time yet. He still had plenty of daylight left.

With the pyre completed, Kenshiro set about the next part of the plan. He walked back to the truck to retrieve the two duffel bags with all the essentials of his life within them. Kenshiro made the trek back and walked casually up to the back door of the little blue house he had been eyeing up all day. It had concrete steps that led up to a faded yellow door. Kenshiro climbed the stairs and let the large bags slide to the concrete of the steps before he gripped the knob. It was locked. Undeterred, he reached down into the black bag and pulled out a small zippered pouch he had found in the glove compartment box of a police cruiser over half a year ago. He unzipped it, and looked at the selection of lock picks that were inside. Trevor had been sure to give him a crash course in the basics of picking locks.

In truth, Trevor himself wasn't very good at it, but Kenshiro had taken what he knew and filled in the blanks of what he didn't know as he went along. The door knob itself was locked but there was also a deadbolt on the door that was probably locked as well. Judging by the looks of the two locks, he would say the one on the knob itself would probably be the easiest. The doorknob looked old, maybe as old as the house. For all he knew, the door knob might be the one they built the house with, judging by the look of the tarnished surface of the metal, but the deadbolt was another story.

It was a Wiser brand deadbolt that was still shiny. It was new, and he guessed probably had a five-pin tumbler in it, whereas the shitty lock on the doorknob probably only had three. He started in on the doorknob first. Kenshiro first pulled the rake pick free. It looked like a thin key that had a handle attached to it. Next, he pulled out the torsion wrench he would use to apply the slight amount of tension to the lock. He put the wrench into the knob's lock first and then put the rake pick in and began to work the pick back and forth in the lock. The whole time, keeping a steady but slight amount of tension on the torsion wrench.

Luckily, the door knob's lock required little patience. The lock was worn, sloppy, and the pins practically fell into place. There was a metallic pop that came from the door knob as the lock sprung free but when he went to open the door, he found the deadbolt had been engaged as well. He let out a disappointed sigh and then went to work on the deadbolt. His assumptions about the lock were correct. It took longer than he would have liked before the deadbolt slid back. He would have made a terrible thief.

Kenshiro could have just kicked the door in. He could reduce an old door like this to splinters with just a few well-placed kicks; but that would have been noisy, and he wasn't at the stage yet where he didn't have to worry about the noises he made. So far, the loudest sound he made all afternoon was the sound of a body being dragged across the ground. Also, it would have ruined a perfectly good door and since he was planning to stay here tonight, he needed to secure the door. It was an absolute must. If Kenshiro resorted to brute force, not only would he not be able to lock the door, there wouldn't be a door to lock, and staying in a house without doors was unthinkable. With the door unlocked, he placed the pick and the wrench back into the zippered pouch, and then stored the pouch back in its compartment in the black bag. He pulled his straight blade free and held it up in front of him as he used his left to open the door.

He let the door swing open slowly. Nothing stirred within, but none-the-less he waited by the entrance. After a time, he used the blade of the knife in his hand and tapped slightly on the door frame, and waited a moment longer. When he heard nothing coming from within the house, he entered with the knife held out in front of him.

The search of the house didn't take long. It wasn't a huge house. The back door opened into the dining area and kitchen. At the front of the house was a modest living room and a small bathroom that only had room for a sink and a toilet. The main bathroom, as well as two bedrooms, were located upstairs. The main bedroom and a sparsely decorated spare room. It was a quiet house. Kenshiro could see no blood or disturbance as he briskly stalked through the rooms. The house was abandoned. It was still in pristine shape and one might have believed the owners would return any minute except for the thick layer of dust on everything.

He didn't relax though, he still held the knife out in front of him in a loose grip, just like Trevor showed him. Kenshiro found the spare room faced west, and when he went to the window, he had a good view of the nightmarish sight of the pyre. *This is where I'll set up*, he thought to himself as he turned away from the window and walked back out into the hall. On his way to the back door, he checked all the closets, behind the doors of each room, and even entered the bathroom and pulled back the shower curtain. Expecting to stab something the whole time, but nothing was there. Then he returned to the bags he left on the back step.

He quickly checked to make sure no zombies were around to see him enter the little house. One of the more predictable behaviors of the undead was that if a zombie saw you enter a building, that zombie would linger outside that building for days, maybe weeks, before losing interest. The whole time it would slowly and clumsily circle the building as if driven by some instinct from inside its rotting mind. Problem with that is, one zombie usually attracted more and more until that building was at the center of an undead whirlpool mindlessly circling their prey. Until they got a look at it that is, once they saw the tasty meat on the inside, then they'd attack the building itself with whatever strength remained in their bodies. Seeing a building under siege from an undead horde was a sight to behold. He had never been under siege like that, and the thought of being trapped inside while undead fists clawed and smashed through the walls, kept him up some nights. Kenshiro released a breath he didn't know he was holding when he saw nothing but his four-foot-high pile of madness he had been creating all day, and he heard nothing but the gentle sigh of the wind through the trees. He sheathed his weapon and scooped up the bags on the step before quietly closing the door and locking both the door and the deadbolt.

He immediately dropped the bags off on the bed in the master bedroom; it faced east, towards the town. After that, Kenshiro went to the window. He saw nothing moving, and was happy to see the street that ran in front of the house was clear. Other than that, it was impossible to tell for certain what portion of the town's undead population remained. There was a giant evergreen on the front lawn that partially blocked the view of the street. What he could see in front was a stark contrast to the landscape behind the house.

Here, was a multitude of mature trees and scrubs that populated the neighborhood to such a degree it was like a natural barrier that blocked the view into the other yards. He could see the house he was occupying was in front of a T-intersection, and he could peer down the road that went deeper into the town to the east. Kenshiro saw two cars parked on the overgrown shoulder of the gravel road, and there were no curbs or sidewalks to be found. The overgrown foliage didn't allow him to see much else. He couldn't even see the houses on the road on the other side, but he knew they were there by the sidewalks that disappeared into the properties. Farther down the road, maybe a block, he witnessed a zombie in a bright orange hunting vest appear through a break in the foliage. It continued to aimlessly walk across the road until it disappeared into some other shrubs on the other side. Kenshiro looked out over the landscape and wondered how much of a problem all this greenery would present, but quickly breathed out and decided it would be a problem for later.

He backed away from the window, content he was safe for the time being. He could relax. So, he pulled down the zipper of the combat vest and let it fall from his shoulders onto the bed beside the duffel bags. The white t-shirt he had on was caked to his body with sweat, and now that he wasn't exerting himself like he was in the afternoon, the shirt just felt cold and clammy against his skin. He peeled it off and tossed it into the corner of the room. Kenshiro took a moment to look at himself in the mirror. It was strange when he did sometimes because he didn't recognize the person staring back at him.

He used his finger to trace a long, ugly scar on the left side of his chest that started at his sternum and rose to his shoulder. It was one of the two bad scars he had gained so far. There was another one on his stomach from when he frantically climbed up a fence that was topped with barbed wire; he didn't even know he had cut open his belly until miles later. He didn't feel too bad about it. At the time he had to climb over that fence or die, there wasn't a third option.

The scar on his chest, though, also involved a life-or-death decision, but wasn't nearly as innocent as cutting himself on a fence. In the new world, the undead were not the only threats out there. It was one of the many hard lessons he had to learn. The man, in his own fervor to survive, slashed at him and cut him deep. He wanted the only possession Kenshiro had, but Kenshiro would not let him have it. They fought. The man wasn't skilled at fighting, but his one advantage was that he wasn't afraid to kill. When the blade sliced through Kenshiro's skin, it was like a switch went off in his head and suddenly the part of him that believed people were good and deserving of mercy, was simply shut off. What happened next changed him forever. Kenshiro had broken the arm that held the knife and choked the man to death with his bare hands, screaming curses at him through tears that ran down his face as he watched the other man's life fade from his eyes.

The only thing he saw in that mirror that reminded him of his old life, was the simple Yin Yang tattoo he had over his heart, with his family name written in Japanese underneath. Watanabe. He had a friend who worked in a parlor in Little Tokyo in Los Angeles, Tenshin. He was the one who did it. Amy took him to get it done on his nineteenth birthday. It was a Wednesday…

Kenshiro turned away from the mirror. He didn't want to think about Amy.

Hours later, after he was cleaned up and found a fresh change of clothes, Kenshiro sat in a large leather recliner that he had moved in front of the living room window. He sat comfortably and watched for the undead while he ate a bowl of pie filling. He ate every spoonful as if it was the last, carefully placing it in his mouth and then using his tongue to swirl it around his gums as if he was trying to paint the inside of his mouth. It was glorious. Kenshiro had never actually ate a cherry pie before the world fell to the dead, and after a few spoonfuls, he reminded himself just how foolish that had been. He had an apple pie once, his father's casual girlfriend, Cindy, had baked them one for some holiday he didn't remember. He recalled thinking it was a little tart for his liking. Kenshiro had another spoonful, and tried to focus on that and not think about Cindy anymore, or how the last time he saw his father he had left to pick up Cindy and bring her back so the four of them could stay together as they evacuated. He put another spoonful into his mouth and tried to focus on that. No point ruining a pleasant moment by pining over the past, and all the mistakes that were made. He couldn't change any of it now but he could enjoy the sweet taste of cherries, so that's what he decided he would do.

When he finished, Kenshiro reached down and simply placed the bowl on the floor by the side of the chair. He then awkwardly pulled the Beretta free from its holster on his leg and double checked to make sure it was loaded, and no surprise, it was. Kenshiro flicked the safety off and laid it down on his right leg just above the knee, so it was within reach if he needed it quickly. He eased back in the chair and placed his arms on the armrests and closed his eyes.

Kenshiro didn't sleep; he wasn't even trying because he knew it wouldn't come. There were still things he wanted to do before he could consider the day as being done. True sleep wouldn't come until those things were completed, but the time to do them wasn't for a couple of hours, at least. The sun still glowed brightly in the western sky. Kenshiro felt his body settle into the chair as his mind settled into the blackness. This was not about sleep, but it had very much to do with rest. Which, he had found, differs from sleep.

People must sleep. It's a biological function that can't be avoided, it's natural like pissing and shitting. Nobody had to teach you how to sleep. Rest however, only came under certain conditions. A man can go to war, for instance, and sleep every night, but he won't feel rested until he gets back home. Only then can he shut off that part of his brain that functions on that higher plain reserved only for survival and other such primal motivations.

Kenshiro enjoyed the blackness he found behind his eyelids. He found the silence of the house calming. Especially because it wasn't dead silence. There were sounds all around him, but they were so faint the sound of his breath drowned them out. He heard the evergreen's branches scratching the roof in the breeze. He was aware of his surroundings but he felt removed from them. This was where he came to rest. The only peace a man could find these days was the peace he made for himself. Inside the blackness, there were no zombies. It was an effort to keep them away, though. It was a talent Kenshiro had to teach himself. '*Down time*, Trevor had called it, and explained that people needed to get away from the fight from time to time. By the look in his eyes when he said it, Kenshiro believed Trevor knew what he was talking about. This was Kenshiro's down time; the blackness was a place he could go to just *be*. He didn't have to think or plan, nor did he try to remember anything. He just breathed and listened to the sound of his breath, felt the air moving across his lips as he did, and simply existed.

-

Kenshiro decided to light the pyre when the sun finally sunk beneath the western horizon. There was still plenty of light out, but the horizon had taken on a deep orange hue and the clouds had a fiery streak along their underbelly from the sun's dying light. All things considered, it was a beautiful sight to behold and, in a way, he was glad for it. If he had to do this, burn a giant pile of corpses in a field somewhere in southern Colorado, he preferred it be in a pleasant setting. It was a send off after all, maybe not quite a funeral, but there was something final about it. Like somehow the indignity of the undead plague had finally ended for those people, and they could rest. That's what he told himself in these times, in a way he was providing them with a service. Ushering their bodies to their final rest. It was a nice thought.

Kenshiro looked up at the pyre and his eyes inadvertently focused in on a tiny pair of shoes that had a big red heart on the bottom of the soles, and the idea of this being noble was shattered. They were pink shoes that belonged to a little girl that he shot in the head, dragged her tiny body across the hard earth, and tossed her small corpse onto a pile of bodies that he was about to burn.

Those were the facts. The cold hard facts of what he did, and what he was about to do. The rest was just a dream he allowed himself. Something in his gut tightened. He shouldn't have looked at the pyre, he knew that. There was still a part of him that screamed out that this was all wrong, that he couldn't be doing what he was doing, and he can't do this one last thing. Kenshiro took a deep breath and this close to the pyre he got a good whiff of rot mixed in with a strong smell of gasoline. It wasn't the calming breath he was hoping for, but it reminded him of what he was here to do and steeled his resolve. He lit the flare in his hand and promptly tossed it onto a spot on the pyre he knew had gasoline. He was standing a good ten feet away but when the fuel caught fire, the whole pyre came to life with flames and he was met with a blast of raw heat.

He didn't stick around to watch the pyre burn. There was a definite difference to lighting a pile of bodies on fire, and watching those same bodies burn. It was hard enough to light the fire, but he didn't think he wanted to be the kind of person who could watch bodies burn dispassionately. It wasn't a campfire, it's not meant to be enjoyed, or even witnessed for that matter. Kenshiro turned and started back to the house, checking his sides as he went. The fire would draw the undead in, and he didn't want to be around when it did. Unlike the sound from the stereo, he couldn't control who saw the flames or the smoke the pyre produced. He had no way to effectively stop it once he had started it. He hurried for the steps of the little blue house, his sanctuary for the night, and after again making sure it was safe to do so, he entered the house and quietly closed the door behind him.

Once inside, Kenshiro checked the windows on the main level for any movement again. True to form, after about five minutes of watching out the window, he saw the undead seep into the street. Each stumbling, hobbling, or limping in their own unique way towards the fire. He could see the light of the pyre flickering onto the street in front of the house, and he knew as the black smoke reached into the sky even more would come. Right now, he counted ten, but more came into view seemingly every few seconds. He stood back from the window unconsciously, even though he knew they wouldn't be able to see him through the lacy curtains. He decided not to risk it anyway.

The spare bedroom faced west, and he went straight to it. He quickly closed the door once he was inside the room and placed the towel he had ready along the bottom of the door to keep the horrendous smell from the rest of the house. There's no way a person could sleep with that odor filling their nostrils. It already saturated the spare room with the horrible smell of the corpses burning in the field. It was a hard smell to describe as it wasn't just one smell but a symphony of offensive odors assaulting his nose. His eyes watered slightly, and he swore he could feel its taint on his skin. Kenshiro reminded himself he might be in this room for a while and that he would get used to it. Regardless, he made a beeline for the stick of deodorant that was on the nightstand and swiped a generous amount under his nose. Kenshiro dropped the stick onto the bed beside his .22 rifle. In preparing for this, he placed the nightstand onto the surface of the bed for a place he could rest his rifle. He didn't want to steady it on the windowsill and have the barrel sticking outside of the house. Any shot he might take would be far more difficult to see coming from within the room itself. Although, experience had shown him, the undead are usually far more interested in the raging fire than whatever muzzle flash his .22 might produce. Why take the chance though?

The orange light from the blaze outside flickered into the room and he approached the side of the window slowly and peered out. He was just in time to see the first arrivals approach the fire.

Zombies had a strange relationship with fire. It drew them to it, but he didn't know exactly how or why. Whether it was the motion of the flames, the light of the fire, or the smell of the smoke, for all he knew it could even be the heat. He didn't know.

The undead approached fire mindlessly. However, when they got within a few feet of the flames, almost to the point you were sure they would just walk right into it, they would simply stop in their tracks. The undead would stand motionlessly, mere feet from the flames and just stare into the fire. When more undead showed up, they would just fill in around the blaze until you had dozens of zombies pressed together shoulder to shoulder, three or four bodies deep, staring into the thing as if hypnotized by the flames reaching into the night sky. It had been a problem, because he would have another collection of undead bodies to deal with in the morning. Hence the rifle, and he was fine with shooting them all from the comforts of the spare bedroom, but in the past couple months he believed he found a better way.

From where he was, he saw the first zombie approach the line of bodies he placed on the ground about four feet away from the actual pyre, he couldn't make out a lot of detail at this vantage point but he could tell the zombie had obviously been a man before, and Kenshiro could see its abdomen had been torn open and something was hanging from the wound. He watched at that critical moment as the zombie mindlessly moved its right leg forward only to have it catch on the facedown corpse Kenshiro had laid earlier, and lacking the coordination to mount any sort of response to the minor obstacle, the zombie pitched forward rather comically into the fire. It didn't even raise its arms to protect itself as it fell face first into the flames. The zombie simply wiggled a bit as it tried to right itself again until the heat of the fire did its work. *Not bad*, Kenshiro thought to himself, pleased with the early results. *Definitely better than last time*. Time would tell of course, because last time he put the circle of corpses too close and some zombies who tripped on it simply bounced off the burning pyre onto the ground. Burned, but other than that, they were no worse for wear.

This time, however, Kenshiro watched with morbid pride as another zombie, this one a shorter looking woman, fell into the fire similarly to the first, and then another, and then another. One zombie managed to lazily lift its leg high enough to avoid the body on the ground only to step into the slight trench he dug between the corpse line and the pyre, lose its footing, and fall forward into the awaiting flames just the same. Kenshiro could see more making their way through the field towards the burning pyre. He didn't stay to watch though, admittedly he was tired.

It had been a long and somewhat hard day. He could still feel the ache in his muscles and joints from lugging bodies around all afternoon. Nothing would be better right now than climbing into the bed of this stranger's house and drifting off to sleep. Except, of course, if it was his own bed in his father's house and Amy was there next to him. The warmth of her body pressing up against his. Kenshiro sighed as he walked out of the spare bedroom and closed the door behind him and replaced the towel along the opening at the bottom to keep the repugnant scent from the rest of the house. *This will have to do*, he thought as he made his way to the master bedroom and tried not to think of that which was lost forever.

Chapter 6

Elliott

Whack.

Elliott felt the ball leave his hand a bit early when he threw it and he saw the ball collide with the bale slightly above the painted bullseye. He smiled contently as Elliott felt it was still well within the strike zone. Elliott bent down and picked up the next tennis ball. He had discovered tennis balls were tricky to throw because they didn't have the same weight as a baseball, which made them harder to throw at any distance accurately. The next one he threw was to the right so much that Elliott saw his imaginary batter scoot away from the pitch. Although nobody was there and this was all pretend, Elliott still waved an apology for the poor throw. In his mind, he saw the batter tip his helmet towards him. Not wanting to hold up the game, Elliott scooped up the last tennis ball, seemingly casually, but as soon as his fingers wrapped around the ball's felt surface, he snapped towards the bale and threw the ball side-arm. Using the momentum of his spin, he launched the ball towards the target.

"Swing and a miss," he whispered to himself as the batter in his mind stood in disbelief by the plate, completely in awe of Elliott's arm. Two strikes, and one unfortunate ball. The softball was next, to his frustration. The softball was the hardest to throw accurately. He rarely hit the target with the softball and with the count what it was he would have preferred to put the batter away using the tennis balls and start a fresh player using the softball. Undeterred, he put the oversized ball in his hand and threw it the best he could. He was happy to see the ball hit the bale but only just. Barely hitting the upper left-hand corner in an obvious ball. He imagined the batter grinning happily at yet another failed pitch and Elliott sneered back at him before he picked up the first actual baseball of the game. Elliott stepped up to the imaginary plate, keenly eyed the imaginary batter using his imaginary confidence, and promptly struck him out with a solid strike, landing the ball squarely in the middle of the bullseye. He stifled a yawn as he reached down for the next baseball and reset the count in his head. The next batter went down easy, three strikes right down the center, nice and clean. He even switched up his last pitch to his sidearm and wowed the imaginary crowd with a real ripper of a pitch. That left him with two rocks left to throw. He rubbed his shoulder, which was filled with the strain of pitching, and he stifled another yawn. So instead, Elliott called it a night. He placed the two-remaining ball-shaped rocks into his pail and then took it to retrieve the others by the bale.

Elliott considered doing a puzzle on the kitchen table while he still had the light of the day to do so. Once all the balls were in the pail, he turned and walked back to the house, but he would get only two steps.

That's when he saw it.

Elliott froze mid-step. On the distant horizon, he saw a dark ink stain snaking its way into the sky. Black smoke that looked like an angry fist that was slowly rising into the clouds. Elliott didn't like how it made him feel. Like there was doom on the horizon in front of him, and he wanted nothing to do with it. Or at least that's how he *should* feel about it.

Of course, it's not the first time he saw smoke on the horizon. That was last night.

Elliott had been on his way to his bedroom when he first saw the smoke in the distance. Not the smoke itself, of course, it was too dark for that. He saw the orange flickering glow from the fire that reflected off the dark smoke that hung in the night sky like a shroud. In a way, it was kind of beautiful, but that was last night. Now, Elliott saw it for what it was, or more precisely, what it could be. After all, it couldn't be a coincidence that smoke was in the exact same spot as last night.

"Shit," he whispered to himself, knowing full well he wasn't normally allowed to curse, but no one was around to hear it and it sort of slipped out. He knew this wasn't something he could ignore or hide from, as much as his instincts told him to. As foreboding as that dark pillar in the distance was, he would have to leave his little coop and venture out into the world to investigate.

After all, that smoke could mean people. Maybe not his parents, well definitely not his parents. But somebody could be out there and maybe they would help Elliott find them or, at the very least, maybe they could give him some food. It was worth the risk, and that was saying a lot because thinking about all the risks that could be involved gave him chills. He also knew there were dangers out there that he probably hadn't even thought about, which frightened him even more. Elliott took a deep breath and tried to steel himself against the ominous sight. Elliott had a plan he worked out at the beginning of the day if the smoke reappeared. He forgot it as he worked through the day, but it was coming back to him now.

He wouldn't go today. Elliott didn't want to rush, and he felt the more time he had to think this journey over, the better it would be for him in the end. He would go tomorrow. Elliott would pack a bag with everything he would need and set out at first light tomorrow morning. He took in and let out another deep breath and started towards the house, casually dropping the pail after a few steps and letting the balls spill onto the ground. It didn't matter, nobody would tell him to pick it up and besides, he had preparations to make that were more important. On his way, he avoided looking at the angry, black pillar of anxiety in the distance and kept his eyes in front of him. He felt the more he looked at it the less likely he would be to follow through with leaving the farm in the morning.

-

The next morning, Elliott stood in front of the large steel pipe that crossed the entranceway into their property and hung about waist high on him which served as a gate into their yard. He didn't bother to unlatch it from the concrete post and swing the giant arm inwards. It was far easier to simply duck under it or swing his leg over and simply climb over it. Thankfully, the grey people never seemed to figure that part out, now and then he would spy one of them stuck on the waist-height gate, both unable to climb over it or duck under it. They simply walked into it, bounced off, and then walked into it again as if they thought they could eventually just move through it, if they only tried harder. It didn't happen often anymore, as he learned to keep quiet when he was outdoors. Elliott tried not to look at the decomposed remains on the ground in front of the bar from the times it did happen, and he had to take care of it. Thankfully, the heaps stopped smelling long ago. When he breathed in, he could only smell the scent of sage on the open plains. He breathed out and looked down at the gate, and then he looked down the gravel road that passed his parent's house in both directions. There was no movement, but worse than that, there was no reason to stay. Elliott had been standing in front of that gate for some time now, idly chewing on his thumbnail, waiting.

He decided last night he should dress for the occasion. Elliott had worn his clean blue jeans, the good ones, the ones Momma didn't like him wearing unless they were going somewhere. He had on his nicest shirt, the long sleeve blue checkered one he only wore for special occasions. He even combed his hair even though after seeing the finished result quickly decided he should wear a baseball hat. If there were people there, he wanted to make a good first impression. They always said the first impression is the most important. Elliott wasn't about to meet the first people he's seen in… a really long time, wearing dirty clothes and a head full of unruly hair.

He also wore his backpack on one shoulder. It was the one he had used for school and when he found it in his room, it still had all his schoolbooks in it. Elliott piled the books neatly on his desk and then got about filling the backpack with all the things he would need. The only things he could come up with were, a change of clothes, a flashlight, and a thermos filled with water. He didn't even really need the change of clothes, but he thought it would be a good idea to have them, just in case. The flashlight probably wouldn't get used either, but again, it just seemed like a good thing to take on a journey of this magnitude, so he dutifully checked to make sure it worked before stuffing it in the bag. With its contents, the bag hung limply from his shoulder, but somehow, he still felt the weight of it pressing into his skin as if he had filled it with rocks. He put his arm through the other strap, then lifted the backpack squarely onto his back and adjusted the straps slightly until he found it to be easier to carry.

Elliott continued to stare at the road beyond the gate that would take him away from the farm. He knew that road well, Elliott had been on it many times and knew where the road led in both directions, but now it seemed different. Less innocent somehow, like it was calling him to leave his parents' farm, instead of reassuring him of his parent's return.

Time to go. Yet, he remained still. What if he was wrong? Like so many times in the past, what if he was wrong about this whole stupid plan? How could he be sure that if he stepped off this farm, something terrible wouldn't happen? What if something happened while he was gone, and the chickens got out, or worse yet, what if a coyote or something got into the coop and killed Molly and Rebecca? Then they would be dead, he wouldn't get any more eggs, and it would all be his fault for not being here. Elliott stepped away from the gate. He hadn't thought of that last night, and now it was all he could think about. He looked back and could see the door to the coop was closed, and the piece of plywood was still blocking the hole in the fence. Right now, those chickens were probably safer than he was. With doom and uncertainty in front of him and loneliness and starvation behind him, he felt like he was being squeezed between two rocks.

"*Elliott,*" he suddenly remembered his father saying. "*Sometimes when you make a decision, you have to stick to it. Sort of ride it out and see what happens. Sure, maybe things will turn out badly, but that's how we learn, son.*"

With tears in his eyes, Elliott abruptly moved towards the pipe and skidded under it. He stiffly pointed his body towards the town and made his legs move. *Time. To. Go.* With each step his legs felt like they were filled with lead. Elliott needed a genuine effort to make them move closer to the town and he felt if he turned around, he would sprint back to the safety of the farm. However, if there was even a slim chance of finding his parents doing this, he had to try. It was terrifying though. Fear drove his senses into overdrive and seemed to put a dark stain on everything. His gaze whipped around constantly from every little sound he heard. He kept a close eye on the overgrown ditch on the sides of the road in case a grey person was hiding, waiting for him to pass by so they could jump out. Elliott kept himself firmly in the center of the road as he went.

The walk to La Veta was a pretty straightforward affair. Once the butterflies in his stomach settled and Elliott could see he was genuinely alone on the road, his feet moved a little easier. Even though it was early and the morning air felt cool against his skin, Elliott still felt tired and it didn't take long for a thin film of sweat to form on his brow. Up ahead, Elliott saw the first bend in the road. It had a collection of trees that grew along the sides that formed a sort of natural barrier. Daddy would often complain about it because you couldn't see oncoming traffic through those trees, and the local teenagers had a habit of taking the bend entirely too fast.

Once Elliott exited the shade of the slight S-bend on the other side, he immediately saw the Hagerty ranch and couldn't help but to think of Jenny. Elliott's heart couldn't help but kick up a notch when he saw a figure in the window, but soon enough his brain informed him that was just another grey person. Same went with all the clumsy figures behind the house that were just meandering around outside the animal pens. Elliott kept his eyes forward and kept walking. The grey people didn't seem to notice him, and he was just fine with that.

Elliott had passed about another half dozen grey people before he got to the edge of Wahatoya Lake, which really wasn't a lake at all, it was a reservoir. All of the undead were just walking around aimlessly on the properties Elliott passed. He tried to make himself as small as possible on the road as he went passed but he kept a nervous eye on them, just in case.

Fifteen minutes after the reservoir Elliott could clearly

make out the first homes on the outskirt of La Veta. An ugly collection of mobile homes that were haphazardly parked on a wide overgrown lot. They reminded Elliott of crooked teeth. Elliott stepped into the town limits eyeing those dilapidated homes, and the spaces in between them, for grey people.

Where are all the grey people, Elliott thought as he carefully made his way down Moore Avenue to Main Street. The few times his father spoke of the town after the grey people came, he said they were *everywhere*. Elliott didn't see any.

Until he did.

There was a trio of them. Elliott stopped in his tracks. He couldn't really make out anything about them, other than all three of them looked about the size of an adult male. One was about a head shorter than the rest, but from what he could see, that one was a bit too round to be a kid. Elliott paused for a second to remember he had once been a pretty round kid back in the day, and if he was the same size he had been and was standing over there, he might look like an adult too. Elliott shook the thought from his head. It didn't matter anyway; he wasn't going over there.

His first instinct was to turn right around and start walking back to his house. Mission accomplished. Elliott wanted to check out the town, well here he was, and as expected, there was nothing to see but forgotten houses and grey people. His next instinct had him look up at the sign on the street lamp, Birch Street, that street ran parallel to Main Street all the way through town before turning into County Road 360 heading south out of town. He couldn't leave yet, he just got here, and those grey people down there didn't even seem to notice him. They didn't even seem to notice each other. Elliott told himself he was still safe, tried to soothe the butterflies in his stomach so he could move his legs. Slowly his body turned away from Main Street and started down Birch. He kept looking back at the trio until they were out of sight, thankfully they didn't notice him as he moved away. Birch Street marked the point where the paved roads ends, and even though many in town considered Birch Street to be a fairly important road, it never got the honor of being paved. It was still a pretty nice street, even with the overgrown patches of grass that ran alongside the road like a buffer zone between the sidewalk and the street. The houses that lined the street were some of the nicer homes in town, and still looked good after suffering their neglect, most of them looked like all they needed was to have the grass cut.

Elliott knew a few people on this street. Up ahead on the left, before that side of the road opened up into the soccer field that the high schoolers sometimes used for track and field, was Mrs. Appleton's house. She was the high school music teacher who also taught piano out of her house, and she had a little dog named Daisy. Elliott liked her. She was always friendly, and he came to realize she would be one person he would be happy to meet again. He looked for her house down the street but instead noticed a bunch of lumpy trash bags scattered around the road up ahead and quickly forgot all about his old music teacher.

He pointed himself to the nearest one and approached it. His first impression had been a lumpy trash bag, but the closer he got, the more that illusion faded away to reveal what it really was. When his brain finally processed the image enough to identify it, he stopped in the middle of the road, and again, his legs refused to get any closer to it.

To the body.

It was lying face down on the road and was facing away from him. The first thing Elliott made out was the shoes. He could see the feet and the tattered, dirty pants they were in and traced them up the legs to the body. Elliott couldn't see its arms because they were tucked underneath its midsection, and unfortunately neither could he see its face, but Elliott was fairly certain if he approached it, he would see the twisted sneer of a grey person. The problem was, he would have to approach it to know for sure. Elliott looked out over the dozen shapes on the ground, and on the road in front of him, and wondered if they were all bodies. The closer ones to him, now that his mind knew what to look for, no longer looked like bags, and he knew the ugly truth of it.

They were all bodies.

On jelly legs he crept forward towards the body on the ground, not wanting to see any more of it, but also knowing he wouldn't know what to do next until he knew whether it was an *actual* person or a grey person on the road. As Elliott came upon the corpse, it became clear it was the body of a rather large man, wearing dark pants with a black jean jacket and a mass of dark oily hair that fell around its head, covering everything. For a brief moment, Elliott thought he might have to roll the body over to have a look, but his brain rejected the idea of actually touching it. It was bad enough he had gotten within arm's length of it. Elliott backed away from the body. There were plenty of others he could check out there. Surely, he could see the face on one of them. Elliott looked around him like his life depended on it, and saw no movement around him except for the windblown leaves. There were tiny noises all around him but nothing alarming, so he started towards the next closest body. Which was maybe ten feet further down the road and lying on the curb on the left side, in such a way the top half of the body was on the grass while the lower half rested on the gravel road. Elliott was about to lift his foot and start towards that body.

He stopped before taking a single step.

What if they were faking? The thought came to him fast, like a freight train crashing into a brick wall. He hadn't considered that. *Would grey people do that?* A nasty scene played out in his imagination. He would walk further down the road to check the body, and when he did, they would all suddenly rise and start chasing him. Elliott knew he was faster than the grey people, but he didn't feel his legs would carry on very far in his condition.

It was his father's voice that spoke up in his head at that moment, telling him he should leave this place, and that he should never have left his home. Elliott didn't belong here, and if he stayed here; he was surely going to die. Elliott squeezed his eyes shut and pressed his fists into the sides of his forehead to make the voice go away. To his surprise, when he opened his eyes again, the voice in his head was silent.

Wasting no time, Elliott took a tentative step towards the other body along the side of the road up ahead, and then another, and then another. He kept his eyes on the bodies on the ground in front of him as he went, almost daring them to move so he could run away and be done with this whole exploit, but nothing moved out there except the leaves that drifted across the road. Elliott shifted his focus to the body he was coming up on. He approached its feet first, and up closer, he could see it had a small frame. Judging by the clothes it wore, Elliott was expecting a boy maybe his own age. The body looked a little bigger than he was, but as he looked on, he noticed the soft mounds of its breasts, and then he saw its golden hair spilling out around its head. Its left hand laid across its chest close to its neck and Elliott could see a ghastly wound on its otherwise delicate-looking hand.

A fair size chunk of her hand had been torn away by

the pinkie knuckle, taking the finger and the knuckle with it. Elliott could see the ragged tendrils of old grey flesh around the wound and he knew he was looking at the corpse of another grey person. Still, he continued on to the face to see the dried, cracked-skinned sneer of its face. Its eyelids hung half open and he could see the grey person's milky white eyes were staring off in different directions. The left one looked almost straight ahead while the other one was looking up. Its mouth hung partly open and between the badly cracked lips, Elliott could see nothing but rotted teeth and blackness inside. The skin of the face looked strangely unblemished but it lacked any color at all and looked horribly dry. Above the left eyebrow was a strange-looking hole where the flesh seemed to dimple inwards. Elliott backed away, disgusted with what he was forced to look upon, but seeing it confirmed the bodies were most likely harmless. Elliott became emboldened enough to give the grey person a slight kick in the middle of its thigh with the toe of his shoe. Elliott jumped back as the body shifted slightly from the blow, fully expecting the blonde-haired grey girl to lunge at him. The body settled and remained still. After a moment, he stepped forward and kicked the same spot but harder, again expecting the body to reach out towards him, but again, the body settled and remained still. It was dead. Elliott straightened suddenly and looked out down the road laden with bodies. They were all dead. He breathed a sigh of relief, suddenly feeling a terrible weight lift off his shoulders. Though, he was still a long way from being safe, by any means.

Elliott continued on down the road slowly, confident the bodies on the ground would never move again, but not wanting to get too close to them either. Just in case. After a few steps, the smell of them enveloped him and he had to fight the urge to gag on the horrible scent. Instinctively, he brought up his arm and buried his nose into the elbow of his shirt, but there was no hiding from it. The breeze was at his back, but he was in the thick of it now. There were rotting bodies all around him. After a short time, he lowered his arm. He stepped around a compact car that was parked haphazardly on the side of the road and as he did; Elliott spied something peculiar up ahead on the sidewalk, it was on the left-hand side of the next block.

Elliott wasn't afraid because it was just a garbage can, but it was upside down on the sidewalk and it had large polka dots on it. He started towards it, wondering if this was maybe what he was looking for. It was clear it didn't belong there; it looked clean like they had never used it, and then he noticed the polka dots weren't dots at all. They were holes. Medium-sized holes had been cut all over the body of the plastic garbage can, and on some cases, he could see right through the can. Then Elliott noticed something was inside it. He stopped ten feet from the garbage can; he was approaching it from the road, and it stood on the sidewalk a good twenty feet from the intersection. Elliott looked up and scanned his surroundings, looking for something else that might be out of place that might lead him to the next clue.

But when he did, his breath caught in his throat.

To get to this point, Elliott had maybe passed a dozen bodies that littered the street. He stepped around them, feeling uneasy at there being so many of them fallen in one place. Elliott had kept his distance, and his eyes on the street in front of his shoes. Then there was the garbage can, so many details to see, and yet he still missed the forest for the trees. How could he miss it?

As he looked out over the grassy field the town used as a running track for the high school and had the town's only ball diamond in the far corner of the lot, he saw the ground of the entire field was littered with corpses. Everywhere in the field he looked, he saw a body, sometimes there were three of four of them on the ground in clumps. Like they had all just simply fallen to the ground where they were walking or doing whatever it was grey people do with their time. Elliott had no words for what he saw. It was like he suddenly stumbled into a nightmare. He didn't understand what he was seeing, but fear crept into his bones. Something horrible happened here, it happened to all these grey people, and he felt if he wasn't careful, it just might happen to him as well. Elliott looked out over the bodies, looking for anything that would confirm the sense of dread that was building in his gut, but there was nothing. The stillness over the field of corpses somehow just added to the wrongness of the entire scene in front of him. He felt his heart thumping away in his chest like a drum as he lost himself in the landscape's insanity.

A noise up the road to his left startled him out of his daze and he snapped his head towards the source. Down the road a short distance from him, was a grey person. The grey man looked to be frantically sniffing the air, his head jerking back and forth like a chicken would, if it had a reason to. The grey man was by a parked truck, near the entrance to the alley that ran between the houses. The noise must have come from when it bumped into the truck's side. The grey man was too occupied with his weird sniffing to even notice Elliott. To confirm this, he gave the grey man a slight wave with his hand, which wouldn't stop shaking and he lowered his stance to ready himself to run. Then when there was no change in his behavior, Elliott briefly checked his surroundings before he turned back to the grey man. He waved more aggressively, actively trying to get the grey man's attention but still ready to bolt in the opposite direction if he got it. He waved his arms until his shoulders burned, which to his surprise wasn't many times. The slim grey man in the shirt and shorts couldn't have cared less he was there. Elliott looked back to the garbage can. He was so close. He couldn't turn back now. Elliott checked to make sure there weren't any other grey people sneaking up on him, and when he saw it was just him and the lone, sniffing grey man; Elliott took the chance.

Elliott thought about a slow, sneaky approach to the garbage can, but when his brain gave him the all-clear to move, he wasted no time getting to the upturned can. Three long hurried strides and he was there. A quick check back to the sniffing grey person confirmed he was still good, but somewhere in his mind, there was a clock counting down suddenly. Elliott felt he had to hurry, but he didn't really know what he was doing or even what he should look for, so he didn't know what he could do to speed it along. He looked back to the garbage can and used his hands to wipe the sweat from his face.

Elliott did a quick walk around the can to see if there was anything of interest and then knelt down and slowly tipped the can back to peer underneath the lip of the can. He could clearly see the stereo in there through the holes in the sides, but he didn't know for sure if there might be something else in there he couldn't see. There were snakes in the area, some of them poisonous enough to send a man to the hospital, and sometimes he heard stories of them getting into the weirdest places. However, there was nothing to see here so Elliott carefully lifted the plastic can up and then checked the insides, maybe there would be a note or something taped inside for him to find, and when he found nothing, he quietly placed the can on the sidewalk to the side.

There on the ground was the stereo. It was a small portable CD player that also had an AM/FM radio and was about the size of a loaf of bread, maybe longer. It was a bright red color, and it looked brand new. No dust that he could see was on it, and it was free of any stains or blemishes that would point to it being well-used. This one looked like it was fresh out of the box. He had seen this kind of device before. Jenny had one like this, but hers was plastered with stickers of all kinds. He understood this kind of stereo was popular because it could wirelessly connect to a cellular phone. It was also pretty cheap. Like Jenny's, this one had the speakers on the sides, the compartment for the CD on top, and the buttons and display on the front in the center. When Elliott looked at the display out of curiosity, he could clearly see a zero and a one flashing in unison next to two vertical bars. With shaky hands, Elliott picked it up.

He felt an energy surge through him when he felt it in his hands. It's turned on. He stared at the display with a foreign combination of awe and disbelief. *It actually works, and it's paused on something!* This is what he was looking for, well part of it, he had actually hoped for a big welcoming party of some sort, but when he got into town, he knew he had to adjust his expectations. The whole town just felt empty, and the deathly silence all around him confirmed it. People made noise. If there were people here, he would know it by now. Finding this, and by some lesser extent, finding the mass of corpses that were choking the green space of the field, was the next best thing. Better than just a clear sign somebody had been through here, which he assumed the bodies were, but he wasn't expecting there would be so many. *This was a message.* This not only meant there was somebody out there, but that wherever they had gone, they would come back, because messages sometimes needed replies, and they would have to come back to see his reply. Looking at the small red stereo, Elliott suddenly wished he had brought a pen and some paper, and some tape would be handy as well. Those things could be gained later if need be and Elliott planned where in his house he would listen to the message when another thought occurred to him in a frenzy.

What if the message was instructions?

He hadn't expected that, but the more he thought about it, the more it made sense. If whoever killed all these grey people wouldn't wait around for people to answer their smoke signal, then why not leave instructions on how to find them or contact them? That worried Elliott slightly because he just didn't have the means to go too far outside of La Veta. He had his bike, but even then, how far could he really go on that?

Elliott decided he couldn't wait to take it home. The clock was still running in his head. He couldn't explain it, but he felt a sense of urgency towards it. Elliott removed his one hand and reached for the play button. He brought the stereo closer so he could hear everything and brought the entire world down to a laser point of attention, focused solely on the message he was about to-.

The tiny box exploded with sound that was so loud and so sudden, Elliott couldn't comprehend what he was hearing at first. It was just shrill sounds that hit him so hard and fast it was almost like a physical force. A sort of blinding fear shot through him like electricity, shorting out his brain. Everything that happened next happened on instinct, and it was like he was helpless to watch the events unfold. He felt the box vibrate in his hand and his brain concluded it was going to explode, and without knowing what he was doing, Elliott pulled the hand holding the plastic stereo away like it was on fire and had scolded his palm. There wasn't even time to register what had happened, let alone try to prevent it. Elliott was still recoiling away from it as he watched the box spin almost gracefully in the air as it fell. The whole time flooding the area with its incredible sound until finally it struck the concrete, and Elliott saw little red bits of plastic shoot out from the body of the stereo. The sound from it died the instant it contacted the ground, and with almost the same force as the music had begun, the silence of its absence struck him as it once again consumed the landscape.

"No," he said weakly at first as what happened sank in. "No, no, no, NO!" Elliott bent down and quickly picked up the wreckage of the stereo and looked at the display. There was a crack that ran right through the center of it. One side of the crack was blank, but the other side was all black. There was nothing else to be seen on the display. With subdued frustration, he stabbed the buttons on the front to make it do… something, but to no avail. It was dead. Like everything else around him.

What have you done? He brought it up to his ear and gave the box a slight shake, and to his horror, he heard little bits moving around inside. Elliott looked at the now useless display again, shook the box a little more vigorously and tried to will it to work. He needed it to work. It had to work. He came all this way. He couldn't go back empty-handed. *What have you done?* He felt like a man on an inflatable life raft in the middle of the ocean watching the air seep out of a hole he had stabbed in the side. Elliott had broken this little red box seconds after he had picked it up. He couldn't blame anybody. Nobody tried to knock it out of his hand. He didn't trip on anything. There was no running away from this one. This was all his fault. He had one chance at… he didn't even know what. Elliott didn't even have time to listen to what was on the stereo, never mind trying to figure out what it meant before his stupid clumsy fingers dropped the thing like it was a hot potato and ruined everything. Maybe even ruined himself. Now he could go home and die in agony, the whole time knowing that he ruined his only chance of survival in less than ten seconds. He made a mess of this, like he made a mess of everything. No wonder his parents left him behind. *What have you done?*!

Another horrible sound broke through Elliott's daze and he instantly recognized the angry snarls of a grey person. He snapped his head back to the sniffing grey man but now he was no longer idly sniffing the air, now his bony black fingers were clawing at the air as he shambled straight towards him. The grey man's milky eyes were fixated squarely on him as his teeth snapped at the air. Instinctively, Elliott backed away from it, glancing down at the now useless hunk of plastic and wires in his hands as if it somehow might have an answer of what to do. The clock in his mind went into overdrive as it counted down to his doom. He had no time left.

"Hello?" He called out meekly as he backed away from the snarling figure stalking towards him. "HELLO?" Elliott yelled louder. The gig was up, after all. There was no time left for discretion. "I'M SORRY I BROKE YOUR STEREO." He whipped his head around to see if anybody was listening, maybe the owner of the small plastic stereo, but his eyes instead locked onto another grey person. This one was a lady that had silently stepped out into view from down the street the way he had come. And then another stepped out from behind a building across the street to the north, now effectively blocking the street he was planning on leaving by. "PLEASE!" He cried out even louder, feeling his vocal cords rattle at the intensity of it. "PLEASE HELP ME!" He turned back to the former sniffing grey person, and it shocked him how close he was. He wasn't close enough to grab Elliott, but he was still far too close for Elliott's comfort. Elliott took a few running steps away from the trio of grey people moving towards him, which forced him deeper into the field of bodies. Which wasn't where Elliott wanted to be, but where else could he go? He was being herded there. Across the field, way on the other side, he saw another pair of grey people, too far to make out anything about them other than they were clearly moving towards him. "IS ANYBODY THERE? PLEASE! I NEED YOUR HEL-."

His words caught in his throat when his foot caught on something and sent him stumbling backwards, though he corrected himself before falling to the ground. When he looked down at what his foot caught on, his eyes locked onto a grey person with the top corner of its forehead missing a sizable chunk. Elliott could see its brains. Black ooze surrounded the wound, its eyes staring up at Elliott. He couldn't help himself, as a little yelp escaped his lips at the shock of it. Tears stung his eyes as it all fell apart in front of him and he faced the inescapable question, whether he wanted to die here and now, or flee back to his farm and die later.

"PLEASE!" Elliott pleaded with the air around him as he watched the grey people close in, "HELP ME!" He screamed, desperately looking for a lifeline over the field of bodies. He repeated it, louder this time, desperation pushing the sounds out and when it was done, his cries echoed off the surrounding houses and he felt a fiery sensation deep in his throat.

He was alone, utterly and completely. Maybe he always had been. He would never know now. He ruined his chance. This venture had been a failure in every sense of the word, and now, alone in a field of corpses and being slowly chased down by crazed grey people, the last thread of his sanity was being pulled taut. He knew what he was going to do, what he *had* to do. Because it was really the only option left, and he hated them for it. Before he did though, there was one last thing he did. Elliott didn't even know he would do it. It sort of burst out from him.

"Get away from me!" The words flew from his lungs with such intensity they were no longer words. The sounds devolved into a sort of roar, primal and unbridled.

He drew back his arm, his eyes locked on the grey man who was close enough Elliott could see its black fingernails reaching for him. He didn't care at that moment. Elliott tried to put everything he was feeling into his arm. With all the pain, the hurt, and the disappointment, he even tried to channel the butterflies in his stomach into his next action. He uttered the last word, then let it all loose. His vision blurred slightly, but that couldn't stop him now. His heels dug into the ground and his body tensed up as his arm exploded forward with such force, he was sure he was going to tear his arm right off. The air kissed the side of his face as his hand travelled towards the grey man hounding him. The stereo left his hand like a rocket and stuck the grey man at point-blank range.

The feeble plastic cover shattered immediately but the bulk of the stereo carried its weight forward. The gray man's head snapped back and the momentum of the stereo, having now been reduced to a simple weighted object, carried on forward until it lifted the grey man off the ground slightly as the lower half of its body tried to keep up with the upper half. Elliott didn't wait around long enough to watch the body fall. His instincts immediately switched over to flight. He turned and ran.

He ran east out of the field, his stressed brain screaming at him. It was the only way as he looked around and his eyes darted from one grey person to another. Elliott zig-zagged through the field of fallen bodies like he was a deer that suddenly found itself surrounded by wolves. With no obvious way out, he simply pointed himself towards home and started running as fast as his legs would take him. Up ahead there was a loose quartet of grey people walking towards him, angrily clawing at the air, their ugly snarling faces fixed on him. He veered north to avoid them, still dodging corpses on the ground until he was finally out of the field and back on the road leading back to Moore Avenue. He would turn back onto that road and he wouldn't stop running until he was safe and sound back at home.

-

Elliott did stop running.

His mind was fuzzy like a dense fog that had moved into his thoughts and memories, turning them into shadows, both real and impossible to grasp. He knew he was passed Jenny's farm, and he was pretty sure he made it around the big bend in the road, but after that, things became intangible. Something had happened on the road. He suddenly felt strange. Before this, he had run through terrible cramps in his legs, he simply ignored them and kept moving. He ignored the fire in his lungs he felt with every ragged pant. He couldn't get enough oxygen when he breathed, and it felt like he was slowly suffocating, but he ignored it and screamed at his legs to keep pushing. Then he felt as if he was a thousand miles away from his body. He felt the same pain, but it wasn't happening to him exactly. Like, he was feeling things remotely and everything had dulled. He had fallen a few times; once in the beginning when he tripped on something on the road, he skinned his knee through the denim of his pants and his hat when tumbling to the side. Elliott left it behind without a second thought. He just wearily picked himself up and started off again with a bit of a limp in his step.

The second time he fell, the ground just sort of jumped up at him. He didn't even really notice; he had closed his eyes for a moment and in the darkness, he felt something shift and then something struck the whole one side of his body. When he opened his eyes, he was on the ground looking out at the road as it stretched off into the distance. His hands fumbled around him as he tried to move them without feeling them. It was like he was trying to use them for the first time. Finally, they found something solid, and he pushed himself up into a kneeling position. *I have to keep going. It's not safe.* Elliott urged his body into motion, but nothing happened. He knelt there, swaying in the breeze that felt like ice as it passed over his skin. Somewhere, a thousand miles away, his body shivered from it. *I have to move*, he thought again, without knowing why he had to and without a full understanding of where he was going or why he had to get there so badly anymore. *Follow the road. The road will take you there. They are coming*! Distantly, he saw dark fingers reaching for him in his mind's eye and his body lurched forward as if avoiding the imaginary hands. His hand caught him before he fell face-first into the gravel again, then he pushed his leg up so he could get his foot underneath him. He pushed up with all the might he had left. His whole body screamed in protest, but he rose to his feet and after a brief couple breaths to steady himself, Elliott lifted his back leg with great effort and brought it forward before he let it come to a rest a few inches ahead of him. Then he did it again, and again, and again. His body fell into an awkward sort of rhythm that felt more like he was perpetually falling forward than walking. He was moving, though.

Elliott recognized the long length of pipe that served as the gate into his parent's property, into his home. It was then that he knew he had reached his destination. This was where he had been going all along. He remembered he had been escaping something, but he couldn't recall exactly what. *The grey people*, he suddenly remembered, and he briefly recalled the mess he had left behind. Elliott almost tripped over his own feet when he turned to look behind him. He anticipated to see a horde of grey people chasing after him in their own weird way. He expected to see dozens of them. When he looked behind him, it seemed like a dream when he saw the empty road stretch out all the way to the bend. There was nothing at all. He knew they were behind him in the town. He had seen them, dozens of them. Now there was nothing, and he wondered in the haze of his mind if it really happened at all. He pivoted toward the gate, towards the safety of his home, and when he went to bend down to duck underneath it, his legs buckled and he went sprawling into the gravel before the gate. Muted pains sprang up from all over but he ignored them. Elliott tried to lift himself out of the dirt only to find his legs didn't work right anymore. He was so close to safety that when he looked up from the ground, he could see his kitchen window. Feeling like he had no other option before him, he crawled underneath the gate and into the yard. With his teeth clenched so tightly he wondered if they would crack, Elliott crawled. Knowing somewhere deep inside he couldn't stand anymore and simply accepted it as an indisputable truth of the universe. He crawled until he could feel the cool softness of the lawn underneath his palms. Then, feeling he had accomplished what he set out to do, and with almost gleeful acceptance, his body called it quits.

A tightness bloomed in his chest, like the side of his ribcage had been put into a vice and was slowly squeezing in on his sides. It was hard to breathe. The world, which felt like it was already loosely swaying underneath him, blurred and darkened at the edges. The ground moved up towards him slowly, almost lovingly, as his cheek came to rest on the grass. It felt like an embrace. He was home. He made it. The difficulties that had happened so far away now were no longer something he needed to worry about. Elliott didn't fight it when the darkness came. He couldn't. It felt so wonderful to just slip into it.

Like he belonged there.

-

When Elliott opened his eyes, he was confused. Warm, comfortable, but very confused. Elliott knew where he was, he was at home. He was currently looking at the very familiar ceiling in the living room. Elliott was on the couch with his head comfortably sunken into the pillow that had always been on the couch, and he was wearing only his white cotton briefs. His feet were lying on the comforter from the hall closet. After a moment, he discovered he couldn't recall lying down on the couch. Nor did he remember grabbing the comforter out of the hall closet. He knew that's where it was because that's where he put it a couple of months ago, but he couldn't recall retrieving it since then. And where were his clothes?

Elliott kept his eyes on the ceiling as he tried to remember. He went to the town, remembered the total catastrophe with the stereo, and then he ran. He ran as fast as he could, criss-crossing across the field any way he could to get away from the grey people. Elliott remembered he had made his way back to Moore Avenue and out of town from there. The last reasonably clear memory he had was passing Jenny's farm. He had been crying by then… and he had fallen. He didn't remember the fall exactly, but he recalled lifting himself off the ground at some point, and he would only have to do that if he had fallen. After that, things got… misty.

They were there inside his mind, the memories but intangible and unrecognizable, but there was something there, something that might be important. Elliott let a big yawn escape his mouth as he swung his legs over and sat up. He decided it was a problem for later. It would come to him. He didn't have the best memory after all, but this felt different. Elliott reassured himself the missing pieces would come to him in time and planned his day. It was then he realized he didn't know what time it was exactly. He assumed it was morning, but as his other senses came alive, he found the air on his face was actually pretty warm. The mornings were usually pretty cool. Also, the light in the room was fairly dim. That meant it was later in the evening. Elliott lazily lifted his head and saw the impossible.

On the coffee table in front of the couch was a bottle of Gatorade, the blue kind he liked, but he never could remember the actual name of the flavor. He would recognize that bottle anywhere. Elliott stared at it incredulously and wondered if maybe he was still sleeping, and dreaming. Or maybe he was having one of those waking dreams crazy people get, hallucinations. *It couldn't be real, there's no way it could be real. Like, how did it even get there?* Elliott certainly didn't remember seeing his favorite flavor of Gatorade just lying around anywhere, and he certainly would if he did, because that would have been the greatest day of his life.

Next to the miraculous bottle of Gatorade were two small pills, which again, he certainly didn't remember being there before. Elliott reached up and scratched his head as if that might wake up his brain so he could get some answers. Before it could though, Elliott then heard the impossible. He had heard it so many times in his life, it was a sound his brain didn't even register when real people were still around.

It was the sound of a man clearing his throat, and it was coming from the far corner of the room.

Elliott knew in that moment that he wasn't dreaming

because you couldn't be this afraid in a dream.

SOMEBODY'S HERE!

A voice screamed inside his head and Elliott's body just exploded into motion on its own, desperate to retreat away from the sudden and deliberate noise. Elliott clawed his way back into the couch where he found to his despair he could go no further. Stuck sitting upright on the couch with his knees to his chest and feeling trapped, he forced himself to look breathlessly at the source of the sound.

There in the corner, in his father's chair, was a large dark figure. The figure had moved the chair to the spot, the darkest spot in the room, but even with the scant amount of light Elliott could see the man was Asian, and a big one at that. His frame seemed to take up most of the chair. Elliott couldn't notice much else because his eyes locked with the man's. Deep chestnut-colored eyes bore into him like a hawk watching a mouse in a field.

"Wha-?" Elliott squeaked and the sound of his weak voice startled him. "Who?" He tried again, but he couldn't form the words in his mouth. His mind cruelly mocked him by reminding him he had wanted to find real people, which was true, but not people like this. He wanted, at the very least, friendly people, but looking at the dark figure in the corner with the dark intense eyes, Elliott knew one thing for sure.

This is not a nice man.

The man moved suddenly and casually, which caused Elliott to yelp and jump from his place on the couch. It was then Elliott saw that the man had a book in his hand, and now he had produced a bookmark which he placed between the pages. He then calmly placed the book on the table by the side of the chair. Elliott noticed him closely as his hand slid to the side of his leg, and to his utter despair, watched as the dark figure then produced a fairly large handgun. Elliott didn't know what type it was, but it was large. Elliott's eyes strained to look away from the weapon in the man's hands, but he couldn't, nor could he help the deep trembling that started in his limbs. The man let it come to rest on his knee. He did it in a way as not to startle Elliott further, but the barrel was pointed right at Elliott's chest. The whole time those dark eyes watched him. The large man eased back in the chair, breathed in deep, and then exhaled the whole breath before speaking slowly and deliberately. His voice seemed to cascade through the room as the man broke the dangerous silence between them.

"Let's talk."

Chapter 7

Kenshiro

Kenshiro saw the boy immediately as he awkwardly made his way down the street. It was the clothes that caught his attention first. They made the teenager stick out like a sore thumb amongst the dirty corpses on the street. Through the scope Kenshiro could easily pick out the soft pink hues of the boy's face, and was struck by the ocean blue coloring of the boy's eyes. He didn't look good though. Kenshiro noticed the frail way the boy made his way down the street, and the weak look of interest that bloomed on his face when he first saw the garbage can the stereo was in. The bored sort of expression showcased the kid's gaunt features and the way his sunken eyes made it seem like he was looking out from shadows on his face. Kenshiro wasn't particularly proud of how he handled the revelation he was looking at another living person.

Bait, his frantic mind thought as Kenshiro hurried toward the weapons bag in the kitchen and started arming himself like he was preparing for a war. He loaded himself up with the Heckler&Koch MP5, which was a personal favorite of his, but he didn't stop there. Kenshiro also threaded his arm through the sling of the large M4 rifle, and packed himself up with enough ammunition to take out a small army. Admittedly, it was an over-reaction. Kenshiro couldn't help himself. His little routine had been shattered.

He crouched down and went to each window and scanned the exterior of the house for threats. Kenshiro only saw the undead, as usual. *Wait a second*, Kenshiro thought as he eyed an undead woman idly meandering around in some bushes on the property across the street to the south. He did some quick geometry in his head and concluded the boy should be in full view of this zombie. *So why isn't it attacking?* Curiosity made Kenshiro check all the windows again. His assumption had been correct, there were no zombies in pursuit of the gaunt teen. Worse yet, when Kenshiro went back to his little sniper's nest and looked for the boy through the scope of the .22, he saw the kid standing directly in front of a zombie, and it was doing nothing. Well, not quite nothing, Kenshiro was quick to notice the weird little twitch the zombie man's head was doing. To him, it looked like a sharp sniffing gesture, but unnatural. Like a seizure of some sort. The teen seems to be surprised by the reaction as well.

Is he fucking waving at it, Kenshiro thought incredulously as he watched the teen frantically trying to get the zombie's attention. The boy did this for a few seconds, and Kenshiro could only watch in utter shock and the zombie stood frozen in front of the boy. Soon though, the kid gave up his attempts and focused his attention back on the garbage can with the holes in it. Kenshiro looked at the seizing zombie dumbfounded. *Why isn't it attacking? The kid is right there in front of him?* Kenshiro couldn't see anything that would physically stop the undead man from lunging at the boy, and yet it didn't make a move towards him.

Kenshiro became transfixed on the impossibility of what he was seeing, so much so that he forgot about the teen altogether. That is, until he noticed the boy pick up his shiny new red stereo, but by the time his attention shifted, Kenshiro could see it might be too late. The boy had his finger raised and poised to press a button on the stereo.

He wouldn't.

Kenshiro spent the first two seconds briefly considering letting it all play out and just sitting back and watching. The music would play rather loudly if he recalled what he set the volume at, and suddenly the bait would lure the wrong target in. Then whoever was out there would have to show themselves or possibly the boy would run back to his masters, giving Kenshiro time to slip away. He figured he only needed maybe two minutes tops to be on the road with all his belongings and make this shitty little town a distant memory. Maybe less, if he opted to just throw everything in the back of the truck and sort it out later. The next second, his mind quashed the idea utterly and completely. More zombies were never a good thing, and the truth of it was he wouldn't know what was out there for sure until he opened the door and stepped out. Kenshiro could deal with the zombies, but if he had to deal with living assailants as well...

The last second, Kenshiro spent frantically reaching for the stereo's tiny remote, which was also bright red, it was lying on the top of the dresser to his left. The remote was inches from his grasp but when he wrapped his hands around it, he knew it was too late. He could hear the music shatter the day's quiet and his heart sank because he knew he had hesitated too long and now he would have to deal with the consequences of that inaction. He looked back to the boy through the window just in time to see his brand-new stereo tumble from the boy's hands to crash on the concrete of the sidewalk. He couldn't see with his naked eye what the damage was, but the abrupt end to the music told him all he needed to know. The sound from the stereo played for only a moment, hardly enough to recognize it as being music before it abruptly ended. However, the effect was immediate. Even from within the room, Kenshiro could hear the undead spring into action.

"Shit," he cursed silently as he went back to the

scope. *Why the fuck would he do that*? He couldn't comprehend what kind of madness would drive a person to do something so obviously suicidal. Looking through the scope, he could see whatever had been afflicting the dead man in the blue shirt and tan shorts had ended. Now what Kenshiro saw was a lot more familiar to him. The zombie's withered clawed hands reached for its meal. Its black teeth snapped at the kid as it started towards him. Kenshiro moved the crosshairs back to the boy, and he was turning away from the tanned shirt zombie that was threatening him. Kenshiro looked through the scope as the kid looked around him with wild eyes before he fixated on the other undead who were coming into the area. He called out suddenly, but Kenshiro missed what he had said until the teen repeated himself, louder this time.

"Hello?" The boy asked while looking wild-eyed for a lifeline from the creeping death moving towards him.

"I'M SORRY I BROKE YOUR STEREO." By the look of his frantic eyes, Kenshiro could tell the boy didn't know he was there in the room. He could see the boy believed he was alone, the desperation coming off the boy was almost palpable, so much so Kenshiro wished he would just run back to his masters and be done with this whole dangerous charade. "PLEASE! PLEASE HELP ME!" He watched the boy's face, searching in vain as he called out. It struck Kenshiro when he heard the boy cry out. Kenshiro recalled calling out like that himself in the beginning.

What if he is alone? The thought invaded his mind as he looked on at the boy backing away farther into the field, retreating away from the lurching zombie in the blue shirt and looking up briefly from the scope. Kenshiro saw two more walking towards the boy. He recognized the one as being the lady zombie from the bushes across the street and he guessed the other one was the raspy breath bastard who was hanging around outside the house. They crossed the street almost in unison towards the kid and his cries.

"IS ANYBODY THERE? PLEASE!"

"Baka," Kenshiro whispered to his rifle. *Shut the fuck up already*! He cursed the boy and his insane stupidity because he was considering what would happen if the scene in front of him was exactly what it looked like. What if there was no trap, no bait, and nobody hiding in the background to save this withered fool from himself? What then? Would he really just sit here and watch?

"I NEED YOUR HEL-." Suddenly the boy stumbled back after his foot caught on a corpse on the ground. Kenshiro felt his heart fall in his chest as the boy faltered. On instinct, he moved his finger to the rifle's trigger, but paused when he saw the boy's other foot quickly and awkwardly regain its footing. He could shoot the lurching dead man easily but then he would give away his position, and he couldn't do that. Not yet. His survival instincts wouldn't allow it, but at the same time, he couldn't watch the first living person he'd seen in what felt like years get ripped apart in front of him. He breathed out forcefully and tried to will the boy to run away from this place. Through the scope, he saw the boy's eyes water as desperation turned sourly into helplessness. "PLEASE!" He screamed, and again, Kenshiro felt something stir inside him for the boy. "HELP ME!" The boy's cries echoed throughout the street. Through the scope, he could see the lurching zombie closest to the boy was almost right on top of the teen. Kenshiro massaged the trigger as he moved the crosshairs over the dead man's head.

He wouldn't let the boy die. The decision came swiftly and absolutely, like a lightning strike. No matter what happened, he wouldn't see another person die by undead hands if he could prevent it. It wasn't an easy choice. The kid had tipped the scales when he tripped. In that instant, fear seized Kenshiro's heart, and he knew then he couldn't let it happen again. He couldn't watch another person die by those cold, dead fucking hands. Ambush or no ambush, he just couldn't do it. Besides which, he was beginning to suspect this boy was alone.

If anybody was out there, the time to step in had come and gone, in Kenshiro's eyes. Their bait was about to get chewed on, and where were they? Plus, the boy had asked for help. He wasn't calling for help. Nor was he looking in any direction. If the kid had been bait, and got in trouble, it might tempt him to look directly at his masters, wherever they were hiding, and call for help, not searching for aid as the kid was. The boy sure didn't look like he was expecting to be rescued soon.

Through the scope he could see the frantic expression of a cornered animal desperately looking for a way out, which confused Kenshiro. The boy could simply turn east and escape between the houses that way, or he could simply run around them because it's not like he was surrounded. Not yet, but soon. Realistically speaking, there was only one threat facing the boy at the moment, and only through his own inaction was it becoming a bigger problem. Kenshiro's finger massaged the trigger as he lined up the crosshairs to the side of the blue shirt zombie's head, right above its ruined ear. Soon, the moment would come when he couldn't wait anymore and he'd have to take the shot or risk the boy being overtaken by the dead.

"LEAVE ME-." Kenshiro watched the boy's expression change suddenly from one of helplessness to one of utter rage as the hand holding the broken and forgotten little red stereo reared back. "-ALOOONE!" The boy howled like a wounded animal and he let the stereo fly straight into the face of the lurching zombie that was mere feet from him. What was left of the tiny stereo flew into pieces after it collided with the center of the zombie's face, plastic and bone alike broke on impact and Kenshiro witnessed the zombie's head recoil away from the blow. The body fell backwards to the ground. Kenshiro took a moment to mourn the loss of his brand-new stereo. It was useful because it took AA batteries as opposed to the larger D cell batteries his usual stereo took, and then forever wiped it from his mind as he watched the boy turn and run to the east. Judging by his sickly-looking trot, he may not be running for too long.

"Baka." *Idiot*. His go-to Japanese curse, he loved the way it rolled off the tongue, sounding like two swords clashing. Except, as he let the .22 rifle come to a rest on the dresser, he wasn't so sure who he was referring to. The boy or himself. Kenshiro would go after the boy, of course he would. How could he not? How could he look upon that kid's deathly face and withered frame and not want to do something about it?

He knew what he *should* do. That was easy. He should pack everything back up and load it into the truck, and then spend the rest of the afternoon looking for enough supplies to cover him until the next town came over the horizon. Two rules he kept close to his heart: avoid trouble at all costs, and don't take stupid risks. Hopping in the truck right now and putting this town in his rear-view mirror would satisfy both those rules, whereas, doing what he was contemplating would break both rules, seemingly needlessly. If he knew one thing, he knew that boy would lead to trouble. At some point, every other person will lead to trouble. It's in their nature, and judging how that kid completely bungled his way through that simple encounter and just barely avoided getting bit, he especially so.

Leaving the boy to his fate would be easy.

However, that's not what he was going to do. Just because it was the easiest thing for Kenshiro to do, didn't make it feel right. From the second that boy tripped, he felt it. He would go after the boy. Part of him was still trying to deal with the fact he actually saw another living being in the flesh. It had been so long. He didn't remember how long ago it was now, but it felt like the memory of the last living person he had encountered had dulled, even though it seemed much more significant now.

The last living person he had seen, Kenshiro had shot dead in the chest and stared into his eyes with muted regret as his life drained from his body. Kenshiro then shot him in the head to make sure he stayed down for good. Kenshiro felt he had to make up for that... unfortunate business. Plus, he felt this boy might have the answers to what caused the zombie to seize up like that. He had never seen that behavior before today. That youth must have caused it somehow. The gears of Kenshiro's mind spun faster as he planned his next move, which at its core was relatively simple. *Follow the boy*, but its implementation would have many challenges and dangers for Kenshiro to face.

He moved through the house swiftly, silently and with purpose. Kenshiro left both the .22 and the M4 rifle where they were, as they wouldn't be much use from now on. The MP5 was still hanging by his side. For the next few hours, he would move outside of his comfort zone. Kenshiro couldn't know what to expect, so he was trying to plan for all things that could go wrong as best he could. Though the more he thought about this plan, the more he realized how reckless and dangerous it could be.

This is crazy. You're not actually going to do this, are you? What happened to not taking unnecessary risks?

He forced himself to ignore those thoughts screaming

inside his skull, demanding he reconsider. Kenshiro moved into the kitchen where he left the green bag, which had all his food, the first aid kit, and the Atlas. All the things he would need, well, all the things he could think of for this little venture anyway. He quickly opened the bag and inspected the contents and did a quick inventory of his food. If it was just him, it would be enough for three days, and that's three good meals a day, but with two people, he knew the food would probably be gone in a day or two unless they rationed it. He closed the duffel bag and slipped it onto his shoulders before heading back to the spot where the black bag was. He dropped the M4 magazines that were in his pocket into the weapons bag. Between the three guns he currently was carrying, he had over two hundred rounds on his person. If he needed more than that, then he wasn't doing his job right. Realistically speaking, the bulk of bullets on him were meant more for the dead than the living.

For his peace of mind, Kenshiro went to the master bedroom and sank down to look under the bed. There, where he had left it, was the cloth-bound bundle. Safe and sound. He briefly considered taking it. Kenshiro didn't like being separated from it, but in the end, he would have to be content with it being secure and stowed away out of sight.

As he moved back into the hallway, he felt the weight of what he was carrying, but thankfully, he didn't feel too encumbered by it. Kenshiro didn't know how far he would have to walk today, but he secretly hoped it wouldn't be too far. Eventually, this weight combined with the temperature outside was going to wear him down. He ran through his checklist of this excursion in his head one last time to make sure he was taking what he needed and nothing more. Satisfied, he gripped the MP5 rifle at his side and brought it up in front of him as he moved towards the door.

He peered out from the safety of the house, fully

expecting to have to dart back inside. He glanced to his right, and then to his left, doing a thorough scan of the area in front of him. Then, without warning, he promptly raised the rifle and stepped out the door. The undead business man was on the road and he immediately noticed Kenshiro. The zombie in the ruined suit awkwardly pivoted and started towards him, but at the moment Kenshiro felt he had bigger concerns than a lone zombie. He looked down the iron sights of the rifle, with his finger touching the trigger, and he looked for threats. First, he looked for possible living threats, just to be safe. When he found none, he moved on to the undead threats that might have heard the excitement and moved into the area. Then when he found no signs of them either, he waited.

A part of him felt suddenly vulnerable on the exposed step of the house, like he was almost daring someone to shoot, which maybe he was, but time was also of the essence. He couldn't let the boy get too far ahead and risk losing him. If they were out there, if there were indeed living people here he needed to worry about, this should force their hand. He stood there for a moment, feeling the warm wind blow across his face, waiting for the shots to come. Time slowed as he felt the beats of his heart within his chest.

Nothing came.

When he decided the moment had passed, Kenshiro moved towards the truck, which was also towards the dead business man. It had stumbled off the street and was between him and the truck. Kenshiro didn't even break stride as he approached the undead figure and planted his boot solidly in its chest in a powerful front kick, fracturing frail undead ribs before sending its victim flying back to land squarely on its back. Kenshiro walked up to it as it flailed weakly, trying to right itself, drew his long straight-bladed knife from his right side and unceremoniously drove it down into its eye socket until he felt it drive home. The business man jerked slightly and then fell still on the grass. Kenshiro yanked the knife free, cleaned it off on the corpse's suit before sheathing it and continuing on to the truck.

On the passenger seat where he had left it was a red handled hatchet he had found yesterday. Kenshiro opened the door to retrieve the weapon before quickly stowing the hatchet in his belt, and closing the door. He checked his surroundings again with an untrusting eye before heading out at a brisk trot after the boy. All the instincts he trusted and obeyed were forecasting doom, but Kenshiro didn't care. It felt like the right thing to do and, besides which, he told himself he hadn't committed to anything yet.

He could still walk away from this at any point.

He made it to the edge of the field with few problems. The hatchet in his hand was still stained with the solutions to those problems, but it didn't faze him. What fazed him were the sounds of the boy's screaming as Kenshiro crossed the field laden with corpses. Kenshiro had stopped to deal with the undead duo that had crossed the field in pursuit of the boy. That's when he heard it. He couldn't make out what he was saying. The distance between them had turned the boy's words into an animal's howl of pain. Kenshiro finished what he was doing and picked up the pace towards the cries. Pursuing the boy had been easy. The undead were in the street stumbling and lurching in pursuit of the crying teen, and were in effect like a trail of breadcrumbs for Kenshiro to follow. Kenshiro came upon them from behind, as silently as he could with the burden he carried and the pace he kept, but when he came within a dozen feet of them their reaction was predictable.

They turned as if guided by some invisible hand to bear upon him, with rotten fingers reaching for him while hissing, snarling, or whatever other muted sounds escaped their lips. His response to each was strikingly similar in theory, but unique to the individual undead he was responding to. He would use his free hand to sweep the outstretched arms to the side, and then, using the same momentum, he would bring the hatchet down and bury it in their skull. Each attack was slightly different because each zombie was slightly different in their own way. Each had a different body type, but each fell the same way once the hatchet blade struck. He must have killed at least a dozen in that way in his pursuit of the boy. At one point, the screams had ended and Kenshiro feared the worst, but didn't dare try to move any faster. If the undead attacked the boy, there was little he could do to help him except maybe to end his misery. If the screaming had stopped, that meant he was probably too late for even that.

Luckily, his fears subsided when he caught sight of the struggling teen off in the distance. Kenshiro had been jogging steadily up Ryus Avenue to what had to be the end of the town. He could see the open fields past the last houses on the avenue, and over the open territory he could see the boy on the road leading out of town. The boy was still struggling down the road going east and was already outside of the town's limit. Kenshiro had expected him to be further ahead but judging by how the poor soul was running, it wasn't a surprise he caught up to the boy so quickly.

Whatever energy the kid had left was quickly evaporating, and he was running on empty. He looked like a marathon runner who had hit their limit. Kenshiro could barely call what he was doing as running. He didn't know why the boy just didn't stop and walk. He himself jogged on, the boy was a good distance away and in the middle of nowhere so he stuck out like a sore thumb out there.

Kenshiro quickly planned out his next moves as he

approached a trio of trailers on his left side at the edge of town. He would move into the field to the north of the road and observe the boy with his binoculars while laying prone in the field, there wasn't any other substantial cover he could use, so he planned to hug the ground and hope the boy didn't look back while he was getting into position. A man laying prone in a field was practically invisible at a distance. Eventually he would have to move up, but he would have to play it by ear a bit when that time comes.

When he was about to turn the corner of the street to the north, he kept a close eye on the boy up ahead. The whole time, one crucial thing eluded him until it was too late. *Where are the zombies that were following him?* Indeed, when he finally realized what was missing from the scene, he cursed himself for not seeing it earlier when he first noticed the boy on the road. Behind his target, Kenshiro could see a vast stretch of empty road. From his vantage point, the lone figure was the only thing on the road he could see. He should see a line of undead followers trailing behind him like groupies, and at the painfully slow pace the boy maintained Kenshiro doubted whether he would even outrun them. They should gain on him, especially after all that noise he had been making earlier. *So, where'd they go?* He turned the corner to the north.

He looked up as he rounded the corner of the street, and his heart sank when he found his answer.

It was a stupid mistake. Admittedly, he should have known better, and when he looked upon the crowd of undead figures ahead of him, he knew instantly what he had done wrong. *You don't just run around blind corners like a scared fool, not unless you know what's on the other side.* Granted, he was on the sidewalk and the immediate area around him was still clear. So, it's not like he ran around a corner and ran smack into awaiting undead arms, though looking at all the undead ahead of him, it kind of felt like he did just that. It didn't register at first, but before he could stop his momentum, he saw it. The same bird-like seizure he had witnessed when he first saw the undead interact with the boy. Their necks craned up, with their heads wildly jerking about... almost like they were sniffing. They were all doing it. That is, until the slight sound of Kenshiro's boots skidding on the gravel beneath him, reached their ears. Then the undead crowd all stopped sniffing, and shifted their collective lifeless gaze upon him.

Run! An old familiar voice inside his head called out as the undead collective hissed and snarled at him. Even from a block away he found the sound shockingly loud and somewhat unnerving, and as a whole he watched them all take their first step towards him. Kenshiro ignored the voice and held his ground for the time being. He turned a full circle and checked his surroundings for any others. Zombies had a terrible habit of showing up in unexpected places, and at the worst times. It wouldn't surprise him if there were others coming. He was careful as he went, trying to stay out of sight as he moved through the town's streets to get here. Kenshiro faced down the crowd of undead faces before him, and he wished the boy had been as careful. Considering how loud the boy had been, he was surprised the entire town's undead population wasn't roused into action. Or maybe that was the point. Maybe this kid wasn't as scared and frantic as he first believed, maybe all his screaming was to lure the undead out of their hiding places so he could zap them with whatever made them seize up like that. Then the kid could leave them for whoever might follow him to deal with. When he first saw it, Kenshiro doubted the kid had anything to do with whatever affected that zombie in the field. From what he saw, he thought the boy was just as confused about the reaction as he was, but now Kenshiro was rethinking that assumption. This was a clever little trap after all, and he walked right into it.

He looked for the boy and found him easy enough. A lone figure painfully trotting down a barren country road. It was hard to miss him. Further down the road, there was a medium-sized body of water beside the lane. There was a curve in the road where a line of small trees was growing parallel along the sides, just passed that tiny lake. Once the boy was past that point, Kenshiro would lose sight of him and possibly lose him all together. Kenshiro tried to judge the distance and how much time he would have until that point came. He couldn't say for sure, but he knew for a fact it wouldn't be enough to backtrack and then try to circle around this tiny horde of undead. He took a deep breath and exhaled slowly as he realized what he would have to do if he wanted to keep up his pursuit of the boy. If he couldn't go around the undead, then he guessed he'd have to go through them.

He moved to a spot on the curb by the stop sign as he unslung the MP5 rifle, and let it drop to the ground, before he took off the cumbersome duffel bag. He also dropped the extra magazines for the rifle from his pockets before he moved back out to the center of the dirt road. Kenshiro didn't need the extra weight slowing him down, he would need all the mobility he could get in the coming minutes.

He devised a battle plan that was familiar to him as he watched the undead crowd come for him. Well, not so much a battle plan as a set of rules for engagement. Plans had a way of falling to shit when things deviated from that plan. 'No projected goals ever survive the first week of development,' his father had said frequently. Rules, however, were flexible. Allowed for improvisation. *Keep them in front of you. Always know what's around you. Maintain your distance. Move in for the attack, and then back away. Repeat as necessary. Stay calm, breathe and keep moving. Know when it's time to pull the pistol and know when it's time to run.* Simple, primal, easy to follow rules that would guide him through this ordeal.

He rolled his shoulders to free up tight muscles from carrying the backpack, twisted at the hips to loosen up his back, then bent down and stretched his legs. He did all the things he normally would do before a big fight. In a different life, he remembered standing beside mats doing the same routine and then later outside of cages. He had one day hoped to do this routine in a dressing room in a stadium at some point, but the world had other plans. It was as much as a mental warmup as a physical one. He was preparing himself for the ugliness he knew lay before him.

In his former life the worst injury he ever saw with his own eyes was a man's arm that had snapped at the elbow. It left the arm bent at an unnatural angle. It was ugly. Kenshiro still remembered how the man's shouts echoed in the gym as he clutched his twisted arm. That injury would pale in comparison to the damage he would inflict on these zombies in front of him. He slipped the hatchet out from his belt and held the heavier weapon in his right hand. He then reached across with his left and pulled the long, straight blade out from his right leg and held it in a forward grip. The hatchet handle was a solid plastic but plastic none-the-less. Kenshiro had concerns the handle might become overly slick in his hand if it were to be covered with undead blood and gore. Time would tell. The beautiful, leather-wrapped handle of the knife had already been tested and wetted with zombie blood many times. He had no such concerns with the knife. Kenshiro stood in the middle of the street feeling the heat of the sun on his skin, a thin film of sweat cooled his forehead from the breeze as he took a couple deep breaths. Kenshiro looked upon all the dead hands reaching for him in the distance. He took a moment and thought of all the lives those dead hands had ruined. All the good people who fell to those hands, those same hands that probably fell upon loved ones and trusted friends and ripped them apart. He thought about his father, about all the things he had taught him, about all the things he could never teach him now. As much as Kenshiro tried not to, he also thought about Amy. About the way her hair smelled, the warmth of her touch, and how she made him feel. He thought about how much he loved her, how he would have done anything to have her with him now.

He breathed out and looked at the undead with their tireless lust for carnage, and he thought of all the things he had to do to get here, all the horrible inhumane acts of savagery that won him his survival for another day. Then he thought about that one unthinkable act and his body tensed as he breathed in sharply. It was time. He felt it in his bones. That old hatred he carried with him had been ignited once again. It burned within him. Now he would harness that fire to a blowtorch's point and destroy them all.

He felt the crunch of the gravel as his foot planted into the dirt road to launch him forward. Kenshiro felt the air move past his skin as his body responded, his senses were hyper aware as adrenalin pumped into his blood as he ran towards the one thing he hated, and feared, the most in this new world. He knew he should feel differently about it, but he couldn't help feeling alive as he rushed towards the undead with weapons in his hands. It was the illusion of beating them. Hurting them in any way he could with his own two hands, it was a visceral urge for retribution.

He ran up on them in a measured sprint, to build up momentum. When the distance was right, he launched his body forward in a leap that wasn't meant to be high, but to cover a significant amount of distance quickly. Kenshiro targeted the lead zombie for the massive flying front kick.

The blow sent all his weight and momentum into the sternum of the undead man in jean shorts and a Metallica t-shirt. The zombie still had dusty aviator sunglasses on, even though it was missing its right ear.

The kick landed perfectly and with such force Kenshiro felt it in his teeth. The intended victim's chest bones shattered with a series of dull cracks as his boot sunk into its ribs. The undead man flew back so violently the sunglasses it wore seemed to hang in the air in almost a cartoonish fashion as its body flew back and bounced off half a dozen others before they all fell awkwardly to the ground.

Kenshiro, however, landed on his feet after the kick with a dancer's grace and wasted no time getting to work. He let the hatchet blade swing down before bringing it up in a wide arc to come crashing down on his right side. The zombie had been a woman with long blonde hair. That was all the detail his brain could process before the hatchet blade obliterated the top corner of its skull. If there was a sound made, he didn't hear it as he quickly reversed his momentum and brought the hatchet down on his left side, to crack open a skull with short hair on it. Two down, but it did not phase the undead in the least. He saw a pair of hands reaching for him on the right side; the zombies were already stepping over the fallen to get to him. Kenshiro used his right forearm to sweep the arms aside and then drove the knife in his left through its milky, lifeless eye. Kenshiro yanked the knife free before he had to turn to his left and thrust his boot into another's zombie's stomach, which folded it from the force of the impact, and he brought the hatchet down on the back of its head during the brief moment it was bent over.

He then swiftly backed away giving himself space to move and reassess; he had blood on him. On his hands, he could feel the black, sickly blood running down his skin, and when he looked down, he could see where tiny droplets had freckled his arm. He looked back to the remaining crowd advancing on him and he knew it would get a lot messier before this was over. There were four corpses in the center of the road. They had somewhat fallen on top of each other, enough that the crowd now had an obstacle to move around to get to him. There was one that managed to step over the fallen bodies without falling, but the others simply shifted their direction to avoid the obstacle. *Not bad*, he thought to himself. Dividing them had been the plan all along, anything he could do to slow them down or divide them was a gain for him. He took in a deep breath and picked a side of the dividing mass of hands and teeth, and move back into the fray.

He picked the left side and moved in with purpose. To the first zombie that approached him, he responded by doing a quick sidestep and lashing out with a hard sidekick to the side of its knee. Kenshiro felt something pop inside the undead's leg and the zombie lurched to the side awkwardly as its injured leg gave way and it was falling to the ground. Kenshiro expected this and came up with his left and buried the straight knife hilt deep into its ear, lifting it back up slightly before he reversed direction and yanked the knife out again. The blade was dripping as it pulled free. As that one fell, Kenshiro stepped carefully forward and swung the hatchet in a wide arc in time to catch the zombie behind it as it stepped closer. The hatchet caught it on the temple and the its blade sunk in and tore through the eye socket as it passed through. Kenshiro grunted with disgust as he saw the shriveled eyeball swing on a piece of tissue from its socket as the body went down. He didn't have to search long for the next target before a female zombie, in a bulky coat more suited for winter, stepped up towards him snarling. Its body fell to the ground quickly after Kenshiro buried the hatchet in its forehead.

He backed up a few steps and then launched himself on the right side of the growing obstacle he had created. Kenshiro lashed out with hard, focused attacks with the hatchet and two more bodies fell to the road. Immediately following that, a zombie suddenly lunged forward and Kenshiro felt the cold cracked skin of the its fingers on his neck, and for a moment, he worried he was going to lose control of this situation. The next moment he brought the knife up underneath its chin until the blade drove into the zombie's brain pan. As the body fell, he pushed the zombie's corpse away from him and freed the knife. Kenshiro felt lukewarm blood drain onto his hand as the knife pulled free. Messy work indeed. He put down three more just as quick with heavy blows from the hatchet that seemed to smash and destroy everything in its path before he shuffled back once again.

He had a moment, so he looked for the kid on the road and quickly spotted him. It renewed a sense of urgency in him as he turned his focus back to the shrinking mass of the undead. There were noticeably fewer now, maybe as much as half had already fallen, and he still felt good. He felt like he could do this all day, but he knew that was just another illusion. Every man had their limit. That was just a fact of nature. He was no different. Kenshiro was far from his limit, though. He was barely breathing heavy. He gripped the hatchet and knife tightly, and he moved in once again to meet his foe head-on.

At this point there had been four that had broken away from the group. Kenshiro guessed they must be fresher than the rest but by looking at them you wouldn't know it. The only real difference he could spot right away is that these four moved a bit... freer than the rest. Like these four didn't carry the same invisible burden as the others. They almost looked eager. Kenshiro wore a hard look of determination on his face as he stepped towards the zombie on the far right with the hatchet raised above his head.

Kenshiro noticed the Hawaiian shirt the zombie had been wearing was stained all down the front of it with old blood, and a moment before the blow landed, he could see the front of its throat was torn down to the spine. It would explain the odd wobble its head made with each awkward step. The hatchet struck the top corner of its forehead with a devastating force. The section of skull first collapsed under the blade and then broke away as the momentum of the hatchet blade carried it through dead flesh. Brittle bone, black blood and tiny bits of spoiled meat sprayed against the neighboring zombie's face a moment before the one in the Hawaiian shirt fell.

Before the body even hit the ground Kenshiro turned and went after the zombie beside it. It had stumbled uncomfortably close, too close for the hatchet and at a bad angle for a good attack with the knife. Kenshiro pivoted and put his weight behind his leg and brutally swept the zombie's feet out from under it. He heard a slight snapping sound emanating from the zombie's leg as he knocked them out from under it. The zombie went down hard. He would come back to it in a moment, but for the time being, it could fumble on the ground while he dealt with more pressing threats. With a slight grunt he thrust the knife between grasping hands and struck the zombie behind those arms in the cheek. The blade ricocheted off the cheek bone, carried on into the eye socket, and straight to the brain.

Once that corpse fell to the ground, the next one, a female with matching pink and blue patterned exercise wear. Its left arm ended at the elbow in dry looking strips of meat, lunged at him with sudden speed. Its one arm reaching for him and its foul mouth poised open, ready to bite down on exposed flesh. Kenshiro took a step back to create some space between them and brought the hatchet around in a wide, powerful arc with the blade turned so it struck with the dull hammer side. There was a sickening crunch as the zombie's whole body was violently thrown to the side and fell in a motionless heap on the dirt road. With cold detachment, Kenshiro turned back to the one squirming on the ground trying to rise and stomped his boot down on the center of its ruined face once and its flailing arms fell to its sides. He looked at the rest with a grim expression on his face, black blood running down his blades, and sweat running down his face to soak into his shirt.

"They're not people," he said to himself out loud in a low voice. It helped to remind him those shambling figures in front of him didn't deserve mercy. There could be no half measures with them.

With that in mind he stalked towards the last ten, the slow pokes, not as withered and ruined as the skeletons, but this lot was well on their way. They all had slight frames, regardless of how they may have looked before. Some had telltale signs of their former selves, loose and sagged skin hung from their bones like loose clothing. Some still had a few patches of their long hair that hung limply from their scalps. All their clothing was threadbare and hung in tatters around them, threatening to fall off at any moment, and the colors had all but worn away completely in the elements and now they all seemed to be the same dark and dirty grey. They moved as if their joints were nothing more than rusty hinges. They were all spaced out well enough from moving forward through a minefield of bodies in their slow pursuit of him that Kenshiro felt this last bit would go quickly and fairly painlessly. He moved upon them. Kenshiro hacked and stabbed his way through them, moving from one to the next with cold indifference. A few managed a last lunge as he drew near, but each time he had been ready for it. Nothing the zombies did changed their ending, just delayed it a second more.

When the last one fell, the job was done, and he was alone. Kenshiro let out a long breath that sounded like a low growl when it passed by his lips. And then another, and another. He still gripped the knife and hatchet with murderous intent, his body still tensed up like a wild animal preparing to attack. A very significant part of him hungered for more. Soon the adrenalin would wear off and he would be left with glimpses of shattered skulls, broken faces, and muted shame to replace the murderous rush. Then he would rationalize and reason his way through it and continue on for another day. It was a process. One he was very familiar with, but right now, he didn't have time for any of that.

The boy, a gentle voice reminded him. Kenshiro gave his head a quick shake and then looked to the east and spotted him just before the bend in the road. Kenshiro had to move. He was running out of time. Unless he wanted to lose sight of the strange boy, he better get moving.

He looked down at his hands and thought, *not like this though.* His arms each had a coating of disgusting, rotten smelling, black blood halfway up to his elbow. He moved to the green survival bag he stowed by the stop sign, dropped the weapons to the grass and lowered himself to unzip the main compartment of the bag. Kenshiro was careful not to smear that foul smelling ooze all over the bag as he pulled out a light blue towel and one of the four bottles of the water he had. He unscrewed the cap and rinsed off his arms. He furiously rubbed his hands together with the water to try to get the blood off his hands. Mostly, he succeeded, but he still made a mental note to give himself a good scrubbing later on with actual soap, preferably an antibacterial brand for good measure. He then used the towel to dry everything off before replacing the knife and hatchet into their respective places.

With his hands relatively clean he dug through the bag until he pulled out his compact pair of binoculars, complete with a carrying pouch he could attach to his belt, perfect for a nice jaunt through the country. Next, he hoisted the bag onto his back once again and was unpleasantly reminded of its weight, he had to shift it slightly on his shoulders to find a comfortable spot. Finally, he slipped the MP5's sling over his shoulder and head and once again let the rifle fall to his right side.

With everything in place, he wasted no more time getting back on track. Kenshiro pointed himself north towards the final intersection where he would have to turn right to follow the boy. He ran with the rifle in his hands as best he could with the weight he was carrying and the distance he knew he would have to go before he caught up to the young stranger. It was more of a sturdy jog but it would have to do. Once he made it to the intersection, he turned right to continue after the boy on the road. Kenshiro veered off to the north side, through the small bushes lining the road, and jogged into the open field. Then once he was a suitable distance from the road, he turned and ran parallel to it after the boy. It wasn't great cover, but at least he wasn't on the road. The boy up ahead stuck out like a sore thumb. He, at least, wanted to make it hard to see him if the boy turned around. Kenshiro ran steadily for the first half mile without incident before he dropped to one knee near a cluster of bushes, where he felt concealed enough from anything up ahead. The boy was simple to find on the road when he pulled the binoculars out of his belt. Kenshiro had managed to half the distance between them, and he could make out the boy much clearer through the binoculars. He didn't like what he saw.

Miraculously, the boy was still managing something that resembled a run down the road. He was clearly exhausted, and he looked like a drunk person running for their life. His feet barely cleared the ground as he pushed forward with his hands weakly clawing at the air like he was trying to run through water. The kid was kicking up a lot of dust on that road as he went. The slight breeze helped, but dust still trailed behind the boy like the tail of a comet. Kenshiro looked around the boy for any undead that might have taken noticed to the display he was putting on. Thankfully for the time being, the boy seemed to be alone. However, he could see up ahead there were houses on the south side of the road.

If there were houses, there would be the undead. That was another general rule that turned out to be true more times than not. If that was the case here, he wanted to be close in case he needed to step in. At this point, it was obvious to Kenshiro the boy could not take care of himself. Judging by the look of him, he probably wouldn't be able to run away from the undead either. *He's fucking useless. Why are you following him? You can't protect him.* Kenshiro looked back to the weak shambling boy fighting his way down the road, faltering on almost every step but still staying upright. *Do yourself a favor and walk away. You can't protect anyone but yourself.*

It was true. He didn't like being reminded of it, but there it was. It wasn't an admission of any sort of failing, but a realization of some ultimate truth. He simply can't protect anyone in this environment he couldn't control, and the only person he has absolute control over is himself. He had failed so many others in the past. *Is that what you want? To go through that bullshit all over again?* Sometimes he couldn't help but to think his journey here was paved with the blood and gore of others. Kenshiro still felt the horrible crushing guilt that crept into his blood, in the dark silence of night as he lay awake on some nights. Breathing. Alive.

It was survivor's guilt. He understood it was all part of

the process of loss. That knowledge didn't lessen the bite, though. He had been on his own for a while now. Longer than ever before. He had learned the hard way not to seek people out.

Kenshiro watched the boy hobble away and thought about going back to town. There would be more undead. He would need to clear them out on his way back to the house he was using, but that was a minor concern. Maybe he wouldn't even have to leave. He would keep an eye out and keep a low profile for the next few days. Kenshiro doubted the boy would make a second journey into the town. That realization left a sour taste in his mouth, but what could he do about it? *That's right. What* can *you do about it? Nothing. You couldn't save her, so what makes you think you can save him?*

Kenshiro's knuckles tightened slightly on the binoculars as he lowered them.

"Shut up," he growled into the open air. He hated that fucking voice sometimes. What could he do? He could do something goddamnit? He could not turn his back on another human being who obviously desperately needs help. "I didn't just sit back and watch her die. I tried."

And you failed.

"Doesn't matter. I will *not* do nothing," Kenshiro whispered angrily as he stowed the binoculars away.

Are you going to help him the same way you helped her? You prepared to do that… again?

"Shut. Up," he hissed and put his hands to the sides of his head and tried to push the voice away. He took a moment to make sure it was quiet inside his head before he grabbed the rifle and continued on after the boy at a steady march.

They made their way pass a few acreages. The boy would just run drunkenly pass the houses and their undead inhabitants. Kenshiro again watched bewildered when the few undead who got too close to the boy froze in place, and start twitching like the one back in town. While all the others just paid the teen no attention at all. Kenshiro, of course, wasn't so lucky. Like in the town, the undead just settled their gaze on him when Kenshiro was in view and approached him the same wicked way they always had. Kenshiro struggled with the heavy pack on his back but he put them all down and then continued after the boy.

They approached a house with a large porch out front and several large windows that allowed Kenshiro to see the lone figure milling about inside the house. There was a rope swing out front that looked like it belonged in a Rockwell painting, and it might have had a nice lawn at one point. What he saw now was a sea of yellow dandelions out front that, in its own way, was beautiful. Here, like a few of the other properties they had passed, had its fair share of undead just sort of lingering around the buildings, and as before, the boy passed by the house and its zombies completely unnoticed. The undead here, too, had the same reaction to the boy as he had seen earlier. Like the others, the effect the boy had over them seemed to end the moment Kenshiro stepped into their view. As before, Kenshiro turned towards the undead and pulled his knife free. There was maybe a half dozen here, all perfectly spaced out. He didn't foresee a problem with this bunch. As the first one was within distance, he saw something out of the corner of his eye that made his heart sink.

The boy had fallen on the road.

Kenshiro forgot what he was doing and instinctively turned to watch the boy settle into the gravel. It didn't surprise him to see the teen fall. The way he had been going, Kenshiro was a bit surprised the teen went this long. The boy kept up that slow, struggled run for almost a half hour, and when he first saw the boy, he looked like he was ready to fall over and die. Kenshiro watched for a moment longer, silently pleading for the boy to get up when he felt the cold dead hands fall upon him.

The next moment, the zombie was on the ground. Kenshiro didn't even wait for its body to settle from the throw before he plunged the knife deep into its milky eye. Once he was back up, Kenshiro made sure the immediate area around him was clear before he checked back to the boy. Kenshiro breathed a sigh of relief when he saw the kid was slowly rising back up off of the road. He somehow kept going, even though now the boy had a noticeable limp in his already struggling stride. For the time being, Kenshiro would have to let him go. There was a bend where the road disappeared into some trees and bushes that lined the sides. He would have to lose the boy in the trees for now and try to catch up to him later. Kenshiro checked his surroundings. He only had the ones in front of him to worry about, and then he could be on his way again. Kenshiro turned back to the house and moved onto the driveway of the property and, feeling a sense of urgency, he moved towards the undead instead of waiting for them to make their way to him.

It was easy. One by one, Kenshiro slowly put them down and tried not to pay attention to the similar features the zombies had, or how they all had the same hair color. Kenshiro forced himself not to look the little blonde girl in the face before he struck. He cleaned his knife off on the brightly colored dandelions beside the girl's body and went to retrieve his pack and continue on.

There was no skulking alongside the road this time once he was at the bend. A thick barrier of foliage lined the road on both sides, and he felt it was more prudent to get eyes on the boy rather than hiding from him. He double-timed it down the center of the road, approaching the lazy bend to the north and was greeted by blessed shade once he rounded the wide corner. The boy was there up ahead. His pace remained steady, albeit hard to watch. A normal person would have stopped attempting to run at this point and just settled into a walk. *What is he running from?* Kenshiro followed behind him at a comfortable walk. There were no undead around, and even if there were, this kid doesn't seem to register on their radar. So, why run? Kenshiro was beginning to worry what kind of mind might be inside that haggard frame.

He briefly considered calling out to the boy, if for no other reason than to get him to finally stop running, but the lizard side of his brain resisted that idea. It wanted to know where he was going and what might wait for the boy once he finally gets there, or who. It was a sad little chase. All the boy had to do was take one glance behind him and it would all be over, but if there's one thing he's learned about the boy so far, it's that he never looks back. Not once in the whole time Kenshiro followed him from the town did he notice the boy looking around himself. He was extremely confident in whatever ability he had over the undead, or he was just plain delusional. Given what he had seen so far from the boy, he could believe the former. The air in the shade was noticeably cooler and gloriously refreshing on Kenshiro's sweat-soaked skin. The sun was beginning its long descent into the western sky, but it would be hours yet before there was any real relief from the heat. For the time being, Kenshiro was enjoying his walk in the shade and he hoped it was as much as a relief to the boy as it was for him. Kenshiro watched him, and the youth certainly didn't look relieved.

He almost willed the boy to stay up because he knew if the boy fell again, Kenshiro would have to step in. Right now, he didn't know which scared him more; the sight of the boy falling to the ground, or having to interact with a living person for the first time in as long as he could remember. People are dangerous, hard-earned experience taught him that. He was either risking his life to save them, or risking it running away from them. It always seemed to come down to that. So why bother? He followed the boy in the cool air, trying to come up with an answer when thankfully he was interrupted by an all too familiar sound.

Hissing.

Out from the tall grass of the ditch ahead to the right crawled a dark and rotten figure. Dead, milky eyes locked on him as its fingers raked at the gravel, trying to get enough purchase to move itself forward onto the road.

First thing Kenshiro noticed was all the hair on its skull. This one had long dark hair that hung in wet looking clumps down to the road's surface, and a full beard covering its face that now seemed to cling to its cheeks in sickening-looking clumps. It made its way onto the road as Kenshiro approached it and he could see the lower half was a mangled, twisted mess of rotting flesh and bone that hung uselessly from its waist as it shimmied along the ground. Kenshiro didn't even break stride as he unceremoniously stomped his boot down on its head. He ignored the loud crack that sounded after his boot sunk into its skull, and something warm splashed against his leg. He snorted loudly as he continued past the now still body. *This is getting fucking messy*, he thought after he decided a change of clothes was going to be in order after this brief episode was all said and done. A change into fresh clothes after a good cleaning, preferable with strong soap and a sturdy brush. The rotting smell of them seemed to follow him now.

Kenshiro approached the next bend in the road, it was a sharper turn this time and the boy had disappeared behind it. Kenshiro approached the bend but he stopped at the corner. The heavy treeline alongside the road ended as abruptly as it began, after the bend was an open territory on both sides of the road. The boy its lone occupant. Up ahead, maybe a couple hundred yards, was another cluster of mature trees on the north side of the road. Even from this distance, Kenshiro could make out the tops of some building that were peeking out above the treeline. He took out his binoculars, let the heavy pack fall to the road, and sat down for a spell. For the time being he was alone, and he had a suspicion the boy would turn into that cluster of trees, *and* he was thirsty.

He laid the rifle across his lap, within easy reach if needed, and pulled a handkerchief from his bag. Kenshiro wiped the sweat from his face before he then moved to his hair and neck. He tossed it to the side of the road in disgust when he saw how soiled it was with undead blood. Then he reached into the bag again and pulled out the second of four water bottles he had brought. He greedily drank half the bottle before he even knew what he was doing. It just felt so good running down his throat, he didn't even mind it was fairly warm. Next, he pulled out a vacuumed sealed package of beef jerky, tore it open and chewed a piece as he watched the boy through the binoculars in the shade's comfort.

He didn't mind the fact he was comfortable and eating while the boy was struggling out on that road in the heat of the dying afternoon sun. The truth of the matter was Kenshiro wasn't entirely convinced he would not end up shooting the boy. One easy word to describe what he had seen of the boy so far would be desperate, and desperate people do stupid things. He watched the boy as he approached where Kenshiro imagined the turnoff was into the property and thought about what he would do if the boy kept walking past that point in the road. How far would he follow this stranger? There had to be a point where he either turned back and let the kid carry on, probably do his death given the shape he was in, or risked confronting him on the road. Kenshiro couldn't follow him forever, not like this. Eventually, he would have to decide. Kenshiro chewed his food as he watched the boy finally come to a stop.

It happened suddenly and with little warning; the boy had been carrying on down the road when his head turned to the left as if his eye caught something, and he just sort of stumbled to a stop. The boy stood on the road for a moment and then, for the first time since they started this journey together, the boy turned around and checked the road behind him. Kenshiro could see the boy had the posture of a broken man, shoulders slumped forward, hunched over slightly and even at this distance he could see the boy's frame heaving with each breath. Kenshiro knew he was concealed from the boy and continued to watch him as the kid looked to the road as if he expected something to be there.

Soon enough, the boy turned to the left and started towards the mostly concealed property, he bent down and lost his footing and went sprawling into the gravel. Kenshiro saw that the boy crawled forward for a bit before he lost him in the foliage. Through the binoculars, Kenshiro scanned the cluster of trees, looking for movement of any kind in between the trees and around the visible perimeter. There was nothing but open territory between him and the property the boy disappeared into. No matter how he approached, Kenshiro would be vulnerable. A damned sniper's dream. No cover to speak of and he would walk towards the shot, assuming there was anybody there to take the shot. Kenshiro didn't see any movement. But that didn't mean there wasn't anybody there, so he waited. He finished the package of beef jerky. He didn't know when he might eat again. Besides which, the second Kenshiro stepped out from these trees, he might catch a bullet. So, Kenshiro took his time finishing his tiny meal while keeping an eye on those trees through the binoculars while he chewed the tough meat. Nothing stirred but the leaves on the tree's branches as time passed by. He was feeling exposed sitting on that dirt road when he finished the package of jerky, but it was better than feeling a bullet puncture his chest. He hoped that wouldn't happen, though.

First off, nobody came out to meet the boy. If there was anybody in that cluster of trees that kid considered a friend, why wouldn't they rush out the second they recognized the state he was in? The haggard teen was obviously in distress. If Kenshiro had been waiting in those trees and saw somebody in his group come half running, half falling along the road, he would rush out to help him back to safety. At least, he would like to think he would, but he recognized this wasn't a world that tolerated foolish heroics anymore. Though, if he was in this hypothetical group, he would never have sent that kid out.

Second, where are all the bodies? If there was some sort of group here, then there should be rotting corpses all around the property. People attract the undead. The more people there are, the more the zombies are attracted to them. One or two people could remain out of sight without attracting a significant amount of undead, maybe three. Anymore than that, would attract fresh undead like sharks to the taste of blood with each new day. If that were the case, he would have expected to see at least a few bodies in the fields surrounding the trees, but Kenshiro couldn't see any. He also didn't see a fence or barrier of any kind around the property beyond the natural barrier of the trees, and that was hardly a barrier at all. The undead may be hopelessly slow and clumsy, but they would have few problems simply stepping through that treeline.

Kenshiro considered another possibility. Maybe the boy finally decided he couldn't run anymore and took shelter in a building. Given what he had seen so far, it was the scenario that made the most sense to him. The next property he could see was maybe another mile away, and across the field to the north. He doubted the boy would get very far over that terrain. It was then that Kenshiro felt a sense of urgency after remembering how the boy had stumbled out of view. He had already witnessed the boy fall once today.

Kenshiro took a deep breath. It was time to go. He couldn't afford to wait longer. His finely honed instincts for survival told him this was a stupid risk he didn't need to take, but he thought of the last living person he had come across. Kenshiro remembered how he died by his hands and he knew what he had to do. If he died, then so be it. If he took a bullet in the next few moments, he prayed the shooter would at least have the decency to shoot him in the head. He rose and hoisted the duffel bag back onto his shoulders. Kenshiro decided he would leave the MP5 rifle hang by his side and come out from behind his cover with his hands empty. The goal being to seem as nonthreatening as possible as he approached, just in case he was wrong about everything he had seen.

As he took the first couple steps into the open territory, Kenshiro held his breath. He kept his hands at his sides, relaxed and swinging freely as he stepped, but was totally aware of where the rifle was at all times, in case he had to reach for it. He let out the breath he had been holding when it became clear he would not be shot, not immediately anyway, and set himself into a good, nonchalant pace.

He feverishly scanned the treeline looking for the trap part of him was sure was there. The less he saw, the more he felt there was to be worried about, but there was nothing. The boy was weighing heavily on his mind as Kenshiro drew closer. He saw the mailbox first, rusted and leaning slightly towards the road. It stood above a tall growth of grass that spread out from its base and reached for the sky. Farther in was a flowerbed that had been left unchecked, Kenshiro recognized it as the foliage the boy disappeared behind. A few steps later, he saw it. The gravel approach into the property, and a thick rusty metal bar that ran across it between two equally rusty posts. On the far end, he could see a chain wrapped around the bar and the post, locking it into place. In front of it, he recognized human remains in various states of decomposition. They were old, real old. Only piles of bones covered in dry tissue and stained clothing.

Kenshiro's hand slipped easily around the pistol grip of the rifle and he brought it up to his other hand, he kept it low with the barrel pointing towards the ground, still trying to seem as unthreatening as possible but he felt it prudent to be ready to be threatening if the need arose. He stopped at the approach, crouched down and took a moment to have a look into the property to see if anything stirred. Kenshiro also listened closely for anything other than the sounds the breeze made as it carried over the grass and through the trees. When he was satisfied, he moved up to the bar and gracefully ducked under it while keeping his eyes, as well as the barrel of the gun, facing forward. Two steps later, Kenshiro saw the boy laying motionless on the ground.

I told you.

He was lying face down in the grass in an unnatural position, like something finally gave out and his body just tumbled to the ground. He wasn't moving. Using the rifle's barrel as a focal point, he scanned the surroundings in front of him for danger as he approached the body. Once there, he stood over the boy and pointed the rifle at the boy's head and slipped his finger over the trigger.

"Hey," he said to the still body. "Hey, kid!" He said louder this time, but there was no response from the boy. Cautiously, he inched closer and used the tip of his boot and placed it under the boy's shoulder. He then nudged the kid over until he flopped over onto his side. A tiny moan escaped the boy's lips and Kenshiro instinctively jumped back, feeling his finger tighten on the trigger as he did so.

He's alive!

The next events happened in quick succession. Kenshiro picked up the boy off the ground and carried him towards the house. He was already carrying a lot of weight but he was still surprised how little the teen weighed in his arms. Kenshiro huffed towards the house and cursed slightly trying to open the flimsy metal screen door and then the sturdy wooden door into the old house. Kenshiro called out frantically for help, but knowing in his heart there wouldn't be a response.

He wasn't a doctor, Kenshiro's talents lie elsewhere but he did what he could for the sandy-haired teen. Kenshiro cut his clothes off his small frame and stood back in horror at the sight of the kid's withered body. Kenshiro's eyes watered slightly, he couldn't help it. He feared he may end up shooting the kid after all. Undeterred, he put wet towels on the boy's legs, chest, and head in an attempt to soak up his body's heat. He made the boy as comfortable as he could, and when that was done, Kenshiro waited.

Out of habit, he searched the house, and then the property. Afterwards, Kenshiro returned to the house and something about a picture that was on the wall caught his eye. He looked at it with idle curiosity at first. The colors were bright and well defined, it was obviously done by a professional. Upon closer inspection, the boy in the photo seemed familiar, and he morbidly wondered if he had put down the zombie version of that kid some time in the past day or so. It didn't take long for him to see it. He liked to think he had a trained eye for this sort of thing, but when he did, he couldn't believe what he was seeing. Kenshiro promptly took the picture off the wall and took it back into the living room, where he held it up to the withered boy on the couch. He looked at the picture, and then at the withered frame on the couch, to the picture, and then back to the couch. It was hard to tell at first glance because the boy in the picture was slightly younger, and the fact the boy in the picture was smiling. There was no mistaking it though, the cheekbones were the same, the nose and the eye placement were identical, the ears were a dead-on match. He saw it with his own eyes, but it was impossible. The picture of the round kid and the withered form on the couch were the same person. The picture was obviously not recent. Maybe a couple of years separated the picture from the actual person, but still. Looking at the contrast of the two side by side was shocking, worse it was heartbreaking, because the boy in the picture looked happy, healthy, definitely well fed. The form on the couch looked like all the life had been sucked out of the body and whatever left had been tossed aside and forgotten about.

This is his house.

The thought came to him suddenly, and he looked around the room again as if he had been seeing it for the first time. That's when Kenshiro noticed the absence of the usual layer of dust on everything, actually the room was quite tidy. *He fucking lives here*, Kenshiro thought incredulously as he went about the room, marveling at the clean surfaces. There were other pictures on the book shelf by the far wall, one was a more recent photo of the boy. It looked like a school picture, and in it the boy looked older than the one that was hanging on the wall, but he was just as large.

"How long have you been here?" He whispered to himself when he returned the picture to the book shelf. How long would it take to transform a person from that boy in the picture to that poor soul fighting for his life on the couch? Dozens of other questions popped into his head. He pushed them all aside, but one remained. *Where were his parents*? Kenshiro breathed in sharply when he realized he should add searching for the boy's parents to his list of things to do and he prayed there were not two zombies stowed away somewhere on the property.

Hours later, the boy had not awoken yet from what seemed like a peaceful sleep. Kenshiro tried not to think about what he might have to do if the boy suddenly stopped breathing, so he read a book instead. He was clean, fed, and wearing a fresh set of clothes thanks to the man of the house, apparently the boy's father, who thankfully was close to Kenshiro's size.

In front of the couch the boy was on, between them, was a long coffee table. On it, Kenshiro placed a bottle of Gatorade he had found in the house he spent his first night in La Veta inside. If the boy woke up, he would need it desperately. Kenshiro only hoped it was still good and didn't make the boy sicker than he already was. Beside the bottle, he placed two pills. The first was a multi-vitamin he was currently using himself, and the other was an aspirin. He thought he heard aspirin was supposed to be good for the heart, and if not, it would be good for whatever pain the boy might be in.

Kenshiro knew little about treating starvation on this degree, but he knew you couldn't just start shoveling food into their mouth. It would shock his system so much it might kill the boy. Kenshiro's plan was to give him the Gatorade first with the pills, and then wait maybe twenty minutes before first trying to feed him a small amount of beans. Kenshiro found, to his absolute delight, the gas stove in the kitchen still worked. He had seen the large propane tank in his search of the property, and gauge on the side showed it was dangerously low, but when he turned the knob on the stove, he heard the gas hiss through the burners and a second later he was greeted with an even ring of blue flames. He would heat some food and feed the kid some small portions and then get him to rest some more. What else could he do? He didn't know, so he stuck with his plan until a better one presented itself. He turned off the stove and retired into the living room to watch over the body on the couch.

He was well into the sixth chapter of the book when he heard the figure on the couch stir. Kenshiro lowered the book slightly so he could peer over the top at the boy, as he had before on the other occasions the boy stirred, but this time he paused. This time, he told himself from this point on, no sudden movements. This time, he saw the boy had opened his eyes.

Kenshiro froze, thinking it best for the boy to notice him first, feeling the gun's weight on his thigh he watched the boy just sort of stare up at the ceiling with a strange look on his face like he was trying to solve a hard math problem in his head. He was debating signalling the boy of his presence somehow. Like the longer Kenshiro went unnoticed, the worse the reaction would be when he finally was discovered. *Stick to the plan.* He quickly reminded himself he didn't know what kind of shape the kid's mind was in. Kenshiro could have a crazy person on his hands, after all. What if the boy's first reaction was to shit himself and then reach around and start lobbing fistfuls of his own shit all over the room? No, better to take this slow and try to gauge what sort of person he was dealing with before he stuck his neck out so far the boy couldn't resist slicing it for him. He would help the boy, but on his terms, the terms set out by the lizard part of his brain. The part keyed for survival. He would proceed with Kenshiro's safety being a priority above the boy's comfort.

Without warning, the boy's head turned towards him and Kenshiro held his breath as he was sure the boy was turning towards him, but the boy's eyes fell onto the Gatorade bottle on the coffee table. The boy's eyes widened in amazement at what he saw. Without taking his eyes off of it, the boy struggled to a seated position on the couch. He yawned and then scratched his head absently, all the while admiring his new treasure on the coffee table. He then noticed the two pills beside the bottle. He was less excited about those as he eyed them with far less wonder in his eyes. Kenshiro was in utter shock at the boy's apparent lack of interest in the figure sitting in the chair not ten feet in front of him. Was he doing it on purpose? Did the boy genuinely just not notice him? Feeling slightly annoyed, Kenshiro signalled the boy by clearing his throat as gently as he knew how.

And the boy freaked out.

Kenshiro couldn't help but to let out a sigh as the boy stiffened up in terror and started crawling his way back into the couch like he planned to disappear between the cushions. Once the boy saw there was no place to go, he pulled his knees up into his chest and kind of made himself into a ball, a ball made of tiny bones and knobby joints.

"Wha-," the boy squeaked out and then stopped himself, like the sound of his own voice surprised him, or maybe it surprised him how hoarse it sounded. He swallowed hard and tried again. "Who?" Again, the boy stopped himself, but this time he looked like he lost the words he wanted to say. Remembering to keep his movements slow, Kenshiro deliberately placed a bookmark to mark his place in the book, in case he came back to it later, and placed it on the table to the side, covering the .22 pistol from the boy's sight. The boy yelped at the initial movement but settled back as he kept his eyes locked on him. Kenshiro then reached down and almost lazily pulled the Beretta free from its holster on his leg and casually placed it on his knee, deliberately pointing the barrel in the boy's direction. His hand calmly rested on top of it. Kenshiro spoke in as clear a voice as he could muster.

"Let's talk," he said simply. Kenshiro didn't know how the boy would react to him, or the gun, or to anything that was happening right now. The boy was terrified, and he was aware of it. Kenshiro could clearly see it from his shaking, huddled form on the couch, with eyes looking at him like a deer would before the wolf was about to strike. Kenshiro had to be ready for the unexpected. Though what the boy said next, Kenshiro had to admit he wasn't ready for.

The half naked boy suddenly stopped shaking and let his knees fall slightly from his chest like his terror had suddenly deflated by what he noticed, and his entire face shifted from one of fear to one of amused disbelief.

"Is that my dad's shirt?"

Chapter 8

Elle

Elle was on the stationary bike, working off some steam while charging several devices that were hooked up to the charging rig that the treadmill powered. She still felt stung by Marty, and maybe a bit over her own over ambition as well. She had come on way too strong, and worse yet she felt foolish for aiming so incredibly high as to propose she fly the helicopter. Of course, he would not agree to let some twenty-two-year-old woman, who he probably thought of as a girl, learn to fly his precious helicopter. Especially when, admittedly, she knew absolutely nothing about them, but she wasn't beat yet. As her legs burned on the bike, she was already planning her next encounter. This felt right to her and she felt an urgency about it, so she would try again.

She heard the door to the stairway slam shut, signalling that somebody had walked onto the floor. When she checked her watch, Elle found Blaine was twenty minutes early to relieve her. She kept pedaling, and soon enough, a figure rounded the corner but stopped at the door to the room.

It was Marty.

"Hey," she said to him with a look that displayed her curiosity as she let the pedal's motion bleed away to nothing. He wasn't one for using the bikes and since this little charging station was really the only thing of interest on this floor, it was obvious he came to see her.

"Hey," he said a bit more sheepishly than she expected. "Listen, about earlier-."

"Don't worry about it." She cut him off. The last thing

she wanted right now was to be coddled by the very person she was trying to convince she was up to the task. She dismounted the bike and moved in front of him in her short shorts and her sweaty blue NYU t-shirt unabashedly and went for it. "I can handle you saying no to me. I'm not some teenager who's been coddled her whole life." Feeling the fire churn in her belly, she took a step towards him, and to her surprise, he stepped back. "I can even handle your little jabs at me. Yeah, I have never been in a helicopter. Sue me. That doesn't mean I can't do it, and it certainly doesn't mean I can't learn. All that shit I can handle, but you want to know what I can't handle?" At that, she took her finger and pointed it at his somewhat bemused face, which enraged her even more. "What really pisses me off? When people treat me like a fucking child. Maybe if you're so goddamn high and mighty important around here, maybe you should do you own fucking laundry from now on. Huh?" She lowered her finger and the air between them seemed to get thicker somehow as she realized she had gone too far.

She didn't think she should let herself slip into a full-blown argument with the man, but it felt like it was pretty close, and now she had nowhere to go but down from this point. They stood there for a moment, just looking at each other. Internally, she was debating apologizing and taking back what she said. Marty turned slightly back down the hall, and she thought he was about to leave.

"Come on," he said softly and motioned her to follow him, and started back towards the stairwell doors.

Elle followed silently a step or two behind him, as expected. He went through the stairwell doors, and started ascending the stairs. Deep down, Elle knew where they were going, but she didn't know why, and to make matters even more confusing, she suspected she smelt a hint of malt liquor on Marty's breath. Which wasn't surprising, but she had to admit it kind of made her question his motives here. Suddenly, she realized she was still wearing her tiny shorts and sweaty t-shirt. A moment ago, she put her sexuality in front of her like a shield, but now, she wished she could hide it away somehow. Soon, however, the concern evaporated with each floor as they ascended in silence. He never even looked back at her as they went.

Marty held the door to the roof for her, and Elle stepped through into the cool evening air. Before Marty showed up, her plan was to finish her shift on the bike, clean up and put on a fresh set of clothes, before gathering up her sister for Jacob and Blaine's movie night. She followed Marty up the metal stairs to the helipad, and there it was. Softly reflecting the retreating light of the sun, was the helicopter. It had the look of a limousine, a solid black color with gold trim around the doors and windows, and a generous streak of gold stretching back to the end of the tail. They tinted the back passenger windows to the point she couldn't see the insides. As she was admiring it, Marty approached the passenger side door and opened it for her.

"Get in," he said simply, and she hesitated for a moment. He smiled slightly and nodded. *It's okay*, so she moved towards the seat.

She climbed up onto the skid and looked into the cockpit and froze as she saw there was a control stick rising from the floor in front of the seat. It looked like something that was out of a Star Wars movie, with the number of buttons and dials she saw just on the stick. *Oh, fuck me.* Her heart sank, and she looked back at Marty in with what must have been a look of absolute terror because he chuckled and held up his hands.

"Relax," he said. "There are controls on both sides. See, look." He pointed over to the adjacent seat and, to her relief, she saw an identical control stick in front of that seat. She breathed out and moved into the chair. "There are pedals down on the floor by your feet. Don't put your feet on them, strap yourself in, and touch nothing." He pointed to the floor, and indeed there were two pedals in front of her. Marty next pointed to the ends of the five-point harness for her to strap into.

Marty closed and latched the door before moving around to the other side, then he opened his door and climbed into the seat next to her. He reached behind her seat and produced a headset, which he gave to her and instructed her to put on. With the headset on, there was utter silence all around her. She watched Marty reach forward and flip a red switch on the center of the console, and the console itself came alive with lights. There were several screens in front of her, but the three main ones were the largest by far, taking up the bulk of the available space. There were two next to each other on Marty's side of the console and one directly in front of her, each display was framed with identical looking buttons. The manufacturers occupied the space between the front seats with a center console that had foreign looking instruments and even more buttons and dials. *It's like the fucking space shuttle,* Elle thought to herself as she looked at the displays with a mixture of awe and horror.

"Mic check? Can you hear me?" Marty asked absently, like he already knew the answer while he was pushing the odd buttons and looking at the various readouts on the display.

"What's going on, Marty? What are we doing?" Elle asked a little more sheepishly than she expected as she watched Marty simultaneously pressed the two buttons marked ENGINE CONTROL and felt a little nervous when they lit up green. Marty sat back in his chair and took in a deep breath before he turned and looked at her solemnly.

"We're just going to take a little trip around the park," he said it like that would explain everything, but it only left her with more questions. "We'll be back before anybody even knows we're gone." With that said he reached forward and flipped the engine start switch to the right.

There were a few loud clicks going off around her and then the engine came to life with a high-pitched drone that was getting higher as the engine's RPMs climbed. Marty pointed to the display in front of him and showed her one of the digital gauges was a tachometer for the engine and rotor speeds. He explained the larger of the two dial indicators on the gauge was for engine speed, while the smaller one represented the rotor's speed. Which she noticed was climbing and then she looked out of the windows and indeed saw the main rotor blade turning and quickly gaining speed. He then pulled the switch to the other side and a second high pitch whine started up and began climbing as well. The sound of the engine was all-encompassing. To her, it sounded like she was standing right next to a roaring jet engine; Elle felt it tickle her insides. She looked over at the rotor speed dial while Marty was busying himself by pressing various buttons along the displays. Elle saw the digital needle climb higher on the gauge; it was almost matching the speed of the engine. Elle looked up to the rotors, but all she saw was a swirling blur above them. Then, some motion on the helipad by the stairway attracted her attention, and when she looked, she saw a shape step onto the concrete of the helipad but before she recognized the form, she heard Marty speak.

"Here we go." The helicopter lifted off into the sky, and it felt like Elle had left her stomach behind.

"Holy shi-." It was all that escaped her lips as her hands clutched her thighs from the shock of the sudden unexpected motion. She collected herself enough to look back at the figure on the helipad, but all she saw was the figure hurry back down the stairwell. "I think that's Derek down there," Elle said, knowing full well she couldn't be sure, but what she was sure of, was the reaction she saw. There was no mistaking the way the figure stormed down the stairs, most likely heading for the stairwell door. That figure was angry about something.

"Yeah, probably," Marty said noncommittally as he continued the ascent off the helipad and into the sky.

The helipad fell away underneath them and Marty shifted the control stick forward slightly, and the helicopter drifted forward. He took the craft up and forward in a slow arc over the buildings in front of them, and before she knew it, the buildings were behind them and they were moving over the park. The view from the craft looked like a postcard depicting the immense concrete landscape of Manhattan. It was a dead city, devoid of life and movement, but in the dying light of the day, the city still held a sort of beauty. A monument of all humanity had achieved and then lost. As they moved ahead across the park, Elle looked down and could make out the odd shapes moving down there like confused ants. Little undead ants searching for food. Her eyes moved back to the front. She didn't need to see them; she knew they were down there, of course they were, and she didn't need to waste her time looking at them.

"This is amazing, Marty. Thank you for bringing me," she said, and she meant it, but after she said it, she feared the possible intention behind this trip.

She looked at the instrument console in front of her with its digital displays, foreign looking instruments each with its own dizzying amount of buttons and little dials and she felt like someone looking at an impossible task. How could she ever understand all that? Where would she even begin? Marty knew how impossible it was and, to his credit, when he realized she wouldn't stop with a simple no, he switched gears and just showed her how impossible it was in the most beautiful way imaginable. She wouldn't ever fly a helicopter, but she would remember this for the rest of her days. The wild freedoms of it were intoxicating, like they could just point the nose on the horizon and just fly away from all their troubles.

"I appreciate you not being a jerk about me bugging you to teach me to fly this thing. I could never fl-."

"What are you talking about?" Marty interrupted her suddenly over the intercom, the sharpness of it gave her a start. "You don't want to fly anymore? I thought you liked it." He was teasing her, she decided quickly, and maybe she had a bit of that coming to her for being so silly to start with.

"I didn't realize I would need a degree in rocket science," she joked. "I guess I didn't really think about it too much before I came to you. I'm sorry about that." She looked over at him, and Marty was shaking his head.

"I think you might be confused." He shifted the control, and the helicopter came to a slow stop and they just hovered there above the city as the glow of the horizon painted it a stunning orange. "I didn't bring you up here to intimidate you." He looked over at her solemnly, and Elle would swear she saw a touch of sadness in his eyes. As he continued, she would find out why. "I just wanted to go for a flight. That's it, no real big conspiracy theory or anything. See this?" He pointed to the bottom corner of his side of the console and there, taped to one of the few empty spots on the console, was a picture of a little girl with brown hair. "That's my daughter, and today is her birthday," Marty said calmly into his headset, and the words struck her like a slap to the face. She didn't know Marty had a daughter. "I have a reminder on my phone and this morning it set off an alarm. She always wanted me to take her up for a flight, but I always put it off because I wanted to wait until she was older. I could have taken her anytime." Then he said it again, quieter this time, as if he was speaking more to himself. "Anytime. Anyway, I thought it would be nice to take someone up who would enjoy it." He smiled awkwardly at that, probably secretly hoping she didn't make a big deal out of it.

"I am, thank you. This is incredible." She gestured to the view all around them.

"Oh, we haven't even started yet," he said with a genuine smile and dipped his head towards the control stick on her side. "Take the stick."

"What?" she shrieked over the intercom. "Fuck no."

"Come on," Marty groaned. "Don't be a pussy." At that, Elle glared at him, and his poor choice of words. He looked down, suddenly realizing what he had said in jest. "Sorry," he said, looking back at her. "You know what I mean, though. Just take it. I'm right here. I won't let you crash. Look." He patted the control stick. "Put your one hand here, and put your other hand down here-," Marty patted a lever that was down alongside of her seat. It looked like the parking brake lever her old car had. "-On the throttle. You don't have to move or do anything just yet. Just put your hands on them and get a feel for it."

"Seriously?" She looked at him, wanting to do it, but the pounding of her heart made her hesitate.

"Do it," he said calmly in such a tone she reached for the controls. Elle put her hand on the throttle first and accidentally nudged the control up as her hands locked around it in a white-knuckle grip and the helicopter lurched upwards slightly. "Easy." Marty cautioned her gently, and she forced her hand to ease up on its death grip on the lever. Next, she placed her free hand on the control stick in front of her. Marty still held on to it as well, which was a comfort as she steadied her hand around the stick's grip. It felt electric in her hands. "You got it?" He asked and as she held the control, she put her whole being into just holding the controls still in her hands.

She could feel her palms sweating, Elle felt like she was about to take the first big drop in a roller coaster. As insane as what she was doing was, Elle did it because at the same time, she hadn't felt this alive in awhile. She nodded firmly while keeping her attention on the controls. In her peripheral, she saw Marty ease his hands away from them and she told herself to just breathe and keep it steady as her heart threatened to explode out of her chest. The helicopter wavered slightly in its hover under her control, and she was sure Marty would take them back from her, but he simply spoke calmly.

"Ok, good. You're doing good. Just relax your grip on the stick a little. Good, now look at me." Elle looked at him with wild eyes, and she expected Marty to have the same expression, but he didn't. He looked... happy? It was hard to tell with him. He was smiling, but his eyes looked serious. "OK, now you're going to take us over to the river over there." She swallowed hard at the idea of doing such an impossible task; it was taking everything she had just to hold the helicopter still in the sky. How could he possibly expect her to maneuver it? She looked at him gravely, but he held that same stupid dad-face. She breathed in sharply, looked down at her hands on the controls. *I'm doing it*, she thought to herself. She was actually flying this craft right now. She might die tomorrow, the last thread of humanity might die out forever in the future, but right now, right here, she was flying a helicopter.

"How?" she asked, and Marty let out a little snort of a laugh.

"Well, alright," he said happily, like it had all been a test and she had passed. "First, keeping your hand steady on the control and only after I say, you are going to take your left foot and press in the left pedal. That's going to rotate us towards the river, push it in real slow until she turns." He looked at her. "You ready?" She nodded firmly and waited for his command, but he only chuckled over the intercom. "I'm going to need you to say the words, Elle."

"Yes, goddamnit, I'm ready," she blurted out over the intercom in a voice that was a little louder and higher pitched than she expected. She cleared her throat and breathed in again. "Sorry," she said, embarrassed at first, but after she once again met with Marty's soft chuckle, she found she was smiling too.

"Do it," he said, and Elle followed his instruction and eased the pedal in and the craft suddenly started turning slowly to the left. She held her breath the whole time until the nose of the helicopter was firmly pointed towards the Hudson River and at his signal, she let the pedal out again. "Ok, now very slowly ease the stick forward, the nose will dip slightly and we'll start to move. There's no need to hurry, just ease it forward a little bit. Ok, do it." She did.

The helicopter responded exactly as Marty had explained, and the craft crept forward. She didn't know how fast she was going. Elle knew one of those displays had a speedometer on it, or whatever helicopters used, but she couldn't have taken her eyes off the horizon if there was a gun to her head. As they went, she had to remind herself to breathe normally as they moved and Marty said supportive soothing words that, frankly, she completely ignored as she focused on what she was doing. Soon the helicopter slipped out over the water and when she heard the signal, she eased the control stick back to the center position. It was at that point Marty reached out and took the controls again.

"I have control," he said gently and she was more than happy to release her grip on the controls. She took a couple deep breaths to try and come down from the adrenalin high her body was on. Elle was shaking.

"Awesome. That was fucking awesome," she said, suddenly feeling giddy. "I will never forget that for as long as I live," she said and instantly regretted it, saying things like that were in poor taste in their situation, but Marty just smiled wickedly at it.

"Really?" He said, strangely amused. "Well, I'm willing to bet you, in the next five seconds, you'll forget all about it," he said with such a seriousness that she frowned in confusion.

Her eyes caught the movement of his hand first. It was sudden and sharp and before she could question him about it; the helicopter fell from the sky.

She had lost the bet.

The helicopter nose-dived towards the river, and for a moment, she felt weightless as the craft dropped at such a speed her breath caught in her throat. Elle clawed at her thighs as her body was coming to terms with what felt like her final moments. Her eyes locked on the dark murky waters of the Hudson in front of her as it rushed up towards them, and she wanted to scream, curse, hell, do anything as she felt her time on this earth was coming to a close, but she did none of that. Crippled by a white-hot panic that seemed to hold every part of her body firmly in place where all she could do was watch. Moments before she was sure the craft would splash down into the river; Elle felt her weight shift violently in the seat and the helicopter swooped up so the view in front of her changed. Elle could now see the horizon in front of them. The helicopter was skimming dangerously close to the surface of the river. Elle looked out the side window and saw the river passing them by in a blur. It was still close enough she swore she could just reach out and stick her hand in the river. *Too close*, she thought as the craft hurled itself through the air above the water at a speed she didn't recognize. She gave Marty a pleading look, not wanting to speak because she didn't trust her voice not to just squeak. When she looked, she saw the look of absolute joy on his face. It was strange to see a man of Marty's age with such an expression, but it reassured her because the operation of the craft completely engrossed him. He gave off the air of being in complete control of the craft.

Marty noticed her looking at him, and he looked over briefly and gave her a sly wink. A wink! She would have given him a piece of her mind right then and there, but her eye caught his hand move the control stick with practiced grace. Before she could protest the helicopter lurched suddenly into the sky. She breathed in sharply as it pushed her weight back into the cushion of her chair as the helicopter climbed into the sky and banked backed towards the city. Marty leveled the helicopter off high above the city and brought the craft to a soft glide back towards the island. Feeling her stomach settle inside her, Elle let out the breath she had been holding and then promptly reached across and slapped Marty several times on his upper arm.

"Asshole," she spat as her open hand struck his shoulder for the last time and sat back in her seat in a huff as Marty just softly laughed at her.

"Come on," he teased. "That was kind of fun. This baby isn't just a pack horse to haul rich people around, you know. She wants to run. What's the point of being the last people on earth if you can't have a bit of fun, right?" He looked at her and must have seen her grim expression, because he grew silent for a moment before adding one more thing to appease her. "I would have done the same if it was my girl in that chair. I'm not picking on you. I thought it would be fun for you, like a roller coaster, you know?" He said and then turned back forward.

"Well," she said without knowing full well what she wanted to say, but not wanting silence to fill the air between them. "She probably would have hit you, too. Jesus, I think I might have peed myself a bit there," she said with a grin. The fear of the moment had passed. Her heart started back at its normal pace and she appreciated what had happened to her. Elle had felt something so powerful it had stolen her breath from her, and now that the taint of fear had drained away, she was left with a sort of giddy feeling that tickled her. For the first time in recent memory, she felt like she was truly happy.

Elle giggled softly at her own joke and when she started, she heard Marty's silly chuckle for the first time. Elle couldn't help herself and she burst out into a full-blown laughter, which Marty echoed from his seat. The moment stretched out until they both had tears in their eyes and when the top of the Prescott came into view ahead of them, the laughter subsided as the end of the ride became clear.

"Thank you, Marty," Elle said, and was meaning to say more, but Marty cut her off before she could.

"Thank you, Elle." She felt he wanted that to be the end. She obliged and looked out over the top of the buildings of Manhattan as they approached home. He brought her attention back when she heard Marty grumble something under his breath as he slowed the helicopter for the approach. Elle looked out to the helipad and noticed a trio of figures standing ominously on the surface by the stairway.

As they got closer, she could make out the silhouettes of Mason, and her least favorite duo in their little group, Dennis and Derek. If those two were together, it couldn't be good. They were like predatory sharks who only tolerated each other when it was time to eat. Unfortunately, they were Mason's right and left hand.

Mason's group had the exclusive right to carry firearms around the building whenever they felt like it, which was all the time. They enjoyed duty-free days where they basically just relaxed all day on the top three floors of the buildings. They ate when they wanted. They drank as much as they wanted. If needed, they could ask for the shirt off your back and they expected you to give it to them. They had the respect of the others in the building, appreciated, but not well liked.

Some days Elle felt like they were the prisoners and Mason's group were the guards. They were here for their protection, but also to make sure nobody got out of line and did their jobs. Her caution level rose sharply when she noticed that Derek and Dennis were both carrying large rifles. Dennis had his strapped to a sling that was over the combat fatigues he came into the group with. Derek was wearing baggy jeans shorts and had on a colorful and entirely tacky Hawaiian shirt with his rifle resting on his shoulder. Elle looked over at Marty and could tell by the look on his face, he had seen them too. Marty also must have noticed the weapons they were caring.

"Marty? What do–?"

"No matter what happens when we touch down, don't get out of the cockpit until I come get you," Marty said in a clear and grave voice that was meant to be obeyed, and not questioned. Elle felt the hairs on the back of her neck rise as a sense of danger flooded the cabin. They remained silent as he brought the helicopter in for what seemed to her as a perfect landing on the helipad. Marty quickly went about flipping switches and pressing buttons and they heard the loud noise of the engine whine down above them. "Remember, stay put until I come get you." Marty promptly exited the cockpit and latched the door behind him. Elle looked out the window as Marty approached the grim-looking trio with his arms outstretched as if he was saying: *What's going on, guys?*

From there, things went downhill fast.

Marty approached Mason and his cronies like they were old friends, like he didn't even notice those large black rifles. But that all ended when Dennis's bulk suddenly moved forward. He forcefully placed his hand on Marty's shoulder, effectively halting any forward movement in an instant. Elle feared the worst as she watched Marty's gaze sink down onto the large hand that held him in place. He looked up at Dennis, and her heart sank as she watched the wide grin appear on Dennis's face. Elle felt the tension of the meeting from inside the helicopter, but what could she do? Mason took a step towards Marty and began talking. Elle didn't know what words passed between the men, but she could tell from his expressions and body language he wasn't complimenting Marty on his fine landing. She couldn't hear anything as the sound of the engine powering down still filled the air in the cabin but she thought Marty must have responded poorly to something Mason said. Mason's face twisted up in anger and he got right in Marty's face and started yelling at him. He then pointed violently towards her in the cockpit and, feeling the attention shift to her, Elle averted her eyes from the confrontation and pretended to be having trouble with her seat belt. She fiddled with the mechanism of the seat's harness and stole small looks at the exchange between the men on the helipad. Mason still stalked menacingly in front of Marty like a jungle cat does when you look at them behind the glass at the zoo, while his two cohorts just smiled as he went on. Those smiles held no amusement and gave her chills as she looked on.

Soon enough, Mason turned to walk away and motioned for his cronies to follow. Dennis forcibly gave Marty a shove back, which sent Marty stumbling back a few steps, before turning away as if bored. Derek just grinned like an idiot and gave Marty the finger before he, too, turned and followed the others down the stairs to the stairwell door.

Marty stood for a moment, as if collecting himself, before he turned back to the helicopter and made his way up to the door and opened it for her. The engine and rotor speed had died down to a mild hum and when she exited the craft, she could still feel the slight down draft from the main rotor.

"Jesus Christ, that was intense. What was that all about?" She asked him as he reached into the cabin to unfasten her seat belt harness and motioned for her to exit the craft. "Marty?" She looked up at him nervously. He must have heard the concern in her voice because he turned to her and smiled the best fake smile he could muster.

"That? That was nothing, just a bunch of macho bullshit. Nothing you need to be worried about." He waved it off casually in the same way men always did when they didn't want to talk about something. "Good news is, I realized after talking to Mason, that I actually *do* need someone to help me with Maggie here," he said and patted the side of the helicopter lovingly.

"Maggie?" Elle remembered the picture taped to his side of the console and wondered what the name of the girl in the picture might have been. Elle was willing to bet it was Margaret. It was an endearing thought, and she felt like Marty was grudgingly showing a side of himself she didn't think existed. "I like it."

"Anyway," he continued, "You still think you're up for the job?" He actually sounded sheepish to her, like he thought she might have said no, but she didn't need to think about it. The answer was obvious. "Now you won't be flying it, but you'll help me with the pre- and post-trip inspections and any servicing she might need. It won't all be sunshine an-,"

"Yes," she burst in and then waited for him to acknowledge her answer. "Yes, I'm in. I'll do whatever it takes." She shot forward and hugged him.

She knew it was something a foolish girl would do and if she was honest about it, part of her did it because she felt it would mean a lot to Marty as well. Feeling his body tense up at the sudden contact, she gave him a quick, simple squeeze and then let him off the hook before he felt the need to reciprocate the gesture. When she stepped back, she looked into his face and saw a broad smile he was clearly trying to stifle. And was he blushing?

"I won't let you down, Marty," she said, and his face darken slightly. He breathed in sharply and let it out in a long, controlled breath. "What?"

"My name is Martin," he said finally and thumbed back to where Mason had been. "Those assholes call me Marty, but my name is Martin."

-

A week into Elle's new apprenticeship and she was alone on the helipad, next to Maggie, staring out over the dead island of Manhattan. It was both thrilling and deeply depressing as the morning air was deathly quiet. Which just felt unnatural.

Maggie, as Martin explained, was a Bell 429 helicopter. One of the finest commercial aircraft ever made, according to him. Elle couldn't help but just be impressed by the sleekness of it. She tried to imagine the sort of people Martin must have flown around in this thing. She made a note to ask him about it sometime.

She was tasked to do the 'A' inspection for the helicopter, which according to Martin, was the most basic inspection one could do. He even had a sheet for her to fill out, and he fucking well marked it after she was done. She and him had done the same inspection every morning since Martin took her under his wing. Today, however, Martin casually informed her she would be doing it by herself.

Elle brought herself a large thermos of coffee, and placed it with the inspection pad on the floor of the rear passenger compartment. She had poured herself a cup and was enjoying the warm taste of it as she looked over the dead city from her perch. The Prescott wasn't the tallest building in Manhattan, but there were few others that rose above it. So, she had a superb view of the park in front of her. Moments like these, the quiet moments, were the only times she still craved a cigarette. She decided to quit the same second it became obvious she would have to ask one of Mason's crew to get them for her. For cigarettes, it was Derek. It was bad enough Elle had to do Jackie's laundry in exchange for tampons and pads, she didn't want to even think what Derek would have her do for cigarettes.

When her coffee was finished, Elle placed the small plastic cup back on the thermos and grabbed her clipboard before she moved to the front of the craft to begin the inspection. Martin had always started at the front when he did it. It just felt right to do it the same way. Elle worked her way down the left side of Maggie and marked off the appropriate boxes as she went. Front landing light lens? Check. Left cockpit door latch? Check. Landing skid front attachment point? Check. Elle carefully checked off the boxes as she worked her way down the side of the craft.

Maggie's skin, from a distance, looked seamless. Martin had explained it was anything but. The helicopter's outer layer was actually molded aluminium panels that are riveted to the body of the craft. Each body panel is listed on the inspection form. Martin instructed her to check these panels by running her fingers along the riveted seams because, according to Martin, *you can feel a lot more than you can see.*

Elle was working her way back towards the front of the craft on the right side. She was onto the lower engine body panel, the one between the engine compartment and the rear passenger door. Elle checked the rivets here in the same manner, she reached up and ran her finger over the black rounded tops of the rivets, and then stopped.

Elle pulled her hand back and rubbed her fingers together. She found something slick was covering her fingertips; she looked down and there was definitely a sort of shine coming off her fingers. *Oil*, she thought. It ran through her like electricity. Maggie's bleeding. She struggled with the implications as she numbly looked down at her shiny fingers. She was no mechanic of any kind. Elle purposefully avoided that entire area of knowledge. Which didn't sound good, and she wasn't especially proud of it, but she preferred to leave that stuff to the boys.

However, she knew oil leaks were bad, and this one was underneath the engine compartment, so it wasn't a stretch of her imagination to be a bit startled by it. She felt she needed to approach Martin with more than greasy fingers. Further thoughts of continuing the inspection were lost as she moved to the left side of the cockpit, Martin's seat, and reached underneath the seat and felt for the roll of paper towel she knew was there. She pulled it out and ripped off a section, which she took back to the oily patch she felt above the compartment door, and wiped the paper towel across the length of the seam above the door. The stain she got when she pulled it back was far larger than what she expected and was clearly a red color, which she wasn't expecting either. She looked up and she couldn't see any oil on the skin of the craft. Against the black skin of the helicopter, the oil was practically invisible, but there it was on the towel, clear as day.

With the towel clutched firmly in her hand, Elle made her way to the stairwell and planned out her path as she struggled with the true weight of the towel in her hand. She yanked the stairwell door open, and burst down the stairs two at a time when suddenly she was reminded of something her dad once said, *you can't yell 'fire' in a crowded theatre, even if it's true.* Elle slowed on the stairs as she remembered asking why. *Because those people will kill each other trying to get out of that theatre. Fear makes people crazy. The more people involved; the crazier things get when the shit hits the fan.* She couldn't remember the situation that prompted the advice, but right now it didn't matter. Elle looked down at the oil-stained towel in her hand and she realized for the first time what she had, and what she was about to do.

Before this, she gave no thought about how to approach Martin with what she found. How she delivered the message didn't seem nearly as important as the message itself. She was about to tell Martin there was a fire in their little theatre somewhere, right in front of whoever was lucky enough to be within earshot of her. Not-so-subtly declaring their only lifeline might be in jeopardy. *Nobody can know about this*, she declared to herself as she stopped on the stairwell to fold the towel so it would fit neatly, and discreetly into her palm with the oil stain facing outward. She took a deep breath before continuing down the stairs at an outwardly calm looking pace just in case she happened upon someone in the stairwell.

Everyone knew she was helping Martin with the helicopter. Some even went as far as jokingly referring to her as his co-pilot, which she wasn't exactly upset about. If someone saw her racing down the stairs with a look that screamed panic, they would infer the worst. Then like in any close-knit community, the rumors would spread like wildfire, and she wasn't blind to their situation. Fear and anxiety had built up to a sort of powder keg that was lingering under the surface, and news like this could potentially be a match.

She opened the door to the fortieth floor with a cool film of sweat on her forehead that had nothing to do with physical exertion. She said good morning to Darcy, who met her in the hallway as he was going the other way. He waved quietly and gave her a weak smile as he passed her. The whole time she kept the hand with the soiled towel close to her thigh as she went down the hallway.

Elle turned the corner into the group's lunchroom. In the far corner of the room, her eyes locked onto Martin who was deep into his morning routine of coffee and a Louis L'Amour novel. As expected, he paid no attention to her or anyone else in the room. She herself took several steps into the room before her brain even registered the others. She smiled innocently as Brenda looked up from the card game she was having with the other two women she usually hung out with. Jolene and Brittany didn't even look up from their cards when Elle passed by their table. There was no animosity there, but after seeing the same people every day for almost two years, there's really no need for hellos and goodbyes anymore.

To her frustration, she saw Kate and Bill had brought the chess set up to the lunchroom and were playing a game at their usual table. When Kate noticed her, she smiled broadly and waved her over, which caused Bill to stretch around in his seat to have a look at who Kate was waving at. Elle shook her head slightly and slowly while smiling widely and waving back, but kept on toward Martin.

Kate's face shifted to one of concern because, of course, she could see something was wrong. In their covert sister language, the look Kate was giving her was clear. *What's wrong*? Elle's response was a subtle but unmistakable look that said, *butt out* or *not now*, she would talk to her later about it. A couple of nice things she could always rely on with her little sister, she had an inexplicably good head on her shoulders and she didn't gossip. Kate nodded her understanding and went back to her game quietly.

When she finally made it to Martin's table, the panic in Elle's head was loud enough she was afraid the others in the room could somehow hear her thoughts. *Look up*, Elle thought as she got close enough to reach out and smack Martin on his head. *Look up GODDAMNIT*! She glared at him and tried to will him to notice her until finally she aggressively cleared her throat.

"Yeah, yeah, I see you there," he said without looking up from his book. She could have screamed at him at that moment, but she forced herself to suck in a lungful of air and waited. After a moment, which felt like forever, Martin marked his page and put his book down. "You can't be done that inspe-," he said before his eyes fell onto the soiled towel neatly tucked into her palm that she was discreetly displaying for him.

She expected his eyes to bulge out of his head in surprise, or maybe even a look of concern, but what she got was a simple nod that was followed by a generous drink of his coffee. She knew he saw it; it was obvious he knew what it meant but his reaction to it was a little underwhelming.

"Okay," he said finally as he rose from his seat. "Let's go."

She followed him in silence to the roof access. Martin took the stairs carefully as he ascended with a flashlight lighting their way up the stairwell. Part of her wondered if she should take comfort in the relaxed way he climbed the stairs. She felt like she was following someone on their way to a dentist appointment.

"You did the right thing," he said finally as he opened the door to the roof access. "There's no telling how some people would react to news like that. So, you did good keeping this to yourself."

"I came as soon as I found it," Elle chimed in as she followed Martin through the door. He led her first to a spot underneath the staircase leading up to the helipad. Where there was a closed off space that served as a maintenance room that came complete with its own door. Martin quickly opened up the door and stepped inside. Elle looked inside after him and saw the space was mostly empty save for a couple ladders and a few things that were laying loosely on the floor.

"Tell me how you found the oil?" Elle did while Martin handed her the smaller of the two ladders along with a black metal toolbox. Elle took the items while finishing her story.

"Good work," he said proudly and then continued on towards Maggie. "On some crafts, it isn't as important to get so up close and personal. If Maggie was white, that leak would be easy to spot from a mile away, but black hides everything. Once we get to a certain point, you can check the mechanical compartment. It won't be as important either, because at that point, you can just check the sources of any leak. Alright," he said as he stopped by the right-side luggage compartment to set up his ladder. "Let's have a look and see what we're dealing with." It was then and with lightening clarity Elle remembered she never actually said which side of the aircraft she had found the leak. All she had said was: above the luggage compartment.

"You son of a bitch," she snapped. "You already know about the leak."

"What?" Martin called back as if he hadn't heard her, but Elle was pretty sure he knew exactly what she had said and why. Elle wasn't so much mad at him as she was ashamed of herself for not realizing this sooner.

"You already know what's leaking, don't you?" She playfully accused him as she placed the toolbox on the ground.

"Set that up over here," he pointed to a spot close to the craft and next to his ladder. "Yeah, of course I knew about it. I've known about it for months now. Started out as just a wetness around the connector, then the fluid seeped out and covered the whole thing, and maybe a month or so after that, the fluid seeped to a point where enough collected for a drip, and so on. I know everything about Maggie there is to know." He affectionately ran his hand along the skin of the craft as he said the last part. "Okay, let's take that engine cover off and I'll let you have a look and see if you can spot the source for yourself."

With that, she smiled because she hadn't expected to get a good look at the actual engine of the craft. She watched intently as Martin pulled out a small ratchet and then fished through the box until he found what he was looking for, a bit, which he popped onto the end of the ratchet and then deftly ascended the ladder. Martin coolly removed the fasteners from the engine cover at the top of the craft almost directly underneath the main rotor. With each fastener he removed, he would stoop down and hand the tiny bolt to her. Elle put each one into the pocket of her jean shorts. When he removed all the fasteners, Martin directed her onto the other ladder and with her at the back end and him at the front of the cover, they lifted it away from the body of the craft.

"Easy." Martin cautioned and for good reason, because when he lifted the cover to a certain point, the top part seemed to unlatch from the craft in a way she didn't understand or expect. She fumbled slightly as the full weight of the cover fell into her hands but she recovered quickly, and helped Martin ease the cover onto the helipad to the side of the craft. After Martin went back to the toolbox, he came back with a small flashlight in his hands. "Go on. Have a look." He nodded to his ladder in an obvious invitation. Elle said nothing when she took the flashlight, but she had a clear grin on her face as she stepped past him and up the ladder.

The massive engine was like nothing she had ever seen before. Frequently, back in her old life, she had often seen car engines. Her step-father had often done some odd jobs on their family's car in their driveway and when she finally could afford her first car, a tan Ford sedan, he had insisted in showing her how to change the car's oil. She was no mechanic, but thanks to her stepfather, she was at least familiar with most engines' anatomy. This engine, by comparison, might as well have been a piece of alien technology for how familiar it was.

"Fuck me," She blurted out in awe at the complexity of it.

"Just follow the leak back to the source. Never mind the rest of it," Martin called up from behind her.

She started at the bottom of the engine compartment around the leak's area. She first found the oil leak farther down the body of the helicopter. Elle quickly found a thin trail of a pale red oily film that seemed to reach out from the engine like a thin tendril. She shifted her weight on the ladder, reached out and grabbed a hold of the sturdy-looking piece of metal to steady herself as she leaned in to follow the trail back deeper into the compartment. She followed the trail up the side of what she assumed was a brace of some sort, and from there, it was a short distance to where four hydraulic hoses that were screwed into the body of the engine. The second one from the left was the source of the leak, it was underneath what looked like an engine mount and was somewhat obscured by a thick bundle of wires that ran the length of the engine compartment, but with the flashlight, she saw it clearly.

"I found it," Elle called to Martin and when she pulled herself back from the engine to looked back at him, he was moving the other ladder closer to hers. Martin quickly climbed up the ladder until he was on the same level as her. As soon as he was in place, she hooked her finger around the hydraulic hose and presented her findings to him.

"Right on," he said with a hint of pride in his voice. Once he confirmed the source, he went into the procedures they would need to follow in order to replace it.

Martin took his time in his explanation, pointing out the individual bolts that would have to be taken off, as well as the order in which some things would have to be removed. Now-and-then, in his instruction, he would ensure she was following and understood what needed to be done. Elle simply nodded her understanding. She didn't ask questions, but not because she felt he would look down upon her. It was just Martin's explanation was so thorough and straightforward, it left little room for misunderstanding.

"Okay, awesome," she said enthusiastically when he finished. "Let's do this."

She was excited to start, and wondered briefly if Martin would insist she change into something more appropriate for engine work. She looked cute in her jean shorts and the simple white t-shirt, but it probably wasn't what Martin had in mind. He looked ready to work in his denim work pants and flannel shirt. Hell, you could put him in the mountains and give him an axe and he'd look right at home.

"Yeah, about that," he started to say and Elle smiled to herself as she thought, *here it comes*. "We don't have the parts, the tools, or the supplies we need to do this job. The job itself is a piece of cake for the two of us, but the real problem here is, we have to go to the service hanger in order to do this." He paused and looked at her as if she understood the full meaning of what he was saying. "Which is at La Guardia." He added and let that sink in.

"The airport?" Which was a stupid thing to ask because, of course he meant the airport. There wasn't a service hanger at La Guardia high school, but she was stunned.

Because of the implications of it.

At the beginning of their tenure at the Prescott, soon after Martin showed up and saved them all with Maggie. Mason and his crew went with Martin to La Guardia to refuel the helicopter for the first time. It ended in disaster. Eight members of their group loaded into the helicopter and six of them returned and one of them, Chris Humberg, later died from a bite he received. They shot him in the head soon after.

Also lost to them, was Richard Hendricks. At the time of his death, some people considered him one of the unofficial leaders of their group. Nobody had really stepped up to lead anyone, but he had the ear of the survivors in the building. He was young, attractive, and persuasive. Richard had worked as an electrical engineer, and when it became obvious their stay in the building would benefit from him, he went to work with a few others to scavenge for useful items. He also made lists of things they would need for the long run. A lot of what they had now, the life they had made for themselves in the building, Richard made possible because of what he had planned for them. When they lost him, the entire group deflated slightly. Their collective light seemed to have dimmed significantly after that first refueling.

That seemed so long ago now, like it may have happened in another lifetime, but the repercussions of that horror were immediate. Before, people frequently discussed the outside world, some even went as far as talking about the possibility of leaving the building. Just get dropped off on the outskirts of the city and head out into the world like they were Huck Finn or some shit like that. After they had to suffer through Chris's brief illness, and even briefer time as a zombie, before Mason finally could put him down for good, nobody spoke of the outside world anymore. The Prescott gave them the illusion of safety; everybody knew it wasn't the truth, and they were okay with that. Especially after they had a small taste of what was waiting for them on the outside. People were more than happy to bury their head in the sand, and try to move on with their lives in the building.

"Shit." It was all she could think to say.

"Exactly," Martin replied.

-

Elle knew Kate had something on her mind, how could she not, but she felt it would be best to wait for Kate to come to her with her concerns instead of smothering her with reassurances. Which would probably do anything but reassure her sister. Elle finished her chapter, and put her book away. The only light in their room was a small candle that burned on the table between them that cast a low soft light throughout the room.

Kate didn't like the total darkness of the night. Early on, she woke up during the night from a dream screaming.

The next night, Elle had produced a candle she found in an office and it helped Kate get through the night. Candles were one item Kate searched for as she explored the building. She liked to have about a dozen on hand, which she kept close by her couch in a neat little cluster. This was when she liked to talk, really talk, when the light was low and the room was quiet. Elle laid there and waited.

She didn't have to wait long.

"So, when would you go?" Kate asked, like she was working her way through a mental list of all the questions she had.

"Martin wants to wait a week to give us enough time to plan out the repair." Elle kept it simple, the truth of it was Martin wanted to take this opportunity the completely service the craft. Then he had plans to pick up what spare parts he could, and bring them back to The Prescott. Thinking they could do any future light repairs he could foresee on the helipad instead of taking this risk again. "We'll probably leave in the morning, I imagine, and he said we should be gone one or two hours." She heard her sister breathe in sharply from across the room.

"That seems like a long time," she whispered.

"It might not take that long. After seven days I'm sure we'll have the entire process down to a science, but it needs to be done. So, it takes as long as it takes, I guess."

"Uh-huh," her sister cut in. "And why do *you* have to do it?" she said with a touch of venom in her voice.

"Martin needs help. This isn't something he can do by himself, and we shouldn't expect him to."

"Okay, but why do *you* have to help?" That was the question she had been waiting for, the question Elle had been dreading because she was still struggling to find a real tangible answer to that for herself.

How do you explain a gut feeling? How could she make her sister understand what she felt was right? She looked over, and in the soft light of the candle, she met Kate's eyes. Elle shifted herself on the couch so she was facing her sister and tried to explain the unexplainable.

"Why shouldn't I help? This is part of the job-," she began, but Kate cut her off.

"No, it's not," Kate said calmly, as if she was stating an undisputed fact.

"Yes, it is," Elle shot back. "It's not a part I was expecting when I signed on, but it's something I can do and there's no reason for me to sit on the sidelines and let everyone else take all the risks for me." She felt some heat enter her tone. Kate had a way of bringing that out in her. Elle forced herself to take a breath before continuing. "Martin is going to make sure nothing is going to go wrong," she said and she couldn't explain it, but Martin's name seemed a better choice for that statement than Mason.

"Who else is going?"

"Mason and his entire crew, there will be room in the helicopter for one more, but I doubt anyone else will be coming." *Who else would be stupid enough to volunteer for this*, she thought it but she didn't dare say it.

"What are you going to be doing?" It was a fair question and one she had been expecting.

"I'm staying with the helicopter." She tried to put a subtle emphasis on it to push the point home. "My job is to take the old hose off and put the new one on, plus Martin wanted to do that servicing, so I may do that as well. I really don't know yet. We haven't worked out all the details. Martin wants to meet in the morning to go through it all," she said with practised ease.

"Hmm," Kate was silent for a moment while she thought about what she had been told so far. "What did Mason say when you told him?"

"He wasn't thrilled." Which unfortunately was an understatement. When the time came to go up to Mason's floor and let him know what they needed to do, she expected their de facto leader to take the news gravely, maybe even second guess Martin's assessment. What she didn't expect was a disheveled Mason to seem to be shaken by the news, angered by it even. She didn't expect to stand there with Martin and have to deal with his venomous complaints and accusations.

"I think after last time he was hoping to never have to go back there again." Elle didn't need to explain what the last time was. Everybody in the building still remembered the LaGuardia disaster. "After he settled down though, he and Martin agreed on a timeline." That wasn't exactly true, either. After Mason regained his composure, Martin told him what needed to be done and when they would be ready to go, and Mason simply nodded and said *his* people would be ready and walked away.

"A week?" Kate asked again.

"Yeah."

"What's the date, anyway?" Kate asked offhandedly. Elle pulled out her phone and checked the calendar app.

"Saturday, June the eleventh." She replied.

"What year?"

"Twenty-twenty four, why?" It was likely Kate didn't know the exact date, and Elle would have bet money on it being Thursday. But Kate knew what year it was. *What was she on about?*

"It might be important later," Kate paused for effect. "You know, when I'm telling my kids about the day I lost my sister because she wanted to be a stupid helicopter pilot." Elle looked at her incredulously through the dim light.

"Jesus Christ, that's a bit dramatic, don't you think? You make it seem like I'm marching off to my death. Fuck." She snapped off the sentence in a sharp tone. She wanted to talk to Kate about this, reassure her, but if she was going to be stupid like that then it was going to make it so much harder to get through to her.

"Last time they went to LaGuardia, it was an effing disaster." Kate had brought the volume and tone of her voice back to a more conversational level, but she wasn't backing down. "And two people didn't come back from that trip." In the darkness, she could see Kate shoot up her fingers as if Elle needed help to figure out how many two were. "And those guys knew what they were doing. Who do you think won't make it back this time?"

"That was the first time they ever went on a run, things are different now. Mason and his crew have been on probably more than a dozen runs since then, and they'll know what to expect. They'll be ready for whatever we come across. Martin said he used to work at the service hanger. Before he flew helicopters, Martin was fixing them. So, he knows the layout of the hanger, where the tools are, the parts. This is going to be nothing like last time." She didn't know if any of that was actually true. Mason and his lot being more experienced in this sort of thing, that was true, but the rest was a bunch of half-truths she pulled out of the air to make Kate feel better about what she was going to do, and maybe at the same time Elle was comforting her own butterflies. "I'm not going to say it'll be easy, but it needs to be done and everybody involved, including myself, is ready to do whatever it takes to get this done because if we don't," She looked at her sister grimly. "If we don't fix that helicopter, we are *all* in trouble. We need that helicopter to survive."

"But *I* need *you* to survive," Kate's voice weakened as she fought through tears Elle couldn't see, but she felt them. Elle's own eyes watered as she rose from her couch to cross the room to Kate. "Like if you died, I... I would..." Kate couldn't finish the thought, but she didn't need to. Elle was on her, Kate sat up and the two Russo sisters met in a teary embrace. Kate sank into her bosom sobbing and Elle's heart broke as she stroked her sister's hair. She hated herself for doing this to Kate, putting her through this. Even as she held her crying sister, though, Elle knew deep down she was doing the right thing. Something that was vital, and this, was an unfortunate by-product of her commitment.

"I miss mom and dad," Kate blurted out suddenly, like it was a confession, and began crying with a renewed vigor.

"Oh sweetie," Elle soothed. "I miss them too, so much." It stung to say because the truth of it was something she had been trying to lock away, and now that they exposed the pain, it still ached like a fresh wound.

"I can't lose you, too. I just can't." Kate's little body shook in her arms under the weight of her sobs. Elle's resolve slipped momentarily as she sat there trying to comfort her sister. They were the last of their happy family. She and her sister were lucky to have each other, and they knew it. They simply assumed all thoughts and discussions of the future that they would be there for each other, and now, maybe for the first time, Kate questioned that. Elle felt the power of her sister's pain in her bones, but it didn't sway her. In the end, she was doing this *for* her sister.

After some time, she didn't know how long, as long as Kate needed for her tears to ebb, they moved with an unspoken synergy until Elle was laying with her sister nuzzled into her arms. She didn't know when, but when she looked down, Kate had fallen asleep in her arms. Her resting face looked so calm and peaceful. Elle prayed it reflected what was happening on the inside.

While she waited for sleep to descend upon her, Elle looked over at the candle burning on the table and her eyes focused on the tiny little flame dancing within its glass cage. Despite herself, her eyes stung with tears and a gentle sob broke free from between her lips.

Not now! Elle couldn't help herself as she looked at that weak little flame that flickered with the slightest breath of air. She saw her and her sister's fate in that tiny little flame that needed to be within its glass cage, or risk being snuffed out. Their entire existence depended on the isolation from the outside elements, but for how long? How long could she keep her and Kate's tiny flame burning?

Elle didn't know the answer.

Chapter 9

Kenshiro

Whump!

Kenshiro's fist hit the bag with a mild force, and the hundred-pound leather punching bag responded with a gentle swing.

He and the boy, Elliott, have been in each other's company for two nights now, and it was excruciating. Since their first meeting, Kenshiro might have said a dozen words to the boy. Mainly questions he needed the answers to, like: *Are you hungry?* Beyond that, he found he had little to say to the boy. Maybe his social skills had eroded from his time alone on the road. Kenshiro regarded the small framed teenager the same way a wild animal might react to something unfamiliar. Like the teen was some unknown threat that, at any moment, and without warning, would cause him harm.

Whump!

His clenched fist recoiled from the bag in a very familiar and almost comforting way. It felt good to hit a bag again. Kenshiro rolled his shoulders to loosen tense muscles and swayed his upper body down and away like he was avoiding an unseen punch before he moved back into the bag for a quick one-two combination. *Whump, whump.* Kenshiro breathed out forcefully through his teeth with each blow like they had taught him so long ago.

"*Stay loose, breathe,*" he remembered his striking coach telling him frequently. "*Tense muscles are slow muscles.*"

Whump-whump-whump!

Of course, the boy, Elliott, didn't seem to have any problems adjusting to Kenshiro's presence. Quite the opposite. The last two nights he wouldn't shut up, almost as if Elliott might drop dead if he went two minutes without speaking. Mostly it was long droning pointless stories from the boy's past. Like when he hit his first home-run, or when he and his parents went on a vacation to the coast. If that was all it was, Kenshiro might be able to tolerate it, but it was the questions that made his blood boil. He would usually give a simple one-word answer and hope the boy would move on to something else. He didn't want Elliott to know anything about him, just in case the time came when Kenshiro might have to put a bullet in his head. At this point in their relationship, that was still a genuine possibility and, in his experience, it was much easier to shoot someone if he didn't like them.

WHUMP

Kenshiro rocketed his fist into the bag, approximately where the head of someone his size would be. He threw from his shoulder and when he exhaled with the blow, it came out like a sort of guttural grunt and the bag recoiled violently away.

WHUMP

That was the other thing about the boy. There was something not quite right with him. As his father sometimes liked to say; *Something was wrong with his head.* It didn't take long to notice; within minutes of the boy speaking, Kenshiro suspected there was a problem there.

At first, it was the boy's repeated use of the phrase 'Momma said'. When he pointed a gun at the boy, he heard it first. Kenshiro wasn't trying to hide the weapon, quite the opposite. Kenshiro was using it as a gentle show of force as if to say: *I'm in control.* The boy hardly noticed it and instead asked if Kenshiro was wearing one of his father's shirts, which he was, and then after that Elliott immediately asked Kenshiro if he would like some tea and then followed it up with,

"I don't have any tea, but *momma said* you should always ask a guest if they would like a beverage." Kenshiro didn't know why the boy wouldn't simply have offered him water, which was the only thing Elliott had, and he didn't ask because at the time it wasn't important.

At first, he chalked it up to the long periods of isolation, when there's nobody around to talk to, or interact with, it was easy to develop little quirks to deal with the loneliness, and he should know. If there had been anyone around to hear some of the bat-shit crazy things Kenshiro has said in his own isolation, they would think he was crazy too. This thing with the boy, though, it wasn't as simple as that. It went deeper.

Whump-whump-whump-WHUMP-WHUMP.

Kenshiro also found out the hard way the kid was irrationally temperamental, and when he lost his cool, the frail teen seemed to fall in a hole of unbridled rage. It happened last night. They argued over sleeping arrangements in the tiny house. Elliott insisted Kenshiro couldn't sleep in his parent's bed, and as politely as he could, Kenshiro argued there wasn't a reason he shouldn't.

Looking back on it, it was a stupid argument and one that Kenshiro could have avoided, but he put his foot down on this issue. A way to get back control of a situation he felt was not entirely in his control anymore, and it completely backfired. He had lost his temper and told the poor boy if he couldn't sleep in the master bedroom maybe he should just leave. Kenshiro would take all the food the boy had been enjoying so much, and they would part ways. It was a childish threat. He then stared down a boy who was probably a decade younger than he was, shorter than him by more than a foot, and had special needs with that ultimatum hanging in the air. It wasn't his greatest moment. The boy's face reflected the storm of emotions raging on the inside.

At first, he looked mad, and then his face shifted to one of terror, and then he glared at Kenshiro with murder in his eyes Finally he cracked, and the tears flowed and he screamed so loud Kenshiro worried he might attract any undead who might be nearby.

"YOU CAN'T!" Elliott wailed repeatedly and his fists suddenly started pounding the sides of his head almost in tune with what he was saying. It was like the boy suddenly became possessed. "YOU CAN'T."

Fearing he might injure himself Kenshiro stepped in and grabbed the boy's clenched fists but the boy shrieked like he was on fire, and violently pulled away from him, unintentionally punching Kenshiro in the face to scramble free. Elliott then bolted up the stairs, once again screaming.

"YOU CAN'T! YOU CAN'T!" Elliott noisily disappeared up the stairs. Kenshiro heard a door slam and for the next two hours he heard the boy switch between his angry chant and pained sobs within his room.

WHUMP-Whump

Kenshiro grunted with every strike. He wasn't hitting as hard as he could, but it was close. His new body, the one formed from the hardships of the undead world, was bigger, more powerful than the body he remembered having. The bag swung with wild abandon under the weight of his strikes. He pushed his punches out from his core, put his hips behind his kicks. Every strike had a crippling force behind it. He didn't plan to stay as long as he did. Taking a break to punch the bag wasn't initially part of it. Nor did he plan on working up a sweat, and he certainly didn't plan on thinking about the boy, but here he was doing all three. His frustration seeped into every blow and spurned him on to hit harder, faster. To feel the burn in his muscles, as if that burn would cleanse him of the shame he felt from the night before. Every breath sounded like the deep growl of an angry dog that seemed to burn in his throat on the way out.

WHUMP!

Kenshiro went to sleep in his prized bed well after dark. Hours after the last sounds escaped Elliott's room. Kenshiro made his way to the room with the use of a small flashlight he had cupped in his hands. Once he was in the room, Kenshiro moved a somewhat heavy decorative wooden chest in front of the door, effectively blocking it from opening. It wouldn't stop someone from opening the door indefinitely, but it would not only alert Kenshiro to the intrusion, but it would give him enough time to shoot whoever was coming through the door.

In this scenario, Kenshiro supposed, it would be the boy. At the time he didn't even care that he had bullied a special needs child so he could sleep in his dead parent's bed, it didn't even register on his radar. He just wanted to get away from this shit hole world for a time. Just long enough to recharge his batteries. He would smooth this all over with the kid in the morning. He pulled the flower print sheet off the bed, and there it was, innocently packaged in a neat white envelope with the prettiest writing on the cover he could imagine.

It read: *To whomever finds this. Please read!*

His first instinct was to throw it away, burn it, but Kenshiro pushed that impulse down. This was different. There might be vital information in that letter concerning the boy. Kenshiro worried there might be a list of medications the boy would need. He worried about that because prescription medications in this day and age would be in short supply, and nearly impossible to come by without taking some significant risks. He took a deep breath and in one sharp motion, like he was ripping off a band-aid, he freed the letter from the envelope and unfolded it.

My name is Emily Newman. If you're reading this, I guess we didn't make it back from my sister's like we had planned. If you're reading this in an empty house, please help yourself to anything you need and good luck to you. If, however, you found my son Elliott and he, by some miracle, is still alive, please look after him. It was too dangerous to take him with us. We knew there was a chance we might not make it back and we couldn't risk taking him. I couldn't bear leaving him, but... He's a special boy in every sense of the word. He can be difficult to handle and he needs a lot of patience and kindness, but he is our son and the most precious thing in this world to me. I have nothing to offer you. Please, please, PLEASE help Elliott get somewhere safe. Somewhere he doesn't have to be afraid. Somewhere he can be loved. We can't provide those things anymore, so I ask you for the impossible. Keep him safe, take care of him, love him if you can, and make sure he knows his parents thought of him at the end.

When he finished the note, the lone piece of paper seemed to become heavier in his hands, like the weight of the words added to the weight of the paper Emily wrote it on. He took a couple of deep breaths and tried to collect his thoughts. The letter added no information that might be useful to his situation with the boy, but it added a whole new level to his dilemma.

Since he found the boy, there had been a looming implication of what contact with him might bring, and his collection of inner voices all spoke out for the same thing, *leave that kid alone and walk away*. All except one, and she didn't even speak the loudest. So, he listened to her, and now he was getting deeper into the emotional muck of the situation. So goddamn deep it felt like he couldn't move, like someone had already planned out his next moves, and Kenshiro had no proper control over it. It pissed him off because deep down Kenshiro knew what he could do, what he *should* do, but that wasn't what he was going to do, because he knew he had to do the right thing here. He knew if he did what the voices wanted, he would give up another piece of his humanity to do it, and he didn't know if he could pay that kind of price. Not just for the opportunity to live another day.

Animals merely survive, son. Kenshiro heard the voice of his father in his head so clearly his eyes watered slightly as he punched the bag. *Human beings should live, because to survive is to only think about yourself and what's best for you. To live, however, you must think about all the people around you because we are only independent when we are alone.* His father would be so ashamed of him if he saw how Kenshiro struggled with such an obviously morally right decision as he looked down at Emily's letter.

Whump!

He made Emily's bed back up, so it looked just the same as it did when he first entered the room, then he moved the large chest back into its original position before exiting the room and heading back downstairs to the couch. He would sleep there tonight, the drama and damage he had done to force his way into Emily's room was a painful reminder of what kind of person he had become, and how far he would have to go in order to make this work.

WHUMP

The next morning, he left before Elliott came down from his room. They could talk it over later after they had some more time to cool down.

WHUMP-WHUMP

Even with his gear on, he moved freely and quickly around the bag, picking his spots and hitting them with lethal force. Constantly alternating between kicks and punches, body blows and head shots. He mixed it all in as he moved around the bag with almost unnatural grace and precision. Fueled by the events of the last two days, he sent his frustration into the bag a little at a time with each strike, punctuated by the deep heavy grunts of air he pushed out with them.

WHUMP

He cursed whatever cosmic force that might be out there running this shit show that brought this helpless boy to his doorstep. He wished he had never even seen the boy. Wished he had never read that stupid fucking letter that was in his pocket. *Fuck Emily, they should have taken him with them, a family belongs together.* Maybe that way, at least when the end came, Elliott would be by his parents' side. You know, where he should be. *Help Elliott get somewhere safe.* Where was that, exactly? What magical place could he take this kid where he would be safe? It didn't exist, not anymore, not anywhere in this world.

WHUMP

With that last hit, he stepped back from the bag. A thin film of sweat covered his face, and it felt like he was breathing fire with each breath. Before he even knew what he was doing, he sucked in a lung full of air and let it out in a deafening howl.

"FUUUUUCCCCCK!" He could feel the muscles in

his neck strain as he screamed at the bag, trying to push all his frustration, fears and anger out in one push. It didn't end quickly, but lasted several seconds, and he forced every bit of air out of his lungs. When he was done, when he finally got it all out, Kenshiro felt spent, but good. Like the end of a long and bitter fight with a rival, whereby the end of the fight, all the hatred and animosity just seemed to evaporate into mist when the last bell rang, and it was over. He stood there in that dusty forgotten garage, taking in long breaths and watching the bag's momentum die a little more with each swing. When it finally became still, he muttered into the empty room.

"Are you done?" By that he meant, *are you done bitching*?

The truth of it had been gnawing at him since reading the letter. Elliott didn't need somewhere that was safe. There was no place on this earth that was safe, so Elliott needed someone to keep him safe. He needed Kenshiro. Kenshiro didn't like it. In fact, he hated it, but it was an unavoidable truth. There was no scenario he could think of where he could walk away from that kid, and still be able to look himself in the mirror afterwards. Maybe that's a good thing, maybe that was something he should try to hold on to. Of course, it was just as likely he was signing his death warrant here. In his experience, there was nothing more dangerous than trying to help someone else, but he had decided what he would do and finally made his peace with it. There was nothing left to do except to get down to it.

Kenshiro walked out of the dusty garage through the same side entrance he entered through. He encountered, almost immediately, a withered figure with long slimy looking locks of hair in a Led Zeppelin shirt and nothing else. The zombie had been a man once and Kenshiro couldn't help but notice something had previously removed the man's penis, and by the look of the ghastly wound, they pulled it off.

Kenshiro winced amusedly at the thought of what that must have felt like, and then smashed the zombie skull into the side of the building. Its hair did indeed feel slimy, but you can't be squeamish about such things all the time. Kenshiro hopped back into the truck, intent on heading back to Elliott's little house. In the north-eastern corner of the town, he was constructing a pyre. He had collected a few corpses on his way out of the town when he first saw Elliott and it was easier than dragging them all the way back to the pyre in the field. He reminded himself they still had to be lit, and that would have to be done at night if he wanted to attract the most undead. Kenshiro opened the door to the truck and wondered if Elliott would like to spend the night in town tomorrow. *First things first*, he thought as he turned the key and the truck's engine came to life. He had some serious repair work to do with Elliott.

Fifteen minutes later, Kenshiro pulled the truck into the Newman property and, because it was an open yard, he drove the truck close to the front door to be easily accessible if needed for a quick exit. By the time he shut off the engine, he was feeling relatively optimistic about the coming conversation he had planned out with the boy. *Elliott. His name is Elliott.*

That wouldn't last, though.

He exited the cab and was heading to the box of the truck to unload the bags. Kenshiro had a surprise for Elliott. When the shrill sound of the screen door of the house came from behind him, Kenshiro turned to look as his hand eased down to his knife sheathed on his leg, out of habit. There on the front step, stood the boy, Elliott.

Red faced, cheeks puffy, sunken-in tortured eyes,

and shaking. One look at that face, and Kenshiro newly appreciated just how badly he had fucked things up between the two of them already, without even trying. Elliott was in agony, not physical agony, but by the look on his face and the tendons straining on his neck, Kenshiro saw an inner turmoil that scared him. He was stunned by it and for a moment he just stood there like an idiot.

"You said you were leaving," Elliott accused him with venom in his voice. The rawness in his tone struck Kenshiro and before he could get out a sound, Elliott continued. "Last night you said if you didn't sleep in the bed, you would leave." Emotion forced Elliott to pause when his voice broke in sobs and more tears streamed down his face. "And you left." He looked at him with pleading eyes. "You... *left.*" He said again and punctuated with renewed sobs so forceful Elliott's slight frame hunched over and his whole body shook with each sob.

"But I came back," Kenshiro said finally, feeling like an asshole because it was the first and only thing he could think of to say, and he had said it like those words alone should be enough to fix it. Elliott continued crying loudly, like he didn't even hear it. Kenshiro straightened up and took a step closer to the boy. He had to do better. "I'm sorry," he started and searched himself for the words before continuing. "I was wrong. I shouldn't have said those things last night."

"You left," Elliott said again between sobs. He wasn't even looking at him anymore, just staring at the ground and sobbing fiercely. It wasn't a display. It wasn't an act. The rawness of Elliott's anguish hung in the air like smoke.

"I know, I know," Kenshiro said, trying to ease Elliott's sobs from a safe distance, and failing horribly. Kenshiro took another step closer to the boy, and sadly, it took a lot more effort than he imagined. When Kenshiro continued on, it surprised him when his own voice broke and his eyes stung under the weight of Elliott's sorrow. "But I'm here now, and I'm not going anywhere." Elliott wasn't looking at him, so he tried to push his meaning into his words. *I will never leave your side again, I promise*, Kenshiro thought as he looked at the frail weeping figure. Elliott looked up and his sobs abated slightly. In his eyes, Kenshiro could see a glimmer of something, hope maybe, but whatever it was, Kenshiro didn't want to see that spark leave the boy's eyes ever again.

"I promise," he said and looked deep into the boy's eyes and tried to will him to believe what he was saying, because it was the truth. At least, Kenshiro hoped it would be. Elliott broke into sobs again, but this time it was a different variety. Kenshiro couldn't explain it, but it just felt different, better somehow, and Elliott ran to him with his arms wide open.

The sudden movement surprised Kenshiro. He braced himself for the boy as he collided with him and, to his surprise, his arms moved on their own and welcomed the boy into an embrace. It felt strange to hold the boy in his arms, foreign. A part of him, maybe the lizard brain, wanted to recoil away from it, but Kenshiro held his ground. *This is okay*, and on some level, maybe even good.

"You can't leave, Kenchurro." Elliott pressed his face into the holster of the .22 pistol on the breast of his vest, and for the first time in a long time Kenshiro wished he wasn't wearing it. "You can't. You can't." Elliott droned on the same way he had the other night except quieter and saying it through sobs of what Kenshiro hoped was relief. How much of an asshole could he be? Last night, he had his head up his ass so far he misunderstood what Elliott had meant when he screamed, '*you can't*'. He selfishly assumed the boy's extrapolated meaning was '*you can't* sleep in my parent's bed', but Elliott was actually begging him to stay.

He *had* to do better.

"I won't," he said into the boy's hair repeatedly. Every time Elliott cried 'you can't' into his chest, he would respond, "I won't." Each time he said it, Elliott sobbed a little less and soon it stopped all together and they stood in silence, holding each other.

None of this was part of his plan.

"Let's go have some dinner," Kenshiro said softly as he pulled Elliott free. The feeling of the boy's spine sticking through his back was still fresh on the tips of Kenshiro's fingers. Looking at him now, he looked like he could drop at any moment. The emotional trauma he felt during Kenshiro's time away had drained whatever reserves the boy still had. "You'll feel better once we get some food in you." Elliott nodded his agreement while looking at the ground and sniffling slightly. Kenshiro moved to the back of the truck and pulled out the green bag. "I have a surprise for you."

"Yeah," Elliott looked up curiously. "What kind of surprise?" Kenshiro approached him and dropped the bag on the ground and unzipped it enough for him to reach his hand in, but not enough for Elliott to see.

It was a ploy, and it worked beautifully. Elliott's dour mood came to an abrupt end as he tried to peer inside the bag, to no avail.

"What is it?" He asked. His curiosity brought a new light to his voice and a bit of a grin to his face, the pain of moments ago was forgotten.

Kenshiro felt his hand wrapped around the prize and pulled it free from the bag. Elliott looked at the blue colored Gatorade with delight and waited for Kenshiro to hand it to him, and even when he did, Elliott still looked up for approval before taking it.

"The blue one is my favorite," Elliott said as he looked down at the bottle in his arms with a sort of muted awe.

"I know." Kenshiro had nearly brought Elliott to tears with the first bottle that was laid on the table for him on that first night. "And there's more."

Kenshiro pulled a box of macaroni and cheese from the green bag. Elliott's eyes grew to the size of dinner plates as he audibly sucked in a lungful of air in amazement. He didn't scream, thank God, but he visibly shook with excitement.

"Come on, let's go eat." Kenshiro laid his hand on Elliott's shoulder, feeling a sting of sadness as he clearly felt the boy's collarbone as he did so, and gently led him back into the house.

The hardest part of curing the boy's starvation was getting him to eat the small portions in front of him first, before he gorged himself into sickness, like he had on the first night. Their feeding routine was simple, two vitamins to be taken twenty minutes before the actual meal, to give it time to make its way into the boy's system, and a small portion of the meal to start with. A few spoonsful at a time in the beginning was all Elliott could keep down.

He would keep Elliott distracted with a board game, or maybe a card game he liked, whatever it took to keep the boy from pouting for more food. Kenshiro developed a system of feeding Elliott a small portion every half hour. Usually after his third portion, Elliott would get tired as what little energy his frail frame had left was being used to digest the food he ate. Elliott slept a lot during those first few days and Kenshiro was fine with that.

Kenshiro didn't dare leave, for fear the boy would wake up and find he wasn't there, but it was nice to have some time to himself. Kenshiro was a little ashamed to admit it, but he found being with Elliott exhausting. He was like Elliott in that way, as he could only handle this new companionship in small portions before his body seemed to reject it. However, instead of throwing up or some other physical reaction, he just felt a strange sort of tension building within him. Kenshiro didn't know what would happen if that feeling ever reached a breaking point and he wasn't about to find out. Thankfully, Elliott's food comas gave him time to settle himself by taking a walk around the property to make sure they were still safe within the small house.

Those walks usually ended with boredom, which sometimes left Kenshiro with a dull sense of disappointment because it would have felt good to release some of his tension towards the undead. The more walks he took, the weirder it became that he found no stumbling, haggard undead figures invading their little piece of Colorado. In the past Kenshiro found that on the days he isolated himself completely from the outside, no light, sound, or visible movement, there would still be at least one zombie bumping around outside the building he was in, after a day or so.

There was no hiding from them.

They knew where you were, even if the undead didn't know *exactly* where you were. By the second day of peace, Kenshiro became suspicious. He searched the property thoroughly, every inch, every building, to ensure they were not unintentionally hiding somewhere.

Every day, the birds chirped on the property. In the past, that was one thing that told him the area he was in was free of the undead. Usually it was a rare occurrence, but now, he had heard the sweet chirps of the smaller native birds every day. *How was that possible? It has to be Elliott. This has to be because of him, but how?*

They spent the bulk of the week playing games and simply talking. To Kenshiro, it felt wrong. He felt he had been in this house for entirely too long, and it made him nervous. Even though, since he had been in Elliott's company, there had been a noticeable decrease in the amount of undead he found in the mornings after they awoke. Like, zero. There had been none around the house and property the whole time he stayed there. There had only been the two on that first day, the day he rescued Elliott. Since then, he and the boy had enjoyed the strange isolation from the undead. Kenshiro couldn't remember the last time he went this long without seeing a zombie.

His/their food supply was draining, and he knew soon he would have to go back into town to resupply, but Kenshiro put that off as long as possible because he and Elliott had a new arrangement. The boy made him promise he wouldn't leave the property without him in tow. That promise complicated things because Kenshiro struggled with how he could keep it, and keep Elliott safe at the same time. They would have to work something out. He had put little thought into that yet; it was a problem for the future that he would address when Elliott was healthy enough.

By the fourth day, Kenshiro felt Elliott's physical progress was coming along nicely. He was no doctor, but Elliott's energy levels seem to be improving. Before, he moved very much like the undead, weak muscles pulling on stiff joints. Elliott moved like he was pushing against some invisible force that restricted every movement. After Kenshiro got some real food through him, the kid's response had been subtle but immediate. The color returned to his skin. Elliott walked around more fluidly and with more confidence, he still slept a lot, but after each sleep the boy seemed to awaken with more life in him.

They spent the daylight hours playing all kinds of games. Elliott seemed to have an endless amount of board and card games he liked to play. Kenshiro grudgingly obliged, feeling a strange pull inside him to do something more… familiar. Like clearing houses of zombies and searching for supplies.

Surviving.

This wasn't surviving. Kenshiro didn't know exactly how he would categorize the time they spent together. During these times, Kenshiro studied the boy closely, looking for cracks in his psyche. He didn't even know what he was looking for, but Kenshiro had a general feeling when the cracks showed, he would notice them. Even if he didn't know what to do about them if they did present themselves. He needed to know what he was dealing with if he was going to move forward with the boy in tow. Eventually the amount of food would run out and it would force them to leave, but Kenshiro wouldn't allow it to get to that point. For now, he would wait and watch. The entire time playing Elliott's games.

The boy talked non-stop during the games. First, he would talk about the game itself, what he liked about it, how long he had been playing it, who bought him the game and so on. From there, Elliott would lapse into stories about other times he had played it, who he had played with and whether he won the game or lost. Kenshiro listened as intently as he could, while now-and-then, asking a few follow-up questions which Elliott was all too happy to answer.

It wasn't all about him though. Elliott was pretty quick to ask Kenshiro questions about himself and the life he left before 'the grey people came'. Kenshiro gently avoided them and simply changed the subject by asking Elliott more questions. He didn't want this to be about him. Kenshiro's past was still a wound he didn't want to expose, though that didn't stop Elliott from trying.

And succeeding.

-

"So, what does your mom do? Like, for a job?" Elliott asked, catching the baseball firmly in his glove. He wanted to be outside today. It was a beautiful day after all, and Kenshiro couldn't see why not. It was then that Elliott produced two baseball gloves from somewhere in the tiny house and came back, almost vibrating with excitement.

How could Kenshiro say no?

"You asked that already." Kenshiro replied, as a matter-of-fact, as he waited for Elliott to throw the ball back.

"I know, but you never said anything," Elliott held onto the ball when he asked, and by the way he was standing, Kenshiro had a feeling he wouldn't throw the ball until he had an answer. "So, what did she do?" Elliott looked at him expectantly, and Kenshiro returned his gaze for a moment. They stood there stubbornly until Elliott added, "Why don't you want to talk to me?" He asked innocently and with no weight to the question like it was just an idle curiosity, but to Kenshiro it was anything but.

"It's not that I…," Kenshiro said without really knowing how to answer the question. "She did nothing. She died when I was young." With nothing to dress it up, he just told the plain truth. Simple as that, she died, nothing fancy.

"Ahh," Elliott cooed. He looked genuinely hurt by what he had learned. "I'm really sorry to hear that." Kenshiro simply held up his glove to signal Elliott to throw the ball.

"It was a long time ago. I don't really remember too much about her," he confessed as he caught the ball. He didn't mean to say it. It sort of slipped out. The truth of it stung a bit. There had been days when Kenshiro had done an inventory of his memories of his mother. He hated to admit it, but pieces of those memories had slipped away from him. Little details, little pieces of a puzzle that went missing over time, and now what he had left wasn't so much an exact memory of her, but an impression of what she might have been.

"What do you remember about her?" Elliott asked absently, like it was the next logical question. Kenshiro took a deep breath, and searched the wisps of what he had of her that would satisfy Elliott as he returned the ball.

"She would read to me for a bit when I went to bed," he said trying to think of something that was the farthest from the sore spot on his soul from the loss of his mother. Before he threw the ball in his hand, Kenshiro had a memory of her sitting politely on the side of the bed, book in her lap with her delicate fingers holding it open and turning the pages.

"Momma says reading is important. She read to me every night too." Elliott then listed off his favorite books that his mother had read to him. Kenshiro was thankful it had taken the spotlight off of him, but truthfully, he wasn't really listening to Elliott anymore. Kenshiro was thinking of his mother and what he remembered about her. It had been some time since he had actually taken a moment to think about her, not the hard memories, not the ones where he sat alone in the hospital with tiny red flecks of her blood on his shirt. He didn't think about her loss, he thought about *her,* and all the things that made her special.

"She liked to dance," Kenshiro said abruptly, cutting off whatever Elliott was saying. He didn't mean to say it, but it was something he had forgotten and when he remembered seeing her in the kitchen moving to the music on the radio, it was like he opened a door to a memory and what was inside struck him.

He caught the ball almost in a daze.

"She would make dinner at night." Those nights, it was usually just him and his mother. Back in those days, his father spent his precious time working or training, and didn't get home until after Kenshiro was asleep. "She would play music on the radio and dance around the kitchen as she made dinner. When I was sad, she would do this silly little dance to make me feel better." She had a dancer's grace. She might have been a dancer, he didn't know. After she had died, who she had been before she was his mother had become less important to him. His father might have known, but he too, talked little about her after she died.

"Are you gonna throw the ball?" Elliott called over, and it shook Kenshiro from his daze, only to look down to see the ball was in his hand. How long had he been holding the ball and standing there with it? He didn't know, but it was long enough to get Elliott's attention. He looked up to see the boy with his gloved hand up and ready. When Elliott could see he had Kenshiro's attention, he shook his glove expectantly.

"Sorry," Kenshiro lazily threw the ball back. What he had said surprised him. How easy it had been, and how he felt after he had said it. It wasn't terrible. There was a stain of sorrow and sadness that went with every memory he had of her. How could there not be? But there was a comfortable warmth to those memories he had neglected as well.

They continued to talk as they threw the ball back and forth, and a few times Kenshiro allowed himself to add to the conversation instead of just being present for it. It had taken five days of them being together, but Elliott had finally worn him down.

At first it slipped out, but in the end, he had decided from that point on that he shouldn't be trying to keep the boy at an arm's length, maybe the opposite. As hard as it was, he shouldn't be so guarded. People are social animals. They carve out social connections and benefit from them even if the individual wasn't aware; it's hard-wired into our brains. Kenshiro didn't like to admit it, but it felt good to hear someone's voice. To listen to thoughts that weren't his own. Elliott was perfect, because he said everything that was on his mind, and he had no qualms about taking the lead in a conversation, and Kenshiro had no problem letting him. He let himself enjoy the small moment the two of them were sharing. It wasn't a big moment, but it was nice to take a break from the ever-present fear of snapping teeth and cold dead hands.

It couldn't last, though.

"Uh-oh," Elliott said as he abandoned his next toss to point towards the road with sudden alarm. Kenshiro didn't need to look to know what he was pointing at, but he did, anyway. By the gate, maybe fifty feet away, he saw two undead figures. One was bumping helpless against the corner of the gate with its arms outstretched and its focus squarely on them, and the other one slipped through the partially opened gate and was slowly crossing the space between them. It was close enough Kenshiro could just make out its weak groans. "I guess we should go inside, huh?" Elliott said, obviously disappointed to have to end their game prematurely.

"No," Kenshiro said, taking off his glove and letting it drop to the ground. "There's only two of them. I'll take care of it." He said, switching gears back into survival mode and hearing the change in his voice. Kenshiro took a quick look around them to make sure those two were the only ones he had to worry about before moving towards them. He didn't get too far before he heard Elliott speak up behind him.

"I betcha I can hit them from here," Elliott said, and when Kenshiro turned back to him he was holding up the ball in his hand excitedly. "I can, just watch." Elliott didn't wait for a reply before he shook his glove off his hand and let it fall to the ground. He then took on a serious look as he wound up severely and launched the ball from his hand with a grunt. Kenshiro couldn't deny the boy had a good arm on him, but at that distance he felt the boy was wasting his time.

"Bullshit," Kenshiro mumbled to himself as he watched the arc of the ball as it left the boy's hand, and travel up and towards the front figure. The closer it got to the target, the more Kenshiro believed the boy might actually strike the stumbling figure, he pictured the ball bouncing uselessly off the zombie's red checkered shirt that had the one sleeve torn off to reveal the badly chewed up arm underneath.

"Fuck off," Kenshiro said quietly, astounded as he witnessed the ball crash into the top corner of the zombie's face, right by the hairline. After which, the ball rebounded off its skull and flew off to the side. The zombie rebounded as well in the opposite direction of the impact, like an invisible fist had punched it in the head. He turned back to Elliott, fully aware of the look of amazement that was on his face.

Elliott just stood grinning proudly as if to say, *I told you so*.

"Ok, that-," he motioned towards the downed body on the gravel of the driveway. "That was pretty cool." Elliott smiled shyly and squirmed over the compliment. Kenshiro looked back to the body on the ground some distance away and he could see it was still moving weakly on the ground. Elliott had hit it, but not with enough force for it to be lethal to the zombie.

Soon enough, Kenshiro was sure the figure in the red

checkered shirt and torn dark pants would soon be on its feet again, stalking towards them.

"You didn't kill it, though," Kenshiro said grimly. He would have to deal with it. This would be the first time Elliott would see him deal with the undead, and he felt this was an excellent opportunity to find out how he would react to it. You didn't have to talk to Elliott for long to know he had a deep fear of '*the grey people*'. He wanted nothing to do with them. Even now when he looked back to him, Kenshiro could see deep concern had replaced his pride when he learned it was still moving.

"Um, Kenchurro?" Elliott called to him weakly. "We should go inside now. It's not safe. Momma said to stay away from the grey people." Elliott shifted his weight between his feet in an obvious display of his unease. Kenshiro took a calming breath and strode over to the boy so he could look Elliott in the eye. He tried to keep his face calm and his tone neutral.

"Elliott, we talked about this." Elliott had asked him many questions about '*the grey people*' and he had answered them honestly, but he had intentionally omitted certain ugly details. "We can't always run away from them. We *shouldn't* always run away from them, there's only two of them, I can take care of this." He wanted to sound reassuring because Elliott was worried about what might happen to him. While Kenshiro was worried about how Elliott would react to seeing the violence required to deal with these bastards.

"But Momma said-," he said, but Kenshiro cut him off when an idea came to him on how to approach this a better way.

"Elliott," he said firmly and then let his tone soften as he continued, "If we go inside now, we'll have to wait inside all day before these guys leave, maybe even tomorrow. It's such a nice day; don't you want to be outside today? Don't you have chores you need to do? You wanted to work in the garden today. How long has it been since you did your chores?"

"I dunno," Elliott stuck his finger into the corner of his mouth; a sign Kenshiro has learned meant the boy's brain was hard at work. "A couple days, I guess."

"Didn't Momma say something about doing your chores?" Kenshiro didn't know if Emily did or not, but he took a gamble that in his life she must have said *something*.

"Yeah."

"Well, okay," Kenshiro said in a singsong voice, as if that solved all their problems. "I'll just go and take care of these guys, and then we'll get back to our game. Then you can work in the garden after we're done playing catch. Does that sound good?" He tried to make it sound convincing. Hell, he tried to make it sound like the greatest idea ever conceived of. Elliott continued to suck on his finger for a moment longer before he looked up at him and nodded.

"I guess." *Good enough*, Kenshiro thought while he put on a friendly smile and gave Elliott a gentle pat on the shoulder before turning away, dropping the facade and moved towards his enemy.

The zombie Elliott had beaned with the baseball was still struggling to get to its feet. Kenshiro approached it as it was on all fours and pushed weakly off the ground, he took two quick strides to bridge the gap between them before kicking its arms out from under it. When the support of its arms left, its whole upper body slapped against the gravel. The undead man raised its head up and hissed angrily at him,

Kenshiro quickly moved to its side and firmly placed

his boot on its neck, effectively pinning it to the ground. He looked back to Elliott and gave him a thumbs-up. Elliott looked like he was trying to make himself look small but he still returned the gesture with a confused expression because he didn't exactly know what he was giving a thumbs-up to. He would know soon enough. Kenshiro raised up his boot and stomped it back down on the back of its neck, right where the spine met the skull, and the loud crunching sound was rewarding as he felt the bone gave way beneath his boot.

When it was over, Kenshiro took a breath and looked back at the boy, and when he did, he saw Elliott had turned away and was walking away. It wasn't the reaction he was hoping for. Kenshiro didn't really know what he was hoping for, maybe something that would reassure him Elliott could handle the ugliness. If this was too much for the boy, how would he handle it when it got really messy?

He threw a baseball at it. Kenshiro told himself that was proof enough Elliott wasn't afraid to hurt them but he couldn't throw baseballs at them all day. Kenshiro couldn't see the boy pushing a knife into their skull. He also doubted Elliott was even capable of summoning the raw savagery to bash their brains out with any sort of bludgeoning instrument. Guns were out of the question; at this point anyway. Elliott was far more likely to injure himself, or Kenshiro, than be able to shoot a zombie in the face. Kenshiro felt it was important to find a role for Elliott when it came time to re-enter the undead world. They couldn't hide in the rundown little house for much longer. Before they left, he wanted to get Elliott adjusted and ready for whatever role he might fit into.

He just needed to give Elliott more time.

Kenshiro started towards the last zombie at the gate. It was a larger one, a lot of mass still on its bones, and it wore coveralls that had the front of it stained dark brown from old blood that leaked down from the ugly gouge that was taken out of the side of its neck. Its face had a large beard that hung in gross-looking matted locks along its jaw line and had a lot of hair that hung limply in front of its milky white eyes. It clawed at him from behind the gate with the ravenous intensity of a starved rabid animal. Kenshiro reached down and pulled the knife on his leg free and was eyeing the spot where he wanted to drive it home.

Then he felt something invade the space beside him.

He didn't see it or hear it, but he seemed to just violently notice its presence in the air beside his left shoulder. A moment later, a black… something, moved passed him with a surprising amount of speed. The tiny hairs of his neck rose by its wake. Kenshiro instinctively jumped to the side away from it.

"Fuck sakes, kid!" Kenshiro cursed silently as the pieces of the puzzle snapped into place in a flash. Suddenly, he recognized the fist-sized rock for what it was, the instant before it crashed into the hair covered forehead of the big zombie. Kenshiro was close enough to see the skin of its forehead split open. The complete structure of its face seemed to shift under the force of the impact, a moment before its frame went rigid and slumped to the ground, motionless. *He could've killed me!* In his mind, Kenshiro pictured that rock striking his own skull and fracturing it to pieces. Fury suddenly burned within him as he whipped back to Elliott, fully prepared to scold the boy for his carelessness.

"Goddamnit-," he started to say, his voice raising to an angry shout, but before he could fully get it out, he saw Elliott wiggling in the distance.

It took him a moment to realize Elliott was doing a dance of sorts, celebrating. When Elliott noticed Kenshiro was looking his way, he gave him an enthusiastic thumbs-up. Before Kenshiro knew it, the fury he had a moment ago disappeared like smoke as he watched Elliott celebrate his toss. Kenshiro looked back to the big new corpse on the ground to make sure it was still, which it was, and then stood in amazement at the distance.

At this distance, Elliott's toss would be comparable to a center fielder in baseball throwing the ball and hitting the batter squarely in the head, on the first throw. His anger over his carelessness gave way to his amazement in Elliott's accuracy and the force of the throw. Kenshiro saw the rock Elliott had used laying on the ground near the body, blood stained with a few bits of hair stuck to it. Kenshiro recognized it as being one of the rocks Elliott had stored in a bucket, with the other baseballs, by the hay bale with a bulls-eye painted on it, and realized he had misunderstood Elliott once again.

Elliott wasn't turning away from Kenshiro and the minor ugliness of stomping down on the zombie's neck, and crushing its brainstem. Elliott was getting another 'ball' to toss at the other one, and he picked a rock because an actual baseball didn't do the job.

Maybe there was hope for him after all.

He turned back to Elliott and raised his thumb high into the air back at him. Kenshiro would have to have a talk with him about certain safety rules, but he could forgive this one instance because Elliott proved himself today. If called upon, he could kill a zombie. He wasn't completely helpless after all, and maybe for the first time, Kenshiro had hope he could make this work.

After that, Kenshiro felt it was time to see what Elliott was capable of. He didn't know what exactly that meant, but he had a good idea how he could find out.

They were deep in the game, with the game board being littered with lettered tiles. He had asked Elliott twice already to check the perimeter, and he had returned each time with the same answer, "All clear".

On the third time, Elliott returned quietly but still with a certain spring in his step and he approached Kenshiro and whispered.

"There's a grey person outside," He reported, "She's by the truck now, and Kenchurro?" He leaned in closer. "She's naked."

This was what Kenshiro was waiting for. He reached into his pocket and found the remote for the stereo outside and turned it off. Kenshiro went to the kitchen window that overlooked the area where the truck had parked.

As promised, there was the naked undead woman of an indeterminable age bumping into the side of the truck. Not exactly active, but the zombie still was mindlessly searching for flesh at the source of the noise. Kenshiro instructed Elliott to take the binoculars and go upstairs and check the fields around them for any more undead. To his credit, Elliott retrieved the binoculars from where Kenshiro left them in the living room and hustled upstairs quietly and followed his directions with no further word. While Elliott was upstairs, Kenshiro went around and checked the ground level floors himself. He didn't see any other figures outside, and Kenshiro hoped with the stereo off, they wouldn't attract any more for the time being. While he waited for Elliott to finish checking the surrounding fields, Kenshiro thought about how he wanted to approach this next part.

The front door to Elliott's house was actually two doors, a large solid looking wooden door that opened inwards and a flimsy-looking metal screen door that opened outwards. Both doors were closed at the moment and Kenshiro walked up to the peephole in the wooden door and had a look outside.

He saw the front half of the truck, and the side of the house that jutted out from the door, obstructing back half of the truck. Where the zombie should be. Kenshiro waited for Elliott to return from upstairs with his report on their surroundings, which Elliott happily announced was clear. Kenshiro considered checking it himself, but decided it was a small concern, and if there were more out there, he had a plan already in place for that. Kenshiro waved Elliott closer and watched the kid closely as he explained what he wanted Elliott to do, to make sure he understood what Kenshiro wanted Elliott to do if things went wrong.

"You got it?" He asked after he said everything he could think of to say. "Questions?" Elliott took a moment and thought it over while chewing the nail on his index finger.

"No," he said finally after fully considering the matter. "I got it."

"Ok," Kenshiro said, getting into position by the door. "Let's do this." He pressed his back against the wall and pulled the .22 pistol free from his holster on his vest. He held it low and in front of him in both hands. He clicked off the safety, checked to ensure a round was indeed chambered, and then pulled back the hammer. He looked at Elliott and nodded to him. He was ready.

Elliott stepped up to the door, and as instructed, first looked through the peephole and then wordlessly looked to Kenshiro and shook his head twice. Kenshiro acknowledged it and Elliott then opened the big wooden inner door. A solid door moving on solid hinges, it opened with little to no sound. None-the-less, Elliott stood in front of the screen door and simply looked out before he again looked to Kenshiro and shook his head twice. Kenshiro turned towards him and pressed his shoulder against the wall with the gun held low and then nodded to Elliott to begin the next phase.

As Elliott stepped forward to push the screen door open, a light metal door moving on cheap tin hinges, the door made a slight metallic groan. Elliott simply held the door open and waited. Kenshiro knew that the slight noise made by the door would be enough to attract the naked zombie by the truck, so the two of them just waited. Beforehand, he had given Elliott a few hand signals to communicate the situation in front of him. It came in handy because, within a few moments, Elliott's hand came up with a single digit. Which meant he saw one zombie and almost immediately Elliott closed his hand into a fist, which meant that the zombie was not moving. This was strange for Kenshiro because being able to see a living person should drive the undead into a frenzy.

"What's it doing?" He whispered, confident he would be unheard by the zombie but prepared if he wasn't.

Elliott looked at him and, as instructed, he remained silent. Instead, he nodded his head upwards, mimicking the movement Kenshiro saw the zombie do when he first saw the boy by the field, and again later on during his pursuit of the boy. Kenshiro thought for a moment about what else he wanted to accomplish. So far, he had indeed establish Elliott influences the undead in some unknown way. It wasn't just a onetime strange thing that he saw and couldn't explain. Now that he had tested it, Kenshiro felt he had confirmed it.

He suspected any additional sound loud enough to alert it would break the effect. However, Kenshiro also knew any additional motion by Elliott would not break the spell. Besides, it occupied Elliott just holding that damned screen door open so it didn't ruin the effect with its noisy hinges.

There was only one other thing Kenshiro could think of that he could test in this circumstance. Feeling the weight of the pistol in his hand, he inched closer to the edge of the door. Kenshiro leaned in closer to look around the corner of the door frame; he saw the haggard naked figure with a mop of dark hair that hung down from its face like a shroud. Its blemish- filled grey skin hung from its bones and looked to be covered with a sort of grime. On its shoulder, he could see a gruesome injury that had stripped the flesh down to the bone.

Then it attacked.

Kenshiro saw the exposed socket joint of its shoulder move as its arm raised and it suddenly shifted its gaze to focus intently, from behind the shroud of hair, on Kenshiro. A weak groan erupted from its throat as it took a step towards the two of them, and that was all Kenshiro needed to see to know the experiment was over.

POP!

Kenshiro shifted gears and brought up the gun as he rounded the corner of the door frame, inadvertently shoving Elliott aside, and shot it in the forehead. Through the mass of grimy locks, he witnessed the pencil sized hole appear on the pale flesh of its forehead where he was aiming a moment before its weight fell to the ground. Kenshiro looked back to Elliott, who was trying to look brave, but it was obvious the sudden turn of events had shaken him.

"Okay," Kenshiro said, trying to sound light. "So, I guess we learned something. We found out that your little special power only applies to you." Elliott smiled. "Why don't you go back inside and set up a new scrabble game and I'll take care of this." Kenshiro used the barrel of the gun to point to the naked corpse on the walkway, "and then I'll meet you inside in a while."

"Okay," Elliott said, happy to have an excuse to retreat back inside. Kenshiro exited the house and watched as Elliott closed the large wooden door before leaving to check the property for any other surprises. The gunshot would bring any zombies that might be near enough to hear the shot.

Kenshiro walked the property with the pistol gripped, and ready in his hands. He scanned over the fields and then walked down to the turnout where he looked down both sides of the roads. For the time being, they were alone again. Kenshiro holstered the pistol and walked back to the truck to retrieve the length of rope he was using to haul the corpses away from the visible yard. He walked back over to the naked corpse slumped awkwardly against the exterior of the house. Kenshiro looped the length of rope around its ankles and pulled the rope tight, and then stood and casually dragged the body away.

He had a spot picked out where he had built a miniature version of a pyre with the bodies they had collected thus far. He had neatly lined the few bodies they had collected next to each other, and this one would be the beginning of the next level. It would be some time before they would need to light the pyre at this rate, and Kenshiro was considering doing it much sooner now that he was seeing the mass of insects of all kinds buzzing around the rapidly decaying corpses. Not to mention the smell. It was bad enough to strip paint off walls. Kenshiro tried to imagine what the corpses he left behind in the town were looking like, after baking in the Colorado sun for almost a week, and whether he should do something about it.

The need to head back into town for supplies hung over Kenshiro like a dark cloud. He considered if he should try to convince Elliott that it would be best if Kenshiro went to town alone. Since that first disastrous day together, Elliott had on some occasions needed some reassurance that

Kenshiro wouldn't leave him again. Kenshiro didn't think he could easily convince Elliott to let him go alone, but he also couldn't be sure he could trust Elliott to deal with the stresses of what might wait for them in the town.

When he left, he was pretty sure he had put a significant dent in the undead population of La Veta and maybe if they were to return, they would encounter fewer zombies. Especially if they stuck to the north-east corner of the town, but *fewer* zombies was a long way from *no* zombies. If he had more time, he felt he could train the kid, ease him into a role where he would fit.

Right now, Kenshiro couldn't see him being of any use beyond that of a look-out. Sure, he was almost supernaturally good at killing them with rocks, but that's when it's one at a time, and he could retrieve the rocks after. What would Elliott do when he ran out of rocks, and there was still undead creeping towards him? If he had time, maybe he could transition into using a rebar spear of his own, or maybe a baseball bat since Elliott already had a predisposition towards baseball, anyway. Hell, he would be happy with a stick with a nail in it. They had maybe one more day on their brief vacation and then they would have to get back to work out there. Kenshiro walked away from the rotting corpses and let out a deep sigh.

Elliott was changing things. It wasn't anything he was doing other than simply existing in Kenshiro's orbit, but that still changed the whole dynamic of his life. It was frustrating. He made a conscious choice not to dwell on that aspect of it. He decided, and nothing had changed about that. However, making it work was a whole other struggle. Kenshiro walked through the main yard towards the truck and thought about Trevor, the man who saved him. Not just by picking him up on that road, but also by forging him into the weapon he was today. He knew how to fight.

He had already fought and bled, but Trevor showed him how to survive. It struck Kenshiro how history had repeated itself with him and Elliott. The student becomes the mentor and lives on to mentor a student.

However, when Trevor found Kenshiro, he was already a weapon of sorts. Trevor just forged the metal and honed the edge. Elliott knew nothing of survival, or fighting, and Kenshiro doubted the kid even had the capacity for the violence necessary. Right now, Elliott could only throw a rock at them like a damned cave dweller. What would he do if a zombie ever got its hands on him? Elliott was lacking in every area, so it was up to Kenshiro to make sure that never happened. But how, and for how long? Kenshiro didn't know and tried not to think about the question. He tossed the length of rope back in the truck's bed and lifted himself up to sit on the tailgate to ponder their future for a moment.

When Kenshiro went back inside, he found Elliott and a cleared scrabble board waiting for him at the kitchen table. Kenshiro smiled covertly as he sat down at the table and saw Elliott had already played his turn, and the word he had put down on the board was 'excitedly', a word that would be impossible to put down on the first turn and a whopping twenty-three points.

"Wow," he said with mock awe. "Twenty-three points, jeez, that's going to be hard to beat. Brilliant move, buddy." Elliott was practically beaming with excitement at the praise. Kenshiro pulled out the remote for the stereo outside from his pocket and pressed the play button. From inside the house, they could hear the muted sounds of Kenshiro's new favorite country singer, Kenny Rogers.

"Whatcha doin'?" Elliott suddenly looked concerned but Kenshiro just put on a reassuring grin.

"We're going to do the experiment again. There

are a few other things I thought of that we can check," he said innocently and looked over to Elliott to gauge his reaction. He seemed to think about it for a minute and then simply shrugged it off.

"Ok," he said finally, lost in the game. "It's your move," Elliott said and motioned to the board and Kenshiro settled in and started arranging his tiles. Elliott sang softly along to the chorus of a song that was playing on the stereo outside. Kenshiro must have heard that damned song a dozen times today.

"You've got to know when to hold 'em," Elliott sang to himself as he waited.

"Know when to fold 'em," Kenshiro cut in softly as he looked up from his tiles to see Elliott's face light up, just like he suspected it would. "Know when to walk away." He straightened up and sang with a little more gusto and then pointed to Elliott to continue.

"And know when to run." Elliott's voice rose as well.

"You never count your money," they sang in unison through their smiles. "When you're sitting at the table, there'll be time enough for counting, when the dealin's done." Elliott clapped in tune with the song, and caught up in the moment, Kenshiro clapped along with him and they started in on the next verse without the aid of the stereo. They were just singing to each other, keeping in time with their own beat. At one point, Elliott started singing into his hand as if he was holding a microphone. They ended the song and laughed as the moment passed. It was stupid, silly, and in a small way utterly glorious because, for a moment, Kenshiro didn't focus on the creeping death that was all around them every day.

They did the experiment three more times, each time changing it slightly, and when they were done, Kenshiro was pretty sure he had all he was going to learn about Elliott's ability. The teen was, for all intents and purposes, invisible to the undead. Kenshiro couldn't explain it, nor could Elliott. It wasn't something the kid was actively trying to do. More than that, though, when a zombie got within twenty feet of the boy, it started doing that weird sniffing seizure. Only sound broke it free from the strange trance, or the presence of someone else. All of which Kenshiro already suspected. He also found out, to his disappointment, the benefits only apply to Elliott. As soon as Kenshiro was in view, the zombie would move towards him. Even if it meant they had to walk right passed Elliott to do it. The only way the zombie would attack Elliott is if he made the sound himself, and if he did, all he had to do to become invisible again is move out of the view for a mere moment. It was like magic.

They ate by the waning light of the late evening. Kenshiro had considered lighting a candle, but the amount of light it would probably provide would hardly be worth it. Luckily, Elliott had been yawning during the last game of checkers, which Kenshiro lost, so hopefully the bowl with the lion's share of the macaroni and cheese in front of him would be enough to send him over the edge and Elliott would call it a night.

Lately Kenshiro had grown to savor the few hours he had to himself after Elliott went to bed and before he himself settled into the couch. Tonight, Kenshiro was looking forward to reading a few chapters of his book by candlelight and soaking up the quietness of the house, but that was later.

Right now, he had other business to attend to.

"Look," he started without the benefit of really knowing how the best way to approach Elliott with what he had to say. He would have to just lay it out for Elliott and see how he reacts. "We're running out of food. This," he used his fork to motion towards the meal they were currently eating, "This is the last of the macaroni and cheese." He paused when Elliott stopped chewing and looked at him with a combination of shock and sadness. Kenshiro nodded sympathetically and continued. "We have one more can of beans left, and a can of pear slices."

"Oh," Elliott breathed out the word like a sigh of relief, "That's good," he said like those two cans were the answer to their food shortage problem.

"It's not enough," Kenshiro said it like it was a fact because it was, and he needed Elliott to understand that. "We need to go to town tomorrow and get more supplies. It shouldn't take too-,"

"I don't want to go to town," Elliott said, staring into his noodles. "There's a lot of grey people in town, and I don't like grey people. We should stay here. I like it here." He started back to his food. "I like it here," he said again with a mouthful of cheesy noodles.

Kenshiro let out a long noisy sigh that Elliott was supposed to notice, but he just went on chewing, completely unaware. That frustrated Kenshiro even more. He had run into this roadblock of Elliott's a few times now and he knew if he pushed too hard, it would lead to a breakdown of sorts, and there wouldn't be any more discussion on the matter. If Kenshiro had to bet, he would put his money on Elliott breaking into tears at some point and storming upstairs to lock himself in his room. It was hard not to view that outcome as a failure on his part. Kenshiro had spent enough time with him to know he might have the body of a regular teenager, maybe around the age of sixteen, but his mind was anything but. Kenshiro didn't know if it was a handicap, or learning disability that Elliott had before the outbreak. At one point, it even crossed Kenshiro's mind that this could be an effect of the isolation and starvation, he didn't know. Even if he did, he doubted that knowledge would help him better navigate these discussions with Elliott.

Kenshiro studied the teen across from him and thought about the dilemma in front of them. With anyone else, this would be a simple problem with a straightforward solution. We need food; we get food. The logic of it was simple, but with Elliott, he felt like a mouse trying to traverse a maze with invisible walls. All he can see is what he wants, but no idea how to get there. Elliott clinked his spoon against the sides of the bowl as he collected the last few noodles into his spoon when he thought of something.

"Okay," he said, finally raising his hands in surrender for Elliott to see. "Okay, that's fine. Just a shame, you know," his face dropped to show his disappointment. "Last time I was in town, I saw a box of chocolate cake mix; I was going to surprise you with it because you've been so good this week." He looked to Elliott, who had frozen with the last spoonful of noodles inches from his face. He locked eyes with Kenshiro's.

"You were?" Elliott asked with a renewed interest in what Kenshiro was saying.

"Yup, but I guess I can't now. That's ok. Probably could have found you some clothes that actually fit too," he said and nodded towards the reasonably clean shirt Elliott had on, that still had remnants of past stains marking the front of it, and was obviously too small for the kid's frame. "And you know what? I bet we could find some of those drink crystals that turn water into juice, jeez, wouldn't that be nice, a glass of grape juice with our dinners?" Elliott looked at him suspiciously as he loaded his last spoonful of noodles into his mouth and began chewing thoughtfully.

"How do you know all that stuff is there? Do you

think we could find some comic books, or maybe another Gatorade?" *Good*, Kenshiro thought.

"Possibly," he said, but made it sound more like a certainty. "Who knows what's out there? You never know what you might find, but the thing is." Kenshiro looked at him solemnly, like he was about to tell Elliott a grave secret. "If you don't look, you're never going to find anything." He let that sink in with Elliott while he cleared the dishes off the table, and walked into the kitchen to place the dishes in the sink. When he returned to the table, Elliott had reset the checkerboard for a fresh game, but by the look on his face, Elliott's thoughts were not on the board in front of him.

"So, we can go into other people's houses and just sort of take whatever we want, and nobody cares? Won't we get into trouble?" He moved his first piece on the board with seemingly no thought, but Kenshiro knew better.

"Who's going to care? There's nobody around to give a shit what we do. I've been doing this for a long time. Trust me, it will be fine. It's how we survive. We'll go into town, we'll clear out the grey people, and then we'll search through the houses for what we need," Kenshiro said in soothing tones. He tried to make it seem like the entire process of clearing a town was relatively safe and fairly straightforward, even though a part of him knew there were a lot of ugly details he purposefully left out. The first obstacle was to get Elliott to agree to go, because they didn't have the luxury of hiding away in this tiny little house anymore. Maybe Elliott didn't appreciate that, but Kenshiro did.

"I don't like grey people," Elliott said as Kenshiro advanced one of his pieces on the board. "They're ugly and they smell really bad. I'm scared of them." He admitted shyly before he moved another piece forward. He solely focused his eyes on the board, but Kenshiro could hear the shame in his voice.

"Yeah," Kenshiro nodded thoughtfully, "Me too."

"Really?" Elliott looked up and he could see the amazement in the kid's ocean blue eyes.

"Sure," he said after he continued his advance on Elliott's pieces. "What's not to be afraid of? And yeah, they're pretty fucking gross."

"You swear too much." Elliott moved his piece into a position where Kenshiro could jump it. "Momma says you shouldn't swear." Kenshiro said nothing to that. He'd heard it before. Instead, he jumped Elliott's piece and was about to say something smug to the teen but then he saw it. Elliott's trap. He had stupidly jumped Elliott's piece and landed into a square that would allow Elliott's one piece on the side to take three of his. With the trap sprung, Elliott moved in for the kill and loudly jumped his three pieces and scooped them up off the board.

"I don't want to fight grey people," Elliott said as he settled back into his chair. "I don't mind throwing a rock at them, but I don't want to do what you do. If we went into town, would I have to fight them?"

"No," he said, seeing an opening of his own. "I was thinking you could just stay in the truck. Probably would be kind of boring for you, really." Kenshiro tilted his head to the side and raised his eyebrow innocently. "Actually, I thought it might be fun if you drove the truck when we get to town. Mind you, there wouldn't be a lot of driving involved and-,"

"Okay." Elliott broke in suddenly while moving his next piece forward and then sat back and said nothing for a moment. Kenshiro let the silence hang in the air as Elliott looked up from the board and met his eyes, he sighed heavily before he spoke again. "I'll go into town."

It concerned Kenshiro, because he expected Elliott to be more excited at the prospect of driving the truck. For a second, he feared Elliott saw through what he was doing, leading him towards the decision with promises of sweets and new clothes, but in the end it didn't matter. He got what he wanted. Kenshiro got over the first hurdle, which was probably the easiest. The next part would be harder, because he had to take Elliott out into the undead world, and keep him safe.

"Okay," Kenshiro responded solemnly, returning his focus to the game he was currently in danger of losing. "Okay."

Chapter 10

Elliott

Elliott tightly gripped the steering wheel of the truck, and stared out the windshield as he waited for Kenchurro to return from the house. He had been getting ready for what seemed like a long time, but Elliott didn't mind. He just waited in the driver's seat and tried to imagine what it would be like to drive. *This is actually happening*, he told himself repeatedly inside his head.

Originally, Kenchurro had said that he would let Elliott drive the truck once they got to town, but this morning that changed. When Elliott came down this morning he found Kenchurro already in the kitchen with a small pot on the stove, and the smell of baked beans filled the room. Kenchurro told him with a disappointed face that this was the last can of beans, and reminded him their food shortage was the reason they were going into town. As they were eating, though, he asked Elliott if he had ever driven a truck before. Elliott had dipped his eyes and told a bit of a fib. Elliott said he had driven plenty, and he had, but that was a riding lawnmower that his aunt let him drive around their property. He had gotten pretty good at it, though. He would have told the truth, but something inside him thought if he did, Kenchurro would not let him drive anymore. So, he told the smallest of lies and then something amazing happened, or more accurately, something else amazing happened.

It had been an awesome week, after all.

"In that case, why don't you drive us into town as well? It's not that far and I don't see why you shouldn't," Kenchurro said and then returned to his meal.

Elliott could only sit there for a moment, stunned at his good luck in finding such a good friend, before a broad smile broke across his face. "Sure."

Now, he eagerly waited in the truck for Kenchurro to finish what he was doing. He had first removed just about everything from the back of the truck and neatly laid them beside the house before he made a few trips inside to grab what items he felt they needed. On the last trip, Kenchurro came back with the black duffel bag he had stowed in the living room during their first week together. Elliott didn't know exactly what was inside the bag, but whatever it was, Kenchurro thought it was important because he practically slept beside it. Elliott watched his friend in the rear-view mirror as he also placed the sharpened length of steel, Kenchurro's spear, inside the truck bed before he closed the lift gate of the truck and moved to the passenger side.

"Ok, are you ready to go, Elliott?" He said when he opened the passenger door and gracefully moved into the seat.

"You bet, Kenchurro," Elliott said with an encouraging smile only to have it drop from his face as Kenchurro seemed to suddenly look disappointed. His new friend sighed heavily, and just sort of looked at Elliott. His heart sank a bit, and Elliott struggled with what he could have done in so short a time to upset his friend. "What's wrong?" He asked sheepishly. Kenchurro put on a reassuring smile and held up his hands as if he was going to surrender.

"It's not a big deal. I don't want you to get upset, but my name is actually Ken-shee-ro," He was still smiling when he said it but Elliott felt his heart fall deeper within his chest. He had been saying his new friend's name wrong this whole time.

"I thought that's what I said," Elliott said shyly. "I'm sorry. Kensheeru?" He said, as if testing the name out against what he had heard a moment earlier. It was close, but wasn't right. "Kenshurro?" That wasn't right either. He looked to his friend pleadingly as Elliott searched for what he was doing wrong.

"Tell you what," he said with a broad grin that made Elliott feel better. "Just call me Ken. That's what my friends used to call me, the white ones anyway. Even the ones who could actually pronounce my name properly, eventually shortened it down to Ken. Just do me one favor, though."

"What?"

"Never call me Kenny, I hate that," he said, looking at Elliott with those squinty eyes that made it hard to tell what he was thinking sometimes, externally anyway. He was smiling, but he had a firm tone that told Elliott he wasn't joking about not liking being called Kenny.

"Okay, yeah. Ken. That's easy. I can remember that," Elliott said, quick to please, and Ken nodded his approval before he reached into his pocket and produced a small key ring with two keys on it and offered it to Elliott.

"Let's do this. Let's hit the road." Elliott took the offered keys and looked at them briefly to see which one he needed to use, but after a close look he saw they were identical, so he just picked one and stuffed it into the truck's ignition on the steering column. He turned the key over in the cylinder and the truck came to life. Elliott's heart rate seemed to kick up a tick inside of his chest.

"Okay," Ken chimed in shortly after the truck started. "Here's what you need to do." Ken started and, to Elliott's relief, he gave him step-by-step instructions.

Elliott breathed in deep and followed the instructions

as he began to first back the truck up, then changed gears, and pulled ahead towards the opened gate. Ken clearly said he didn't want Elliott to drive fast. He mentioned something about not wanting to leave a dust trail behind them for the grey people to follow, but Elliott was only listening half-heartedly as he approached the gate. Elliott held a steady pressure on the brake pedal, and he saw the needle on the gauge that told them how fast the truck was going had barely moved, and yet to Elliott it felt like he was practically flying towards the gate. His heart raced and his palm felt slick as he gripped the steering wheel, but he told himself to just keep breathing.

A moment later, Elliott eased the truck around the corner of the driveway and then they were on the road heading towards town. It was exhilarating. Elliott felt a sort of electricity flow through the steering wheel and run through his body, causing the tiny hairs on his neck and arms to stand at attention. The tires of the truck crunched noisily on the gravel as they made their way to the first bend in the road.

"We can probably go a bit faster," Ken said from the passenger seat. Elliott didn't dare look over to him as he had his eyes locked on the road ahead, looking for any dangers, but also unable to tear his eyes away from the sheer excitement of the motion of the truck that *he* controlled. "Just ease your foot off the brake a bit and just let it coast forward."

"Okay," Elliott said through his concentration and did as he was instructed. He felt the speed increase all the way to his bones. Ken must have felt his apprehension because he told him to relax and just keep the truck in the middle of the road. Ken said it in the soft voice he sometimes used when he talked to Elliott. It was reassuring to hear his voice so free of worry, even if Elliott knew better.

"You're doing good," Ken said it like it was a fact that pleasantly surprised him, and Elliott risked a quick glance over to the passenger side. Ken was looking out over the vast emptiness around them like a hawk looking for a field mouse. *He's looking for grey people.* Elliott couldn't help but feel safer in his new friend's presence. Ken wasn't afraid of the grey people, quite the opposite as far as Elliott could see, he *hated* the grey people. Elliott quickly returned his gaze to the front just as they approached the first bend in the tree-shaded section of the road. Out of instinct, he slowed the truck down a bit as Elliott maneuvered around the corner and there on the road in front of them was a dark shape.

"Umm, Ken? There's a body on the road." Elliott looked over to Ken, who just looked ahead solemnly and calmly told Elliott to just drive around it, which he did, but as the truck glided by the body on the road, Elliott took a moment to glance over to it. He immediately wished he hadn't.

Are those brains?

He had only glanced at it, not even a proper look, but what Elliott saw reminded him of a watermelon that somebody had smashed onto the ground, and he saw its dark contents spilled upon the tiny rocks of the gravel road. Elliott felt a tiny spike of fear course through his body as he snapped his head forward again, and a moment later it was behind them. In front of them was the nicely shaded section of the lonely road before the second bend ahead. The fear ebbed quickly, but in his mind, Elliott still felt its shadow linger with the memory of the body with the smashed in skull.

"My best friend jenny's house is up ahead," Elliott said. He tried to push the ugly memory of a moment ago out of his head and looked for a distraction that would help. "She's been my friend forever. She's younger than me, but she is still cool, and she's really smart and nice. Our parents are friends too and sometimes in the summer we will go over to their house for a big barbeque and-, "

"Elliott?" Ken said suddenly.

"Yeah, Ken." He looked over to his friend who was staring at the road ahead of them as they turned the bend, and exited the shade of the tree along the sides of the road. His friend casually pointed ahead.

"Best keep your eyes on the road for the next bit. There are a few nasty bumps ahead I don't want you to hit. It might damage the truck." Elliott looked ahead of them to roughly where Ken had been pointing, but as the truck rolled ahead, he failed to see anything of concern. None-the-less, Elliott kept his eyes fixed on the road as they drove on.

"I don't see it," Elliott confessed.

"That's okay, you're doing great. Just keep your eyes on the road and keep going." Ken scanned up ahead and said nothing further. So, Elliott let the truck coast forward and was sure to keep a steady eye on the road for the bumps Ken warned him about. The road ahead of them was arrow-straight until they got to Wahatoya Lake, and then he had to negotiate the slight bend as it moved around the corner of the lake. After that, the first few outlying buildings of La Veta came into view. Elliott's foot stepped on the brake slightly, almost like a reflex, to slow the truck as he noticed the figures on the road off in the distance. They were too far off to make out any real detail other than that they were people, and they were upright. They were just five shapes looming in the middle of the first intersection that led into the town. Elliott knew they were grey people. Who else could it be? Ken had said there were no normal people left, and the way he said it, made Elliott believe him. At the time, Elliott had asked him where the normal people had gone to, thinking maybe

Ken might know where his parents had gone, but he didn't answer the question. Instead, Ken changed the subject.

"Ken," Elliott began nervously. He had been hoping there wouldn't be any grey people out today, and seeing the small collection of them ahead just seemed to put a dark stain on his day out with his new friend.

"I see them. Just keep going," Ken said, and when Elliott looked over to him, Ken locked his gaze forward. It reminded Elliott of how a cat looks at its prey.

"Should we turn around?" Elliott asked hopefully. Ken glanced at him in a way that made him feel a slight sting of shame.

"No, Elliott. I'll take care of them. Just pull the truck up closer to them and then stop." He reached down and started putting on a tan pair of leather work gloves that were on the seat between them. Elliott's gut instinct was to turn the truck around, but he didn't think he could do that without Ken's help, and worse yet, he didn't want Ken to look at him again like he had a moment ago. So, against his best instincts, Elliott did as Ken instructed. By the time he had brought the truck to a stop, the group of grey people were still some distance away, too far for Elliott to throw a rock, at any rate. "Stay in the truck," Ken said almost immediately after Elliott placed the transmission in Park.

"Ken? I don't-," Elliott said before Ken sharply cut him off.

"Elliott," Ken snapped, and then let his voice soften. "Stay in the truck, it'll be fine," he said as he reached for the door handle. "I've done this before."

With that, he exited the truck and moved to the rear of the vehicle. Elliott's eyes followed him and saw Ken pull the long, sharp steel rod from the bed of the truck. With the skinny rod in his right hand, tip pointed down, Ken passed by with his eyes forward and walked towards the figures in the distance.

Elliott nervously gripped the wheel, and in his mind, he pictured the dark figures descending upon his friend. Sweat slicked his palms as he pictured the dark shapes overwhelm Ken and force him to the ground. What would he do then? What could he do? This differed greatly from the grey people who came into the yard. Those came one at a time, but this was an entire group Ken was walking towards. Elliott sucked in a sharp breath and when he let it out, he was disappointed to find it came out as a soft moan, as he watched the group of grey people and Ken approach each other. Elliott knew he didn't want to see what would happen, but he couldn't look away.

The strange scene unfolding in front of him, reminded Elliott of those showdowns he would sometimes see in the westerns he watched with his father. The lone gunman walking towards the five desperados in the dusty main street of the road. However, here, instead of a heroic lone gunman, there was only his friend with a long metal pole in his hand. While the desperados were the five drunkenly shambling figures, that were ghastlier the more Elliott watched them approach. They looked like five angry, tortured souls that were belched up from the pits of hell. Ken had said that the grey people actually ate real people, and at the time, Elliott had a hard time believing something as monstrous as that could be true. Here though, watching his only friend in the world walk so casually towards them, he saw it. Elliott saw five ruined beings claw and limp their way towards their next meal. He saw monsters, and in his mind, those monsters would overwhelm and consume his friend right in front of him, and there wasn't anything Elliott could do about it.

Elliott wanted Ken to drop that stupid pole and take out

his gun and shoot them, or at least use those knives he had, and seemed to be pretty good with. But what was he going to do with that thin little pole? Elliott then remembered something Ken had said before he had left. When he spoke the words originally, Elliott didn't know what Ken meant by them exactly, but when the scene went to hell in front of him, it helped explain what he was seeing.

I've done this before.

Elliott practically had tears in his eyes with worry when he remembered those words, and in front of him Ken moved the pole in his hands to grip it with two hands. Not how a normal person might hold it, though. Ken held it with his right-hand way down on the pole, and his left hand about halfway up the shaft. Elliott had never seen anyone hold a long pole in such a way. *I've done this before.* As if on cue, Elliott saw Ken's body tense briefly and then, like a snake, he struck forward with alarming speed and force.

The sharpened tip of Ken's pole disappeared into the face of the front-most grey person. It was a lady with long slimy looking dark hair in coveralls with reflective strips on the shoulders. It almost looked like he didn't make contact until Elliott witnessed the grey lady's body tense up, and then using his whole body, Ken pulled the pole back out, swung it overhead and brought it down on the next grey person. It was a man, and the pole struck the man in the side of its head with such force its body just sort of pitched over to the side. Before that body could even hit the ground, Ken was bringing the pole around to bear down on another grey man on the other side. Ken struck him in the head with enough force Elliott saw his whole grey, ugly face shift as the pole crushed its head, and the broken bits of its skull shifted beneath the rotting flesh of its face. A blink of an eye later, the body came to settle on the ground where it landed.

Ken didn't slow down. He kept moving with lethal grace as he moved the pole low and caught the next grey lady who stepped forward in the leg, and swept it right out from under her. Her body tilted back like she was looking at something in the sky overhead, and before gravity could pull the body down to the gravel road, Ken brought the pole down on her face and drove her skull straight into the road like a sledgehammer.

The last grey person, a stoutly built woman, moved in and Elliott felt his heart spike as a part of him thought, *this is it*. This was when he would see his friend die, but Ken straightened and pivoted on his front foot to spin his body around in a circle before he kicked out with his boot. The blow landed squarely on the grey lady's chest and launched her backwards into the gravel. Dust kicked up around her body as she landed hard on her back. Ken stepped forward towards her before she could even get her bearings, with the pole raised overhead. Elliott flinched away as the pole came down, just in time to miss the impact. He hadn't meant to, but it was a reflex response to turn away when you knew something horrible was about to happen. Like the moment right before two cars collide with lethal force. When Elliott looked back, he noticed that Ken had knelt down beside the grey lady and was using the hem of her dress to wipe off the end of the spear mechanically as he carefully surveyed the surroundings.

The entire ordeal was over in mere seconds. Elliott gawked at his friend as his mind tried to process the sheer amount of violence that he witnessed in such a short amount of time. Elliott has never seen anything like it before. He would never admit to having any love for the grey people, but for a moment there towards the end, maybe the last second of it, he kind of felt sorry for them. *Like, they didn't even have a chance*, Elliott thought as he reflected on what he had witnessed. *He totally murdered them.* It was true. Ken had dealt with the grey people with equal parts of savagery and grace, almost like they planned the movements out beforehand, and all Ken had to do was perform them. Like a fight scene from a movie.

Thinking on it more, Elliott inexplicably felt that it was beautiful, like if you removed the grey people and the cruel intent behind the movements, it would be pretty much like figure skating, but with a sharp stick. Elliott straightened up in his seat when he saw Ken was heading back. His face was hard and determined, and he had a predatory gaze in his eyes. Regardless of how serious he looked, Elliott couldn't resist himself when he walked up to Elliott's open window.

"That was awesome!" Elliott exclaimed loudly when Ken bent over and leaned his bulk in the window. "Like, so awesome. I can't believe you just did that. You were like," Elliott imitated what he had seen his friend do from the confines of his seat.

He knew he must have looked ridiculous at that moment, but he didn't care. Elliott had so much excitement his little body just couldn't seem to contain it.

"That was like the coolest thing I have ever seen. Where'd you learn to do all that stuff, anyway?" He looked at his friend wide-eyed with wonder and admiration, while Ken seemed… Well, normal. He wasn't even breathing hard.

"Coolest thing you've ever seen, huh?" He asked with a smile and a slight chuckle. "You need to get out more," he joked dismissively, while leaning the pole against the side of the truck. "Look, I'm going to clean up the bodies up ahead-,"

"Why?" Elliott asked before he had finished. He couldn't imagine why Ken would want to spoil the day more by lugging around a bunch of smelly bodies. Ken sighed and looked at him with a neutral face before answering.

"Because we can't leave them on the road. We drive on the road after all, and we can't drive over them, and I sure as hell don't want to drive around them all day. Just sit tight and I'll move them off to the side, and there's also another group farther on I want to clean up, so it might be a while. Are you okay to wait in the truck while I work?" Elliott didn't want to wait in the truck but he worried the alternative would be to help clean up the bodies of the grey people, and he *really* didn't want to do that.

"I'll wait in the truck."

"Cool," Kenshiro said. "Keep an eye out for anymore zombies while I do this. If you see any, just give the horn a quick honk." He gave Elliott one of his trademark thumbs-up, which Elliott enthusiastically returned, and then Ken stepped to the bed of the truck to retrieve the length of rope he liked to use to haul the grey bodies away.

Elliott watched him walk back to the bodies, haul them off the road, and onto the shoulder on the left. He wasn't overly gentle about it, and Elliott wondered if maybe he should be. They were dead after all, but the more he watched, the more he noticed Ken wasn't overly mean about it, either. Ken just looked like he was working, like he would have the same expression on his face if he was hauling lumber from point A to point B. To Elliott, something about that didn't feel right, because he wasn't just working. That wasn't just random pieces of wood he neatly stacked on the ground beside the road. It didn't feel right to do such a gruesome job so casually.

When Ken had finished moving the five bodies from the road, he looked over to Elliott from where he stood. Ken pointed to some other bodies, that were maybe twenty feet farther up the road, and used his hands to communicate that he was going to haul them away as well. Elliott responded with a thumbs-up before Ken could signal that he also wanted Elliott to wait in the car.

The air inside the cab was getting warm, so Elliott turned on the air conditioner, and enjoyed the cool breeze coming from the vents. He put his hand to the vent and felt the blessedly cool air smash into his sweaty palms, pass through his open fingers, and up his exposed forearm. Elliott saw where Ken was walking, and looked farther ahead to the pale brown gravel of Spruce Street. It led south and was the unofficial town line, because there was nothing to the west of it except open territory for maybe half a mile before the lake's border. There on the road, he saw the dark shapes and before he could even look away, his mind had already given him the tally of how many bodies were over there. Twenty-six, and Elliott was thankful he wasn't close enough for his wicked little brain to give him any more details of the scene. He didn't need to know, but he knew enough right now to know Ken was going to be there awhile. So, Elliott eased himself back in his seat, adjusted the air vents so the cool air hit him smack dab in the face with an increasingly cool stream of air, and did what he was told. He kept a lookout for the grey people, and when they came, he gave the horn a slight honk. In the distance, Ken would perk up, check his surroundings, and deal with the grey person with cold efficiency.

Elliott had to honk the horn three times before Ken could finished stacking the bodies on the road.

Ken dragged the last body over to the pile he had constructed on the side of the street by the intersection. It was large enough to be an official mound of bodies. Elliott purposely averted his eyes from it. There was something about it he didn't like, so he just didn't look at it, besides there were plenty of other things he could look at after all. He watched Ken's bulk walk towards the truck's passenger side and he opened the door and hopped into the truck. Elliott felt the heated air invade the truck and run across his cooled skin.

"You kept the truck running with the air conditioning on the whole time I was out there?" Ken asked calmly. Once Ken settled into his seat, Elliott could see the sweat had soaked through his shirt and was running down his face in tiny droplets. He was clearly hot, so Elliott knew he must enjoy the coolness of the air inside the truck as much as Elliott was.

"You bet," he said with a smile. "It's hot out there." Ken smiled and breathed in a deep lungful of the cool air.

"It sure is. What's the gas gauge at?" He asked, scanning the road ahead of them even though they were parked. Elliott figured he was searching for grey people, so he quickly checked the instrument cluster for the right gauge. It took a while.

"Umm... It's at the first line on the thing," Elliott finally said after his brain gave up searching for the words. In the end, Ken just leaned over and checked for himself.

"A quarter tank," he said.

"A quarter tank," Elliott repeated gleefully, and Ken just sort of looked at him for a moment. With his smooth features and those narrow, dark eyes it was hard to tell what Ken was thinking, but it was clear to Elliott something was out of place. Sometimes, Elliott felt he said things wrong by how people reacted to his words, and for a moment Elliott wondered if he was supposed to say something different.

"OK, from now on, let's maybe not run the truck for an hour with the air conditioning on. We are trying to save gas, after all."

"That's a good idea," Elliott said, not missing a beat. "It was starting to get cold in here." Ken did something Elliott hadn't seen before, nor expected. Ken burst out laughing. It made Elliott suddenly uncomfortable. "What did I say?" He pouted slightly.

"You just said something really funny. Don't worry about it," Ken said, and waved him off before telling Elliott it was time to go into the town. Elliott felt his heart get all jittery, but Ken knew where he wanted to go, and he assured Elliott they wouldn't be there long. Soon enough, he added, they would be playing catch in the yard and enjoying some tasty snacks for dinner.

Ken quickly picked out the first house he wanted to enter. Elliott nervously pulled up to the front of the quiet looking single-storey house that was a block into the town on Moore Avenue. It was a yellow house with white trim and was nestled into the middle of the open lot. As soon as Elliott parked the truck, Ken reached over and gently punched the center of the steering wheel. The truck's horn barked out a slight noise that startled Elliot.

"Every house we stop at, I want you to press the horn quick like that. Just once," Ken instructed before he exited the truck.

Ken quickly, and brutally dealt with the trio of zombies that appeared from behind the house. Once they were settled onto the ground, Ken moved into the house. Moments later he returned with a white garbage bag that was only partially filled and then placed the bag quietly into the back of the truck. Ken looked to him and Elliott guided his attention to the grey man walking on Moore Ave towards the front of the truck. Ken nodded and went back to the house to retrieve his spear before stalking towards the man.

Elliott watched his friend yank the pole free from

the dead grey man with a sudden jerk of his hand. Then Ken looked up with that face that was so hard to read, and did a slow look around himself. Elliott looked at his face and noticed that it wasn't his friend out there, not exactly. The face he knew was one of quiet amusement, and was warm. The person out there with the pole in his hand was, without a doubt, Ken, but a different Ken. This was Business Ken.

Over the last week, Elliott had seen glimpses of Business Ken, and each time the intensity of Ken's purpose radiated off him like the heat of a white-hot ember. It was Business Ken who first showed up in Elliot's living room, a dark shape hiding in the corner with darker eyes peering at Elliott from across the room. He was only there for a moment, and then regular Ken shifted into place as the shadows seemed to recede from his face. It was strange because physically nothing about him changed. He still looked the same as he had before, and Elliott couldn't explain it, other than to say his wave changed.

Since as long as Elliott could remember, and that was a long time, he had noticed a weird sort of energy that people had coming off them. He didn't see it like he saw the world, nor could he feel it in the sense he felt his clothes on his body, or the way the wind felt on his skin. But it was there, and he was acutely aware of it, even if nobody else was. Worse yet, if he concentrated hard enough, Elliott could go inside that energy. Then Elliott would find himself on the *Mind Shore*. That's when things got weird.

For the longest time, he didn't know what it was, or why it was the way it was. Elliott occasionally asked momma about it, but she would only flash that same grin whenever she didn't understand something. After a while, she just called it his gut-feeling. *Are you having another one of your gut-feelings?* She would comment when Elliott would shy away from someone he didn't want to be around.

As far as Elliott could tell, no two people had the same waves. He supposed a person's wave was unique to them, like fingerprints were. However, as unique as they were, they were also a lot of things waves had in common. Over the years, Elliott had only put them into two fairly basic categories. Smooth waves, and spiky waves. Smooth waves were like waves on a quiet lake shore, water coming in to wash the shoreline almost affectionately before quietly retreating. Those people Elliott got along with the best, Jenny was like that, gentle waves coming up to kiss the shore before scampering away.

His mother too, mostly, a deep blue ocean reaching out to stroke a sandy beach and smoothing out all the jagged edges and filling in the holes. Like all things in life, the waves scaled up. Some waves started out calm but then right before the beach they would swell and then crash onto the beach. While others, they would be like the wave a surfer might ride where it swells and crashes well before the beach and waters forcefully lap against shore like a grasping hand pulling whatever it can back into the water with it.

Angry people were like that, that's part of the reason he didn't enjoy being around his uncle. Mostly it was his breath, but also whenever he was around him, it felt like he might risk being pulled under somehow.

Beyond that were the Spiky waves.

They were like storm surges that crashed against the rocks with an explosion of force that sent water spraying in every direction, before its riptide sucks everything in its grasp back down into the depths. Elliott didn't like being in the company of those people, and would actively try to distance himself from their loud, destructive waves that seemed to crash inside his head, making it hard to think straight.

Ken's wave was blessedly calm, but deep, like the edge of the shore that dropped sharply into an abyss of black water. In the distance, there was a massive swell, bigger than anything he had felt before. Elliott had felt those types of waves before and didn't really know what to think about them. However, this was different. Ken's swell was like a mountain of water that just waited, in view of the shore. Never moving, never changing. Except for when Ken switched into *Business Ken*. Then that massive swell surged towards the beach, threatening to reach the shore but never actually doing so, because if it did, Elliott felt it would consume everything in its wake. He didn't know what that meant, though, or how that sense translated into the psyche of the person. The shore was serene. That was the part that seemed to affect how Elliott felt about a person. If the shore was calm, then Elliott felt he could grow to like them. So, the ease of Ken's shore was a good sign, but there was something ominous about that coolly, threatening swell in the distance that made Elliott wish he understood people's waves better.

The next two houses went the same way. Elliott would bark the horn once after he parked, and Ken would exit the house and deal with any grey people who arrived. After that, Ken would head back into the house, deal with whatever greys might remain inside, and then he would exit with a trash bag filled with what he found.

Ken exited a nice blue house that had an overgrown hedge surrounding the yard with a number of trash bags in his hand.

"Good news," Ken said after he deposited the bag in the truck's bed. "I think I found some clothes that might fit you."

"I like my clothes," he stated simply and with not much

conviction behind it.

"Maybe, but they don't fit. Trust me, if we find you some clothes that fit, I'm sure you'll like them just the same," Ken said while keeping a keen eye out for the grey people. Elliott wordlessly started the truck and allowed it to creep forward down the road under its own power.

It was true his clothes didn't fit. There was no use trying to hide that fact. His t-shirt sleeves didn't go all the way down to his elbows like they should, but instead stopped about halfway down his biceps. Even with his small frame, the shirt was still tight in the shoulders, and if he was to lift his hands above his head, his shirt would sort of jump up and expose his belly to the world. His pants fit better, sure the hem of his pant leg was above his ankle, but they went on just fine and didn't cause a problem as long as he didn't crouch down in that certain way that seemed to apply some uncomfortable pressure on his boy-berries. He couldn't argue with Ken that he needed a new wardrobe, but Elliott also didn't want to tell him why he liked his clothes.

His mother bought him this shirt when they went to the Target in Walsenburg, during their yearly back-to-school shopping trip. That would later become the last August before the world changed, and the grey people started popping up all over the place. The lady behind the counter at the check-out had on a name tag that said Terri, and her waves were gently lapping against the shoreline, but Elliott felt that farther out, there were turbulent waters swirling and churning in the darkness. Elliott told her it would be okay, and she looked confused for a moment, but then smiled kindly while continuing to ring through their purchases. On the way back, his momma was singing along with Travis Tritt on the radio, and he sat back and soaked in the warm afternoon sun through the car window.

The jeans were a hand-me-down from the Hagerty family. Elliott didn't know for sure who owned them originally, but he suspected Russell, the oldest boy in the Hagerty family, may have owned these first and then they made their way through Joshua, the younger of the two brothers, before they had made their way to him. Both the Hagerty boys were older than Elliott and they both were a little on the round side themselves. Mama said, "Only fools turn down a perfectly good pair of jeans. You're gonna wear 'em or you can run around outside in your ginch." She had a way with words.

On the right thigh was a tiny black dot that was a bit of paint he got on himself when he helped his daddy stain the bathroom cabinets. Mama got upset when she spotted that little dot later on that evening, but Daddy calmed her down by telling her how hard he had worked and what kind of help Elliott had been to the project. He then winked at Elliott and gave him a toothy grin, because he knew Elliott knew he was lying a little. He hadn't been that helpful that afternoon. The clothes he wore, sure, they were ill-fitting but like everything else he had, these clothes came with their own unique history.

He could also agree that, yes, these new clothes would have their own history and it would be with his new best friend, but that was the recent history. The recent history didn't have his parents in it... yet. He didn't want to let go of the old history. It felt like that would be a betrayal somehow, but he also remembered his mother's words.

Only a fool turns down a perfectly good pair of jeans.

"I guess," Elliott finally said sometime later to an empty truck. They had parked at the next house down the road. Ken had exited the truck some time ago and gone inside the house.

Throughout the morning, Elliott's superpower kept him safe and unnoticed inside the cab of the truck. A few times a grey person would walk into view while Ken was inside. When that happened, Ken instructed Elliott to bark the horn a single time and then he was to duck down under the dash for a ten-count until his special ability kicked in again. Ken told Elliott if he was ever in trouble he was to press the horn button three times in quick succession. That was the danger signal. So far, Elliott hasn't even considered using it.

They both knew the next house was going to be a problem before they even parked. The front door was already open and through the large window out front they could see a number of grey people moving around the inside. Ken wasn't phased by it though. After Elliott honked the horn, Ken used his spear on the grey people on the outside before he unsheathed the long-straight blade on his right leg and entered the house.

Elliott saw a large shadow moving quickly amongst the grey people like black lightning, obviously Ken, because wherever the fast-moving shadow went, another shape fell away. Ken bolted to another shadow that was in front of the window, and the shape sort of jumped up suddenly, with a crash that shattered the front bay window of the house, but also the calm of the day. So much so, Elliott jumped up in his seat in shock, but his eyes still registered the grey person flying through the air. The grey person, Elliott thought it looked like a man by his clothing, pierced the window in an explosion of glass and sound that seemed to fill the inside of the truck, and Elliott watched the graceful arc the grey man's slack body made as it sailed through the air with tiny fragments of glass around him that sparkled in the sunlight. Its body had a slight rotation as gravity seemed to pull his upper body down and forgot all about the lower half. As his momentum ended, the grey man's body crashed to the ground in an ungraceful way. Landing first on his shoulder and then his legs kind of carried on past him overhead until they, too, crashed into the ground. Then the stiffness in the grey man's joints kind of pole vaulted the upper half another half rotation, until the body came to rest some distance from the house.

Elliott looked on dumbfounded for a moment, he had only seen something like that in the movies. Like in a western, where the whole bar breaks out into a fight, or maybe in one of those other movies daddy watched sometimes. Seems like there was a lot of movies where people got thrown out of windows now that Elliott thought about it. To see it in real life, though.

"That was awesome," he exclaimed inside the empty cab.

Elliott was suddenly thankful he had been in the truck and was looking in the right direction when it happened so he could see the whole thing from beginning to gruesome, bone shattering end. He looked back to the space where the window had been and with it gone; he had a clear view inside the house, just in time to see Ken finish his work.

There were two more grey people left inside the room that he could see, a man and a woman, and before his weird little mind could discern too much else, it was all over inside the house. Ken kicked out low at the grey woman, who was considerably shorter than Ken and Elliott saw the impact ripple through the upper half of her body as the grey woman kind of tilted violently and tumbled to the ground. Ken then turned and Elliott saw a flash of light reflected off the steel in his hand briefly as Ken struck. First coming in low with his weight behind him, Ken brought the knife in his hand in an uppercut that caught the grey man under the chin with the knife point. Ken drove it home with such force he lifted the grey man's body off the ground and sent it crashing over the side of the couch and out of sight. Elliott looked at the stern darkness on Ken's face and it stirred something ugly inside him, like a rabbit that caught sight of a wolf hunting another animal. He saw Ken turn back to the grey woman who was out of sight on the floor. Elliott knew exactly where she was, he just had to follow the death glare on Ken's face to know. Elliott watched his friend face scrunch up in anger as he raised his boot up and stomp down with considerable force, once, twice, three times. On the third time he brought his boot down, Elliott could see that whatever it was he was looking at, Ken looked satisfied with it. Elliott was secretly glad he couldn't see the full scope of the scene Ken was standing in the middle of.

Ken didn't seem bothered though, he seemed to look around the room for something until he finally found it and he then went to the space where the bay window was and casually hopped out of the house and onto the lawn. Ken made his way to where the grey man he had kicked through the window lay on the ground, essentially motionless, save for the odd movement that looked more like an involuntary spasm than an actual intended motion. Elliott could see the angle of his neck didn't quite seem right, as he was lying on the ground. Soon enough, it no longer mattered because Ken walked up and casually sunk the blade into the side of his skull and the spasms stopped.

When Ken looked up to Elliott, he had a grim look on his face and Elliott could see dark spots on his face that, at first, looked like blood but only much darker. For a moment, he was worried Ken was injured until he realized that wasn't Ken's blood on his face. It was the blood of the grey people, and with a closer look Elliott could see that blood was in a lot of places on Ken's body.

Elliott was about to say something to his friend when he saw motion from the far side of the house the garage was on, it was another grey person. Ken had noticed it as well. His grim face turned, and Ken started off towards it with his one knife clutched in his hand. It was the long straight one that he kept on his right leg with the large pistol. It occurred to Elliott in that moment that the only time he had seen the large pistol out of its holster was when Ken had it on his lap when they first met, and wondered why that was. He didn't have long to think about it because Ken pulled his attention back to him, stalking up to the grey person who was halfway across the driveway. Ken collided with the grey man with his knife raised and punched it into the grey man's eye socket as Ken guided the body down to the pavement of the driveway. Ken quickly pulled his knife free and stepped back from the body.

"Ken?" Elliott called out to his friend from the open window of the truck as he walked back to the front door of the house. Elliott wanted to ask him if everything was ok, because the look on his face scared him a little. At this distance, he could just barely feel Ken's waves but he felt that monstrous swell churning angrily like a storm surge that would swallow up anything that was in its path.

"Stay in the truck, Elliott," Ken said. No, he commanded, and Elliott shrunk a little in his seat from the raw emotion in his voice.

Ken disappeared into the house and a minute or two later, Elliott heard an angry shout come from the house, and Elliott couldn't be sure, but to his ears it kind of sounded like a curse word. Then there was a crash from inside the house. He couldn't tell what it was, but whatever it was, it was loud and it made Elliott nervous. Ken came back out, same grim face that told Elliott that whatever was inside that house was bad enough to shake his friend, because Ken wasn't just angry. Sure, he looked plenty angry, and Elliott didn't so much see it on his friend's face, but he knew enough about people's waves to recognize sadness when he saw it. It was there, buried far beneath the angry churning swell, small enough to be overlooked but still significant enough to affect the surrounding swell. Elliott avoided his dark eyes when they focused on him and he raised up his one hand.

"Everything is fine," he lied. "Just stay in the truck while I clean this mess up."

Ken put his pole in the back of the truck, pulled out his length of rope, and dragged the bodies of the grey people from the house to the corner of the lawn. He started with the one on the driveway, and then the one in a crumpled heap that was surrounded by glass. Then the four from the other side of the house that showed up when they first arrived. After that, Ken moved into the house and moved the corpses out from the house to the pile.

Ken first pulled out a large grey man and wrestled the body to the ever-increasing pile on the corner of the lawn. Next, he pulled a smaller grey man from the house, followed by a smaller grey lady in khaki shorts and a tan shirt with a smashed-in face that forced Elliott to look away in disgust. After that, Ken brought out a smaller grey body. This time he carried it in his arms effortlessly as he made his way to the pile. The body looked so small in his arms. Unlike the others, Ken laid this one on the pile with a measure of care, and when it was done, his friend took a deep breath and headed back inside.

A short time later Ken re-emerged from the house with a small white bundle in his arms. Elliott watched him cross the lawn with it, and when he approached the pile of bodies, Ken gently laid the tiny bundle on top of the pile. Ken nestled it in the lap of the smaller one he had just put there. Ken turned back to the house, but not before locking eyes with Elliott, who looked at him through the windshield with a worried face. Elliott held up his thumb to his friend, as more of a question than a statement.

Is everything alright?

Elliott could see on his face that something had changed from when they arrived, and it worried Elliott because he didn't know what it was and therefore grew concerned that maybe it was something Elliott did, or didn't do. Ken looked at him and he could see his chest swell and fall with a deep breath before he lifted his hand and raised his thumb up unenthusiastically, but his face remained blank and distant, before he moved back into the house.

When Ken didn't reappear after a few minutes had passed, Elliott got worried that maybe he ran into more trouble while he was in the house and pondered if he was going to see Ken haul any more bodies out.

Sometime later though, when Ken did finally re-emerge from the house, Elliott saw he was wearing different clothes than he had when he went in. Ken entered with blue jeans and a white polo shirt that he wore underneath that vest he always had on. Now, his blue jeans were clearly more faded. Plus, Ken replaced his father's white polo shirt with a tan button-up shirt. Ken had a clean face again and Elliott noticed that his hair was also wet. He had a refreshed look to him, but his face still held a grim expression. Ken made his way to the truck with two heavy bundles in his hands.

He said nothing as he approached the bed of the truck. Ken easily tossed the two bags into the back of the truck, then he simply turned back to the house, and later returned with two more bags in his hands, which he again deposited into the truck bed. On the third trip, he had yet another white kitchen garbage bag in one hand and in the other; he carried another large water jug. Elliott couldn't believe that after he placed those items in the truck bed that Ken was going in again. *How much stuff is he going to take?* Elliott wondered if maybe Ken wanted help with all the bags, but he quickly surmised that if Ken did indeed want his help, he would ask. On the last trip, Ken came out of the house with one object Elliott recognized and another he didn't. In Ken's left hand, was a fairly large red plastic jerry can that Elliott just assumed had gasoline in it, because he couldn't think of anything else people would put into a container like that. In his right hand, was what looked like a short, fat suitcase and judging by the effort Ken put into carrying it, Elliott could tell it must weight a lot. As he got closer, Elliott could see on the side of it was a dial and a couple switches. At a loss, Elliott looked at Ken with a quizzical look.

"It's a generator," Ken said, seeing the look on Elliott's face, "A little one. These guys turned their basement into a bunker of sorts," Ken said as he approached the truck. "Things must have gone to shit pretty early on though, because they still had a ton of stuff, including this little beauty."

He first lifted the jerry can up over the side of the truck to place it in the bed, but for the generator he quietly opened the tailgate before hoisting it into the back. Ken slowly clicked the tail gate closed and jumped into the passenger seat.

Once the door was closed, Ken sank back into the seat, closed his eyes and let his head fall back onto the headrest. He took in a deep breath and when he let it out, it came out sounding like a low, deep throaty growl. Ken let the moment draw out for another breath before saying: "That was a messy one, that was a real messy one, but we got a lot of good stuff. So, it was worth it, but still…" Ken left the sentence hanging in the air, like halfway through he had run out of words.

"What kind of stuff?" Elliott asked casually, but his rumbling stomach focused his mind on one thing, even though he didn't want Ken to know that.

"All kinds of food," Ken said while keeping his eyes closed, "I also found clothes for you and me. The guy's clothes are a bit large for me, but they'll work for the time being, and I think the clothes I found for you should be about the right size. We'll see." He opened his eyes then and sat up straighter in his seat to have a quick look around the area before returning his gaze to Elliott. "We should probably get going. You okay to drive back, or do you want me to?" Elliott shook his head and reached for the ignition.

"No, no, I can do it." Elliott turned the key and the truck came to life around them. "Can we turn on the A/C?" Even with both windows open to allow a breeze to blow through the cab, it was still uncomfortably warm inside the truck. Elliott had a thin sheen of sweat that seemed to cover every inch of his body, and he had just been sitting the whole time.

"Fuck, yes," Ken exclaimed suddenly and Elliott flinched slightly at the curse word, but Ken didn't seem to notice as he reached for the controls, and turned the fan on high. Soon enough, blessedly cool air ran across Elliott's face. "That's the best idea I've heard all day."

Ken positioned the vent on his side to blow into his face while he leaned back in the seat and rested his arm on the window.

"Let's go." Elliott nodded and threw the transmission into gear as Ken guided him to reverse the truck into the driveway of the house they were at, and then pull forward and turn back down the road, heading for home. It was a simple enough drive, no real turns involved, just a few slight bends to be considered. Besides which, Ken again instructed him to just let the truck coast under its own power. Reminding him they didn't want a dust trail the grey people could see, and then follow to its source, but also, that they weren't in any real hurry. It was mid-afternoon, judging by the sun in the sky, and Elliott thought they had plenty of day left ahead of them.

"Umm, Ken?" Elliott asked when the truck had settled into a pleasant cruise on the road and Elliott felt he had a handle on the vehicle enough that his mind went to other things. "Did you find any chocolate cake mix?"

"No, sorry buddy, I didn't find one," Ken said dismissively while looking out the window as they moved out of town, probably for grey people. Elliott didn't see any, but then again, he was concentrating his focus on the narrow strip of gravel ahead of him. He almost missed the sudden ripple in Ken's wave.

"Oh," Elliott sagged a bit in his seat. He couldn't help it. "That's ok"

"That's good," he said, and in the corner of Elliott's eye, he could see Ken had turned to look at him, "Because I found THREE!" Ken then exclaimed loudly, and Elliott heard the news and turned, and saw Ken had a big grin on his face. That confirmed it.

Elliott cheered loudly and took one of his hands off the wheel to do a fist pump in the air, which caused the truck to swerve slightly on the road, Ken laughed as Elliott frantically scrambled to get his hand back on the wheel, and then over-corrected for the slight swerve which caused the truck to skip in the other direction. His heart jumped in his chest but Elliott got the truck under control and soon enough they were moving straight down the center of the road again. Elliott let out a breath when the excitement was over and Ken chuckled in his seat as he looked out over the countryside.

It was nice to hear Ken laugh. He didn't do it often, not genuinely, anyway. Even though Ken was quick to offer a smile and usually spoke with merry tones, Elliott found the expressions hollow. It wasn't the real Ken. It was the mask he wore when he was around Elliott. He knew it because he recognized the signs. Ken wasn't the first person he ran across who tried to hide their genuine feelings from the world. Quite the opposite, most people hide who they were from the world. It was one challenge Elliott had with people, because there was who they really were, and then there was the face they put forward for everyone else to see. Like an image that was superimposed over another.

"Now, before you get too excited, I think there are some things we should do when we get back, you know, before we pig out on chocolate cake," Ken said from the passenger seat and snapped Elliott out of his thoughts. "It kind of smells in this truck. I think we should take today and clean ourselves up good. God knows I'm feeling a bit shaggy." He said as he ran his knuckles along his jawline, feeling the tiny black hairs of his patchy pre-beard scruff. Elliott took a careful moment and sank his nose cautiously down to his armpit and took a timid sniff. There was definitely something funky there, but Elliott didn't think it was too bad. "And it probably would be a good idea if we gave you a bit of a haircut."

"Yeah," Elliott said quickly, checking the rear-view mirror and seeing his sandy brown locks hang down from his forehead.

He needed a haircut. This was the longest his hair had ever been. Momma would have a fit if she saw the state of his hair. In the front it hung down past his eyebrows, and Elliott had made a habit of using his hand to brush his hair out of his eyes. On the side, his hair hung well past his ears, and the hair in the back was close to touching his shoulders. Normally, his mother would cut it every couple of weeks. She liked to keep it short and neat with a part to the right, because that looked best. For whatever reason, his hair didn't seem to want to part in the other direction. It just refused to settle if he tried parting it to the left, or at least it used to. Now it just seem to hang in whatever direction it wanted. It looked unruly. Elliott didn't like it.

"I *do* need a haircut," he agreed, and if Ken will do it for him, well, that was just fine with Elliott.

Ken quickly explained his plans for the night. A bath for them both, and a haircut for Elliott. Ken said he wanted to shave the scruff off of his face. It had been a few days since he had shaved. Ken didn't need a haircut, he said he cut his own hair a few days before he met up with Elliott and it still looked too short to grab, but Elliott could see patches that were clearly longer or shorter than the rest and secretly hoped Ken would do a better job when he was cutting someone else's hair than he did on his own. If Elliott ended up having the exact haircut as Ken, well, he supposed that would be alright as well. He didn't mind looking like his friend.

After they had cleaned up, Ken wanted him to go through the clothes he found for him and see if anything fit well enough to keep. Ken was sure to note that he shouldn't be choosing clothes based on how they looked, but if they fit and were comfortable. Which made sense to Elliott. Ken added they weren't competing in a beauty pageant after all, and Elliott laughed at the thought of the two of them on stage. Ken said they would eat dinner, and then after that he would bake the cake so they could eat it for dessert before bedtime. It was a good plan to Elliott, but if he was being honest, any plan that ended with him eating cake was a good plan to him. He nodded his agreement to each point of the night's itinerary as he drove on. The day was looking up like Elliott hoped it would, but he still had a lingering thought that bothered him.

"Ken? What was in that white package you put on top of the pile?" Elliott knew he didn't need to say anymore by how Ken's waves suddenly shifted, Ken knew exactly what Elliott was talking about.

"Oh, that?" He said dismissively while looking down the road in front of them. "Why do you want to know?"

"When you came out with it, I could tell it was…" Elliott paused and searched for the right words. *I could tell whatever it was made you really sad.* "Important." He looked at Ken, hoping he had chosen the right words. Ken nodded slowly before he spoke.

"I suppose it was, at one point." Ken paused. He seemed to be searching for words of his own. "I could tell you, but the problem with that is once you knew it would change you forever, at least, that's what I'm afraid of. You stick with me long enough, you will see your fair share of nasty things. Some of those nasty things are so bad, they dim your light a bit." Elliott had to admit, he didn't know exactly what Ken was talking about. By the way he looked in the seat next to him, Elliott believed Ken knew what he was saying, and Elliott would do well to remember what he said, even though he wasn't exactly sure of Ken's meaning. "I guess what I'm trying to say is it's not really important what it was, it's not something you want to know about. Better to forget all about it and try to focus on something else." He paused for a moment before adding, "That's what I try to do, anyway."

"Okay, Ken." That was good enough for him. Even though, he found he was slightly more curious than ever about what Ken could wrap up in that package, he was ultimately content that maybe he really was better off not knowing.

They were more than halfway home as the truck slowly moved down the road, hardly fast enough for a decent breeze to blow in the windows if they were open. Elliott was thankful Ken left the air conditioning on, but he was getting a suspicion that Ken was enjoying it more than him. Elliott looked over and saw him relaxed into the chair with his arm resting on the window's edge. He looked at peace, sort of. Ken was still alert and aware. Elliott caught him a few times checking the surroundings, his eyes suddenly became intensely sharp as they fluidly moved over the landscape, taking in every detail as they went, and when they finished, they would once again settle into a dull, lazy gaze that just sort of took in everything as they went.

Elliott replayed the day's events in his mind as they went along. He felt he had a good hold on driving the truck at this speed, and it had been an exciting day. There was a lot to think about, a lot to mull over. One thing he noticed in his memories that he missed in the moment's excitement, was the look on Ken's face when he dealt with the grey people throughout the day. It was a simple thing to miss when that pole of his was in the air, hitting the targets Ken chose with lethal force. It was like nothing Elliott had ever seen before. Ken moved his pole with a sort of familiarity that gave it the illusion that the pole was an extension of his body, his will, like a scorpion's stinger or a tiger's claws. Ken struck out with that pole like it was a part of him, like something ingrained him with the knowledge of how to use it into his DNA. Seeing that, it was easy to miss the expression on Ken's face when he struck, especially since it was only really visible in that hair-width length of time right before he made contact. After that, it was gone, until the next time he struck. Once Elliott saw it and recognized it for what it was, though, he couldn't avoid seeing it.

One image stuck out over the others in his mind.

Ken was standing alone in the living room of the last house, and from the truck Elliott could still see the dark blood on his face oozed down his cheek. It gave his face the illusion he was wearing war paint, his chest swelled and collapsed as he just stood there with his fists clenched by his sides. His fury radiated off him like an intense heat that distorted the surrounding air. For two short breaths, he stood in that living room like a wild beast who was about to rip its prey to shreds, a dark bloody specter on the edge of murderous motion, and after that second breath left his body, somebody flipped a switch somewhere in the cosmos and that dark specter became his friend again.

"Umm… Ken?" Elliott practically whispered.

"Yeah, buddy?" Ken said, soaking up the cool breeze coming from the truck's dash.

"Do you hate the grey people?" Elliott asked, feeling himself shrink slightly.

Once he heard the words leave his mouth, he regretted the question. He was still concerned about the answer, but not at the risk of being too nosy. A fault his mother had warned him about frequently, and sitting there with that question hanging in the air, it suddenly felt like one of those times. He shot a nervous look, and half expected to see a scalding look on Ken's face, but his expression changed little as he stared off down the road.

"I guess I do," he said thoughtfully and then turned to look at Elliott. "Does that bother you?" He asked, and Elliott was relieved to hear the sincerity in his voice.

"Momma said people who hate are blind, and that

people shouldn't hate because it doesn't accomplish nothing and just makes people hate more."

"She did, eh? I see where she is coming from there," Ken nodded thoughtfully as he spoke. "And I guess I can agree to that to a point, but I think that is just one way of looking at it. I like to think of it as a lighthouse. It gives you something to focus on so you don't lose your way. I think if more people hated the grey people when they first showed up, and feared them less, we probably wouldn't be in this situation. But everyone was either too busy trying to contain them for their safety or running away from them, to deal with the problem." He said *grey people* like it was a dirty word when he spoke, but other than that his voice held no anger, which Elliott was thankful for.

"Is that why you hunt them?" Elliott continued.

"Oh," Ken smiled, "Make no mistake there either, I'm not hunting them. They're hunting us."

Chapter 11

Elle

The helicopter slipped over the deep blue waters of the East River. Martin expertly flew them straight to there destination. *La Guardia.* Elle sat numbly in her chair and squeezed and released her hands to keep herself from going insane.

During the last week, her days had been filled with training. In the mornings, Elle trained with Martin as they went over the repair process from beginning to end. Martin was like a drill instructor as he stood by with a stop watch in his hand. He timed her while she went through the motions of removing the various parts of Maggie she would need to get remove the leaking hose. Martin had a time in his mind for how long it should take her to complete the job. Forty-five minutes, from beginning to end. Elle didn't even come close in the beginning, but Martin kept on her. By the end of the week, and after a few arguments, they had it down to a solid fifty minutes, with a few attempts being under the time limit.

In the afternoons, after a quick lunch, Elle did firearms training with Nathan. She had never spent much time with the quiet, blonde soldier before and to her surprise she found him to be pretty good company. Unlike Martin, Nathan was gentler with his lessons. During those seven days Nathan taught her how to fire and reload a variety of handguns, assault rifles, and the smaller submachine guns. When shooting, Nathan brought his lesson down to three easy-to-remember points. *Ready* your weapon, *aim* down the sights, and *fire.* Ready, aim, fire. It seemed idiot-proof.

"What if I miss?" Elle asked once during a lesson.

"Repeat steps two and three," Nathan quickly quipped.

Elle's evenings were spent with her sister. They simply spent their time together doing whatever they felt like. They didn't talk about the mission, though every now and then Elle would slip in a few words to try and reassure her sister. Kate wasn't interested, and soon, Elle found it was safer to not talk about it. It was easier to actually enjoy the time she spent with her sister when she didn't have to pretend not to be worried.

Now, she was actually on the mission. Elle was eager to start, well, she was eager not to feel this anxiety inside herself. But she knew that wouldn't happen until she set her feet back down onto the security of The Prescott. Only then, would it be over.

Elle nervously caught movement coming from Martin's seat. Elle whipped her head to the side and saw Martin reach over and tap his leg to get her attention. She was about to say something when her gaze went to his face, her heart sank a bit when she saw him shake his head slowly. She frowned at him and followed his hand as it went to the center console, to a component with dials, buttons, and a digital readout that currently read double zeros. Martin motioned discreetly to her side of the console, and she looked to the same place on the bottom corner on her side, and sure enough, she had a very similar looking component tucked into the console. Complete with the same dials, buttons, and a digital read-out that currently displayed double zeros. When she turned back, Martin held up two fingers so the others wouldn't see and then she watched closely as he moved to the component and turn the dial until the read-out had a zero and a two. *The intercom!* Elle went back to the intercom control on her side, and now that she had an idea what she was looking at, she recognized one dial had the symbol she recognized as volume, which meant the other one was the channel select. She quickly switched her intercom over to channel two and immediately heard Martin's smooth voice in her ears.

"They can't hear us in the back. This channel is just for the pilot and co-pilot. We don't have a lot of time before we get there," Martin said quickly and yet still maintained an air of quiet, steady calm. "If I don't make it out of that hanger, I want you to high-tail it out of there, head south towards the parkway and follow that east for about a mile. There's a marina there, find a boat and get the hell out of dodge." Martin kept his gaze forward the whole time he spoke, and she could tell even with his hushed tones he was deadly serious.

What the fuck? This wasn't part of the plan.

"What about the others?" She whispered into the mic. Following Martin's lead, she kept her eyes forward, probably to conceal their conversation from any prying eyes in the back.

"Fuck them," he said bitterly. "They can take care of themselves. Trust me, it's what they're good at. If I don't make it out, just point yourself south and start running, and you don't stop running until you get to that marina. You don't owe them anything." Elle's mind was doing circles in her head, *you're telling me this NOW!*

There was so much more she wanted to ask, to talk about, to discuss so she could get her head around what exactly he was saying and why he felt now was the time to be telling her this. It's no secret Martin had some reservations about Mason's bunch, and one could even say Martin didn't like them. The feeling was definitely mutual in some regard, but what he was implying went far beyond that. What he was suggesting was leaving them behind to save herself. Not that she could imagine they would really feel her absence, but just the idea of it felt wrong. Once she thought about it, though, the idea of them leaving her behind to save themselves didn't seem outrageous. Until something else struck her entirely.

"What about my sister?" She asked and risked a quick glance at him. She could see his face darken as he kept his eyes forward. "What about the rest of the people at the Prescott?" She pressured him further when she returned her gaze forward. If he didn't make it out of that hanger, they were all fucked. He was the lynchpin of their success and the continued survival of the people back at the Prescott.

"I don't have all the answers, Elle," Martin answered defensively, and she didn't blame him. He knew the stakes involved. He wouldn't be careless with their lives if he didn't have to. If there was anyone else who could go into the hanger and retrieve the parts and tools they needed, Martin wouldn't be going. But he is the only one who knows the building, and where to locate those items.

"Exactly," she snapped softly, "So you make sure you get your ass out of there with the shit we need so it doesn't come to that." There was definitely venom in her voice as she spoke. She couldn't help it. The thought of being in a situation where she would never see her sister again was unacceptable.

"Yes, ma'am," he said with what Elle imagined was a grin on his face.

She didn't doubt his conviction about the success of this... *mission*. She didn't doubt anyone's conviction who was inside the craft. They all needed this to succeed, even Jackie. There might be hostility, but Elle trusted it would be pushed aside when they touched down at the airport. They might not like her and Martin, but Mason's crew understood success depended on everyone doing their parts.

Once they were over Roosevelt Island, Martin banked the craft gently to the north-east. Seconds later, they crossed the river and were over Astoria. She had a step aunt who lived in Astoria somewhere. Since Carl came into the picture, Elle had only been there once or twice. Looking out over the city, though, she couldn't find where her aunt's apartment building would have been. From this height, the city blended together into a vast topography of concrete and steel where none of it was identical, but nothing was so unique as to stand out from the rest.

Elle looked out ahead of the craft looking for some sign of where she was, and in the distance, she saw a tiny emerald patch of land that stood out against the grey. Elle figured that had to be St. Michael's Cemetery, and on the northern edge was a massive-looking road that stood out on the landscape like a vein on flesh, Grand Central parkway.

They buried her father at St. Michael's. From the air, she saw the section of the cemetery they laid him to rest and, in her mind, two images flashed by. One was the wildly infectious smile her father had. She still remembered how the corners of his grin curled slightly and little dimples would pop out on his cheeks. The second was the front of his tombstone. It wasn't anything fancy. From a hundred paces away, it was invisible amongst the other tombstones. Elle hated that. She remembered the first time she had gone to visit his grave alone. She had skipped school to do it. When she first arrived, she spent what seemed like hours wandering through the tombstones sobbing uncontrollably with frustration until an attendant noticed her and took pity on her and showed her to his grave.

Moments later the craft was upon it and the green of the

cemetery disappeared beneath them. Up ahead, on a giant piece of man-made real estate that stretched into Flushing Bay, was LaGuardia Airport.

LaGuardia Airport hugged the northern side of the Parkway where it curved north around East Elmhurst. Here it looked like its own city, complete with the massive unique structures of terminal A and terminal B, that helped separate the airport from the rest of the city. Out front were the two massive parking structures and behind them were the equally impressive two main terminals of the airport. Between the two parking garages was the control tower. It rose above all the other structures and sort of looked like the mast of some giant mechanical ship, complete with a crow's nest at the top.

Further east were the smaller terminals, C and D, and behind those smaller terminals were hundreds of abandoned jetliners. The magnitude of it struck her when she first saw it. Elle had never seen so many jumbo jets parked in one place like that before. The planes occupied every free inch of asphalt of the Apron. From her viewpoint, the planes on the tarmac were so close they looked like puzzle pieces loosely placed together. She swore a few of them might actually be touching. Before the outbreak had become apocalyptic, the government had shut down the airports, and with nowhere to go, the airport just started parking the planes where they could.

Before the outbreak, the parking structures in front of the main terminals were in the process of being renovated with newer, more efficient structures. The terminal B parking structure and concourse had been completed a year before the outbreak. It stood shiny and new with reflective glass windows that protected no one from the elements. The shiny solar panels stood out on the roof in sections, and Elle wondered briefly if there was any real electricity left in the building. *Maybe we should put up some solar panels?* She thought as she marvelled at the newly completed structure.

The other parking structure, it had been abandoned mid-way through construction. The concrete and steel skeleton of the parking structure for Terminal A rose above the ground like the bones of some giant creature that had bleached in the sun. *It looks undead, it looks like a goddamn undead building.* As stupid as the thought sounded when it popped into her head, as the craft slipped nearer to the abandoned project, it seemed to match too perfectly for her to be completely comfortable with it. Martin dropped the craft down as they passed over the parkway and Elle saw figures down on the street level. Everywhere she looked, she saw at least one of them. She looked over to the airspeed gauge, one of the few she recognized, and the feeling she suddenly got in her gut had been correct. They were slowing down.

As Martin steered the helicopter past the side of the incomplete structure, Elle spotted a figure inexplicably wandering near the edge of the top level of what would have been the parking structure. There was a patchwork of concrete that led to the top level, and Elle wondered how the zombie had even gotten up there on its own. A moment later, she saw the figure casually walk off the edge of the structure in pursuit of them as they flew by, and calmly fall six stories. It hit the ground hard enough to kick up a cloud of dust around the impact point.

"One-minute warning," Martin stated over the cabin intercom as he aimed Maggie towards the north-western tip of the airport's property.

There, amongst the vast emptiness of the runways, was a paved area with three hangers that were clearly separate from the main terminal with marked portions she assumed were the parking stalls for some sort of aircraft. There were three wide hangers in a row. Beyond them, Elle could see the drab waters of the East River, and further out into the bay was the infamous Riker's Island. All three hangers were identical in size but only two of them were a drab grey color while the one on the far north had brighter colors, and even at this distance she could make out the Skyways Limo Service logo on the billboard above the massive retractable hanger doors.

In front of their hanger, painted on the ground, were three large squares that looked like giant bulls-eyes. *This is it*, Elle thought to herself as Martin was making a fast approach to the landing zone. Then she looked down only to see her clenched fists resting on her lap. Elle willed her fingers to relax and when they finally opened, she saw that she had dug deep divots into the flesh of her palm with her fingernails. Elle forced herself to take a few deep, steady breaths as she ran through the checklist for the first couple of minutes after they touched down.

She quickly located the scaffolding she would need to maneuver in beside the helicopter as they descended. There was only one, which was fine because Martin had said he didn't need a ladder to change the motor oil. Over the last week, Elle had been so focused on her own job she didn't even bother to inquire what Martin's task entailed, nor had he offered anything about it. For him, though, it was probably pretty routine, except for the constant threat of the undead menace, of course.

Elle looked out the window as they neared the landing zone and she saw them. The undead. Even in this deserted section of the airport, she didn't have to look very hard to spot one. She saw loose patches of zombies that were still wandering all around the hangers, the paved area in front, and all over the open area of the runways.

There was no hiding from them, and with the thunderous sound of the engine, she assumed every fucking zombie in a two-mile radius knew they were here, and God only knows how many that might be. She looked at them, feeling sweat moistening her palms. The undead were already making their way towards them and, like true New Yorkers, no two were the same. The only things the zombies had in common were that they all had their arms out like their prey was always just out of their reach, and they were all walking towards the helicopter as it was landing.

Somebody in the back had opened the side door to the passenger compartment before the skids slapped down onto the asphalt, and it triggered an alarm which made her jump. Martin didn't even notice because he already had his headset off and was quickly flipping switches and pressing buttons to power down the engine. The effect on the sound of the engine was immediate as the RPM's of the engine bled away.

She was the last one to unhook her seatbelt and exit the craft to step into the windstorm of the craft's rotor wash, everyone else was already moving with a sense of purpose. Elle furrowed her brow and started moving towards the maintenance scaffolding, being sure to keep her head down until she was out from underneath the rotor. Martin met up with her as she was coming around the front of the nose. He grabbed her arm and pulled her close so she could hear his words over the sound of the dying engine.

"Don't forget, wait until the rotor comes to a full-,"

"Yeah, yeah, I know," She said, pushing him in Mason's direction, who she could see was aggressively waving for him to follow while Martin was busying himself telling her things she already knew. Like honestly, did he really think she needed him to tell her not to get on the scaffolding until the blades stopped moving? They were called *blades*, for Christ's sakes.

And then the shooting started.

It was to be expected, but she still jumped slightly when the first shot rang out. Elle looked up, and Martin was hustling behind Mason, Dennis, and Nathan as they made their way toward the hanger door with their rifles raised in front of them. More shots rang out as the dead in front of them fell. They were calm and professional as they moved. With each shot, another undead person fell to the ground in front of them. While they were gone, Derek took up position by the helicopter side that was facing the hanger. Jackie was covering the side that faced the wide-open expanse of the runways. Elle started towards the service scaffolding that was maybe twenty feet away off to the side of the hanger. She stopped when she saw a trio of undead beyond it, awkwardly and angrily making their way towards her. They would reach the scaffolding well before she would.

A moment before, she saw Martin's group disappear into the man-door of the hanger and the darkness beyond, so she pivoted and called out to Derek in his silly looking Hawaiian shirt who was scanning the surrounding area for targets. There were plenty of undead to shoot at if he wanted to, but Elle knew the perimeter team would not shoot until absolutely necessary. Right now, the closest threat to Derek's side of the helicopter was a hundred yards off yet.

"Hey, Derek." He turned to look at her, and par for the type of person he was, he looked pissed off. "Give me a hand." She didn't ask. Maybe it was the situation, or the adrenalin, but she didn't have it in her to ask. She commanded. She pointed to the scaffolding and the trio of undead moving towards it. For a moment, given her history with the man and given what Martin had said on the way here, *they would leave you behind in a heartbeat*, she considered the possibility he would just shrug, or give her the finger and leave the scaffolding to her.

To his credit, Derek simply nodded and approached the scaffolding with his rifle out in front, and she followed close behind. Derek moved with purpose as he walked up on the trio of zombies. Derek got what she felt was dangerously close before he raised the rifle up and fired three shots in fairly quick succession and, one by one; he popped the heads of the undead in front of them.

Elle watched in muted horror as their heads snapped back violently and she could see the explosion of gore and bone out the back of their skulls, as the bullets passed through with ease. The last one to fall, Derek had hit slightly off center and a decent-sized piece of skull broke away from the impact and flew off to the side. As the body sank to the ground, Elle could see inside its skull and it took a moment for her mind to register what she saw spill out of the wound when it hit the ground. *Not now*, she told herself and took her eyes from it and focused it on what mattered.

The scaffolding.

When they approached it, Derek quickly informed her that the casters on the bottom were the locking type, and they had to be unlocked before they could move it. Then she watched him as he used the toe of his boot to press down on a small pedal on the one side of the caster. Elle followed suit with the casters on her side and when all the wheels were unlocked, she was glad to see Derek grab the opposite side and help push the scaffolding towards the helicopter.

It wasn't exactly light; Elle knew she could have managed on her own but she was glad to have Derek's help, because the two of them could maneuver the scaffolding a lot faster than she could have on her own. The faster they could get this into place beside the helicopter, the sooner she could start her part of the operation. The two of them pushed the scaffolding up to a good speed as they came around to her side of the helicopter. By then Jackie was firing at a slow but steady rate and behind them she could hear muffled shots from inside the hanger, those shots were far more frequent. Elle said a silent prayer for Martin's team as she and Derek positioned the scaffolding underneath the compartment where she would be working. Derek locked the caster on his side and turned to her.

"You good?" He shouted even though the noise of the engine had died down and the rotors were lazily coming to a stop. Elle thought nothing of it, *probably just adrenalin*, she told herself. Behind him, she could see a group of undead approaching from beyond the tail of the craft.

"You got some behind us," she pointed behind him, "Go." She pointed again, and Derek nodded once and turned to head towards them. She turned away and a moment later, she heard shots come from behind her. He and Jackie were responsible for covering all sides of the craft until Martin's team returned from the hangar. However long that was.

Jackie was about twenty feet away from Maggie, facing out towards the runway. She had her feet planted squarely with her knees bent, and Jackie looked very comfortable with her rifle tucked into her shoulder. Ahead of her was a massive open area that was littered with too many undead to count. They were all spread out over a large area, with few zombies being closer than twenty feet from each other. Jackie started on the right side and scanned left with the rifle, lined up the ones within her comfort zone and fired until they fell. Jackie didn't hit her mark every time, but it was damned close, far better than Elle felt she could do. Jackie was one warrior holding back a slowly advancing army.

She's the one keeping me safe.

Elle jokingly thought how dire a circumstance she must be in if she was putting her life in Jackie Orr's hands. Elle watched Jackie pause her firing only long enough to pull out the spent magazine and slap in a fresh one, then she shouldered the rifle and sighted a new target and fired.

Elle snapped back to the job at hand. With the scaffolding in place and the main rotor still lazily winding down, she moved on to her next phase. It was time to gather the tools. She turned to move around the nose of the craft when her heart sank. Elle didn't remember seeing the red toolbox Martin described where he said it would be out in front of the hanger, but she kept moving because it *had* to be there, and not seeing it didn't mean it wasn't there.

After all, it felt like it had been a lifetime since they had touched down on the tarmac, and maybe it was there and her mind just didn't register it. She rounded the nose and immediately spotted the large red upright toolbox in front of the hanger, close to the door Martin's team entered through.

How could I have missed that? She scornfully thought before she hurried over to it. She knew what she was looking for. Martin made her memorize the socket sizes. She already had the quarter-inch ratchet and hexagon socket she would need for the engine cover bolts in her pocket. So, she would just need a three-eighths ratchet, and the four other sockets. A nine-sixteenth wrench for the hose connectors, and a flathead screwdriver to help with any prying she might need to do with the motor mount bracket. She knew where she would find everything because Martin explained it was actually his toolbox.

As she approached the large red steel tool box, she saw the color had faded, and she could see a film on the outside where the dust had collected from its exposure to the elements. *How long had it been out here?* She wondered briefly how long it had been since the last doomed mission to the airport, but quickly abandoned the thought as she stepped up to the box. The way Martin explained where she would find the tools left nothing to the imagination. The sockets displayed on the very top of the box, along the front of the compartment, had metric sizes on the left, and standard sizes on the right. Behind those, were the three-eighths sockets. This time the sizes were by row with metric being in front, and standard directly lined up behind those. The last four rows were all half-inch sockets, with the first two rows being regular sockets organized like the others, and the back two rows were all flat black impact sockets.

Martin instructed her to grab the three sockets in the three-eighths ratchet size. Which thanks to Martin's abnormally organized tool box, she readily found and quickly stuffed them into the pockets of her jacket. Martin had explained the box down to a tee during one particular sitting they had. Now standing in front of it, even though she was seeing it for the first time, Elle felt like she knew it. She moved to the lower section of the box, to the first left-hand drawer. When she pulled out the drawer, it didn't surprise her when she found that Martin filled it with a small assortment of ratchets. Martin had three different three-eighths ratchets for some reason. She picked one she felt would work best and stuffed it into the back pocket of her jeans.

That's when she heard it. That unmistakable groaning.

Even with the gun fire popping off all around her and from within the hanger, she heard it. That low sort of gurgling snarl that made her heart seize up for a moment. She leaned to the side to look past the toolbox and there he was, there *it* was. Maybe twenty feet away, coming around the corner of the hanger, and it was limping its way straight towards her. An undead man in the soiled orange coveralls that had reflective strips up the arms and down the side of the pant legs. The badly soiled zombie had a bloody patch torn out of the side slightly above where she imagined its hip would be. Its face was slack and lifeless except for the area around the mouth. There, it peeled its lips back to expose the dry, gross looking teeth that it used to snap and snarl at her.

Out of instinct, Elle looked back to Derek, but he had his hands full with a group that was making their way towards them from the giant parking lot to the south, as well as a few that were making their way to them from between the hangers.

Where the fuck are they all coming from?

She marvelled as Derek held his ground and simply sighted his target, fired and then moved on to the next one. Elle would be on her own, and this, this was why she needed firearms training.

She looked back at her undead stalker; he was closer now, but he was still far enough away that she had time. This one was the only one that was threatening her, and for the first time she felt the weight of the pistol that was holstered to her leg. Her hand slipped down and opened the first full length drawer on the bottom portion of the toolbox to reveal an orderly array of wrenches placed neatly into small plastic racks for storage. Her eyes locked onto the wrench she needed. Elle snatched it up, and quickly stuffed it into her other back pocket before closing the drawer. She looked back to her zombie stalker. He was closing in on ten feet, so close she was sure she could smell the sweet stink of its rotting flesh. *Raise the weapon, sight your target, and squeeze.*

Pop!

The recoil from the pistol traveled up her arm and

seemed to spread throughout her entire body like a shock wave. Elle didn't know where the shot went, but the zombie in the soiled coveralls snapped its head back as if an imaginary fist had struck it, before all remaining life faded from its body and it just slumped down to the ground.

She didn't even remember pulling the pistol from its holster. She was looking at her stalker as the zombie stepped closer to her, and then something in her mind told her if it got any closer, that would be the end of her, the mission, and her sister's life. The rest seemed to happen automatically, like her brain decided but didn't trust Elle to go through with it. So, it took over and left her in the passenger seat to watch the action. She didn't hear the shot, and the world seemed to be enveloped in silence until the body came to rest on the ground, then suddenly the sounds of the gunfire around her came flooding back in. She blinked hard once and her senses came back to her. Elle could feel the weight of the gun in her outstretched hand. She took a breath and slowly lowered the weapon to her side and holstered it.

A flat-head screwdriver.

She looked at the box helplessly for a moment before it came to her. *Top section, bottom drawer.* Her hand shot out and pulled the drawer open and she grabbed the first screwdriver she felt would do the job if it came to it. She clinched it in her hand as Elle made her way back to Maggie. The main rotor still had enough momentum for a slight motion but she figured it would settle by the time she was setup, and if it wasn't, she could probably stop the motion all together with just her hands. She didn't want to do that, but she would if it came to it.

Elle couldn't wait any longer.

She felt that truth in her bones, like she'd go crazy if she didn't have something in front of her she could focus on. Elle made her way back to the craft, taking hurried steps that were as close to running as she could get without actually running. Elle felt if she ran, she would lose her tenuous grasp on her ability to control her anxieties. She didn't know what she would do if that happened, so she just put one foot in front of the other towards the scaffolding. She pushed out all thoughts of her sister, the Prescott, and especially the zombie she had just killed so she could focus on the here and now.

She looked over to her right and saw Derek firing at a spread-out crowd of undead that were encroaching on their position from the southern parking lot. Jackie seemed to hold her line as best she could in front of her. The proof of her success was a noticeable line of bodies across her field of view, maybe twenty yards out. Elle guessed Jackie may have put down over a dozen of them by now, maybe more.

Elle got to the scaffolding and pulled herself onto the reinforced wooden platform and went to work. She forced herself to breathe normally and not pay any attention to the constant but random gunfire that was going on all around her.

She first took out the tools from her pockets and laid them all out neatly on the platform, far enough away from where she would work so she wouldn't have to worry about tripping over them or knocking them off the platform. That would cost her precious time to hop down and retrieve. Time she would need later on. She laid the ratchet, the wrench, and the screwdriver on the surface of the scaffolding. Beside them she laid out the sockets in order by size, smallest to largest. Elle held the quarter-inch ratchet, with the strange bit she had never seen before last week, in her suddenly weak and awkward fingers and went to work on the engine cover bolts. *For fuck's sake, don't drop these little bastards*, Elle reminded herself as she removed the first bolt. From her experience over the last week, she knew what kind of pain in the ass it was to locate these tiny little bolts on the concrete once it slipped from her grasp. Again, time she couldn't afford to lose.

As soon as she worked the tiny bolt out far enough to get her fingers on it, Elle used her free hand to secure it. Once completely out, she tucked the bolt away into her jacket pocket and went to work on the next one. She soon built up a cautious rhythm, which made the work go by quicker, it helped her regain some of her confidence in her finger dexterity again.

After Elle removed all the bolts, she eased the reinforced fiberglass panel away from the craft and immediately she felt the heat radiating off the engine. It felt like she had just opened the door to an oven. Elle pivoted on the platform and leaned the panel against the railing on the other side so it would be well out of the way. It was when she turned back to the furnace-like engine compartment that she remembered what she had forgotten and why it was important.

"Listen," she suddenly remembered Martin saying, *"It's probably going to be pretty hot in there so you better bring some gloves or grab a rag from my box when you're there. You will not want to grab those bolts with your bare hands."*

RAG!

You stupid cunt! Elle screamed inside her head, she forgot to grab the fucking rag, and she didn't bring gloves, because why *would* she when she can just grab a rag from the toolbox when she was there? Out of pure cruelty, her mind flashed to the memory of the toolbox, and there on top in plain fucking view was a pile of probably a dozen rags, and there she was, moving one of them aside to pluck the five-eighths socket she needed.

Fuck.

Elle didn't even consider hopping down and running back to the toolbox. Her brain wouldn't allow it, instead, her mind made a snap decision. *A rag was just a cloth, after all. There was nothing really particular or special about it, and I just happen to be wearing a rather large piece of cloth.* Elle bolted up straight, unzipped her jacket in one smooth motion and frantically took it off like it was on fire. Underneath she had on a full-sleeved blue cotton shirt with the Yankees logo on the right breast. It was one of the few shirts she still had that fit really nicely, which made it one of her favorites. She grabbed the bottom hem and pulled the shirt over her head without a thought. The warm air kissed her bare skin and a part of her was thankful there was no one around to see her topless, except for the faded pink bra she had on, but she knew it wouldn't have mattered if there was. The sense of urgency she felt demanded it. Elle hung her shirt within easy reach on the railing of the scaffolding and scooped up her jacket. She rolled up the sleeves before zipping it back up and continued her work.

"Problem solved," she said congratulating herself mockingly for fixing a problem she created, and promised herself that going forward, she would do better.

With practised efficiency of motion, she scooped up the ratchet, snapped in the five-eighths socket, and went to work loosening the bolts on the side of the engine mount that locked the bracket to the frame. She didn't have the large ratchet or socket she would need for the two larger bolts on top of the bracket that connected the piece to the motor, for that she relied on Martin to retrieve the tool she would need from the hanger. As she worked the bolts loose, she tried to get a sense of how long Martin had been in the hanger so far and, to her frustration, Elle found she couldn't. She had lost any genuine sense of time since she killed her first zombie.

The smell of it still haunted her, and all she could do now was say another prayer for Martin and keep working.

The heat of the engine compartment was intense, but bearable. She was soon disappointed to find that the bolts on the bracket did not seem to want to loosen off. Sure, she expected there to be some resistance at first, but surely after she got the large bolt turning it would eventually get easier, Elle found that wasn't the case. The bolt was moving... slowly. She coordinated her breathing so that when she braced herself on the platform and used her weight to pull on the end of the ratchet, she breathed out. Just like she would back in the day when she was at the gym, lifting weights. She pulled the ratchet the length of its travel and then, as she was pushing the handle back into position, she would breathe in.

After a while, she felt like she was trying to row a large boat. Her shoulders shamefully ached from the exertion, and beads of sweat collected on her forehead. Finally, the bolt freed up to where she could use her fingers. She stuffed the ratchet into her back pocket and pulled her shirt from the railing to turn the bolt the rest of the way out. The bolt was longer than her longest finger and wider, too. She didn't take too long to admire it. Instead, she knelt down and placed the bolt on its head on the platform, some place she was confident was out of the way. She went to work on the other bolt on the bracket and found it was just as resistant to turning as the first one. By the time she had the other bolt out of the bracket and neatly placed next to its twin, she had sweat freely running down her face. She didn't bother to wipe it away, just stood back and wondered what she could do from here.

By this point in the trial runs she and Martin had done over the last week, she would take the other bolts off the engine motor mount, but Martin wasn't here yet and she didn't have the tool. Her mind wouldn't allow her to rest and wait. Instead, it searched frantically for what she could do.

With the bracket still in place Elle wouldn't have room to remove the hold-down for the thick bundle of insulated wires that ran through the compartment, and if she couldn't move the bundle of wires out of the way, she wouldn't be able to maneuver the wrench enough on the hose connector to remove it. So, she looked to the other end of the hose. Elle would skip a few steps in her process, but she didn't see any reason she couldn't start taking the other end of the hose off, so that's what she did. With her mind set, she switched gears and exchanged the five-eighths socket on the ratchet for the half inch size and went to work on the two bolts of the u-clamp that secured the back portion of the hose to a metal frame piece. Thankfully, those bolts were a lot more agreeable to coming off, and she had both bolts and the clamp put to the side next to the bracket bolts she had just taken off. With that out of the way, she could remove the back portion of the hose off after she unscrewed the connector.

Where the fuck is Martin? She wondered bitterly as she reached down for the wrench and as she did, she couldn't help but to steal a glance to the south. She couldn't see him because of the tail section but she could hear Derek's sporadic shots and she could see what she guessed was dozens of undead, maybe more, about thirty feet out and looked to be locked in on Derek's position as they awkwardly crept forward completely oblivious to the gunfire they were walking into. That was the direction she was to escape if things went bad, and she was ashamed to admit it, but for a moment she considered her escape, and at what point she would have to make that decision? How much longer before she realized Martin wasn't coming back? Would she recognize it in time for it to make a difference?

You're wasting time you don't have.

It was only a moment, a glance, but still. Elle turned back and leaned into the sweltering engine compartment to reach the back hydraulic connector on the hose, there was plenty of room to maneuver the wrench and as she put the first twist on the wrench, Elle felt the ease of movement after the initial twist to break it free. She was sure this would end up being the easiest part of the whole repair. She noticed a bead of red fluid aggressively seep through the top seam of the connector, which she was told was to be expected as the line would still have pressure in it. Without giving it a second thought, she repositioned the wrench and gave it another good pull.

Then the world exploded in pain.

Elle knew there would be pressure, but didn't expect the heated fluid to spray out from the partial loosened connector like a damned geyser. Her survival instinct took over and did what it could by having her body pull her face out of the engine compartment immediately. Her hands came up to protect her face out of instinct as she was pulling back, just in time to prevent her face from being horribly scalded.

Instead, the boiling hot oil splashed onto the back of her left arm and an atom bomb of pain exploded in her head. She had burned herself with hot water before, and that was bad, but the water fell away. Here, the oil coated the back of her hand in lava and, unlike water, the heat just stayed there. Cooking the flesh of her hand.

Elle grabbed her arm out of instinct and sucked in a lungful of breath through her teeth. She didn't scream, her agony caused her vocal cords to seize up and the only sound that came out was a pained wheeze. The pain was unrelenting and panic took over and she reached out for her shirt-like rag with her good hand and without a thought to what it might feel like; she slapped it down hard on her hand to soak up the hot oil. The pain changed somewhat, but it still consumed her, so much so Elle was sure she felt it in her teeth. She sank to her knees on the platform cradling her hand to her chest like it was a baby and, for a moment, the sounds of the surrounding gunfire faded, or maybe the burning sensation just overpowered her senses. Elle felt alone as her brain tried the process the intensity of the signals her arm was sending up her nerves like lightening, and all it could manage was a kind of steady roar that filled her head.

"Hey!" A familiar voice broke through the pained void and then she felt a hand press onto her back, warm but firm, Martin. "What happened?" He asked behind her, his voice filled with concern. "You okay?" He asked first, and then, "Are you bit?"

"I burned my arm," Elle managed to say and turned to him with what felt like tears in her eyes.

"Lemme see.," he asked kindly, but she could feel the urgency in his voice.

She eased her hand away from her body and when it was far enough, Martin held her firmly by the forearm and used his free hand to pull her shirt-rag off. Like a child, her first instinct was to turn away. After all, if she couldn't see it then it couldn't hurt her further, but she held firm. She knew she burned her wrist, but when Martin lifted the rag off, she could see the flesh of the back of her wrist and forearm was a deep, angry red and in several places, blisters had already formed. The largest of which was right in the center, which Elle assumed must have gotten the bulk of the fluid.

"Jesus! That looks bad," he said, and she could tell he meant it. Hell, it *did* look bad. Then her eyes caught sight of something on the platform by Martin. There on the reinforce wood was a large ratchet which was easily the length of her forearm with a large socket on it. Beside it was a clear plastic bag with the new hose inside. "Maybe I should-,"

"I can do it," she said, reaching past him with her good hand for the ratchet.

Her hand throbbed horribly. Pain bloomed from the center of her palm and seemed to spread out to the tips of her fingers. She didn't know if she could trust her hand to work properly before going forward. She wanted to hug Martin and tell him how glad she was that he made it out of the hanger in one piece. There were a lot of things she wanted, but when she saw that ratchet and the part that she, *they*, needed all other desires evaporated. Save for one.

"I can do it," she said again, rising to her feet with the ratchet in her hand like a weapon.

"Okay, get it done." Martin nodded like he understood. "You've got twenty minutes, and then I want to be airborne." He turned and hurried away without another word.

Elle held her hand tight to her chest and she risked a moment to look out over the airfield. Just in time to see Dennis's bulk come into the picture on Jackie's right with his rifle raised to take up his position for the second phase and began firing. On Jackie's left, Nathan appeared from behind the nose of the craft to take up his position by her side. The three of them held back the undead from the runways. Then, for a moment, Elle felt reassured until her gaze went out past the trio. Out past the large scattering on the undead in front of them, to the terminals. She saw a wave coming towards them from the structure. There were too many to count. From this distance, the undead pouring out of the terminals looked like a solid, undulating mass. There was no way those three could hold that back.

She turned back to the engine with a renewed sense of purpose. Her hand still throbbed, but she forced herself not to pay any attention to it. Elle locked the large socket over the large bolt of the motor mount, and moved the handle into position. Elle growled as she forced her injured hand to close around the handle of the ratchet for extra leverage. The skin on the back of her hand flexed and shifted painfully, but she closed it around the handle. She didn't pull; she was too deep into the panic of her situation to begin with half measures like that.

With a grunt, she planted her feet and yanked on the handle of the large ratchet with as much force as she could muster. The bolt reluctantly turned. Elle repositioned the ratchet and did it again, and again. Her blistered skin seemed to soak up the heat of the engine like a sponge and her brain was basically screaming at her that her arm was on fire. It begged her to stop and put it out. Pain went off in her head like an electrical storm, but Elle refused. She had come too far already to quit just for something as immaterial as pain. She clamped her mouth shut to keep from vocalizing what she felt and she attacked that bolt.

Soon, the bolt loosened off enough that Elle felt she could use her hand. With her bare hand, she turned the bolt and pulled it free. It was hot, sure, but it wasn't sizzling the meat of her hand, so her brain hardly registered it. She put it with the others, fought the urge to look behind her, and went to look at the last motor mount bolt. By this time sweat was freely running down her face while her shoulders and her lower back were having a debate over which one ached worse. They were just more distractions she had to push out of her mind as she cranked on the large ratchet.

Once that bolt was free and put away, the motor mount slid right out, no prying needed. A minute later, she had removed the bolts for the wiring harness bracket and the bundle of wires tucked up and out of the way. Then there was only the last connector. Elle put the large ratchet on the platform by her feet and scooped up the wrench she needed and dove back into the engine compartment. She didn't even feel the heat anymore except on her burnt hand. Elle worked on loosening the connector relentlessly.

She didn't even consider the possibility of burning hot oil spraying up at her. Maybe she should have, but thankfully, the only fluid she saw was a small amount that drained out of the hose. Elle was at the halfway point. There was gunfire, shouting, and danger all around her while the pain from her hand throbbed unrelentingly throughout her entire body. She felt it pushing against the back of her eyes.

Elle stuffed the wrench in her back pocket because she would need it again soon and bent down and grabbed the plastic bag her part was in. She bit down on the corner of the bag and used her teeth to rip it open. She grabbed her part out of the bag and, without a look, tossed the bag away. *Thread it with your fingers first, then use the wrench when it tightens up.* Martin's instructions somehow pushed past the fog of pain in her head. She forced her fingers to work slowly and carefully, to put the hose in place, and then threaded it to the corresponding connector as Martin had showed, and then the other. Elle used the wrench and tightened down both connectors, and for good measure, she checked the torque one last time before Elle was satisfied it was good.

There was no celebration, though. Elle just began the entire process in reverse and worked as fast as could with one good hand. Her injured hand reluctantly followed along numbly, but threatened to make her pay for it later on. Elle saw the light at the end of the tunnel now. She was doing it; she was going to finish. Elle got the wiring harness back in place and secured it to its bracket. The motor mount went back in to place like it wanted to, and she wasted no time bolting it down. Elle had just finished tightening the last motor mount bolt when she heard Nathan's voice from behind her.

"Elle." She didn't have to see his face to know something was wrong. She heard it in his voice. "We need to reload these mags." He dropped maybe a dozen spent magazines onto the platform, as well as a metal container that was painted a military green.

"But I-," she protested, but he shot her a pleading look and cut her off.

"If we don't refill these mags, we're dead." He didn't shout, but the urgency in Nathan's voice made it clear this had to be done. She looked to her protectors, and it disheartened her to see their position was closer than it had been. *They're retreating.* She realized suddenly and to punctuate it, she saw Dennis and Jackie take one measured step backwards as they continued to fire.

We're losing.

Without a further word, Elle stowed the tool in her hand,. She grabbed a spent magazine and a fistful of loose rounds, and began loading them into the magazine like her life depended on it, because it did. She held the magazine painfully in her left hand because she knew her injured hand wouldn't have the dexterity to push the rounds into the channel of the magazine. Elle frantically filled the magazines by jamming the cartridges into the channel one after another. When she finished one, she placed it to the side next to the one Nathan finished and started in on the next one.

In her head she was counting the seconds as she loaded the cartridges. She guessed she took about a minute to fully load the magazine, Nathan was slightly quicker than she was, which wasn't a surprise. She looked at the ones they had left to do, and did some quick math in her head. It would take almost five minutes, five goddamn minutes, to fill all the magazines. It felt like a lifetime.

"What the fuck are you doing?" Martin shouted from the nose of the craft so they could hear him over the constant gunfire. She didn't know who exactly he was talking to, but Nathan spoke up first as he approached them.

"We're running out of bullets," he said it like it was a matter of fact. "We won't make it if we don't fill these fucking things." Nathan's frustration was palpable. He knew this wasn't part of the plan and he wasn't happy about it either, but what could Nathan do?

"Is the hose on?" Martin asked. Elle didn't need to look up from her task to know he was speaking to her.

"Yeah, all I have left to do is put the clamp on the back and then get the cover back on." She shouted back to him as she worked.

"Okay. The oil's draining." Martin moved in between her and Nathan so they both could hear what he had to say. "Once the oil is done, I'll fill it back up and top up the hydraulic fluid. Ten minutes." Then he leaned into Elle. "Ten minutes, and we leave. This job has to be done by then." Elle said nothing. She understood, and Martin patted her on the back. Elle's overworked nervous system barely noticed it. "Give me your weapon," Martin said to Nathan. Nathan unslung his rifle, reloaded it with one of the magazines from the platform, and handed it to him without a word.

"What are you going to do?" Elle shouted, suddenly turning to him.

"I've got to load up the tools, no point having parts if we don't have tools," he said, and the bastard even managed a slight grin before he turned and disappeared around the nose of the craft. A second later, she heard shots coming from that direction too.

Elle did the math in her head; she could do maybe one or two more magazines after she finished the one she had just started, and then she absolutely had to get back on her own job.

"I'm out." Someone shouted from the line behind her. Elle thought it might be Dennis, but she couldn't be sure. Nathan said nothing or even really give any outward signal he even heard it. Instead, he just scooped up as many refilled magazines as he could carry in his hands and bolted for the firing line. A moment later, he returned with more magazines to refill, which he dropped onto the platform.

"Nathan, I can't-," she said as she neared the end of the magazine she was refilling.

"I know." It was all he said, it was all he needed to say. Elle finished the magazine and put it with the rest and then picked up the three-eighths ratchet from the side and went back to work.

"Grenades." She heard someone say and for a moment the gunfire ceased all together, only to be replaced with the low drone of the thousands, maybe tens of thousands, groans and snarls of the undead all around them.

Seconds later, the explosions came. She was expecting a loud and fiery explosion that would rattle her bones. What she heard were loud pops that went off in the distance like large firecrackers, which she doubted would've made much of a difference given the sound it gave off.

The gunfire had returned earnestly as soon as the sound of the small explosions faded. Elle was busy tightening down the bolt for the rear bracket. She gave the wrench one last good pull before she put it away and grabbed her shirt-rag and frantically wiped and dabbed the oil that had sprayed the rear of the engine compartment. She reached for the engine panel, put it in place, and partially twisted in a few bolts with her good hand from her pocket to hold it in place, before screwing in the rest of the tiny bolts. She cursed as Elle fought with the panic inside her to slow down, and carefully twist in each of the impossibly small screws of the engine cover. With the tiny ratchet she brought with her, she madly tightened each of the tiny bolts home. When the last bolt was torqued down, she slipped the tiny ratchet into her back pocket and stepped back from Maggie, somewhat dumbly because she had come to the end.

I did it!

She turned to declare she was done. They could leave, they had accomplished their mission. The words caught in her throat before she could speak them, because she saw the five soldiers constantly firing into the approaching wave of undead. Beyond the shooters, she saw the countless slack faces of the undead tide from the terminal. The soldiers had been at least twenty or thirty feet out from the side of the helicopter when they had started. But now, the undead had pushed them back so much Elle felt like she could reach out and pat Dennis on the shoulder from the edge of the platform.

From her slightly elevated position, Elle could see over the heads of the dead in the front of the firing line. Only to see a black writhing mass of teeth and outstretched clawed hands reaching all the way back to the terminal. *We're going to die,* Elle thought out of reflex when she saw the undead sea in front of them for what it was, a wave of death, and Mason and his crew were trying to keep the tide from coming in, but it was beyond impossible. She didn't think there was enough bullets in all of New York City to kill each one of the undead in front of them. To their credit, the hopelessness of their task didn't phase the soldiers. They continued to pick their targets from only about ten feet in front of them and shoot, and at the distance they were working with there was no chance they would miss what they were aiming at.

The problem was as soon as one zombie went down, another stepped forward almost immediately to take its place.

A movement snapped her out of her trance and she turned and saw Nathan running to each member in the firing line and stuffing a full magazine into their back pockets before bending down and retrieving what spent magazines he could and running back to the platform. Elle dropped behind the metal case of loose cartridges, ready to refill magazines even though she secretly knew it wouldn't save them, but was glad to have something she could focus on except their imminent deaths. She looked into the case as she was about to scoop out a handful of cartridges and her heart sank when she looked down and only saw four cartridges at the bottom.

"Don't bother," Nathan said, almost shouting, so she could hear him over the constant noise of gunfire. He looked up, saw that the job was done, and she could see in his eyes that he was shifting gears. "Load up all the tools into the cargo hatch." he commanded and Elle simply nodded and did as she was told, like God himself commanded it to be done.

Nathan dropped the spent magazines he was carrying into the metal case, and quickly dumped the metal case onto the floor in the back passenger compartment. Elle barely had enough time to collect all the tools off the platform before Nathan unlocked the casters and pushed the whole platform away from the craft. Elle fingered the latch on the cargo door and immediately saw what Martin had been up to. He filled the compartment with labeled cardboard boxes of all sizes, clear plastic bags filled with numerous things Elle didn't recognize, and tools. The compartment looked like Martin had literally thrown everything into the space in a panic. Elle followed suit and simply tossed the tools into the compartment with little regard and latched the door shut.

"Elle!" She heard Martin's raised voice over her shoulder. Elle turned to him and was about to report her success when Martin cut her off. "Get in, right now, we're leaving." He unslung the rifle he was carrying as he walked past her and handed it back to Nathan, who was striding back from the platform he abandoned close to Derek. "It's empty. Two minutes." He shouted over the gunfire and held up his two fingers to nail the point home. Nathan simply nodded while reloading his rifle before he turned back and headed back to the line. He walked past each member and slap them twice on the back.

"I'm out," Derek declared, let the empty rifle fall to his side by its sling and pulled his sidearm and started firing.

Elle retreated into the helicopter. She threw open the door and practically dived into the supposed safety of the cockpit before closing the door behind her. A second later, the pilot's door opened and Martin burst through the opening. One hand was closing the door while the other hand was already flipping switches and pushing buttons.

A low whine came from the engine above them as the fuel pump primed and the turbines spun up. Martin hit the dual engine start buttons on the console at the same time using the index and middle fingers of his hand, and the engine responded. The engine's whine rose to a steady increasing roar as the main rotors moved above them. Elle turned in her seat to watch the firing line as they retreated slowly, step by step, towards the helicopter. Nathan had his firearm out and was firing towards the rear of the craft at what Elle couldn't see, but as soon as the slide locked on his pistol, he turned and took three quick steps and jumped into the passenger compartment.

"Rear rotor's clear. Good to go," Nathan shouted into the front so Martin could hear him over the increasing sounds of the engine, as well as the constant echoes of gunfire going on just outside the cabin door.

Martin kept his eyes on the instruments but nodded his acknowledgement, and a second later shouted throughout the cabin for everyone to put on their headsets. Elle reached over her shoulder and quickly put her headset on as well and the sounds of the surrounding madness dulled slightly, but not enough for her liking. She didn't think Martin realized that the only person in the back had been Nathan, who was putting on his headset and soon his voice was added to Martin's on the intercom. Elle wanted to tell Martin nobody was inside the cabin but her throat clamped shut from the strange brew of chemicals her brain dumped into her body to help her cope with the pain from her hand. It still throbbed mercilessly but somehow felt a thousand miles away. She risked a look down at the injured hand she cradled in her lap. The entire back of her hand now was an unnatural shade of red and ugly clusters of painful blisters ran a straight line up her arm from where the oil had made initial contact. The hand trembled, and no matter how hard she tried, Elle couldn't make it stop.

Don't look at it, she told herself. *We'll deal with that later.*

The wash from the main rotor was kicking up a good wind which blew the sticky, sweet stink of decay into the cabin. Mason was the first one from the firing line to enter the craft. He cautiously stepped back until he felt the skid of the craft on his boot, then he turned and jumped in, fired two more shots out of the compartment and then reached out and patted Jackie on the back, who promptly turned and hopped in. They repeated the same process until all members were aboard, and shooting out the open door of the compartment, filling the inside of the cabin with the sounds of rapid little explosions that Elle felt to her core. Elle jumped when something struck her window.

It was an undead fist.

When she turned, she found she was staring into the milky eyes of some dead woman of unknown age who was trying to bite the smooth glass of the door's window. Elle could see into the moist decay of its mouth. Elle wanted to turn away, but then another one appeared beside it and began clawing at the door with its dark, cracked fingers.

It was chaos inside the helicopter; the engine roared loudly, sporadic gunfire erupted inside the cabin as Mason, Dennis and Jackie still continued to fire at the encroaching zombies. Someone in the back was shouting for Martin to take-off but the main rotor wasn't up to speed yet and all Martin could do was to shout back for them to close the door which went largely unnoticed, as they continued to fire out of the open door. Even with the headset on, it still seemed impossibly loud.

Everything seemed to happen in slow motion. Elle just wanted to close her eyes to it all, but she was in the passenger seat inside her own head as she looked around wide-eyed at the craziness inside the cabin. Martin shouted into the back for everyone to put on their seatbelts. Or maybe he said, *headsets*, because the tiny space of the cabin amplified the shots of the gunfire as the sounds turned into shock waves as they bounced around inside of Maggie. Even with the headset on, it seemed loud. She didn't want to imagine what the sounds would be like without the headset.

"Come on, you fucking bitch," Martin cursed over the intercom, and it took a moment for Elle to realize he was talking to Maggie. "Come on!" He growled over the intercom. She looked over and saw Martin gently pulling on the collective, but the rotor still wasn't up to speed, so no lift was being generated.

In the back, Nathan was shouting for someone to close the door and when she looked, Elle saw Mason and Derek had pushed themselves up against the opposite side of the cabin. Mason was shouting for Martin to take-off and Derek had a wide-eyed, wild look in his eyes as he constantly pulled the trigger of his empty sidearm at the zombies threatening to climb into the cabin.

At the door, Jackie and Dennis were crouched on the seats, firing their rifles into the faces that popped into their view. Holding back the tide. Elle saw Dennis had a grim look of determination as he picked his targets and fired.

Jackie, however, was a different story. She laughed madly as she fired with abandon into the mass of snapping teeth. Elle couldn't believe the impression her brain was giving her of what she was witnessing. *Is she enjoying this?* Elle saw Jackie was shouting something as well but with all the other noises filling the cabin, it was impossible to hear what she was saying. To Elle, it looked like whatever it was, Jackie was saying it to the undead in front of her.

Maggie trembled around them slightly, threatening to liftoff and take them to safety. Elle could feel it. Any second now, and this would all be behind them.

"Jackie, don't-," she heard Dennis's voice roar from behind her.

Elle looked behind in time to see Jackie had her sidearm raised now, the rifle hung by its sling in front of her. Elle couldn't see what she was aiming at, but Jackie reached outside the door to fire at her target.

A moment later her body jerked forward as something was pulling Jackie out of the helicopter.

Jackie growled as she fought to pull herself back, and then in the next instant her growl turned into a shriek of terror and pain. Elle saw Jackie's expression change on a dime and Elle was sure she was going to see Jackie get pulled from the craft and devoured before their eyes. Elle saw the events unfold from inside her mind and morbidly wondered if the undead would leave anything of Jackie Orr after the sea of death washed over her.

Dennis reached out and his massive hand clamped down on Jackie's shoulder, and with a look of effort he pulled her one-handed back into the cabin. With his other hand, which still held onto the pistol grip of his rifle, he shot the zombie that had clamped down on to Jackie's left hand in the side of its head, but inexplicably its jaws still held on. Dennis didn't miss a beat and simply lifted his boot and kicked the zombie off Jackie.

Jackie screamed like a wounded animal as the flesh from her arm tore off in a strip that traveled down to her thumb. Elle looked away when her eyes locked on the pasty white of the exposed bones of Jackie's hand. Jackie pulled her hand back and held it close to her body, and blood freely poured from the wound and down the front of her ill-fitting fatigues.

It was at that moment when Maggie decided she was ready to take-off and the craft rose gently off the tarmac. Elle looked out the window to the side and watch the zombies that had surrounded the grounded craft fall away beneath them. The craft rose to a safe height above the sea of death and just sort of hovered there inexplicably.

"Close the door!" Martin shouted into the intercom, his voice blasted into her ears and she was stuck by the rawness of the sound. In the back, Jackie was screaming at her gushing hand. Derek was tearing the sleeve off his shirt and saying something to Jackie she couldn't make out while Dennis stood over her, and held her writhing body still as

Derek worked.

"Will you fucking go?" Mason shouted angrily forward and slapped the back of Martin's chair.

"Close the goddamn door," Martin shouted back again in response. Nathan carefully stepped past Dennis and braced himself on the handhold by the entrance before he reached out and closed the passenger compartment door and latched it shut. "Hold on." It was the only warning the people inside the craft got before the craft shot into the sky while Martin rotated the helicopter so the nose was facing back towards Manhattan.

The sudden movement shifted the people in the back wildly as the craft spun like a ride at an amusement park. Those who could brace themselves did, and those who couldn't cursed, as the motion tossed them gently to the sides before the craft settled in its direction and sped off into the sky.

The passenger compartment was in chaos as everyone was shouting at everyone else and nobody seemed to know what to do about the bite. It was Mason's voice that cut through the drone suddenly when he spoke.

"We have to cut it off!" His stone-cold voice came over the intercom.

It seemed to cut through all the other sounds in the craft and effectively silenced all the other voices. Even Jackie seemed to take a break from her screaming when she heard it. Elle looked into the back in time to see Mason's chiseled features give each member of his team a hard look.

"WHAT!?" Jackie screeched throughout the cabin. Jackie wasn't wearing a headset, but Elle could still hear her screams clearly. "What the fuck did you just say? You're not cutting off my arm! Get your fucking hands off me, you motherfuckers!" Jackie howled wide-eyed at Dennis and Derek, who were currently on each side of her, holding her in place on the floor between the seats in the back.

She looked like an animal that was fighting her captors wildly, thrashing around on the ground, trying to escape their grasp. Now and then, Jackie's leg would kick up into view as she fought.

"What the fuck is going on back there?" Martin called to the back over the intercom, panic and concern were mixed equally into his voice.

"Jackie got bit." Nathan was the first to speak up. "On the hand, it looks pretty bad too."

"Jesus, it hurts, it hurts so bad," Jackie growled through her clamped jaw and then she turned to Derek with pleading eyes and said something Elle couldn't make out, but Derek's response was clear as day as it came through the intercom.

"They have to," he said to her in a soothing tone Elle didn't think Derek was capable of and then he added, "I know, I'm sorry but this has to happen, and it has to happen right now before it spreads."

"Don't cut it off," Martin chimed in over the intercom. "We'll be back within ten minutes. Just tie it off and let Bill look at it when we get back."

"Just fly this fucking thing and mind your own business," Derek snapped over the intercom, and Elle watched as he looked down at Jackie solemnly. He nodded once and then looked up at Mason. "Do it."

"Give me a knife," Mason said.

"I don't have a knife." Elle heard Derek confess.

"Me, neither." Dennis added.

"Here." Nathan's voice came over the intercom and

she saw him hand Mason something.

"What the fuck is this?" Mason said as he pulled open the three-inch folding blade knife. "It will have to do. Okay, hold her down." It was at that point Elle's body decided it didn't need to see anymore and she numbly turned back and faced the front of the craft.

Elle then reached down and turned the tiny knob that controlled the volume of the intercom in her headset. She turned it way down until the voices she heard were mere whispers in her ear. In her mind, she pictured the knife she had seen. It reminded her of the pocket knife her uncle on her father's side, Uncle Brent, always seemed to have clipped to his belt. They would hardly consider the knife she saw intimidating.

A small blade that was roughly the size of two of her fingers put together, and had a small portion of serrations near the handle. *That's the knife that's going to cut Jackie's hand off?* She thought to herself incredulously. Try as she might, she couldn't imagine a knife that size being capable of such a grievous injury as a severed hand. A nasty cut on the finger, sure, but to cut off someone's hand, you'd need something... bigger. Morbidly, and from the safety of the passenger seat inside her head, Elle imagined the effort needed to use that knife to cut off something as substantial as another person's hand. Sure, you could saw through the meat of it, but what do you do when you get to the bone?

And then the screaming started.

It started out like a panicked scream, much like what they had heard, but then, as she imagined the knife bit into the flesh of Jackie's wrist, the sound changed. It became a guttural, animal sound that filled the cabin, and had such an intensity to it Elle felt the tiny hairs on her arm move in tune with it. Elle couldn't turn down the volume on Jackie's anguish. She kept her eyes looking forward, but she barely registered the city view as they raced back to the Prescott. Elle didn't look at anything, but just tried not to let the pained animal howls penetrate the fortress of her mind.

Please make her stop. Make her stop.

She pleaded silently inside her head. Elle refused to listen to their words, but she got the impression the amputation was not going well. In the cabin, Jackie's fevered howl rose sharply and then sort of died away, and the cabin was quiet.

"Is she…?" Someone asked cautiously. Elle thought it was Derek, but she couldn't be sure.

"No. Just passed out." Elle recognized Dennis's deep voice say. "Probably the best thing for her right now."

Elle reached down and turned her intercom off with a final twist of the volume knob, and then her world reduced to the steady whine of the engine, which at this point was strangely calming. She wanted to close her eyes and put this all behind her, but not yet. There was more to do, and she'd come this far. *I've shot a man, for fuck's sake.* Elle would see it to the end. Right now, she felt like she needed to be doing something. There was nothing she could do for anybody. Elle wanted to close her eyes, but she was afraid of what she would see in the darkness behind her eyelids.

Elle remembered the zombie she saw walk off the top of the unfinished parking structure and thought for a moment that she felt like that zombie falling to its death. She couldn't put a finger on when it happened exactly, but at some point, she started falling today. Her body has been living off the thrill of the fall all day without the concern of the sudden stop, but now she sat in her chair feeling like her seatbelt harness was choking her, and Elle dreaded the end because she realized when the sudden stop occurred, she would then have to deal with the consequences of the fall itself.

Elle made a checklist of things she would have to do when Maggie finally came in to land at the Prescott. There were a lot of things that would need to be unloaded from the cargo hold, and then they would have to figure out what they had, and what exactly they were going to do with it. They also would have to find some place to put Martin's tools. There were a lot of decisions to be made yet. Elle wasn't done. When she was truly done, then she could deal with the events of the day.

Martin raced over the rooftops of the city. Elle didn't feel the same giddy excitement in her stomach this time, though. This time she just felt numb as the buildings passed by in a blur beneath Maggie. She caught the slightest motion from Martin as he shifted the control stick between his legs and the craft banked dramatically to the south.

And there it was, The Prescott.

Martin wasted no time on the approach. The craft felt like it was falling out of the sky as Martin brought them in to land. Elle's good hand made a white-knuckle fist as they came in to the landing at a speed that was more reminiscent of crashing than landing. Martin pulled up at what she imagined was the last moment, and the craft's fall ceased suddenly. The skids of the craft slapped down soundly on the helipad and the craft bounced once before it finally settled. Martin flew through the shut-down procedure and the high pitch whine of the turbine engine died away as the engine powered down.

Just a little longer, and then we're done. She told herself as she reached for the door latch and exited the vehicle, not really knowing what her role was going forward. They never trained her for this part.

The passenger compartment door flew open and Nathan was the first one out. He held the door open as Dennis jumped out and then reached around and grabbed Jackie by the legs and pulled her to the door of the craft where he then lifted her up in his massive arms, without a word he and Nathan bolted for the stairwell that led down to the roof access door with Jackie. Mason and Derek quickly followed. They all had blood stains covering some part of their clothes, *Jackie's blood.* Elle saw Jackie's slack and strangely peaceful face as they hurried by. Jackie had turned a ghostly pale color, but that was no real surprise. No one could lose that much blood and not be in terrible shape.

Jackie's entire upper body was slick and stained with her body's life fluid. Inexplicably, even her normally sandy brown hair was wet with crimson and stuck wetly to the side of Jackie's head. Mason's hands were painted red, and it stained the sleeves of his fatigues to his elbows. On his cheek, there was a spot as well. The amputation had splattered him with some heavy drops and streaked his face crimson as it oozed down and into his salt and pepper beard. Dennis and Derek both had bloodied hands and forearms as well, but nowhere near as bad as Mason had. *He must have done the cutting,* her brain informed her morbidly as the group made their way down the stairwell at the edge of the helipad and out of sight.

"I should go too," Martin's voice came up behind her. "She's going to need blood, and I'm a universal donor." He finished as he strode past her to follow the others.

Just like that, she was alone on the quiet platform. Nervously she looked around her, certain she had heard something carry on the slight breeze that blew around her, something that sounded a bit like a groan. She looked all around the platform to confirm she was alone before she let out the breath she didn't know she was holding.

Standing beside the passenger compartment, a morbid

curiosity drew her gaze to the interior. The back passenger area of the helicopter looked like a murder scene. The floor of the compartment looked like someone had poured out blood into the center of the space between the seats and then tried to spread it out over the whole area of the floor, down the center was a long line where it was clear they dragged Jackie away.

The seats had spots where the blood had sprayed onto the leather material and then gravity pulled those drops into streaks. In more places than she could count, there was smears where something bloody brushed across the seats, in several places she recognized bloody hand prints that were left behind. Looking at it, she felt there was no way anybody could enter that compartment without getting blood on themselves, and as the wind blew through the open compartment, her nose caught a whiff of something that smelled metallic to her.

Her eyes soon locked onto an object on the floor she, at first, didn't recognize. Possibly because her mind simply refused to believe what she was looking at. What are the chances someone would see something like that in their lifetime?

Jackie's severed hand.

She looked at it cautiously, almost as if she expected it to hop up and start running around on its fingers, but thankfully as she stared at it, it remained motionless amidst the drying blood of the compartment. She looked at it dumbly for a second, knowing she should do something about it, but not knowing exactly what. *Would Jackie want that back?* She thought inexplicably for a moment as she looked at the severed limb.

Just keep it together a little longer.

Elle tried to focus on what was next. She decided

it would be best if she started unloading the cargo they had brought with them. She would leave the passenger compartment for later. Something inside her told her she shouldn't try to take on that ugliness right away. Elle opened the hatch to the cargo compartment, unpacked the boxes and then piled them neatly on the helipad off to the side from the helicopter.

Elle heard the sound of her sister's voice before she got very far into the job. She turned just in time to catch her sister's wild embrace. Elle absently squeezed Kate's tiny body as she spied Jacob and Blaine climb onto the helipad as well. Elle couldn't explain it, not exactly, but she didn't want to see them. Not now. Not like this, not when she still had so much to do before she could stop. Elle replayed the broad strokes of the mission for the boys. Recounted the polite points of Jackie's injury and the following amputation. All the while she hid her injured hand behind Kate, she didn't want them to see it. Elle didn't think she could stand the way they would look at her if they saw it. Like they were looking at something that was tragically broken.

"Come on, sweetie," Jacob said in that infuriating motherly voice of his. "Let's get you out of here."

Elle could have slapped him for suggesting such a thing. She didn't because she could appreciate where he was coming from, but he didn't know what they went through for these parts and tools. Jackie lost her fucking arm for it. Elle wasn't going to just walk away now. Not with the job half done. Not a chance.

She tasked the boys with finding a shelf while she and Kate moved the parts and tools down into the storage room. Kate didn't object, though Elle didn't appreciate how closely her sister was watching her.

"Elle!? Your arm!" Kate shrieked in surprise when

Elle inadvertently revealed a part of the ruined flesh of her forearm.

"It's fine," Elle responded numbly and kept working. "I'm fine. Don't worry about it." Elle suddenly moved out of the room like suddenly all the breathable air had been sucked out of the small space. Elle walked up to the helipad, and rebounded away from the ghastly sight of the passenger compartment and just faced the dead city and tried to catch her breath. When she found she was ready to return, Elle found Kate had gotten bored and moved on to something else. Probably went exploring somewhere. Actually, it was a bit of a blessing because now Elle could focus on what needed to be done instead of reassuring her sister. *Just a little more.*

When Jacob and Blaine returned with the flimsy metal shelf, Elle had them maneuver it into the tight space before she shooed them away as well. It took some doing. Especially after Blaine questioned Elle about her right hand that wouldn't stop shaking. A few stern looks and sweet reassuring words was all it really took to send the boys away as well.

-

"Elle?" A voice came from outside the door. She jumped at the unexpected sound and took a step back, away from it. "Elle?" It came again. She recognized Nathan's voice and she found it strangely reassuring. "It's Nathan," he said calmly, and Elle wanted to respond but she had a feeling if she opened her mouth and spoke, the only thing that would come out would be sobs. "Hey," he said as he slowly came into view in the doorway. Elle was worried he would have the same worried expression, but his face was blessedly neutral.

"Hey," she said weakly back to him.

"Whatcha doing?" He said with a slightest amount of surprise in his voice, like he didn't expect her to be here.

"Not much, just you know, cleaning up and putting the stuff we brought back away." She said innocently.

"You've been up here for hours," he stated, like he was accusing her of something.

Hours!? She felt a pulse of panic and disbelief ripple through her and she tried to make sense of where all the time had gone. She and Kate couldn't have taken over twenty minutes to unload the helicopter, or was it longer than that, and where did Kate get to, anyway? Did she tell her where she was going, or when she left? How long did the boys take to retrieve that piece-of-shit shelf? Elle wanted to ask Nathan how many hours had she lost, but then she would be admitting she lost track of time, and that felt worse somehow.

"Okay." It was the only thing she could think to say, and for good measure, Elle made it sound like she didn't know what his point might have been.

"It's time to go. Bill's waiting to look at your hand, and besides that, you shouldn't be here by yourself," Nathan stated as a matter of fact, and then pointed to the holster on her leg. "Also, I'm going to need your weapon," he said plainly and held out his hand.

She didn't want to part with it. Elle had grown used to the weight on her leg and come to rely on it like it was the only thing anchoring her to this world, and without it, she would just float away. It was a minor comfort, though. A larger part of her was happy to be rid of the burden.

"Sure," Elle said and briefly considered sticking out her hip for him to grab it from its holster himself so she wouldn't have to touch it, but that would have been strange, and he might have noticed that.

She reluctantly reached down, eased her hand around the pistol, and pulled it free. Elle mindlessly handed it over to him butt first, like she was supposed to. But she was ashamed to see she had just given Nathan a live weapon. A round was chambered, and the safety was off. Nathan specifically had warned her about that, but during the day, she had forgotten that bit of the lesson. Nathan was unphased by it. He just flicked the safety of the pistol on and stowed the pistol in the waistband of his pants, which she just noticed were different from the ones he wore this morning. Now that she was looking, she noticed Nathan had not only changed his clothes; he seemed washed and rather refreshed. "Tell Bill I am just going to finish up here, and I'll-,"

"No," he said flatly.

"Excuse me?"

"You don't need to do this now. You need to come with me and get yourself checked out, and then Emilio has some food for you, and you're going to eat it. Every. Last. Bite. That's what you need to do right now." He then gestured about the room. "Not this. This can wait." He was stern, and maybe even a touch preachy. He was right, though. And yet...

"Did Jacob or Blaine send you?" She asked, knowing exactly how paranoid it sounded. Nathan only sighed deeply.

"No. If you must know, Kate went and found Bill, and Bill asked me to come up and get you. He seems to think you'd be more likely to listen to reason if it was coming from me. And seeings how Martin is out of commission," he said and must have seen the change in her expression because he held up his hands to calm her. "He's fine. Martin just gave a lot of blood and he's resting right now. He wanted to, but he's in no shape to be walking up and down stairs yet."

"How's Jackie?" She asked, partially ashamed she

didn't ask earlier. Nathan moved back away from the doorway and motioned for her to exit as well. She did, and he quietly closed the door behind her.

"She's going to make it. She's one tough lady. I wouldn't bet against her being back on her feet soon enough," Nathan said, leading the way to the stairwell. "Hey, for what it's worth, I think you did good today. I was worried about Martin bringing you along, but you really performed well out there." He finished and opened the stairwell door for her. After she had walked through the doorway, he carefully slowed the door so the only genuine sound it made was the click of the lock when it finally closed.

"Thanks."

They did the rest of the trip down the stairs in silence, which Elle didn't mind at all, the peace and quiet of the stairwell was oddly calming. She had a fleeting thought that it would be so relaxing to walk these darkened stairs all day, just up and down, with nothing but the dimly lit stairs in front of her. Nathan led the way with his tiny flashlight in hand and Elle numbly followed behind. She thought they might go to the group's make-shift medical area, which Bill organized after the last trip to La Guardia.

However, when they passed the floor without stopping, she then suspected the next logical place, the common area on the fortieth floor where the group normally share their meals. She didn't know what time it was exactly, and Elle got anxious about other people being there. She didn't want to answer their questions and reassure them of things, nor did she want to look into their accusing eyes.

As she expected, Nathan opened the door to the fortieth floor and held it open for her before he quietly closed the door and then hung his flashlight up on one of the hooks crudely screwed into the wall. Leading the way once again, they walked to the common area where Bill sat at a table alone with the briefcase he used to store the medical supplies he sometimes carried. Nathan paused at the entrance to the open area and let Elle pass and make her way to the table. Elle stopped.

"Nathan?" She looked back at him shyly. "How long were we there? At the airport."

"I don't know what the exact mission time was, but we were at the airport for fifty-two minutes, give or take."

"Oh, okay. Thanks." She started towards Bill's table feeling a little dumbstruck.

Fifty-two minutes? Elle didn't know what to expect. She remembered how long Martin had originally said it would take, and looking back on it, she had no sense of how long things took. Her memory of it was just a cold chronological series of events. If she tried to get a better sense of it, everything became foggy inside her head. Fifty-two minutes. It didn't seem like enough time. How could something so big fit into such a small amount of time?

Bill was looking at her the entire time she approached with that wide smile of his on his face. The whites of his teeth stood out against his dark skin. Bill had a warm smile, the kind people looked forward to seeing in the morning. From a distance, he could be mistaken for Morgan Freeman's brother, except his skin tone was a little darker and his face a little wider. He had a three-day growth of stubble on his face and his eyes regarded her warmly.

"Hey," she said as she sat down in front of him. "How's Jackie and Martin doing?" She got right down to business. Bill's smile faltered slightly, but mostly remained in place. She had struck a nerve.

"They'll be fine," he said and then added, "I

think." Bill then motioned for her to place her injured hand on the table. "Jackie's arm looked like a pack of rats gnawed her hand off. I had to cut it back another two inches to do the amputation right. If I left it like that, Jackie would be in constant pain for the rest of her days. When you amputate an arm, it's not like the movies. You can't just hack off a limb and cauterize the end with a hot iron," Bill said, not trying to hide his frustration, as he looked over the blistered, red flesh of her hand.

"You know how to do that?" She knew Bill had been in the Vietnam War. He didn't talk about it and people rarely asked, because most people at The Prescott didn't know. What they knew was that Bill was the resident doctor. No one questioned where that knowledge came from. He was the only one of them that had any medical training, even though that training was forty years old, so he kind of fell into the role.

"I've done four of them," he said as he began slowly draining the remaining bulbous blisters that hadn't already broken open. "One of them unsupervised, three of them lived." He added with calm seriousness. "It's easy really, only takes about twenty-five minutes to do it right, but that's the trick. You have to do it right. You have to smooth the end of the bone off, cut the nerves in just the right way so they retract back into the muscle tissue, tie off the arteries, and shape the muscles over the end of the bone to protect it. When that's all done, you tie it all back up and call it a day." He dabbed up the fluid gently from her hand, but still each dab sent a hot bolt of lightening up her arm.

"Is Nathan here to keep me here, or keep everyone else out?" She asked half-jokingly as she looked back at Nathan, who was standing guard at the entrance to the open area.

"What does it feel like?" Bill asked and looked at her

with an alarming amount of seriousness before his smile cracked over his face. "Don't worry about him. He's here because he wants to be here, and I think we'd all agree we don't need a bunch of people crowding us right now." With the blisters drained, Bill then took a pair of tweezers in one hand and a comically small pair of pointed scissors in the other. Elle watched as Bill lifted the dead skin from her burn and cut it away, he put the dead chunks of skin in a Styrofoam cup.

"I'm fine, really." She felt she had to say.

"Oh, I know, believe me I know just how *fine* you are." Bill looked at her with those dark eyes that just seemed to look right into her. But not in a judgemental way, more like how her mother would smile while seeing right through her lies. "Thing is," he began slowly, "people are a lot like a horse and rider," he said and then looked at her to see if she was following.

"Okay," she said, not really sure where he was going with this. He simply nodded and continued.

"Now, when things work right, the horse and rider work together as one, and it's a beautiful thing. For many people, it's normal and they don't even think about it. But sometimes," Bill said, returning to his work removing the dead skin from her wrist. "Sometimes, the horse gets spooked," he said it and the word resonated with Elle on a level she didn't expect.

Spooked. Suddenly, she knew exactly what he was talking about, and more importantly, why. Elle's eyes watered, but she listened intently to what he said next.

"An experienced rider can recognize the signs of a spooked horse, and there are ways to calm it, mostly just time and understanding. However, if the rider doesn't recognize the signs and just carries on business-as-usual, eventually, *something* will happen." He let that hang in the air for a moment before he continued. "There's a lot of things a horse can do, it can bolt, it can kick, sometimes it even tries to buck the rider clean off. What it does isn't important. What's important is that the rider isn't in control of the horse anymore. He's just along for the ride. Wherever that horse takes him, he's gotta go because the rider can't get off the horse. Not really. Do you understand what I'm saying?" He looked at her and saw the tear rolling down her cheek. She didn't bother to wipe it away. There was no point in hiding it anymore. Thankfully, she felt like there was no *need* to hide it. She didn't say the words, but she nodded. "Me and Nathan, we're just experienced riders, that's all. We see it because we've been there."

"Tell me what to do." Her voice broke after she burst in. Elle wanted to be in control again. Suddenly, it became crystal clear why Nathan took the pistol away from her. She couldn't blame him. She was thankful it was gone. "Tell me how not to feel... like this," she said without the benefit of knowing she was going to say it. It just sort of came out.

"Well," Bill said calmly, even though she felt like she was breaking apart in front of him, his calm voice was probably the only thing keeping her grounded at this point. "First thing we're going to do is get this all cleaned up, and then we'll get some food in you, and we will play it by ear from there. How does that sound?" He asked gently and squeezed her good forearm the way her mother used to.

"That sounds fantastic," she said, using her good hand to wipe away the wetness on her cheeks.

She sat there quietly while Bill tended to her burn. He removed all the dead skin and then gingerly cleaned the wound with soapy water. She felt each soft dab a thousand times more than she felt she should. Each time he touched the red exposed flesh, hot needles shot up her arm. Elle flinched and sucked in air through her clenched teeth, but she sat there and let him work.

It didn't take long, and when he was through, Bill packed his supplies back into his fancy looking brief case he obviously found from some office in the building. Kate probably got it for him. Almost on cue, Nathan appeared by her side with a warm bowl of fresh oatmeal. It was a larger portion than what she usually received and had a good amount of brown sugar on it. On top was a small red strawberry in the center.

"Emilio sends his regards," Nathan simply said and held the bowl out for her. Elle took it and looked up at him and tried to smile.

"Thank you," she said, fully aware of what she must look like right now. "For everything." Nathan smiled warmly.

"Us soldiers have to stick together, right?" He said with a wink, and then took the seat next to her and Bill. *Us soldiers*? Elle didn't feel like a soldier, she felt like a failure. However, for the first time since she got back, Elle questioned those feelings. Maybe those feelings were her own inner horse running amuck and taking her along for the ride.

She ate the rest of her meal quietly in peace while Bill and Nathan made conversation. They talked about baseball. The outbreak occurred shortly after the start of the baseball season, and they theorized about how certain teams would have done in the year. It was clear about how he talked Bill was a Mets fan while Nathan, who was out of his league talking baseball with Bill, seemed to mention certain players from certain teams just to see what Bill thought of them.

She had a feeling they were doing it for her to make

her feel better, normal, maybe, and on some level, she appreciated what they were trying to do. So, she just let them chat while she scooped down the oatmeal before it got cold.

When she was done, Bill said he was going to check on Martin and refused Elle when she offered to come with him. He said she had other things to focus on.

"Like a bath, you kind of smell." Bill wriggled his nose at her and smiled.

She gave herself a quick whiff and had to agree there was a definite funk about her. She said her goodbyes and took Nathan up on his offer to walk her down to the floor she shared with Kate and Bill. They walked in silence down to her floor and before they parted ways, Nathan once again told her she had done a good job today, and stressed that she could talk to him if she needed to. Elle thanked him again before she said goodbye and walked back to her room.

Kate was waiting for her. When Elle came around the corner, she hopped up from the couch she was sitting in, letting the ancient Gameboy she was playing fall to the couch in her haste.

"I'm sorry I narced on you. You were acting weird, and I didn't know what to do," Kate said, explaining herself as if she broken some unspoken, sacred sister-code or something. "I was really worried." Elle stepped into the room and pulled her sister into an embrace, but unlike the hug on the helipad, she allowed herself to feel this one and didn't feel any rush to end it.

"I'm fine," she said into Kate's hair, knowing it was a lie, but feeling that maybe it wasn't as big a lie as it had been when she said it earlier. She doubted her sister believed her, but it was something sisters said to each other.

When they did separate, Elle felt selfish when she told her sister she was going to have a bath, which was code for washing herself with cold, soapy water and a sponge in the bathroom. After which, she might just try to lie down for a bit and read the book she was working on, and maybe try to have a nap. Kate agreed with her she needed a good scrubbing, and added in a description of the smell that followed Elle around with her, for good measure. Kate smiled and took the cue Elle had given her and said she would leave her alone for a bit and check on her later, if that's what Elle wanted. Elle had to admit it was.

Elle felt heavy, weighted down by the fatigue she only now was feeling. Kate gave her three hours, which would put it around dinnertime. So, Elle suggested she bring their meal down here so they could eat together. Kate called it a picnic. Even though Elle didn't exactly share her enthusiasm, she still liked the idea of a quiet meal with her sister. Once Kate was happy with the agreement they made, she hugged her once more and asked Elle if she was okay again, looking into Elle's eyes for good measure.

"I'll be fine," Elle said, changing her words slightly, so she didn't have to lie to her sister anymore. Kate made her promise, which she did, and then Kate reluctantly said her goodbyes and left. Elle waited until she heard the stairwell door close before letting out a heavy sigh.

I'm done. She admitted to herself and felt an uncomfortable stirring in her belly. Elle ignored it, and went to the file cabinet on her side of the room that she used as a dresser to store her collection of other people's clothes that she wore.

Elle picked out a pair of jeans and a plaid button-up shirt she liked and after a moment of consideration, she pulled a fresh pair of underwear out of the packet of six she had. She didn't remember how long it has been since she wore a *brand-new* pair instead of just handwashing the ones she had. It was a luxury she didn't give herself very often, but today she needed it.

The other items she would need should already be in the bathroom. She just hoped the watercooler they put in there still had plenty of water left in the jug. She needed only a little. Elle really didn't want to go hunting for another full water jug just to lug it back down here. Elle just wanted to have a '*bath*' and be done with it. She packed up the new clothes into a bundle and walked to the bathroom. She clicked on the flashlight by the door and opened it.

The darkness of the bathroom was almost all-consuming as she stepped in. Elle held the flashlight so the beam pointed up to the roof and reflected a low light back down into the entire room. As she moved, Elle saw shadows all around her shift in unison with her steps. She walked up to the long counter and dumped the clothes onto the countertop. Elle carefully balanced the flashlight on its end so the light kept shining on the ceiling above her. She studied herself in the mirror, as if the anxiety she felt could manifest itself physically on her like a pimple or something, and all she had to do to be rid of it was just pop it once and for all.

She started by unzipping her jacket; it was a dark blue color fitness jacket fashionable joggers would wear while jogging in the fall or spring, before the actual heat of summer hit. Elle had soiled the right side with hydraulic fluid and although the jacket was a dark color and she could probably save it with a good washing, Elle tossed it on the floor in the corner by the door. She was done with it.

Elle found she was done with all her clothes and couldn't think of a better future for them except to be thrown away and never thought about again. Before she removed her pants, she, out of habit, pat down each of the pockets to make sure they were empty. Elle felt something in her back pocket, and now that she felt it with her hand, she remembered something was poking her in the butt when she sat down with Bill and Nathan.

Elle reached back to retrieve it, and as soon as her fingertip touched the smooth metal of the tiny ratchet, she knew what it was with dread certainty. She none-the-less pulled it from her pocket and held it out in front of her for a moment before her hand shook and she felt she should probably just put it down on the counter. Which she did, and then slowly sank to the floor.

You're done, she told herself on the way down. *You don't have to pretend anymore. You don't have to be strong for anyone, and nobody needs you to do anything.*

The sobs broke before she settled herself onto the floor, which seemed to be the best place for this to happen. Elle brought her knees up to her chest and hugged them tight to her body as the tears formed. All her defences she had put up to protect her from the ugliness she knew was in there had been shattered by the simple, tiny metal tool. When the tears came, they came in full force.

She didn't fight them, quite the opposite. She tried to push the tears out. Elle wanted them to come because if experience taught her anything, it was that tears had a way of cleansing the soul, and that's what she desperately needed right now. So, she cried, and let the sobs break free from her. And when that wasn't enough, she screamed as silently as she could into the croak of her elbow until her throat was raw. Behind her eyelids she saw it all again, and she let it wash over her like a giant wave that consumed her completely, and for a time she felt lost to the world. *Let it out,* she told herself, *let it all out.*

Soon, it ended.

Not all at once, the torrent of emotions shrank down to a stream, and then finally to a trickle, until she felt she could breathe normally again. She felt better. She still didn't feel good, but at least she could say she felt more like herself, her old self. That's seemed important right now. That really seemed like a win for her because, although they had succeeded in their mission, Elle felt like she had lost something along the way.

Something important.

To my new readers

Thank you. Thank you so much for taking a chance in me, and this book. I put a lot of work into it, and I sincerely hope you enjoy it. Ultimately, that's why I wrote it. For people to enjoy. This is a new venture for me. A scary one. I swear to you now, I will never take my readers for granted. If I can squeak out a living for myself doing this, it will be because of you, and I will be eternally grateful. However, new readers who enjoy the book and wish to read more, have a bit of a responsibility. It's simple, really. All I need you to do is tell people you liked it, maybe suggest it to a friend, or possibly buy it as a gift. Hell, there might be someone at work who hates zombies, and are generally a bad person, buy this for them and anonymously leave it on their desk, to spite them. And hey, if you wanted to leave a review on Amazon, that would be a big help to me. Or facebook, or twitter, or whatever. And don't worry, the next book in the series isn't dependant on it. I got your backs. There are three more books to complete the story. I will be painstakingly releasing them all. However, they would probably be released sooner if I didn't have to go to my day job anymore…just saying.

Preview from

Ronin of the Dead: Book two

Chapter 1

Elliott

"Ow!" Elliott hissed quietly as he yanked his hand back out of the bag and instinctively shook it as if the sudden motion would shake the pain off his hand. "That hurt," Elliott complained quietly and looked down at the offended hand just in time to see the first bead of crimson peek out from the wound.

It wasn't deep at all, just hurt a lot, and bled a bit. Elliott inspected his hand with great interest and immediately found the wound. A tiny puncture wound stood out red and angry against the gentle pink of his palm right in the meaty part by the thumb. He watched the tiny red bead of blood on his palm swell slightly before it broke off and drained to the center of his palm. That's when he heard it.

Elliott couldn't explain the sound. At first, he wasn't even sure he was hearing it. The slight breeze around him just seemed to carry this weird buzzing noise with it. It was there for a moment, a quiet sigh that seemed to come from all around him, just enough time to register with his brain, and then it was gone. Elliott cautiously looked around him, like Ken often did, to see if he could spot the source of the noise while his brain replayed the slight sound repeatedly in his head to see if it could identify it. His brain liked puzzles, and this was as good a puzzle as any. The weird thing that struck him was that the sound came from all directions at once. Maybe it was a little louder to the south, but with the short time he had to listen to it, it was hard to tell. His brain tried to place the noise but the best it came up with was a heavy, scratchy sort of sigh, the kind his great aunt would do after a coughing fit when they would visit her in the old folks home in Colorado City, but that made little sense. He listened for a moment while cradling his injured hand to see if the sound would return. It didn't, and after a few moments Elliott dismissed it altogether. He had more pressing matters, like his hand.

With nothing to clean the wound properly, Elliott settled on simply licking the small amount of blood off his palm, and lacking any sort of proper medical training, Elliott resorted to simply sucking on the tiny wound until it stopped bleeding. When he looked down, there was only a tiny speck of blood that still covered the wound. His solution satisfied him. He felt he had dealt with the problem sufficiently, so Elliott opened the bag wide to have a look to see what was inside it that had poked him.

Elliott carefully shifted some contents to the side and then he found it. It was an old style metal can opener. Momma had one just like it, though Elliott couldn't recall a time she ever used it. He admittedly didn't know exactly how this style of an opener worked. It looked more like a tiny blade that had a little hooked thumb on the top of the short blade. Elliott retrieved the pokey item from the bag and tossed it into the miscellaneous bin with the flashlights and the compass. With that taken care of, he considered the matter closed and returned to emptying the bag, more carefully this time, just in case there were any other surprises.

Elliott was digging into the bag and sorting the contents

into the three bins. Well, two really, because Elliott didn't feel the third bin would fill up. Elliott was delighted to find the previous house had a score of Macaroni and cheese boxes. There were other pastas there as well, and Ken made a pretty good spaghetti and tomato sauce. It wasn't as good as Momma's, of course. She made hers from scratch. His palm still throbbed a bit. It wasn't bleeding anymore, it was just a flesh wound, but those sometimes hurt the most. Elliott pulled out a can of apple pie filling and smiled broadly because pie filling had become his new favorite treat. Cherry was his and Ken's favorite, but Elliott liked apple too. He placed it in the can bin with sudden disappointment because Ken had said these supplies would go into the storage unit. Elliott thought briefly about hiding it away for later, but then he simply placed it in the bin and made a note to ask Ken if they could keep that one can for themselves. He was pretty sure Ken would agree to that. Elliott looked into the bag. There wasn't much left inside and reached his hand in for the next can.

That's when he noticed the movement from down the road.

The moment he noticed it, his eyes snapped to the source. Of course, it was a grey person. What else would it have been? Elliott noticed the grey woman's denim pants that stopped halfway down the shin, *Capris*, his Momma had called them, and on top was a simple black shirt but she had a vest on like Ken had, but this one was green and kind of raggedy. She was missing her arm, and to Elliott's displeasure, he could see ragged pieces of meat swing from the stump with each uneasy step. Elliott immediately noticed the snapping teeth and clawing arm, as well.

She can see me.

Elliott did a quick inventory of all the sounds he made

in the back of the truck; he was sure he had been utterly silent. Even when he pierced his palm on that weird looking can opener, he had hardly made a sound. However, there was no mistaking what he saw. Something else struck him as odd, this one was moving more nimbly than he'd seen other grey people move. Still awkward and slow compared to normal people, sure, but the grey woman was stumbling ahead at a pace that was almost a fast walk. Which, for grey people, was practically sprinting.

The sound at the driver's door startled him. Elliott turned, expecting to see Ken's bulk standing by the door and was about to comment about the grey woman almost trotting down the street, but what he saw was dark hands reaching for him.

"Whoa!" Elliott couldn't help yelping when he felt the nails of the grey person's claw-like hands scrape across his back as Elliott jumped instinctively in the opposite direction.

He tumbled backwards across the bed of the truck and landed awkwardly in the back corner of the truck's bed, his arm knocked painfully against the tailgate. He hardly felt it, though. His blood stream was spiked suddenly with adrenalin, the pain in his arm was a distant thing, his wild eyes focused on his attacker. The dark, grimy figure that was now angling himself towards the back of the truck to get to him. Elliott scrambled to his feet and hopped out of the truck on the passenger side.

His first thought was to run away, but he had to get to the horn to alert Ken inside the house of what was happening outside. Elliott ran for the open door on the passenger side and climbed into the seat and reached over and gave the horn button three quick presses.

Honk-honk-honk

Panic had set in. Something *was* wrong. He knew

it. The grey people shouldn't be acting like this. After all, Elliott had his superpower. It was something Ken had tested and agreed with. It was real. Ken said it made him special, so what happened? Elliott didn't know, and he had no time to think about what went wrong. Something was wrong, and he needed Ken to come out and fix it. Elliott locked his eyes on the front door, confident any moment Ken would appear through the doorway with his trusty knife in hand, and he would know what to do.

Ken wasn't coming, though.

Made in the USA
Monee, IL
30 April 2024

57768272R00213